BLUE WATER
A Tale of the Deep-Sea Fishermen

BY
FREDERICK WILLIAM WALLACE

INTRODUCTION BY
M. BROOK TAYLOR

Formac Publishing Company Limited
Halifax

© 2006 Formac Publishing Company Limited
Introduction ©2006 M. Brook Taylor

All rights reserved. No part of this book may be reproduced or transmitted in any form or by any means, electronic or mechanical, including photocopying, or by any information storage or retrieval system, without permission in writing from the publisher.

Cover Illustration: Courtesy Sobey Art Foundation.

Formac Publishing Company Limited recognizes the support of the Province of Nova Scotia through the Department of Tourism, Culture and Heritage. We acknowledge the financial support of the Government of Canada through the Book Publishing Industry Development Program (BPIDP) for our publishing activities. We acknowledge the support of the Canada Council for the Arts for our publishing program.

Library and Archives Canada Cataloguing in Publication

Wallace, Frederick William, 1886-1958.
    Blue water : a tale of the deep-sea fisherman / Frederick William Wallace ; introduction by Brook Taylor.

(Formac fiction treasures)
Reprint. First published: Toronto : Musson, [1907?]
ISBN-13: 978-0-88780-709-1   ISBN-10: 0-88780-709-7

1. Fishers—Newfoundland and Labrador—Fiction. I. Title. II. Series.

PS8545.A472B55 2006   C813'.52   C2006-904371-X

Series Editor: Gwendolyn Davies

Formac Publishing Company Limited
5502 Atlantic Street
Halifax, Nova Scotia B3H 1G4
www.formac.ca

Printed and bound in Canada

Presenting Formac Fiction Treasures
Series Editor: Gwendolyn Davies

A taste for reading popular fiction expanded in the nineteenth century with the mass marketing of books and magazines. People read rousing adventure stories aloud at night around the fireside; they bought entertaining romances to read while travelling on trains and curled up with the latest serial novel in their leisure moments. Novelists were important cultural figures, with devotees who eagerly awaited their next work.

Among the many successful popular English language novelists of the late 19th and early 20th centuries were a group of Maritimers who found in their own education, travel and sense of history, events and characters capable of entertaining readers on both sides of the Atlantic. They emerged from well-established communities that valued education and culture, for women as well as men. Faced with limited publishing opportunities in the Maritimes, successful writers sought magazine and book publishers in the major cultural centres: New York, Boston, Philadelphia, London and sometimes Montreal and Toronto. They often enjoyed much success with readers at home, but the best of these writers found large audiences across Canada and in the United States and Great Britain.

The Formac Fiction Treasures series is aimed at offering contemporary readers access to books that were successful, often huge bestsellers in their time, but which are now little known and often hard to find. The authors and titles selected are chosen first of all as enjoyable to read, and secondly for the light they shine on historical events and on attitudes and views of the culture from which they emerged. These complete original texts reflect values that are sometimes in conflict with those of today: for example, racism is often evident, and bluntly expressed. This collection of novels is offered as a step towards rediscovering a surprisingly diverse and not nearly well enough known popular cultural heritage of the Maritime provinces and of Canada.

Frederick William Wallace

INTRODUCTION

In the summer of 1911, when Frederick William Wallace was a freelance journalist and illustrator working in Montreal, one of his assignments was to write a series of articles on the Canadian fishing industry for the weekly *Canadian Century*. Seeking light on the subject, he contacted Alfred H. Brittain, Managing Director of the Montreal-based Maritime Fish Corporation. During one of their interviews, Brittain issued an invitation to the 25-year-old journalist: "Look, Mr. Wallace, if you want to get some first-hand dope on Nova Scotia fisheries, you'd better come down with me to Digby in August. They're holding a Fishermen's Regatta and a couple of schooners are going to race for a cup which I am presenting. If you'd like to come along and write up the story, I'll see that you get on one of the schooners in the race."

Wallace quickly agreed, but as he later wrote, "Little did I think at that moment that I had unconsciously embarked on a series of events which were destined to influence my future career."

In many ways Frederick William Wallace had been preparing for such an offer all his life. He was born on December 11, 1886, at Govan, a working-class district of Glasgow next to the docks of the River Clyde. His father, William Wallace, was then a first mate in the service of the Allan Steamship Line, sailing regular runs between Glasgow and various ports on the eastern seaboard of North America. A commanding but frequently absent figure, William Wallace had fought his way up through the ranks from the lowly position of apprentice seaman. Before joining the Allan Line in 1881 he had spent almost two decades on the great ocean-going square-riggers, rounding Cape Horn more than a dozen times, roving from port to port and vessel to vessel. The move to the Allan Line and steamships afforded him professional stability and permitted marriage to Frances Hurditch in 1885. Fred was the first of their five children (one of whom would die in infancy). When William finally reached the rank of captain in 1896, the family was able to move to the middle-class suburb of Langside.

William and Frances intended that their children leave behind the world of manual labour. Young Fred was, in any event, a sickly child, bothered by a weak digestion. This condition kept him at home for lengthy periods in the society of his mother. As if in compensation, Fred developed a passion for drawing and music, which his parents indulged with paints, drawing books and piano. Despite concerns for his health and parental disapproval, Fred loved nothing more than to venture down to the docks with his friends. "We boys," as he later wrote, "always tried to outdo each other in our ship knowledge, which led us into an intensive study of rigging, ships lines, house flags, etc. As we all intended to go to sea, the acquisition of such knowledge seemed to be necessary to fit us for our future vocations."

And whatever the Captain's injunctions against a life at sea, they were undone by his obvious pride in his work and the respect in which the community held him. With each visit home between voyages he brought a new round of stories from his vast repertoire, a new shanty or a new present from a foreign land, all fuelling the young man's determination to get out into the world upon graduation in 1902 and live up to the hard-won standard set by his father. Writing many years later to a nephew on the verge of a similar decision, Wallace wrote, "Father and Mother wanted me to go to University, but I thought that I had had enough of schooling and I wouldn't go."

A life at sea nevertheless remained elusive. Although young Fred's health improved, his parents remained set against his going to sea. A more practical impediment to the fulfillment of his boyhood dreams was the passing of the great age of square-riggers, as wood and sail gave way to iron and steam. Shovelling coal into a boiler could not, in his mind's eye, compare with furling canvas in the midst of a gale. So instead of fulfilling an improbably romantic dream of life before the mast, Fred reluctantly accepted work as a clerk in the passenger office of the Allan Line, a position no doubt secured by his father. Fred's frustration with life in crowded Glasgow was matched by that of his parents, who feared for the health of their children in the city and bridled at class barriers to advancement. As a consequence, in 1904 the family decided to move to Hudson, Quebec, beside the Lake of Two Mountains. Fred took to the new environment with a passion, hunting, fishing, canoeing and sailing on weekends and holidays. Unfortunately his weekday existence did not change at all. Instead of working as a clerk in an office in Glasgow, he now worked as a clerk in an office in Montreal, to which he commuted each day by train.

Apart from weekends out-of-doors, Frederick William Wallace's other form of escape was writing and illustrating adventure stories. As he later told a reporter for the *Montreal*

Herald, he delighted his fellow workers by throwing off "bits of impromptu verse of the red-blooded kind with which Robert W. Service first broke into fame." Some of these early verses and short stories survive in his notebooks and cover everything from tales of the Wild West to the Boer War, but more often than not the heroic deeds were set aboard square-riggers on the high seas. His colleagues' reception of these literary efforts inspired Fred to think of commercial publication.

A market certainly existed for such efforts: turn-of-the-century offices were filled with desk-bound young men with frustrations similar to his own. Many escaped the routine of their lives by turning to adventure stories, dreaming of a rugged life in "Indian Country," up the Amazon or Congo, or anywhere else far from a desk, a clock and authority. Cheap novels and magazines proliferated to meet this demand. Sufficiently encouraged by his friends and discouraged by a succession of clerkships, in 1908 Fred quit his job and embarked on a life as a freelance writer, journalist and illustrator. He bought a typewriter for $40, put up a trestle table in his attic bedroom and set to work, often writing late into the night by oil lamp. Here he turned out his first publication, "The Phantom Ship: An Adventure Off the Bird Rocks," which appeared in the June 1908 issue of *Dominion Magazine*.

Where did Fred get the inspiration for his stories? Usually from tales told to him by his father. The old Captain wrote down autobiographical fragments, reminiscences and shanties for his son, who turned them into fiction and non-fiction, prose and verse. This was not all Fred wrote, of course. As a reporter and illustrator for various Montreal-based newspapers and magazines, he covered comings and goings in the harbour and generally took on any assignment

INTRODUCTION ix

to do with subjects marine. Still, it was the experiences of his father the captain — not his own — that Fred relied on for most of his more substantial stories. Now heading toward his mid-twenties, living at home and in part financially dependent on his family, he had yet to find a secure career or prove himself. This existence was not only vicarious, it was also precarious, and it was threatened when Captain Wallace died in April 1911. Frances found it difficult to maintain the house after her husband's death, and it fell to Fred as the eldest son to take the lead. It was at this moment that fate intervened in the form of the invitation from Alfred H. Brittain.

The First Fishermen's Regatta of Southwestern Nova Scotia, held on August 12, 1911, was a daylong series of races involving every class of vessel within range of the town of Digby, from the working dories and motorboats of fishermen to the slim yachts of the leisured well-to-do. The highlight of the day was a race between two new banks fishing schooners, the *Dorothy M. Smart* captained by Harry Ross and the *Albert J. Lutz* captained by John Apt. The Maritime Fish Corporation owned the former, and Brittain made sure that Wallace was aboard the *Smart* for the 11-mile run from Digby wharf up the Annapolis Basin to a buoy off Goat Island and return. The journalist was enthralled. "Though I had sailed in plenty of steamers and had handled many sailing yachts, this fishing schooner trip was something new. My eyes took in spars, sails, running gear, and I made mental notes of equipment and the manner in which the vessel was handled." Here were men still living in the manner of Wallace's boyhood dreams, sailing wooden vessels powered by canvas and wind. As Captain Harry Ross brought the *Smart* home to victory by one minute and thirty-five seconds,

Wallace came to a decision. He would ask to go on a working trip to the banks aboard the schooner in order to experience a life he had until then only imagined. The next day, presuming on his connection with the Maritime Fish Corporation and the sponsorship of Alfred H. Brittain, Fred obtained reluctant permission from Captain Ross to sail aboard the *Dorothy M. Smart* in a few days' time.

The Digby fishing community into which Frederick William Wallace insinuated himself in the late summer of 1911 specialized in the fresh fish trade for markets in New England and central Canada. With ice-filled holds, schooners designed for speed made quick trips of a week to ten days' duration to the nearby banks off the southwest coast of Nova Scotia. Each schooner carried nine or ten double-man dories from which longlines were set to catch such groundfish as haddock, cod, hake, pollock and occasionally halibut. Crews were paid by shares in the catch, either even shares or "by the count" according to their dory's effort. Captains earned and maintained command by their ability to bring in highline catches, ensuring profits both for the crew and the owners of the vessel. Ross was only 25, the same age as Wallace, but had already won a reputation as a "fish killer," a driver and a hustler. The men who followed Ross were those who knew him best: his relatives, neighbours and friends. Almost all were drawn from small communities at the base of Digby Neck near his home village Culloden. Aboard the *Smart* in 1911, for example, were Ross's brothers William, Ensley and Wiley, his brother-in-law W. J. Murphy and such neighbours as dory mates Jim Tidd and Judson Handspiker. All were uncertain about carrying a lightweight "city feller" from Montreal to the banks.

INTRODUCTION

They need not have worried. The *Dorothy M. Smart* departed from Digby on August 25 and headed to Yarmouth to purchase bait. When Ross called the crew out in the black of the first night, Wallace fell out with the others and made his way forward in a southwest wind and heavy rain to furl the balloon on the exposed bowsprit. In the forecastle afterwards, the Captain exclaimed, "What are you doing out of your bunk at this time in the morning? Hell, man, I didn't mean for you to turn out." One of the crew responded, "don't think you need to worry about this lad, Skipper. Him and me stowed the balloon. He knows the ropes." No words could have meant more to Wallace. "From that moment all [the Skipper's] paternal solicitude on my behalf ceased, and for the rest of the trip I turned out and gave a hand at whatever was ordered." After so many years of trying, Wallace had made the transition from observer and passenger to participant and shipmate.

The succeeding days on the banks gave Wallace his first taste of the life of the schooner fishermen. When the *Smart* returned to Digby with a full hold on September 14, he was determined to go out again. Such was the reputation he had earned that he found no difficulty in finding captains willing to oblige. In March 1912 he returned for a second voyage aboard the *Smart*, this time in harsh winter seas and under the command of Captain Arthur Longmire. A square-built, ruddy-faced man of around 45 years, Longmire came from Hillsburn, a small village on the Fundy or Bay Shore of Annapolis County. It was from here and the neighbouring communities of Delaps Cove, Litchfield, Parkers Cove and Youngs Cove that he drew his crew.

Such was the rapport that Wallace developed with the crew that when he returned to cover the second Fishermen's

Regatta in August 1912, he took the opportunity to visit his friends on the Bay Shore. The setting caught his imagination: "In spite of its ruggedness and isolation, the Bay Shore to me was picturesque and inspiring. The air was charged with the odour of the spruce forests and the new-mown hay in the clearings, and one was lulled to sleep by the murmur of the surf on the beach. On windy nights, the darkness was sonorous with the sough of the gale in the trees, the thunder of the breakers and the clamour of boulders and gravel rolling in the wash." If the beauty of the setting inspired Wallace, the warmth of the people engaged him. His shipmates from the winter trip aboard the *Dorothy M. Smart* threw open their homes to him. He met wives, sisters and children, attended a wedding and was never without a meal and a bed.

Wallace's subsequent voyage to the banks in December 1912 was exceptional. Harry Ross was now in command of the American-registered but Digby-owned and -crewed *Effie M. Morrissey* sailing out of Portland, Maine. (The schooner is still afloat today as the *Ernestina*, based at New Bedford, Massachusetts.) It was there that Wallace joined the *Morrissey* on December 10. After a few days in Portland, the crew was a little the worse for wear and had to be winkled out of barbershops, poolrooms, taverns and other less respectable spots. Probably in part as punishment, Ross decided to race the *Morrissey* in high following seas and wind to Yarmouth, making a record run of 200 miles in 20 hours. Wallace would later write a song variously titled "The Log of a Record Run" or "Mary L. Mackay" that would make its way into folklorist Helen Creighton's *Songs and Ballads from Nova Scotia*. The return journey to Portland from the banks between December 18 and December 20 was just as eventful, run in the teeth of a fierce

INTRODUCTION

gale that shredded the riding sail and jumbo and shattered the foregaff. This adventure, combined with the experience of the two earlier voyages, inspired Wallace to spend January and February of 1913 writing his first novel, *Blue Water*.

Wallace had experienced a way of life few other writers ever had, and he wanted to open a window on a world unfamiliar to most readers. The story opens in the village of Long Cove on the Bay Shore, and the hero is Francis James "Shorty" Westhaver, a youngster in his early teens. His father was the captain of a fishing schooner who went down with his vessel ten years before the novel opens, leaving Shorty to be raised by his widowed mother with the occasional assistance of his uncle, Captain Jerry Clark. Shorty is a spirited youth, skipping school and getting into mischief, including one incident involving alcohol. His uncle pulls Shorty aside to tell him that his father died because he was drunk and lost control of his schooner, killing both himself and half of the crew. This revelation sobers young Shorty, who now begins to work hard at school and apply himself to working with the inshore fishermen around the harbour. Having proved himself in this way, Shorty is asked by Captain Clark to join his crew fishing on a schooner out of Gloucester, Massachusetts. After a gap of several years Shorty emerges as a respected fisherman, who exhibits talent at sea and intelligence ashore. These qualities win him a following among his fellow crewmembers and, by good fortune, command of his own schooner.

Shorty is infatuated with Carrie Dexter, a young girl from Long Cove who moves to Boston to become a nurse. There she becomes so enamoured by the lights of the big city that she loses interest in a simple schooner captain who works with his hands. But Shorty — now Captain Frank Westhaver — finds love elsewhere, when he comes to the assistance of a sinking barque carrying timber out of Yarmouth. Among those he rescues are Captain Denton and his beautiful daughter Lillian. Lillian sees the sterling character that lies beneath the rough exterior of Captain Westhaver and, unlike Carrie Dexter, sees nobility in his profession. However, Captain Denton will only permit Lillian to marry Captain Westhaver if he quits the perilous occupation of fishing and finds employment ashore. As the focus of Westhaver's love shifts from Carrie to Lillian and he finds a way to build a career ashore that retains a connection with the sea, the tension of the last half of the novel builds until the story reaches a happy, if somewhat improbable, conclusion.

The plot would be familiar to anyone raised on *Boys Own Annual* tales of adventure. The hero — brave, intelligent and sensitive — overcomes great odds and through unexpected twists of fate wins the girl and riches. But if the story is fanciful, the context is not. Long Cove and neighbouring Anchorville — stand-ins for Hillsburn and Digby — lovingly portray the mixed fishing and farming communities of the Bay Shore and Annapolis Basin. The characters may act to a formula, but they are often recognizable as individuals with whom Wallace sailed. Shorty Westhaver is clearly based on Harry Ross, and the likes of Judson Handspiker and others make barely disguised appearances. But it is work on the sea that Wallace most wanted to bring to life, and he describes in full and accurate detail the technicalities of raising, reefing and lowering sails, putting a dory over the side, laying and hauling a trawl and dressing down a catch. He works the *Morrissey*'s record run into the story, and the great squall.

INTRODUCTION

He includes detailed explanations of how voyages are financed and fishermen paid. He brings to life the fisherman's lot, both in the forecastle and cabin at sea and in the dives of American port towns, and he explores the nature of the relationship between schooner captains and their crews. The realism of his context makes up for any lack of realism in his plot.

Advertised as a sailing adventure by someone who had experienced the life first-hand, *Blue Water* was a commercial success. First published in Toronto and London in 1914, it was subsequently republished in 1920, 1922, 1924 and 1935. More gratifying to Wallace than sales were the letters and praise he received from fishermen, and the knowledge that the novel was read aloud in the forecastles of schooners fishing on the banks. *Blue Water* was sufficiently noteworthy — and simple — that it was made into a movie by producer Ernest Shipman in 1922 in Saint John, New Brunswick. Wallace, who was paid an undisclosed (but likely modest) sum for the film rights, was enthusiastic and arranged for the participation of his friend Captain Ansel Snow and the crew of the Digby schooner *Robert and Arthur*. With the yet-to-be-famous Montreal-born actor Norma Shearer in a starring role, filming began in the unlikely month of October. Not surprisingly, the production crew encountered cold, rain and fog and retreated to indoor sets in the St. Andrews Roller-Rink. Eventually the entire cast and crew quietly left town to complete filming in Florida. The movie premiered in Saint John in 1924 to good reviews, but there were distribution problems, and it was consigned to a vault in New York. The film subsequently disappeared.

Wallace was not yet done with the fishing community of Digby. Between 1913 and 1918, he would make four more trips to the banks aboard fishing schooners and two aboard trawlers. These voyages provided the material for another novel, *The Viking Blood*, published in 1920, a dozen short stories collected and published in 1916 as *The Shack Locker* and a regular series of articles in magazines and newspapers. Wallace's journalism was remarkable not just for the vivid accuracy of his descriptions but also for the superb photographs with which his articles were illustrated. In addition to pencils and notebooks, Wallace took "a cheap little box-form camera" on all of his voyages in order to record the men, the vessels and the work. Over the course of his seven schooner and two trawler trips he took hundreds of photographs that provide a window on the banks fishery in the last age of unassisted sail, a window that is unparalleled. Wallace's photographs, like his novels and short stories, have been too-long neglected, and are only now being assessed by scholars and placed back before the general public.

Wallace's unique expertise and connection with the industry — from fishermen on the banks to directors in the boardrooms of Montreal — recommended him to J.J. Harpell, owner of Industrial and Educational Press, who specialized in the publication of such industry journals as *Pulp and Paper Magazine* and *Canadian Miller*. Harpell was looking for an editor to launch a new publication, the *Canadian Fisherman*, and Wallace seemed ideal. When the first issue appeared in January 1914, Wallace's name was on the masthead. Apart from a brief break in the 1920s to edit the American equivalent, the *Fishing Gazette*, Wallace remained with the *Canadian Fisherman* until he retired in 1953. This position allowed him to haunt ports and vessels for the rest of his life, and left him sufficient leisure time to

INTRODUCTION xvii

continue writing short stories and another novel, *Captain Salvation*, based either on his own experiences or those of his father. Originally published in 1925, *Captain Salvation* was republished in the *Formac Fiction Treasures* series in 2005. In later years Wallace turned more directly to historical works, the first and most famous of these being *Wooden Ships and Iron Men*, first published in 1924. The best, and least recognized, was his autobiography, *Roving Fisherman*, published in 1955. Frederick William Wallace died on July 15, 1958.

M. Brook Taylor
Halifax, Nova Scotia, July 2006

M. BROOK TAYLOR is a member of the Department of History, Mount Saint Vincent University, and author of *A Camera on the Banks: Frederick William Wallace and the Fishermen of Nova Scotia* (Fredericton: Goose Lane Editions, 2006), upon which portions of this introduction were based.

To
THE MEMORY OF MY FATHER
A Sailor
AND TO MY MOTHER
A Sailor's Wife

INTRODUCTION

BLUE WATER WAS WRITTEN DURING THE WINTER OF 1913 immediately after the writer had returned from a stormy fishing trip in the schooner *Effie M. Morrissey* out of Portland, Maine. I had been to the Banks in fishing vessels prior to that, but certain experiences in the *Morrissey* in December, 1912, inspired me to write my first novel, incorporating therein something of the deep-sea fisherman's life as I had seen it, or heard about from various shipmates. While the tale is fiction, much of the material is actually drawn from life.

That was over twenty-two years ago at this writing and many changes have taken place in the conduct of the Atlantic Coast Banks fisheries in that period of time. Steam, oil and internal combustion engines have relegated sails into the background as a means of getting the vessels to and from the fishing grounds. The otter-trawler — an importation from European methods — drags its cone-shaped bag-net over the sea floor; the fish are thus scooped up without the use of hooks and lines. The great sailing schooner fleets of Boston, Gloucester and minor ports, using dories and trawls (long-lines), have practically vanished and the "draggers" have replaced them. Some few American schooners remain to carry on with the old methods, but the majority of the lofty, sleek clippers of the Banks have gone like the snows of yesteryear.

Only in Nova Scotia and Newfoundland has the intrusion of the otter-trawl been repulsed. In these sections of the North Atlantic, the schooner, the dory and the long-line trawl still retain the favour of the fishermen. But the vessels employed no longer lift tall masts to be clothed with canvas. Diesel engines furnish power to drive the schooner and the shortened masts support just enough canvas to steady the vessel, aid the engine in fair winds, or save fuel when hove-to.

Conditions in world markets have seriously restricted the output of salted and dried fish of late years and the large Nova Scotian and American sailing fleets formerly engaged in "Salt Banking" have diminished considerably. It is doubtful if we will ever see such fleets again. The majority of the vessels fishing from North American ports today are engaged in producing fish for domestic consumption in fresh or frozen form. The demand is for strictly fresh products and in consequence the fishermen make much shorter trips than used to be the case. It is a fast-moving age, and the deep-sea fisherman, like every other industrial worker, is keeping in step with the times.

But if the dory-fishermen have modernized their vessels with the adoption of Diesel engines, electric light and radio, the work of the dory-mates remains the same as described in *Blue Water*. The schooners no longer race off to the Banks under press of sail but forge direct to the fishing grounds under power. But once on the Banks, the old systems of fishing, with some minor changes perhaps, still hold sway. The dories go over the side as of yore and the men pull away, set and haul their miles of gear under the same conditions as outlined in this book. In some instances, perhaps, they take more chances than formerly. Knowing the ability of a powered vessel to pick them up quickly in threatening weather, they'll hang on longer than would ordinarily be the case with the purely sailing craft mothering them.

The Nova Scotian deep-sea fisherman of today has broadened his outlook with the coming of the radio, the movies, the automobile. But in his character, and the qualities required by the nature of his work, he hasn't changed much since the time *Blue Water* was written. He is the same independent, sturdy and courageous type; hardworking, kindly and hospitable. If he has lost anything—I speak of the generation since 1913 — it is his ability to handle a vessel under canvas. Only those who were brought up in the days before the adoption of the motor engine in the schooners are thus familiar.

Only in such vessels as the famous Lunenburg fishing schooner *Bluenose* do we see a survivor of the old-time craft. But the *Bluenose* is probably the last of her type in the Nova Scotia fishing fleet. Without an engine in her, she would find it hard to keep pace with the requirements of the fisheries in this day and age. And when you put an engine in a vessel, you find it more profitable to make her full-powered and capable of logging from ten to twelve knots. Sail plan is cut down to save the expense of spars, rope and canvas since it will be but little used.

The entry of the otter-trawler or "dragger" and the powered schooner into the American and Canadian fishing fleets has eliminated much of the romance and colour which enhaloed the days of sail. Then, the Banks fisherman was a sailor as well as a fisherman. Skippers and crews took a pride in the swiftness and weatherly abilities of their craft; took a daring delight in "putting it to her" in a breeze of wind and ramming her home in heavy weather or seeing how long she'd carry her sail without rolling over or jumping the spars out of her. The vessels themselves, and their skippers, acquired reputations which were known to every Banksman from Georges to Grand. When these clippers and skippers passed away, this inspiring, heroic atmosphere went with them.

Much as one regrets the passing of this colourful age, one's practical experience and intimacy with the fishing industry for a quarter-of a-century would not permit sentiment to turn back the pages of the years. Fishing is a business, and like every other business, it must keep pace with the times. The demands of an exacting market will make no allowance for the employment of methods which contain an element of hazard. There is enough gamble and hazard in fishing even as it is today without adding to it the uncertainty of dependence upon sailing vessels to run the catch to market. When one has been eight days sailing four hundred and fifty miles with a catch of fish slowly deteriorating, one recognizes and admits the value of power.

In company with the tall-sparred Bankers of *Blue Water* days, the coasting schooner fleets are also vanishing from the seas. Only a few remain in the lumber and pulpwood trade with one or two survivors making West India voyages from Nova Scotia ports. The square-riggers, formerly common sights in the Maritime Provinces' harbours loading lumber for South America and Australia, have passed entirely from the scene. Their place has been taken by small tramp steamers, usually of Scandinavian origin.

The fishing villages are not so isolated nowadays. The popularity of the automobile brought good roads in its train and speed of communication. "Goin' to town" is no longer an event for the residents of out-of-the-way hamlets. The ox-cart may still be seen in parts of Nova Scotia, but the motor-truck and the tractor are displacing them.

Since its first publication early in 1914, *Blue Water* has been favoured with several printings. It has even been dramatized in a motion picture, providing Miss Norma Shearer — a Canadian-born actress now world-famous — with possibly her first starring vehicle. Viewed in the light of mature years and wider experience, one might be tempted to rewrite parts of it which hold an amateurish flavour. Yet, on reflection, and casting one's mind back to the days when it was written, I am constrained to hold my hand. We were young then and life was full of romance and adventure. Inspired by what we had seen and heard, the story flowed forth as though dictated by an unseen mentor. It was completed in two months, start to finish, with little or no alteration to the original manuscript. I harbour no illusions as to its literary quality, but as a description of fishing and the characters of fishermen of those days, I could not, at this date, add or subtract anything from the narrative.

FREDERICK WILLIAM WALLACE

Gardenvale, Que.
September, 1935.

BLUE WATER
A Tale of the Deep Sea Fishermen

CHAPTER ONE

Th' sun's arisin' o'er th' hills, an' th' breeze blows down th' Bay,
An' th' towboat's got our hawser, for we're outwardbound to-day.
So break away the anchor to a chantey's rousin' sound,
An' fare-ye-well, my sweetheart, for we are outwardbound.

Our barque's a Bluenose clipper, an' th' skipper's Bluenose too,
Our cook's a Bluenose nigger, an' we're 'most a Bluenose crew.
Heave hearty to the chorus, there, as lusty as ye can!
For we're outwardbound this mornin' on a Nova Scotiaman.
—*Ballad of the Outwardbound*

THE BROAD WATERS OF THE BAY OF FUNDY SHIMMERED as a vast steel-blue expanse in the glare of the hot June sun and merged into the azure of the cloudless sky with but a streak of faint mistiness at the horizon. Apparently oblivious of the heat and the exertion, two barefooted boys ran down the dusty Bay Shore road and threw themselves upon a patch of bush-shaded grass fringing the highway. The older of the pair, a stocky, sandy-haired youngster endowed with all the aggressive cocksure manner which goes with twelve years of earthly existence, was the first to speak.

"Got th' pipe, Lem?"

"Yep!" replied the younger boy, wiping his face with the sleeve of his blouse.

"Here's th' terbacker. Gimme a knife an' I'll cut it up."

Lem fished in his pocket and handed over the article called for.

"Cal'late that's good American plug," he remarked, regarding his chum's awkward efforts to slice the hard cake of Mayo's with an expectant eye. "Whar' did ye git it, Shorty?"

The stocky youngster closed a keen grey eye and answered gravely, "Found it——"

"Where?"

"In my Uncle Jerry's coat pocket."

"That's stealin', Shorty!" murmured the other, with an ominous shake of his tousled head.

"No, 'tain't! Leastways, not from Uncle Jerry," asserted Shorty in extenuation. "Fair exchange ain't no robbery. Uncle Jerry took my pistol an' ca'tridges away from me las' time he was to home. It cost me a dollar, an' I cal'late I'm due a good many plugs o' terbacker for that weppin. He took my pistol away 'thout askin' me, an' I'm jest takin' his terbacker 'thout askin' him. Gimme th' pipe naow. I got a fill cut up."

The pipe—a dirty malodorous clay of the commonest variety—was produced reverently by Lem, and his companion fingered the blackened article with the appreciation of a would-be connoisseur. "Good pipe that," he remarked after a critical examination. "Coloured up dandy. Does she draw well?"

"Yep!" answered Lem. "I tried her out two days ago with some tea. Tea makes good smokin', but pow'ful strong. Here's a match. You kin try her out first——"

Shorty made a negative gesture. "No, Lem. I ain't no hog. You kin hev th' first shot——"

"No, no! You smoke her, Shorty. I—I ain't sure that I like that kind o' terbacker."

The other sniffed disdainfully. "Huh! Make ye sick, I cal'late. 'Member how sick you was las' time I give ye a pull o' my cigar?"

"That warn't th' cigar," indignantly answered Lem. "'Twas th' green apples I was eatin' afore. Takes more'n a cigar t' make *me* sick."

Lying flat on his stomach, Shorty pulled away at the pipe while his companion regarded him with admiration in his eyes. Shorty Westhaver was something of a character—a veritable Napoleon among the boys of Long Cove, and Lemuel Ring ranked as his trusty lieutenant. Though young in years, both were old and steeped in juvenile crimes. When Hank Garvey found his berry patches raided of their best and most luscious fruits he immediately made but one deduction. "Shorty Westhaver an' Lem Ring!" When Deacon Elisha Small missed the best of his apples and cherries he used long-forgotten oaths and levelled them at the tousled head of the Widow Westhaver's kid. Even the parson wasn't spared, and many a time the worthy cleric was disturbed in his studies by the shouts of an enthusiastic crowd of Long Cove youngsters applauding the equestrian abilities of Shorty as he careered around the field as a cowboy on the bare back of the clergyman's old horse. Tom Crosby, a cranky, cross-grained old fisherman, and the terror of the Long Cove boys, once fell foul of Shorty and next day found his dory gone from the beach and floating bottom-up in the mill dam a quarter of a mile away. How the youngster got it up there is a mystery to this day, but some folks say that Captain Crawford's yoke of oxen had been purloined for the purpose.

But in all the boy's tricks and escapades there was nothing spiteful or vicious. The inhabitants of the tiny Nova Scotian settlement characterized him as being "sassy an' bold," and liked him in spite of his impish qualities, while the school-teacher, to whom he was a sharp thorn, regarded him as one of her most promising pupils—when he attended school and it suited him to be so—and at times her most incorrigible and unruly. He was truthful and plain-spoken to a truly remarkable degree—traits which redeemed many of his mischievous pranks—and being fearless, pugnacious, and determined, Master Francis James Westhaver, at the tender age of twelve years, had gained a reputation.

He wasn't a big boy for his age, being short and stocky, but when he had his tousled sandy hair brushed and his clean Sunday collar and suit on he looked a fine, smart little fellow. Round-faced, eyes of clear, cool grey with just a hint of blue in them, and freckled as all fair-skinned boys are, men said the youngster was the "dead spit" of Captain Frank Westhaver, drowned these ten years in the chill waters off Sable Island Bar. "An' he's like the ol' man in every way," they said. "Reg'lar devil he was with his tricks an' games. Allus jokin' an' stringin' a man, but a great favourite with th' gangs what shipped with him, an' even his last crowd 'ud forgive him for what he done. Let's hope th' young 'un don't imitate his father in that respect." Whatever men said of the boy's father, they never clearly elucidated the veiled hope which invariably ended their remarks. What it was, many men knew; the Widow Westhaver knew and locked the secret in her bosom; but the majority of Long Cove and Bay Shore folks were familiar only with Captain Frank Westhaver as the man who had gone down on Sable Island Bar with the *Grace Westhaver* and half his crew years agone.

Shorty's companion in most of his plots and tricks was Lemuel Ring—a youngster six months his junior. Lem was the son of another fishing skipper who, having a fine house and a large farm, was regarded as one of the "big" men of Long Cove. Lem trailed after the redoubtable Shorty in all his escapades, and whenever the sandy thatch of young Westhaver was bent in outlining a plot the black mop of Lem Ring would be seen in whispering proximity.

At the time this chapter opens it was summer, and the idea of attending school at such a season proved distasteful to Shorty. He had little use for school anyway, and infinitely preferred the fish shacks and the society of the boat fishermen and lobstermen along the beach to the gloomy schoolhouse and the severe and staid, teacher. Whatever Shorty thought was right, Lem accepted, and ever since the snow went the school saw but little of the two worthies.

As he lay upon the grass at the side of the road, jaws working as he puffed assiduously at the feeble spark in the bowl of the pipe and a seraphic smile on his freckled face, an observer would have said that Shorty was at peace with the world. So he was—but lengthy contemplation on

Shorty's part usually meant mischief—the calm before the storm as it were. Turning sharply, he reached out with a dusty, sunburned foot and kicked Lem in the side.

"Lem!"

"Ouch!" Master Ring acknowledged the command with a grunt.

"'Member when ye hed them red-jacks o' yours on this winter?"

"Yep!" growled Lem suspiciously. "What about them? They was good boots."

"'Member what teacher said about ye?"

The other grunted. "Uh-huh! Said I was clumsy on my feet."

"Yep, an' so ye were, Lem, an' ye'll remember when ye fell down an' knocked her desk over she said you was worse'n a bull in a china shop."

Lem frowned, and the other continued after a pause: "I've often wondered jest what a bull in a china shop 'ud be like. It 'ud be lots o' fun, I cal'late?"

"Huh?" Master Ring's eyebrows arched questioningly and he showed interest. "What's th' game, Shorty?"

"Let's git along to school, Lem," proposed the other.

"To school?" cried the younger boy in amazement. "Why we're an hour late already. What's th' use o' goin' back now?"

"Jest you wait an' see," answered Shorty, rising. Lem followed, grumbling at the senselessness of such a suggestion. "We'll git a lickin' for being absent this mornin'——" Then a light dawned upon Lemuel and he smiled knowingly. "I cal'late I know why ye want to git back to school naow. You want to see that Dexter girl, hey?"

Shorty blushed. "Maybe I do an' maybe I don't," he replied.

Lem sniffed. "Bob Morrissey is kinder strong with that kid, Shorty. I reckon you ain't got no chance while he's around——"

"Shut up," snapped the other. "That ain't what I'm goin' back for. I've got a good game on."

"What? Let's hear it."

"Let's drive Tom Phinney's ol' daygin inter th' schoolroom."

Lem stood appalled at the suggestion. "Drive that old ox o' Tom's inter th' schoolroom?" he reiterated, and the humour of the thing caught his boyish fancy. "Bully idear! Let's git along an' do it. Gee! won't teacher be scared!" And chuckling with mischievous delight the plotters ran along the road to the little pasture where Tom Phinney's old ox Beauty was meditatively chewing the cud under the shade of a giant spruce.

Shorty rapidly cast the halter adrift from the tree, and with many a "Haw, Beauty! Gee, Beauty!" he steered the lumbering animal out and along the dusty road in the direction of the schoolhouse.

This was a plain one-story building, shingled and whitewashed, situated upon a knoll of bare rock which seemed to heave itself suddenly out of the earth at the roadside. It seemed strange that the only rocky land in Long Cove should have been relegated to the schoolhouse and the Anglican church, but teachers and clergymen were wont to apologize for the ruggedness of their respective territories by sundry references to education and religion being founded on a rock. Long Dick Jennings—a local fisherman and a character—used to affirm that both were rock-bottom propositions and hard to butt against, but, as Dick had no education and very little religion, he was no authority.

As soon as the schoolhouse opened itself to view Shorty fetched the ox up with a jerk when he caught sight of a horse and buggy tied up outside the door. "Whose is that?" hissed Lem apprehensively. "'Tain't th' minister, is it?"

Shorty, with the pipe still in his mouth, scrutinized the buggy and horse closely before replying.

"No, 'tain't th' parson," he said finally. " 'Tis a hired team, an' I reckon I knows whose it is."

"Not th' inspector's?" queried Lem in a half-panic at the thought.

"Naw! It's Cal Jenkins. He's a-goin' away second mate o' that three-master down to Anchorville an' he's a-callin' on teacher afore he sails. Give th' daygin a prod, Lem. Giddap! Gee!"

Up the bare rock path they scrambled, and opening the schoolhouse door with a bang, they leaped behind the bewildered ox and drove him through with thumps and wild yells of encouragement. There was a chorus of girlish shrieks from the interior of the room as poor Beauty, frightened out of his bovine senses, crashed through the narrow doorway and into the apartment, with the framework of the summer door entangled on his brass-knobbed horns.

"Aha! I've got ye, ye consarned imps!" Shorty and Lem turned on hearing the voice, and instantly found themselves grasped by the horny fingers of Beauty's master, Tom Phinney. Inside the schoolroom the ox was bellowing thunderously; girls were screaming in fright, and as Tom Phinney lugged them up to the door, both boys heard a familiar voice—a man's voice—driving the animal out of the room. "Uncle Jerry!" gasped Shorty, and while he squirmed in the farmer's clutch, the ox came lumbering out of the exit with horns down and tail upraised, and with the red-faced Uncle Jerry thwacking it with a wooden pointer the bewildered quadruped drove head first into Mr. Phinney and the two culprits, and ox, boys, and man rolled to the earth in a cloud of dust and profanity.

When Shorty came to himself after Beauty had rolled over on him—a chaos of staring bovine eyes, frothing jaws, and lashing hoofs and tail—he found himself being dragged inside the schoolroom by his avuncular relative Captain Jerry Clark, and in a daze he looked into the eyes of Miss Prim, the schoolmistress, and snapping and indignant eyes they were.

"Give them a lickin', Miss," cried Tom Phinney, dusting himself in the porch. "Tan 'em good. They desarve it——"

"I'll look after him, Miss Prim," interrupted Jerry Clark. "I'll fix him when we go home——"

"Thorough bad boys," the teacher was saying. "Playing truant from school, and full of wicked tricks. And just look at the pipe and tobacco which has fallen out of your nephew's pocket. Such depravity——"

Shorty was not listening. He was staring over at a back bench where a pretty little girl was drying her eyes and regarding him with a look of admiration not unmixed with fear. Shorty, the bold and wicked, seemed every inch a hero to little Carrie Dexter then, and the boy, ragged, dust-begrimed, and at outs with authority, felt heartened, like the Red Cross Knight of old, with the glances from his Una's eyes.

"Boy! go to your seat until school is over. I'll attend to you later." And Uncle Jerry gave his nephew a shove towards a vacant bench, behind which a big, heavily built boy of fourteen was seated. Lem had mysteriously vanished and Shorty was wondering what had become of him when the boy behind prodded him through the bench with his foot and whispered nastily. "You're a-goin' t' git socks from yer uncle for this racket, Shorty. I hope he tans ye good."

The culprit disdained to answer, though his anger rose at such a malicious observation. Bob Morrissey had very little love for Frank Westhaver, and as both were rivals for the affections of little Miss Dexter, relations were rather strained between the pair.

"Yah—you quitter!" Morrissey jammed his foot a trifle harder into Shorty's back. "Carrie's gittin' on to you now. She ain't got much use for your kind. Smokin' a pipe! Huh! Fancy a kid like you tryin' t' smoke. Carrie—— Ouch!"

There was a resounding smack of a fist on flesh, and Morrissey clapped his hands to his nose and yelled, while Shorty, blazing with rage, jumped over the bench after his tormentor. In a moment the schoolroom was again thrown into confusion. The girls screamed, and Uncle Jerry rushed from the platform, where he had been talking with the teacher, to separate the combatants, who were rolling upon the floor and under the forms and pounding each other with the gusto of the primitive savage. In a snarling, panting heap they tussled, thumped, and squirmed, and when the uncle threw the benches to one side, he arrived in time to pull his nephew away from the prone body of the Morrissey boy. "Reg'lar wild-cat, you are!" he growled as he piloted the pugnacious Shorty to the door. "Ye've disgraced me an' yer ma with yer monkey shines——"

"Lemme git at him! Lemme git at him!" howled the boy, struggling in his uncle's grasp.

"You'll git along to home at once," snapped Captain Clark in a voice strident with vexation. "I'll set ye up good an' taut with a bit o' ratlin stuff when I git back. Away with ye!" And Shorty was thrust ignominiously outside the schoolhouse door. As one of the school trustees, the worthy captain was annoyed with his nephew's misdemeanours, and when he returned to listen to the children's exercises he vowed a sharp retribution upon his sister's son.

Bedraggled and begrimed with dust, Frank ambled along the road, bitter at heart, and like Ishmael of old, with his hand against all men. How was he to know that Uncle Jerry had arrived home from the fishing? Why couldn't he keep out of messing around with the affairs of the School Board? His uncle—a man who couldn't read or write—mixing in with the parson as school trustee and always talking of the advantages of education! Pah! It was disgusting. A man like his uncle should know better. A fishing skipper to be in league with Miss Prim and the Reverend Mr. Westley in forcing a boy to cram book-learning into his head! It was unheard of! Thus soliloquizing, he ambled gloomily towards home until the padding of bare feet behind him caused him to turn and behold Lem Ring.

"Gee, Shorty, but you've certainly raised a rumpus," he panted. "I saw it all . . . through th' window . . . skipped 'raound th' schoolhouse when th' daygin knocked you'n Tom Phinney over. Miss Prim's madder'n a cat in a gurry butt, an' yer Uncle Jerry's right savage——"

"Humph!" Frank found no solace in the information.

"Where ye goin' naow, Shorty?" enquired Lem after a pause.

"Home," replied the other tersely.

"No use goin' yet. You'n me's a-goin' t' git a lickin' anyways, an' we don't need t' be in a hurry t' git it. Let's go down to th' wharf for a spell." The other nodded moodily, and both boys trudged down the hill.

Long Cove wharf was a short pile-and-crib erection constructed on the southern side of a small creek which flowed down from a cleft in the rocky, tree-covered hills which flanked the Bay of Fundy for many miles. At low water the wharf stood high and dry upon the stony, weed-strewn beach, and the small sloops and pinks belonging to the place hugged the festooned piles with their keels grounded in the trickling stream. No large vessels ever called at Long Cove, and with the exception of Captain Daley's thirty-ton packet schooner, which came in and departed on a tide periodically, the wharf was used principally by a few fishing pinks and sloops for landing their fares.

At the shore end of the pier were a number of sheds used by the local fishermen for cleaning and dressing down their catches of fish, storing their lines and gear, lobster traps and seines, and here and there upon the wharf would be an old dory used for salting fish. The clean, sun-bleached rocks and boulders of the beach above tide-water were strewn with drying hake, haddock, cod, and pollock, and numerous lath-built flakes were erected across the tangled hill-side. In summer the wharf was quite an animated spot, but in winter the place was practically deserted, as the boat fishermen usually went away vessel-fishing out of Gloucester and other great fishing ports.

"Where you a-goin'?" asked Shorty when they came

out of the path and entered the alleys of fish-flakes piled with circular heaps of dried hake.

"Drop in an' see Dick Jennings, I reckon."

Entering the first of the sheds, the boys came upon a man overhauling a tub of trawl. "Howdy, Dick!" cried both in chorus.

"Hullo, thar', fellers," returned Dick, without looking up from his work. He was a long, rangy man of some thirty-five years with a clean-shaven, leathery face creased by a thousand little wrinkles which seemed to multiply whenever he smiled. When the boys entered his shack he was seated upon an up-ended trawl tub with another between his sea-booted legs. With a tangled heap of seven-shot haddocking trawl beside him he was engaged in deftly stripping the old herring bait off the hooks, clearing the gangins, and recoiling the trawl back in the tub again. Occasionally he would reset a straightened hook and give a blunt barb a rub with a file, or with an incredibly swift series of movements, snap off a frayed gangin, open up the back line with a fid, and stick and hook up another and have it coiled down before an observer was aware of what he had done.

"Makin' a set next slack, Dick?" ventured Lem easily.

"Cal'late to," replied Jennings, squirting a stream of Niggerhead into a bait bucket.

"Fish strikin' good?"

"Not bad," answered the man, coiling away. "Pow'ful lot o' pesky dogfish last set I made. Fed most my baitin' to them." There was a pause, during which the fisherman coiled a good shot of gear into the tub. "Ain't you kids at school these days?" he asked suddenly.

Lem replied, "Yep! We was an' we wasn't. We're in an awful scrape, Dick."

"So? That ain't nawthin' new. What hev you two done this time?"

"Me'n Shorty drove Tom Phinney's daygin inter th' schoolroom——"

"What?" Long Dick stopped to look up at the redoubtable pair.

"Yep!" continued Lem, throwing out his chest. "We drove th' daygin in an' ye sh'd ha' heard th' racket. Shorty's Uncle Jerry was inside 'spectin' th' school an' he caught Shorty."

The fisherman's eyebrows raised in arched curves and his sunburned forehead paralleled them in numerous corrugations. "Whew!" he whistled, fixing the stolid, unblushing Shorty with a pair of keen brown eyes.

"I didn't know yore uncle was home from Gloucester."

"Neither did I," growled Westhaver.

"No, son, I cal'late you didn't. Ha! ha! ha! That's a good one!" Long Dick burst into a roar of laughter. "Lord Harry! Drove the ox inter th' schoolroom an' got cotched by yore Uncle Jerry. Dodgin' school too, I reckon——?"

"Yep! An' that ain't all, Dick," continued Lem. "Shorty had a pipe an' a plug o' terbacker in his pocket, an' it fell out, an' teacher saw it, an' he has a fight with Bob Morrissey right after he was sent to his seat. His uncle kicked him out th' room an' sent him home. He'll git some lickin' t'night, I'll bet——"

Shorty grunted. "Aw—an' so'll you, I reckon. Ef ye don't, I'll lick ye myself——"

"Ha! ha! ha! guffawed Dick. "What a pair o' wild-cats! Ho! ho! ho! An' he had a fight with Bob Morrissey right in th' school. My! Won't yore uncle be pleased with his nevvy! He'll tan ye some, I cal'late, for disgracin' him—an' him so strong on eddication an' sichlike. Never mind, son! Yo're th' right stuff for a fisherman. Don't let them spile ye by too much schoolin'. Book-l'arnin' don't l'arn ye how t' catch fish or pull lobster traps. Look at me! I never l'arned a thing at school in my life, an' ain't I one o' the best fishermen on th' Bay Shore? Ain't I 'most always high dory?"

"You sure are, Dick," exclaimed both youngsters.

"Thar' now," continued Long Dick. "That shows ye what book-l'arnin' ain't done for me. Look at Ted Small, th' deacon's son! He goes t' school an' gits full to th' back teeth with eddication an' then goes a-fishin', an' what is he a-doin' now? Tallyin' kintles o' salt fish on Lunenburg wharves 'most likely 'cause he was never no good at trawl haulin'. Eddication has taken th' backbone outer him, an' 'tis makin' strokes an' crosses on a tally-board he is at this moment, I cal'late. Yes, siree! T' Jericho with eddication an' joggraffy an' grammar an' 'rithmetic an' sich-like trash. They're no good to a fisherman. Pass me over that long-neck ye see in th' corner, son!''

A black bottle was passed over by Shorty, and Jennings, after drawing the cork with his teeth, indulged in a ''little touch.''

''Great stuff, that,'' he remarked, corking the bottle and smacking his lips. ''Never saw revenoo did that rum, an' rale West Indies at that.''

''Give us a swig, Dick,'' entreated Shorty.

''No, no, son,'' answered the fisherman. '' 'Twould make ye sick, I cal'late.''

''Sick, nawthin','' returned the boy. ''Sure I've had a swig o' rum afore now. Lem here got drunk once on a bottle we found down in his dad's fish shed——''

The fisherman flashed a strange look at the youngster, and rising, he placed the bottle inside a locker. ''No, son,'' he said decisively, ''I ain't got much left an' I ain't a-goin' t' spile good liquor by pourin' it down yore throats. Wait ontil sometime I git another jug.''

While he returned to his trawl combing the boys sauntered off to the pier-head, and for an hour they sat on the cap log and threw stones into Judson Morrell's dory. The dory was almost awash with the weight of them, when Lem gave Shorty a sharp nudge.

''Shorty,'' he exclaimed, ''Long Dick's gone home an' th' door of his shed's open.''

''What about it?''

For answer Lem screwed his face up in a knowing wink and beckoned to his chum to follow him. Entering the shack, recently vacated by the rangy fisherman, they stumbled over the trawl tubs, and, after groping around the dory sails and oilclothes hanging upon the rafters, Lem produced a black bottle.

"Rum," he explained, holding up the bottle for Shorty's inspection. "Dick thinks I ain't hep to his rum-sellin' game, but I know whar' he keeps his stuff. Here's for a drink." And opening his clasp-knife, he soon prised out the cork. With all the ease and abandon of a confirmed toper he placed the bottle to his lips, and, tilting it up, sputtered and shed tears as the fiery liquid went down.

"Hev a touch, Shorty." And passing the long-neck over, Master Ring began to feel all of a man.

Frank gingerly took a sip, but seeing his chum regarding him with the patronizing air of a professional for an amateur, decided not to be outdone, and gulped a wholesome nip.

The nip, in Lem's estimation, was more than he himself had taken, so in order to even matters up, he indulged in another. "Bet I kin drink more'n you at a gulp," exclaimed Lem.

"Bet ye kain't," returned the other. To back up his words Lem called his chum's attention to the high-water mark on the bottle neck, and, tilting it up, proceeded to lower it by the process of absorption into his own.

"There!" he grunted with a gasp as he passed the rum over. "I've drunk it down to that nick. Beat that ef ye kin."

Shorty beat him, and a species of Bacchanalian Marathon ensued between the pair until the rum defeated them both. Lem was the first to succumb, and he sat on an up-ended trawl tub holding his head and trying to regain an equilibrium which seemed to be whirling and gyrating like a chip in an eddy. Shorty lay prone inside a dress keeler or gutting-table, feeling very dizzy and sick at times and happy and hilarious by turns. The long-neck lay between them, its remaining contents spilled on the floor, and thus they lay until Uncle Jerry, Long Dick, and Ezekiel Ring found them late that evening.

"Waal, I be everlastin'ly cussed ef this don't beat all my

goin' a-fishin','' ejaculated Dick Jennings when he discovered the pair. "They've bin in here all afternoon a-broachin' my rum—th' young devils."

Zeke Ring strode over and yanked his young brother on to his feet.

"Whashmarrer?" mumbled Lem sleepily.

"I'll matter ye, you young swab," growled Zeke. "Home ye come now, an' ef I don't set ye up good an' proper, my name ain't what it is."

Frank was dead to the world, and repeated shakings, nudgings, and punchings by his uncle and Long Dick failed to elicit a sign of consciousness from him. Uncle Jerry's rage gave way to fear, and he turned to Long Dick. "What kind o' rum was that ye had? 'T'ain't no cheap rot-gut, is it?"

"No, siree," replied the other regretfully. "'Twas th' best Jamaica rum there is. I got it from Joe Spinney, mate o' the *Ella McKay*, what jest come up from th' south'ard two days ago, an' now 'tis wasted on a couple o' young sculpins——"

"Go'n git a bucket o' water, Dick," interrupted Captain Clark, and when the fisherman returned, he poured it liberally over his nephew's head.

"He gimme a kick," muttered the boy, feebly protesting against the cold douche. "Lemme git at him——"

Uncle Jerry gave him a shake. "Wake up, Frank. Rouse yourself!"

Shorty began to exhibit signs of consciousness, and Captain Clark turned to the other. "I'll carry th' lad home, Dick. Don't say anythin' about this to a soul. His mother 'ud go crazy ef she thought th' boy had bin drinkin'. Keep it quiet, an' tell th' Rings t' do th' same." And shouldering his inanimate burden, the big skipper trudged up the hillside in the dusk.

CHAPTER TWO

FRANK WAS AROUSED BY HIS UNCLE AT AN EARLY HOUR next morning, and, feeling sick and penitent, he dressed without taking the usual precautions. His mother was still a-bed, and Shorty, with a bad taste in his mouth, and his mind a complete blank after his recollection of the first two drinks of Long Dick's rum, was oppressed with a foreboding of trouble.

"Uncle's a-goin' t' tan me good this time," he muttered dismally, and, feeling very seedy, he crept quietly downstairs. His uncle was waiting outside the house, and engaged in whittling a stick. His face was stern, and he addressed his nephew harshly. "Follow me!"

Leading the way to a seat under a giant spruce, the Captain seated himself and motioned to the boy to follow suit. It was a glorious morning, sunny and clear, the bright blue of the sky flecked with fleecy white clouds racing past on the wings of the fresh westerly breeze which ruffled the waters of the bay into foam-streaked azure. The surf was thundering in on the rocky beach, and as far as the eye could see the blue water stretched before them with the white sails of the inshore fishermen's dories dotting the watery expanse. A large lumber-laden square-rigger was standing out of Anchorville Bay, and her dingy topgallant sails could be seen flapping in the fresh breeze as she made sail. Yes, it was a grand morning, when one felt glad to be alive, but to Shorty's jaded soul these things appealed not.

"Boy," began his uncle, whittling away, "do you know that you are goin' a bit too far?"

Shorty said nothing, and the captain continued:

"Yesterday's shine in th' schoolroom has jest about

cooked your goose, my son. A fine character you're a-makin' fer yerself. First dodgin' school, then smokin', then drivin' that ox, fightin' with one o' yer schoolmates right afore my eyes, an' finishin' up by stealin' a bottle o' rum an' gittin' drunk. Boy! what d'ye think ye're a-comin' to?"

Shorty made no answer, and his uncle proceeded: "You don't seem to understand what ye're doin'. Think o' yer ma. Ain't she got a bird of a son for people t' be gossipin' about? I don't mind yer tricks, but what I mind is yer sneakin' off an' drinkin' that rum. What made ye broach that liquor? Did ye go down a-purpose?"

"No, sir. I jest blundered in thar' with Lem."

"Who broached the bottle first, you or Lem," queried the skipper. "Give me a straight bill now—no yarns. Was it you?"

"No!" answered the boy. The big skipper seemed relieved.

"Then I cal'late 'twas Lem that found the rum, eh?"

Frank nodded. It went sorely against his grain to inform on his chum, but there was an underlying severity in his uncle's questions which brooked no subterfuge.

"What did ye do when ye broached the stuff? Sit down an' enjoy it?"

"No," replied Shorty. "Me 'n Lem had a try t' see who c'd drink th' most at one gulp."

"Huh." Uncle Jerry nodded grimly. Staring hard into the blue-grey eyes of his nephew as if to read his soul, he suddenly enquired:

"D'ye like th' taste o' that stuff, Frank?"

"No, I don't," replied the boy firmly. "Sooner hev lemonade or apple cider."

Uncle Jerry grunted again, and seemed to be debating in his mind what to say next. Picking up the stick, he commenced whittling deliberately.

"Boy," he said at last, "I want t' tell ye a story, an' you listen. See? Once there was a very fine man—name was Frank too— a fisherman he was, an' a big, handsome, strappin' feller—smart as a steel trap, an' a great favourite with all th' gangs what sailed with him. He had only one bad fault, and that was a kinder love for rum. He warn't a soaker, ye know, only he jest liked t' have a jug allus handy so that he c'd git a nip whenever he felt like it. He was a smart man, as I said afore, an' got on t' command his own vessel. He was more careful in them days, went easy on th' boose, but as he got on, his wife c'd see that it was gittin' a hold on him. Now he was a good feller, an' only laughed at his wife when she'd tell him about th' drinkin', but th' men as sailed with him was beginnin' t' talk aroun' th' ports about th' rum their skipper took t' sea with him. He'd stay sober at home, an' be half drunk all th' time at sea, and it warn't long afore this skipper an' his wife hed a quarrel. Then he goes off on a fishin' trip, an' when they got their salt wet they swung off for home, but not afore th' skipper takes a shoot inter Sant' Pierre for a little rum. It was breezin' up for a proper November blow when they left Sant' Pierre, but th' skipper, he started broachin' his liquor an' wouldn't take notice o' signs, an' swinging his whole four lowers, he starts running for Glo'ster afore a no'the-easter. All that day they carried their kites—even though it was blowin' a breeze o' wind with rain an' snow at times—an' when th' gang asks th' skipper t' shorten sail he only laughs them out of it an' passes his jugs aroun'. Purty soon half o' th' crowd were feelin' good an' not carin' a hoot for anythin'. Th' skipper had been below drinkin' all day, an' he gave th' course for t' raise Cape Sable 'thout botherin' t' check it up by th' log or lead. As I said, it was blowin' some, an' thick o' rain an' snow, an' long about two in th' mornin' they found themselves gittin' nervous as to their whereabouts.

"Th' skipper was still purty full, an' when th' gang asks him about haulin' up for a cast, he jest laughs, an' he was for broachin' another bottle when th' vessel hit th' Sable Island No'th-East Bar. She had all four lowers flyin', so she struck hard, an' with a howlin' gale drivin' a wild sea on th' lee shore where they lay, th' vessel soon went t' pieces, but before she went, ten o' her crowd went too. Jest fancy, boy! Ten men—all friends o' th' skipper—droppin' from th' riggin' inter th' sea an' drownin' afore his eyes. The captain knew it was his fault—knew that these men had bin sacrificed through his rum-swiggin', an' he had t' hang on t' his vessel's cross-trees an' watch 'em drop inter th' sea. He h'ard them prayin' for their wives an' children, an' with never a word t' say to him they'd let go an' drop. Ten o' them he saw go out that night, an' then he goes himself. All through a little nip o' rum, Frankie! Eleven good men drowned, an' many a widow an' orphan t' mourn them! D'ye know who that skipper was, Frankie?"

"No," replied the boy in horrified wonder.

Slowly and quietly the fisherman spoke. "Frankie, it was your own father!"

"My father?" cried the boy incredulously. There was a trembling of his lips and a suspicious mistiness in his eyes. He swallowed hard upon a lump which rose in his throat, and his uncle regarded him with a sympathetic gaze strangely out of keeping with his burly, weather-beaten appearance. "Will you want t' tech liquor agen, Frank, after what I've told ye?"

"Never!" replied the boy vehemently, and his uncle believed him.

"Now, son, I've jest a few more words I want t' say t' ye. Frank, you've got t' stick t' school, an' quit this dodgin' an' skulkin' game. I want ye to, an' yer ma wants ye. It's for yer own good t' git all th' l'arnin' ye kin, even ef you don't think so. Now take me, f'rinstance, I kin only jest sign my own name, an' I hev t' do all my figgerin' an' tallyin' by notches an' strokes—"

"Aye," interrupted Shorty, "but you're a high-line fisherman all th' same, Uncle. I'm a-goin' fishin' when I git old enough, so what's th' use o' l'arnin' a lot o' stuff that ain't no good a-fishin'?"

"Now that's whar' you make a big mistake, son," returned his uncle. "I may be a high-line fishin' skipper an' all that, but all th' same I wish I had had a decent eddication. I kain't pass a pleasant hour in readin' a noospaper; I kain't figure up a simple sum 'thout cal'latin' on my fingers; I'm cut off from writin' a letter—things what any T Wharf lumper kin do, an' here I am, forty-two years of age, an' more ignorant than you are. Many's th' time, Frank, I'd wish t' God I c'd ha' had th' chanst t' git th' schoolin' you're gittin,' an' here you are deliberately chuckin' yer chances away! Boy, ye must be crazy! D'ye think yer mother hez no pride? D'ye think she wants ter hev a son what kin hardly sign his own name? An' let me tell ye, if I'd ha' bin eddicated I c'd be in a better position than I am to-day. I c'd ha' bin runnin' a plant o' my own instead o' runnin' a vessel, but there's whar' I've got t' stick until I die. Livin' a dog's life at sea 'count o' knowin' nawthin'. You're goin' a-fishin', ye say, but ye want t' be somethin' more'n a fisherman all yer life—at least I hope so—but, mark my words, boy, ef ye keep up th' game ye're playin' now, ye'll pass yer days as a poor, miserable, ignorant fisherman, fit only for baitin' up an' haulin' trawls. By th' Lord Harry, Frank, ef ye only knew what I'd give t' go t' school again, ye'd never be in a hurry t' git away from it.'' Shorty was listening with bowed head, and with his bare toes he was nervously tracing patterns in the dust. His uncle regarded him with earnest eyes.

"Frank!" he resumed, after a pause. "What are you a-goin' t' do?"

The boy looked up gravely. He had never heard his uncle speak like this before, and it impressed him. "I'll go t' school, Uncle," he said finally.

"An' l'arn all ye kin?"

"An' l'arn all I kin, Uncle!"

The square-rigger had her topgallant sails and royals set by now, and, braced sharp up to the westerly, she was standing out the Bay. From the house came a suggestive rattle of pans and crockery, and a number of vagrant chickens made a sudden scurry for the kitchen door. Uncle

Jerry threw the stick away, and put his knife in his pocket. "Come on, Frank. We'll hev breakfast an' drive over t' Anchorville to-day. Don't say nawthin'.to yer ma 'bout what I was a-tellin' ye. She don't know nawthin' 'bout th' drinkin' but I cal'late she's got somethin' t' say about the rumpus in th' schoolhouse yesterday." And she had, but Shorty's young mind was obsessed with the tale he had heard, and he gave but little ear to his mother's scoldings.

The summer passed all too swiftly, and Shorty and his maternal uncle busied themselves around the homestead. The house was given a fresh coat of whitewash, new shingles were nailed on the roof, and with the garden and the orchard the boy was kept busy. Lem's father had returned from a Lunenburg vessel, and under parental authority he was set to work among the fish flakes. "Keep a boy outer mischief—keep him busy!" was Captain Ring's motto, and, like Shorty, Lem spread, turned, and piled dried fish; strung hake sounds on the wire fences; picked off potato bugs, weeded, hoed, and raked the garden until suppertime placed a halt upon his labours.

Bob Morrissey went off to sea as cabin-boy with a relation who was mate of the *Ella McKay* barquentine. Carrie Dexter had left to spend the summer with an aunt in Boston, and with these two gone Shorty's life was peaceful and almost free from untoward incident. The summer was a busy one for the Long Cove folks. An addition to the wharf had been completed, and it was now possible for a boat to float alongside the addition at ordinary low tide. A flag- and lantern-pole had been erected on the end of the wharf, and Long Dick Jennings was granted a small annual salary by the Government to keep the lantern and look after the wharf as a sort of harbour-master. As he could neither read nor write he depended upon Shorty to make out his reports and collect his wharfage dues. "Assistant or Depitty Harbour-Master o' Long Cove, I app'int ye," said Long Dick. And Shorty felt strangely proud of the title.

Judson Morrell was building a small schooner upon the

shore near the wharf, and with a number of new barns and sheds going up, Jim Hawkins, who owned the small waterpower saw-mill built alongside the creek, was kept busy. With the men nearly all back from the Banking fleets, the settlement took on a bustling and populated appearance. There were a number of "bees," picnics, clam bakes, and tea meetings, and though the Bay Shore folks were remote from the railroad—without telephone or telegraph, and dependent for news of the outside world by a weekly mail delivery—they were as happy and contented as dwellers in the large cities. Anchorville, the nearest town, was fourteen miles away, and though the distance was not great as the crow flies, yet it was quite a journey to get there. One could take a sloop or a dory and sail around if the wind was favourable, but the Bay Shore coast with its stretches of deserted, rock-bound beaches and beetling cliffs, dangerous underwater ledges and unknown tide-rips, was not an ideal shore to skirt, and the duration of such a journey was problematical. The most popular route was by the road, but as the highway climbed deviously over a steep mountain range, the drive was a six-hour ordeal and by no means easy on the horse. Thus Long Cove, Folsom's Harbour, Rock's Cove, Amiro's Cove, and Port Stanton, though practically adjacent to a town and all the luxuries of modern progress, yet remained a *terra incognita* to all but its own inhabitants.

After haying time the men and the older boys began to leave and join their vessels. Captain Jerry Clark left for Gloucester with a crowd of Bay Shore men, and one by one they departed—some to join American fishing craft out of Portland and Gloucester, others to make up the crews of Anchorville "shackers" and Lunenburg "salters." Thus they went, horny-handed toilers of the Banks, the true blue-water men which only the rock-bound shores of Nova Scotia seem to rear.

Shorty committed his uncle's admonitions to memory, and after listening to a lengthy dithyrambic upon the advantages of education, he regretfully bade his guardian good-bye. The packet schooner, which was taking the crowd to Anchorville, had swung miles down the coast ere Shorty turned away.

"Waal, Depitty, thar' gone agin for another season. Here's wishin' 'em luck an' high-liner's stocks." It was Long Dick who spoke, and the boy felt a strange vacancy enter his soul.

"Oh, Dick," he cried, "I wish I was a-goin' too. I'm gittin' tired o' this. I want t' git out t' sea like them."

"Time enough for that, youngster," replied the other. "Another year an' ye sh'd be ready t' go in th' dory. Come up an' help me bait a tub o' trawl."

The August days drew to a close and school was opened once more. Shorty had kept in touch with his books during the summer, and mindful of his uncle's advice, he made up his mind to study, and as he was a naturally smart boy, Miss Prim entertained hopes that she would be able to do something with him. He wrote a decidedly good hand, was smart and correct at figures, and had a remarkable aptitude for geography and reading. Grammar was his *bête noire*, history was distasteful, and drawing and geometry were hopeless propositions. Carrie Dexter had come back from her aunt in Boston, and now that Bob Morrissey was gone, Frank Westhaver had the full share of her affections. Frank and Lem still went around together as of yore; each indulged in occasional sorties of apple and berry robbing, and now and again a surreptitious smoke. One escapade was chalked to their account when they took a cruise in Jud Morrell's new schooner *Mayflower* and had the irate Judson chasing them all over the Bay in Long Dick's dory. Still, even Judson forgave them when he noted the able manner in which Shorty handled his little craft and brought her alongside the wharf.

It was getting along towards Christmas when, on a cold, dull December morning when the frost mist was obscuring the Bay, Shorty spied from his bedroom window an occasional vista of a large ballast-laden barque beating up and down the Bay. It was blowing a fresh breeze, hazy, and with the prospect of wind and rain or snow before nightfall, and the boy speculated upon the vessel's probable destination and the reason for her standing off and on. After breakfast he met Lem and both strolled down to the wharf to see Long Dick or Jud Morrell, but as both had made an early set they were at home in bed. It was beginning to snow a little by now, and Shorty caught sight of the wind-jammer standing very close inshore.

"Lem," he said suddenly, "I cal'late that craft's tryin' t' git inter Anchorville Bay, an' she's a-waitin' for a pilot."

"What about it?" queried the other, sensing something.

"Waal, I was thinkin'. What's t' hinder you an' me takin' her in? I know th' channel, an' I reckon ef we jest take Long Dick's dory we'll be aboard of her in twenty minutes."

Lem shook his head. "Kinder rough lookin', Shorty," he demurred. "How're we a-goin' t' git back?"

Shorty was pushing the dory off. "We kin git back all right. Come round in th' packet an' tow th' dory. There's twenty dollars in this bit o' work. Come on, tumble in."

Reluctantly Lem helped get the boat off the beach, and, shipping the oars, the boys pulled out from the lee of the wharf and swashed over the cresting combers in the direction of the vessel.

It was very cold, but the boys soon began to perspire with their exertions at the oars, and as they pulled the dory over the miniature hill and dale of sea, Lem was panting and gasping for breath.

"Keep it up, Lem," cried Shorty cheerfully. "She's stoppin' for us. Ten minutes more an' we'll git aboard."

Under the impression that a pilot-boat was coming out the barque had backed her maintopsail and a mile offshore was rolling her rust-streaked hull in the short Fundy seas. Under her stern went the boys, and the swart-visaged officer on the vessel's poop made a gesture of annoyance when he saw that the supposed pilot-boat contained but two curious boys.

"She's a Dago," surmised Shorty as they read the

name on her counter. "*Stelora Carmello* of Genova—that's what it reads." Then hailing the officer on the poop above him—"Hey! want—a—pilot—for—Anchorville?"

The officer nodded. "*Si! Piloto*—Anchorville. Yaas, pilot!"

Lem hove up the dory painter and a seaman grasped it, while another lowered a Jacob's ladder over the vessel's rusty iron sides.

"Up you go, Lem," cried Shorty, and jumping out of the dory, they soon threw their legs over the barque's topgallant rail and landed on her grimy decks. Up on to the poop strode Shorty, and the officer who had first hailed them shouted in rapid Italian to someone below deck. In a moment a stout, black-bearded man appeared, and by his self-conscious air, Shorty deduced that he was the captain.

"*Per la vita mia!*" he cried on beholding the boys. "*Il piloto di Anchorville? Caramba! Ella scherza, signor!*"

The officer turned to Shorty. "You able *pilota* dis—a ship—a Anchorville?"

"Sure thing," replied Shorty confidently.

The captain shrugged his shoulders. "*Ne dubito,*" he said, but young Westhaver started to take charge.

"Get her a-goin' agen," he said to the officer, who appeared to understand English, and the man bawled a gabble of orders to the shivering mob of Latins cowering under the shelter of the weather rail. The maintopsail was swung, and the barque gathered way.

The man at the wheel was a stupid-looking Italian hardly able to understand his own language, and the amateur pilot motioned for the English-speaking officer to take it himself. This was done; the helmsman shambled forward, while Lem and Shorty hovered around the wheel swinging their arms to keep warm.

"Cal'late you've taken on a job," muttered Lem dismally. "See'n don't pile her up, or that skipper'll hang us to the gaft, sure!"

"Leave it t' me," growled his chum. "I c'd sail a

schooner in, an' I cal'late steerin's th' same in all kinds o' craft. Gee! ain't this a big vessel. I wish Uncle Jerry c'd see me now!"

"Snow's comin' away harder," croaked Lem. "Looks as ef we were a-goin' t' git a blow. Where'll ye take this feller?"

"To th' ballast ground, I cal'late. He'll be for loadin' lumber at Anchorville Mills, but they gen'ly hev t' heave out their ballast afore they go alongside th' dock. Geehosophat! it cert'nly is snowin', but thar's Nub Head yonder. We'll put her square afore it an' run for th' Sound in a spell."

It was snowing very hard by now, and the rocky coast to leeward was almost blotted out. The barque was under double topsails, lower staysails, and spanker, and the wind was coming in puffs which heeled her well over.

"Cal'late she's abreast o' th' Upper Head naow," cried Shorty confidently, then to the officer at the wheel he cried, "Up helm, sir. Let her run in." The officer, who later proved to be the mate, nodded in comprehension, and before spoking the wheel over, he sung out to the captain, who was pacing excitedly back and forth across the poop.

"*Come comanda!*" the latter ejaculated, with another hopeless gesture, and striding to the rail, he spat out a volley of orders. The yards were squared, and bowing and curtseying as she swung off before the wind, the barque forged ahead for the narrow entrance to Anchorville Bay.

"*E un tempo orribile!*" remarked the captain to Shorty, with a shudder.

"I'll take your word for it," replied Westhaver, with a grin. "What's he a-sayin', sir?"

The mate elucidated. "The ol' fool saya disa bad weather. He ver' frighten. Dam' fool."

Shorty laughed. Such remarks about a superior in his presence seemed particularly humorous.

"There's th' fairway buoy, Shorty," cried Lem suddenly, as out of the snow-mist came the dismal tolling of a bell. In a minute they spied it on the port bow.

"Steady!" commanded Westhaver.

"Steady, *signore!*" repeated the mate.

The buoy seemed to come rapidly towards them, and when it rolled into the mist astern, Shorty spoke again.

"Starboard yer helm!"

"Sta'borda it ees, *signore!*" And the mate hauled the spokes over and chattered orders at the same time.

"Steady!"

"Steady, *signore!*"

At this point they had to stand in very close to the shore by the Upper Anchorville Head, and Shorty began to realize the responsibility of his position. The tide was running in very strong, but off the Head there was a rip which could always be depended upon to knock a vessel off, especially with a flood tide. On the wings of the breeze they drove in for the land—Shorty gauging his distance by the mournful hoot of the Upper Head fog alarm—and then the thickness lifted to reveal the surf-washed rocks of the Head rising a scant half-mile in front of them.

The Italian skipper gave a howl, and rushed to the wheel. Shorty saw him, and guessing the reason for his fright, yelled to the mate: "Keep him away, sir. It's all right— plenty of water here. Keep her steady, for heaven's sake, or we'll go on the Man-of-War."

With a contemptuous push, the officer kept his superior away and snarled: "*Tacete*—(be quiet)!"

Waving his arms dramatically and sputtering "*Misericordias!*" and "*Sono perdutos!*" between the rapid fire of Italian he was launching at the phlegmatic mate, the fat skipper danced all around his quarter-deck firmly convinced that Shorty was running his vessel on the rocks. Lem enjoyed the sight immensely, and sat upon the broad poop rail laughing derisively at the shipmaster's antics.

The rocks were coming close aboard by now, and Shorty raised his hand.

"Hard a port!" he yelled, and at the same moment the vessel's way was perceptibly checked as the tide-rip, deflected from the rocks, caught her on the port bow. Round came the lumbering vessel, and the yards were braced just off the backstays for a stretch on the port tack. The rocks vanished again, the hoot of the fog whistle died away, and the little skipper mopped the perspiration off his swarthy forehead.

"*Che fortuna*—(what luck)!" he exclaimed, while the mate regarded him with a look of ill-concealed contempt.

"Stand by to let go your anchor!" cried Westhaver, and the mate translated the order. The sea was comparatively smooth now, and though the snow veiled everything from sight, yet the boys knew they had fetched well inside the Bay.

"See the can buoy on th' ballast ground?"

Lem was half-way up the mizzen rigging looking for it.

"Yep! thar' she is!" he cried, and catching sight of it well to port, the pseudo-pilot passed the word to the officer.

"All right, sir. Round her up right here an' let go yer hook! You're all right now!"

The tatterdemalion shellbacks congregated on the foc'sle head, the cock-billed anchor was dropped from the cathead and swung free from the hawse, and as the jibs and foretopmast staysails were hauled down the vessel shot up into the wind, and when she began to make sternway with the wind in the backed topsails and the push of the flood tide the anchor dived for the bottom with a thundering roar of rusty chain.

While the crew were leisurely stringing out on the footropes aloft and furling sail, the snow ceased, and in a very short time the outlines of the town and wharves of Anchorville could be discerned. The fat skipper rubbed his hands and strutted around with humorous pomposity. "*Va benissimo*—(all is well)," he said, with a smug smile to the redoubtable Shorty, who was leaning over the poop rail and watching the men aloft. "*Quanto costa questa, mio fanciullo?*"

"Costa? costa?" repeated Shorty in perplexity.

"Yep," broke in Lem knowingly. "He wants t' know

what this is a-goin' t' cost him. He says don't make it too fancy, I cal'late."

The skipper nodded. "*Si, costa, costa?*"

Shorty considered. "Twenty dollars, I reckon."

"*Venti dollars, capitan,*" translated the mate.

The skipper looked up sharply. "*Venti dollars?*" he growled. "*Cielo! Ella scherza! Cinque dollars por piloto abbastanza!*"

The mate translated with a deprecating shrug. "He say you-a make-a joke. Twenta dollar too much-a. Five dollar enough!" And he added, "Make-a heem pay-a twenta dollar. He's peeg! dam' fool."

"Twenty dollars is what we want. Th' regular pilot from Anchorville 'ud charge ye more'n that t' take ye in from th' Heads thar'," said Lem.

"Twenty dollars is my price, an' I'm a-goin' t' stick to it." And Shorty nodded his head in determination.

On the boy's reply being translated the fat skipper indulged in a series of violent gestures, and almost choked Shorty with his garlic-laden breath while giving him a broadside of voluble protestations. "*Cospetto! Venti dollars pilotaggio troppo. Cinque dollars abbastanza. Povero me!*"

"He say-a he give-a you five-a dollar for *pilotaggio*. Him dam' peeg! Make-a heem pay-a twenta dollar!"

The captain nodded excitedly. "*Si, si!*" and the olive-skinned mate laughed. "He say-a for you-a to stick for twenta dollars. Yes, yes, he say-a."

"Twenty dollars," repeated Shorty steadily.

"No, no," said the skipper. Shorty sat down on the skylight. "I'm a-goin' t' stick here ontil I git that money, so ye kin tell him that, sir." And Lem nodded aquiescence. The captain, on hearing the boy's reply, swore in choice Genoese and clattered below. The mate busied himself for a few minutes superintending the clearing-up of the decks, then, with a shiver, turned to enter the cabin. Spying the boys, he beckoned for them to follow him and he led the way down to his room.

"Capitan ees peeg," he whispered as he ushered them into the tiny apartment. "Seat you a-down. I getta you-a somet'ing to eat-a. Leetle boys like-a somet'ing to eat-a always. Hah?" And his white teeth glittered in a smile. Singing out for the steward, a greasy-looking individual answered, and in a few minutes returned with a tray laden with a wicker-covered bottle, two glasses, and two steaming plates of spaghetti mixed with some kind of chopped vegetable. The boys had never seen macaroni or spaghetti before, and tackled it rather gingerly.

"Looks like worms," remarked Lem suspiciously. "Ye kin niver account for tastes. Some folks'll eat anythin' nowadays——"

Shorty had tasted. "It's all right, Lem. 'Tain't what you think. Tastes good." And he rapidly demolished his portion.

"You-a take-a *vino Chianti*—leetle wine?"

"Sure thing," assented Lem, passing his glass, but Shorty shook his head. "Not for me, sir, thank ye!"

"What's th' matter, Shorty?" queried his chum. "Ain't you a-goin' t' try a drink o' this?"

"No!" Shorty's memory was still fresh with the incidents of the last drink. Somehow or other his thoughts turned to the story he had heard, and his imagination pictured that bitter, black night on Sable Island North-east Bar when the *Grace Westhaver,* his father, and ten men went to their long home on account of a few bottles of Saint Pierre rum. No! he would never touch liquor of any sort again.

Lem quaffed his glass of wine with evident gusto, and the mate laughed at the boy's air of insouciance as he gulped it down. "You *Americano* boys are veree devil boys!"

"No," said Shorty. "We're not American—we're Nova Scotian."

"Aha! Novva Scozian. Dat ees not Americano. Dat ees Canadian, eh?"

Shorty shook his head indignantly. "No, no," he

replied. "Nova Scotian is kinder different from Canadians. Canadians belong away up th' west aways. Ontario, Quebec, an' Manitoba. We folks down east are Nova Scotians an' New Brunswickers."

The officer seemed perplexed, but accepted Shorty's explanation on face value.

Producing a bundle of long cigars with quills inserted in the mouthpieces, he passed them around, and in great goodfellowship the three were chattering away in the tiny smoke-filled room and admiring the mate's stock of curios which he was taking home to a certain Marghareta who lived in Spezia. The barque had just come up from the River Plate, and the officer exhibited a number of fine grebe skins, oily and high-scented with native tanning, but beautiful in their downy creaminess. Then came a huanaco robe which had doubtless graced the form of some belle of the Pampas, but the most wonderful thing about it was the manner in which the little deer skins were sewn together by the sinews of the South American ostrich. Souvenirs, *Recuerdos de Buenos Aires y Rosario,* photos of the Movediza del Tandil —the wonderful rocking stone which, though it weighs countless tons, can be set in motion by the push of a baby; gorgeous-coloured representations of the Plaza de Mayo in Buenos Aires on the glorious 25th of May—anniversary of Argentinian independence—besides countless other nicknacks which set Shorty's seafaring blood afire and awoke in him a determination to learn more about the great world he lived in at some future date.

Like a trio of old cronies, the boys and their Italian friend smoked countless *cigarros* and listened to yarns of adventure by sea and land: doublings of the dreaded Cape Horn in wintry weather; Garibaldi's great fights in Italy and South America; and stirring tales of wharfside fracases on the Buenos Airean Boca and the moles of Monte Video, Valparaiso, and Callao. The mate was just in the midst of a mutiny yarn, and the boys listening intently and with eyes aglow, when a discordant and yet in a manner welcome interruption came in the raucous voice of old Captain Spinney—the Anchorville harbour-master.

"Below thar'," he rumbled. "Ain't thar' a dam' soul on this blasted hooker t' heave a ladder over th' side? By Godfrey! them Dago barques are th' limit for attendin' t' th' business an' regulations o' th' port of Anchorville. No report made—no quaratine—no customs examination or nawthin'. Hey, thar', Capitan! *Intendete?*" Captain Spinney was an old windjammer skipper, and he started hailing for the barque's captain in the Lingua Franca of the seas—a language which every deepwater-man knows and which sailormen of all nations can understand.

The mate excused himself. "The capitan peeg ees asleep. I go." Then to the harbour-master who, with the doctor and the Customs officer, was waiting in the cabin, he said, *"Buon giorno, signores!* the capitan I call heem."

The Italian shipmaster was eventually roused out, and for a few minutes there was some lively language in the hallowed precincts of the cabin.

"Why'n Tophet didn't ye bring yer papers ashore when ye arrived?" bawled Captain Spinney. "D'ye think I'm a-goin' t' come out t' every blasted Dago hulk what brings up out here for the dues o' th' port o' Anchorville? Bring out yer register—*registro,* savvy?—an' yer quarantine papers from yer last port—*quarantena,* savvy?—an' call all hands aft here for to pass th' doctor. Make yer Customs declarations as well—*spedizione doganale,* savvy?—an' be thumpin' quick about it!"

Captain Spinney thundered these commands out in a foretopsail-yard ahoy voice, and the boys in the mate's room listened in keen appreciation. "Ain't ol' Spinney givin' it to him?" murmured Lem admiringly. "Jest listen t' th' way he kin swear, an' yet he an' John Muise was up to Folsom's Cove at the Revival meetin's last week a-prayin' an' a-groanin' for th' poor sinners."

"Who fetched ye in here?" was the harbour-master's next question. "Where's yer pilot? I cal'late ye never came in that snowstorm without one——"

Shorty stepped into the cabin. "Me'n Lem piloted her in from off Long Cove——"

The harbour-master's eyes opened wide in surprise, and the doctor and Customs officer stared at the boys in evident astonishment.

"Waal, I swan!" cried Captain Spinney.

"Yaas!" It was the Italian mate who spoke. "Dese-a lettle boys piloto de barca into de porta—ver' good—ver' smart—but capitan no want-a pay-a dem for piloto."

"He don't wanter pay ye, son?" asked the harbour-master addressing Shorty.

"No! He would only give me five dollars, sir," replied the boy. "I kinsider that it's worth twenty. Ye see, it was snowin' hard—an' breezin' up for a blow—"

"You're blame well right, son," cried the Captain. It's blowin' half a gale in th' Bay now, an' t' take this lumberin' box in here when it's thick is worth double th' money. Wait a bit, boy—I'll see that ye git it or I'll libel th' hooker."

The Italian shipmaster passed a very unpleasant hour at the hands of the old Nova Scotian harbour-master, and the two boys, after viewing the might of his authority, made up their minds that a harbour-master's job was a position of great importance.

"Long Dick's harbour-master at Long Cove," said Shorty, "but he ain't a shine t' Cap'n Spinney."

The crew were all mustered in the cabin, and little Doctor Manson examined tongues and pulses with a thoroughness not to be equalled at Ellis Island, and the horde of shivering, dungaree-clad Latins were declared physically free from any infectious disease and dismissed. Protesting and swearing, the barque's captain brought out his cashbox and paid his accounts in American money, almost giving way to tears at handing twenty dollars to a couple of schoolboys for pilotage.

"Thar's yer money, son," said Captain Spinney. "Naow see'n don't spend it in luxuries an' riotous livin'." And the doctor and Customs officer laughed.

They pulled ashore to the Anchorville Long Wharf in their own dory, accompanied by the Italian mate, who seemed greatly pleased that the boys had screwed the money out of his superior.

"Il capitan di porto—he ees smart man," he remarked, smiling. "Novva Scozian—Bluenoze—bucko! I sail Bluenoze ship one time. *Abbay Ry-er-son* of Yar-mout', Novva Scozia."

Before they parted with their Italian friend, Shorty spent some of the money in purchasing a pretty Blomidon amethyst brooch from an Anchorville jeweller and presented it to the delighted sailor.

"For Margaret in Spatechea!" said Shorty, and the mate's swarthy face flushed with pleasure. "*Grazie! grazie! signores!*" he murmured. Before he left them he had their names and addresses written in a notebook, and, emptying his pockets of all his cigars, he went his way. "*Addio, signores! Vada con Dio!* (God go with you!) *A rivederci!* (We shall meet again!)"

The boys regard that visit to Anchorville as one of their most treasured memories and one which gave them a topic of conversation for many days to come. Just imagine two country boys loose in a town with twenty dollars to spend! Boys who had seldom been any further than twenty miles from their homes, and who had passed all their lives in a quiet settlement hemmed in by the mountains behind and the sea in front. Will they ever forget the ecstasy of it? The freedom to do as they like? To stroll around looking into the shop windows and price things with the consciousness that they could buy them if they wanted to? It was glorious! With pockets bulging with candies and oranges the boys felt as if they owned the town. Italian cigars in their mouths, they strolled into the stores and made their purchases with an air of wealth which impressed the storekeepers and caused some busybodies to wonder "ef they had come by it honestly."

And they had a fight—a most glorious fight—to add zest to the occasion, when a lout of a pool-room loafer passed some disparaging remark anent "Bay Shore kids goin' on a ten-cent spree!"

After Lem and Shorty had pummelled him he was glad to run away, while the victors continued their round of pleasure. And in the evening when they went aboard the packet and hugged the genial warmth of the stove in her cabin, they spun the yarn of their adventures to the skipper, Cap'n Bill Daley, and he smoked their cigars and agreed with them in all they said. And the presents they had bought were characteristic of their natures, and a source of extreme pleasure to both as they opened the parcels and viewed them again. Lem's red-and-white jersey, his belt and sheath-knife, tobacco-pouch and two pipes—one for himself and the other for his brother—a cheap Swiss nickel watch guaranteed to tick if nothing else, and a few pins and brooches for his mother and sisters. Shorty's purchases were of more use, consisting as they did of a good briar pipe for his Uncle Jerry, another to conciliate Long Dick for borrowing his dory, a brooch for his mother with the name "Grace" engraved upon it, another brooch to be held in reserve for some person at present unknown, and two books—one Stevenson's "Treasure Island" and the other "Dana's Two Years before the Mast." These, with the addition of a pipe and a plug of tobacco for himself, constituted the boy's outlay of eight dollars, and to his mind he had wonderful value for his money.

They slept upon the lockers in the little packet's cabin and awoke in time next morning to assist Cap'n Daley and Joe Small in getting sail hoisted. It was still dark when they left the wharf, but the wind of the previous day had died down to a light breeze. Past the great light hulk of the barque they glided, and the boys wondered what their Italian friend was doing then. "He was a decent kind o' feller," commented Lem. "I don't think he had much use for that greasy-lookin' skipper o' his'n. Got'ny o' them Eyetalian cigars left?"

Shorty passed one over, and the youngsters enjoyed a smoke while the schooner slipped past the Upper Head.

"Hey, Pilot Westhaver," cried Joe Small. "Come'n take th' wheel while I go git breakfast!" And while Lem and Cap'n Daley were clearing up the gear and chocking up the numerous kerosene barrels which littered the decks, Shorty sat astride the wheel-box smoking a lengthy Italian cheroot and steering with a watchful eye on the luff of the mainsail.

The sun had risen clear of the wooded hills to the eastward, and the waters of the Bay stretched cold and blue under a cloudless sky as far as the eye could see. Here and there the anchored dories of shore fishermen waiting for their trawls to set could be seen, while far over towards the New Brunswick shore the smudge of a steamer's smoke hovered low over the horizon.

>"Lively on th' chorus thar',
> Ez hearty ez ye can—
> For we're outwardbound this mornin'
> On a Novy Scotia-man!"

It was Joe Small who was singing, and his voice rolled up the hatchway amid the clatter of pans and the sizzle of frying bacon. "Keep it up, Joe," cried Shorty, who was fond of music and singing. "I'm listenin'."

"Oh, I ain't no blame' primmer donner," cried Joe, "but take it from me, son, when I starts a-chanteyin' it's somethin' t' listen to.

> Whin we manussed Skipper Penny o' th' schooner *Nip an' Tuck*,
> 'Cause he drove her east an' drove her west, an' didn't have no luck.
> So ter stop his wicked squeals,
> We laid 'un by th' heels,
> An' we lashed 'un in buoy line an' run 'un to th' truck.
> So it's Hey ho! my hearties o' th' schooner *Nip and Tuck!*
> We'll manuss every skipper whin he's lost his bloomin' luck!"

Shorty applauded with a stamp of his feet. "What's that, Joe?"

"Oh, some blam' cod-hauler's chantey I ha'rd up in Noof'nlan'."

The fragrant odour of coffee came up the scuttle, and the boy sniffed hungrily. The breeze was freshening, and the beamy old packet was swashing and curtseying in the short seas, and whisking a dash of chilly spray over her blunt bows. The patched mainsail was as full as a balloon, and the cool breeze sang a low sibilant song in chorus with the snore and splash of the water under the bows.

"Great morning, son," remarked Cap'n Daley. "We sh'd make Long Cove in an hour at this clip——"

"Grub, ho!" bawled Joe, sticking his head out of the scuttle. The skipper grasped the wheel. "Go below, boys, an' git a bite." And Shorty and Lem piled into the cabin with alacrity.

Harbour-master Dick Jennings was standing on the string-piece of the Long Cove wharf when the schooner swung in. He spied his dory towing astern, and addressed himself to Shorty.

"Consarn ye, ye imp o' th' devil," he bawled. "Run off with my dory 'thout so much as by yer leave. Some kids hez cheek for a whole ship's comp'ny—— Oh, ah, is this for me, son? Waal, by th' Lord Harry! ef that ain't a pipe an' a half. Will I smoke it? Jest give me a fill an' I'll be for breakin' it in right now. Ye piloted a barque inter Anchorville? Waal, I'll be goshswizzled! 'Tis as smart as a steel trap, you boys be! An' in all that snow yestiddy? Waal, by gosh, ef that don't beat all my goin' a-fishin'." And Long Dick regarded the youngsters in unfeigned admiration, while he proceeded to enjoy a smoke in the new pipe.

"Smart kid that Westhaver boy," remarked Cap'n Bill Daley after his passengers had departed for their respective homes. "They sure had a great time 'round Anchorville yestiddy on th' money they got for pilotin'."

"Warn't drinkin', were they?" queried Long Dick anxiously.

"Oh, no," answered the packet schooner's skipper.

"Jest buyin' up th' town, hevin' a little fight or so, an' smokin' cigars. I reckon Tim Evans—th' town policeman—was kinder scared t' handle 'em kids. Tol' me he never saw a couple o' thirteen-year-olds with so much sass. Lord, Dick, ye'd ha' laughed t' ha' seen 'em strutting 'round Water Street with them Dago cheroots in their faces. How many bags o' salt d'ye want?"

Dick scratched his head. "Let me see! Zeke Ring'll take five, I reckon. I'll take five an' a bar'l o' kerosene. Th' parson wants a bar'l o' flour. Ted Harley'll take two rolls o' tar-paper an' ten bundles o' shingles. Them dory oars you got thar' are for Jud Morrell, I cal'late. Did ye git his noo mains'l from th' sailmaker? No? Waal, I reckon that'll be about all for Long Cove. Down in the cabin, ye say? How many bottles did ye git?" And Dick Jennings, Long Cove harbour-master, entered the schooner's cabin presumably "to check up his accounts."

CHAPTER THREE

CHRISTMAS AND NEW YEAR CAME WITH SEASONABLE weather, and for a week Long Cove entered into the festivities of the occasion. A number of the men came home to spend the holidays with their folks, and for a while there was a continual round of dances and tea meetings. Uncle Jerry came over from Gloucester, and in exchange for his nephew's present of a pipe produced a bulky bundle of books which he had purchased in Boston.

"I cal'late you kin read them, Frankie," he said. "Th' man I bought them of said they were useful an' entertainin' readin' for a boy. See! Thar's some good seafarin' pictures in 'em—that's how I sized 'em up. Look at this yarn—a couple o' pinks firin' guns at each other. Cal'late they must be Frenchies a-scrappin' up on th' Treaty shore. What's th' name o' th' yarn, Frank?"

" 'Westward Ho!' Uncle."

"So! That's a good-soundin' name for a book. Now what's this feller here with three 'O's' and an 'M' in th' name——?"

" 'Omoo,' by Herman Melville—a tale of the South Seas," answered his nephew delightedly. "I'll bet that'll be a dandy like 'Treasure Island.' What are the others? 'The Wreck of the Grosvenor,' by W. Clark Russell——"

"Aye!" interrupted his uncle. "That's a book I was told t' git by one o' th' gang. Said it was a great yarn, tho' I don't remember 'bout that wreck. Cal'late she warn't a fisherman. An' this book here—what's that about?"

"That's not a story book—it's a book on figures—'Arithmetic Simplified,' it's called."

"Eh? eh?" cried the skipper in surprise. "Arithmetic, is it? Now I wonder haow I come t' git that derned thing? Better heave it away, Frank— we don't want 'rithmetic books, do we?"

Shorty was looking over the pages. "No," he said quietly, "I'll keep it. 'Tis a mighty useful-lookin' book, an' I kin see thar's a lot o' good things in it. Gives the answers to th' problems as well. Cal'late I'll work 'em out this winter——"

Uncle Jerry seemed to be pleased at the boy's reply, and when Shorty's back was turned he winked knowingly over at his sister.

While he was upstairs conning his literary treasures, Uncle Jerry turned and enquired of Mrs. Westhaver: "How's he gittin' along at school, Grace? Ain't bin dodgin', has he?"

"No, he's been going regular," she replied, "an' Miss Prim's very pleased with him. She was jest a-saying yesterday that Frankie was the smartest boy in the school this year. If he passes the examinations in the spring he'll have gone as far as he can go."

"Humph," grunted the other in content. "I cal'late he'll do. Next summer when school closes I'll git him out in th' dory with Jud or Dick, an' long about fall I'll git him off on a Bankin' cruise."

Mrs. Westhaver's brow clouded. "But I don't want him to go to sea, Jerry. There's enough on the farm here to keep him going, and 'tis lonesome enough I am now without—— Oh, Jerry, keep him to home if you can." And the appeal in her voice came from the heart.

Uncle Jerry blew a great whiff of smoke. "Grace," he said slowly, "kin ye keep a duck from th' water? C'd mother keep me from goin' t' sea? It's in our blood, an' 'tis salt water that runs in our veins. Frankie's a Westhaver an' a Clark, an' did ye ever know any o' th' menfolk o' them families linin' up with a longshore job? Never! An' by th' Great Trawl Hook! I'd never want t' see chick or relation o' mine settlin' down 'thout doin' his time on blue water." He paused for a moment while his sister bent over her sewing. "That boy is a born sailor," he continued. "See him handle a dory in a chop! See him put that little schooner o' Jud Morrell's through her paces! Jest think o' him pilotin' that lump of an Eyetalian barque inter Anchorville that day—thick o' snow an' blowin'! Why, Jesse Collins—lightkeeper at th' North Head—thought that 'twas Cap Spinney himself a-bringin' her in. Jest fetched her about at th' Knock Rip as nice as ye please. An' d'ye think ye'll keep a boy like that away from th' water? Ye can't do it, Grace, an' 'tis better for him t' go with our consent than t' run away. Ef he runs away he'll go coastin' or deep water—jest what I don't want him to do, for a fisherman I want him t' be, but not such a fisherman as I am—ignorant an' uneddicated. No, Grace! leave him t' me an' I'll make somethin' outer him."

Mrs. Westhaver said nothing, but in her heart of hearts she knew that her brother was speaking truth and being born and bred in a seafaring community, with the sea ever before her eyes and the breath of it in her nostrils, she knew that the day was coming when her only child would answer to the call. It was hard, but the womenfolk of that sea-washed coast were steeled to bear it; nerved to endure the racking anxieties of days and nights when the great Atlantic combers thundered in acres of foam upon the iron rocks, and the grey scud flew low before the spite of the gale; when the spindrift froze in the biting air and slashed through the howling snow-grey nights when wind and sea arose in rage and shrieked for victims. God! They need His help when their men are at sea!

The New Year holiday passed: the men returned to their vessels, and the Bay Shore settlements became bleak and deserted. The ground was covered with snow to the water's edge, and the hills towered gaunt and sullen with their ragged spruce-clad crests serrating the sky. The rocks on the beach were scaled thick with ice, and the shore fishermen went about their bitter work on the waters of the Bay clad in heavy clothing, and always with a bit of grub in a parcel and fresh water in the dory jar.

Around the farms the only evidence of life came in the wisp of blue smoke from the chimneys and the chop-chop of the axes in the bush lands. Slow-footed oxen trailed logs over the snow-covered roads to the rollway at the mill dam, and occasionally the silent echoes of the creek gully were awakened by the rasp and ring of Jim Hawkin's water mill.

Shorty broke the ice in his water-jug of a morning, and his pre-breakfast hour was spent in milking the cow, splitting and drawing wood and water. Clad in warm woollens and with mittens on his hands, he walked to school a little before nine o'clock, and got the stove going for Miss Prim. Until four he applied himself to his lessons, and the remaining hours of daylight were usually spent down among the fishermen at the wharf or up in Skipper Ring's barn, where sprawled among the hay, he read "Treasure Island" to an awed assembly of listening youngsters. The grotesque chorus of "Fifteen men on a dead man's chest!" became as popular as a music-hall ditty around the Cove, and hoarse shouts for "Darby McGraw! Bring aft th' rum, Darby!" set Miss Prim wondering as to their origin. And they had a deal of fun out of it too, for with Shorty as Long John Silver and other youngsters taking prominent parts they acted passages from that wonderful story upon the deck of Jud Morrell's schooner until that gentleman wondered "what in tarnation thunder hed come over th' kids?"

And "Westward Ho!" Who can describe the pleasure Shorty got out of that book? How he longed to emulate the men of far-off Devon and go a-sailing down the Spanish main in search of gold-laden galleon and carrack! How Carrie Dexter cried when Shorty read her the unhappy outcome of Rose Salterne's love for the Spanish Don Guzman; how she shuddered at the terrors of the Inquisition and gloated over the merciless hatred of Amyas as he searched the Invincible Armada for the man he wished to kill! To her romantic imagination Shorty was an equal of the daring Amyas. Had he not boarded a galleon and wrested a treasure from the black-bearded Don in command? Had he not returned triumphant as did the men of Devon laden with presents and with one for her? True! the circumstances were slightly different—the galleon was typified by a rusty-hulled Italian barque big enough to carry a galleon on her main deck—but, as she gazed at the Blomidon amethyst brooch he had given her out of his prize money it seemed as valuable as the great emerald of Don Francisco de Xarate.

Bob Morrissey was forgotten, although sundry letters from him had reached her from West Indian ports; but Bob was far away galley fetching and brass polishing on a barquentine, while Shorty was near and to home. And Shorty was no end of a man in her eyes. He could lick any boy in the place—small and all as he was—and the way in which he could smoke a pipe had even old Captain Crawford hull-down for style and aptitude. And he wasn't a bad-looking boy either. He had nice grey-blue eyes and white teeth: his freckles "became him," and matched well with his sandy hair. Yes, as Carrie gazed at him reading aloud the adventures of the bold Amyas she could picture in her imagination that it was Amyas himself who was telling the tale, and the fancy pleased her mightily.

The winter was not without its adventures for the boy, for both he and Long Dick had spent a whole bitter night out in the Bay unable to make the Cove in an easterly blow. It was wild, exciting work keeping the dory riding the seas, but when the grey morning broke, the storm eased down and they had a long pull in. Then there was a fire in Colin Baker's barn, and Shorty manipulated an almost red-hot pump-handle while the bucket brigade saved the homestead. Though his hands were blistered and painful, yet he felt it was worth it when Carrie Dexter gave him a kiss and a piece of real chocolate for his heroism.

Altogether the winter was a very fair one, with no storms to speak of, and good fishing both in the Bay of Fundy and on the Banks, and when the men came home in the spring to attend to their farms there was all the evidence of a prosperous winter's fishing among them. Houses were painted up, sheds built, new dories on the beach, and a nine days' wonder in the shape of a piano in Skipper Ring's house. The piano was brought around from Anchorville in the packet schooner with Captain Ring and Zeke to convoy it, and the whole of Long Cove crowded the wharf when it was unloaded under the supervision of old Captain Crawford, who rigged a complicated web of tackles for its safe discharge. Up to the skipper's house the crowd followed the oxen, and when it was finally unpacked, carried into the "settin'-room," and Miss Prim played a few old ballads upon it, the Long Covers "cal'lated that th' place hed purty well all th' luxuries of a taown!"

Then came the examination of the school with a saturnine inspector, the English Church minister, and Captain Jerry Clark to superintend. Shorty and Lem were both in attendance, and as the children bent over their papers Uncle Jerry kept a vigilant eye upon his nephew. When at last they had finished and the boys and girls advanced to the desk with their completed tasks, the inspector glanced over Shorty's work and remarked: "You write a good hand, my boy. Ah, let me see? Are you not the youth who misbehaved himself and failed last year?"

Shorty nodded calmly. "Yes, sir, I cal'late I did!"

The inspector allowed a ghostly smile to flicker across his austere visage. "Humph!" he said, and dismissed him.

Vacation time came in due course and also the intelligence that Frank Westhaver had passed his examination successfully with high percentages in arithmetic, geography, reading, writing, and spelling. Poor Lem had failed dismally, and his parents wrathfully decided that he would spend another year at school.

Closing day came, and a sunny afternoon saw an apparently endless procession of buggies trailing up and down the Bay Shore roads. All the Long Covers were present in the schoolhouse, including many who had neither son nor daughter at the school, but by reason of their being alumni of the ancient whitewashed building they found a reminiscent pleasure in being there on Closing Day. Captain Jerry Clark, resplendent and awkward in a stiff white shirt and high collar, was seated upon the platform in company with Mr. Westley the Anglican parson and Mr. Letteney the Baptist minister from Folsom's Harbour. Captain Asa Crawford—an old sea captain, dressed in an ancient black beaver hat and a "square-mainsail" coat— was seated close to the platform amid a bustling, rustling crowd of elderly mothers, who passed remarks upon everybody and everything.

"The ol' Captain's keepin' his age well," commented one portly dame in a stage whisper.

"Yes," assented her neighbour. "Seventy, I cal'late."

The old skipper heard and corrected. "No, I ain't, Mrs. Pusey. Ye know well enough that I'm jest eight years older'n you——"

While the worthy captain was raking up comparative dates Mrs. Pusey was vainly endeavouring to change the subject from an uncongenial topic. The children, with cheeks shining, hair brushed, and dressed in their best, were nervously awaiting the commencement of the exercises. Mr. Westley arose and tapped the desk for silence. Instantly the hum of voices died down with the exception of Captain Crawford's, and he was still laying down the law to the portly lady red with rage and mortification behind him.

"Yaas," he was saying, "you were 'zackly twenty-five years of age when I was a-courtin' you 'long in eighteen-fifty, an' I was mate o' th' *Freeman Collins* then, an' jest thirty-two. Clem Pusey married you in 'fifty-nine, an' folks was a-sayin' then that you were gittin' along an' consarned lucky t' git a man——"

The clergyman tapped the desk ominously, while the assembled parents tittered. Mrs. Pusey was a notorious gossip, and the old sailor was providing an unconscious play for their delectation.

"Captain Crawford," interrupted the minister, who was a diplomat, "I think we should have you seated with us up here on the platform." And greatly to Mrs. Pusey's relief, the old man accepted the invitation and squeezed himself between Jerry Clark and Mr. Letteney.

The recitations then commenced with a sextette of little girls, wonderfully arrayed in vari-coloured ginghams and sashes, who, after their initial coyness had passed, sang to the accompaniment of the school harmonium, played by Miss Prim. This was liberally applauded by the delighted parents of the girls, and praised in glowing terms. A studious-looking boy got up next and delivered "Mark Antony's address to the Romans," and his oratorical effort was hungrily followed by his admiring father—a horny-handed trawler of the Grand Banks.

"Great work, son," he rumbled when the boy had retired. "Ye'll be in Parliament yet afore ye're through." And chuckling to himself, he broke the stem of a favourite pipe in his nervous pleasure.

For a reading Shorty read from that portion of "Westward Ho!" which describes the approach of the *Rose* to La Guayra, and it moved old Captain Asa Crawford to make some reminiscent remarks.

"That's dead t' rights," he said, smacking his fist on the desk. "I bin off'n that coast a-runnin' guns inter La Gooayra an' Cartyena. An' didn't I get shelled by one o' them blame' Venezooalian *guarda costas* an' forced t' run for Jamaica with nigh' six feet o' water swashin' 'round in th' brig's hold? An' that Saddleback Mount'in is thar', for I seen it with my own eyes, an' I also saw that governor's house up th' hill-side, tho' it seems t' me they were usin' it for a *calaboose* when I was in La Gooayra last. I remember havin' t' go up thataways 'bout one o' my crew who'd got in th' sun an' took a *vigilante's* rifle away from him!" And with the old captain's elucidation, Shorty came in for a round of thunderous applause.

The usual speeches were made, and feeling very proud

of himself, Shorty left the schoolhouse for the last time as a scholar.

"Now, boy," said his uncle as the pair strolled along the road, "you're through with school, but I hope you ain't through with l'arnin'. Don't think 'cause ye've l'arned all they kin teach ye at Long Cove that ye ain't got nawthin' more t' know! Don't go an' heave yer school books away or make a bonfire o' them, for ye never know when ye may need them again. Ye'll hev t' make use now o' what ye hev l'arned, see? An' I hope ye will too, Frank, for I'm much set on ye, an' wish ye t' be a clever man. Did ye do anythin' with that arithmetic book I made th' *mistake* o' buyin'?"

Shorty nodded. "Sure, Uncle, I've gone all through it an' worked out nearly all th' sums. It hez bin good fun too at nights, figgerin' out th' problems an' seein' by the answers ef ye were right—'most good as a game."

The uncle nodded. "That's fine, Frank, an' I'm glad that th' book was some good after all. Now d'ye think ye c'd go t' work an' figure out th' runnin' an' cost o' a vessel —say a fishin' vessel like?"

"Yes, I think so."

"Waal now, jest suppose we git home an' git some paper, an' I'll give ye some little problems t' work out, eh?"

Vaguely wondering what his uncle was driving at, Shorty got out paper and pencil when they arrived at the house, and seating himself at the table, announced that he was ready.

The skipper lit his pipe and, screwing his eyes up in deep thought, began. "Suppose, Frank, we hev a sum of ten thousand dollars between us—got that, ten thousand dollars in hard cash. Now we go git to work an' buy a vessel— a new vessel—ninety tonner, Bank fisherman, carryin' ten double-trawl dories. She costs, with gear an' all complete, say nine thousand five hundred dollars—got that?"

"Yes," replied Shorty. "That leaves five hundred dollars and the vessel."

"Good!" continued the other. "Now we ship a crew on th' share system for fresh fishin'. I go as skipper with a ten-dory gang, a cook, an' no spare—I cal'late I'm limber enough yet t' catch dory painters an' ship pen-boards—an' we make a trip o' ten days, say—off th' Cape Shore or Browns—an' git a fare o' one hundred thousand at one dollar'n seventy-five cents a hundred. How much is that, Frank?"

"One thousand seven hundred an' fifty dollars!"

"Good! Now cal'late that th' vessel takes a fifth o' that as her share. What's that?"

"Three hundred and fifty dollars!"

"Now say we make twenty trips at th' most with an average fare o' eighty thousand at one seventy-five. What 'ud that make?"

Shorty did some figuring. "It would make a total stock of twenty-eight thousand dollars for the twenty trips——"

"And th' vessel's share 'ud be?"

"Five thousand six hundred dollars."

Uncle Jerry nodded. "In two years, I cal'late, she'd pay for herself, 'thout counting my share an' c'mission. How'd we stand at the end o' th' second year, Frank?"

"Waal, Uncle, ye'd hev a good vessel fully paid for an' eleven thousand two hundred dollars in hand, sides th' five hundred balance outer yer original ten thousand dollars—makin' th' vessel an' gear complete, an' eleven thousand seven hundred dollars in hand——"

"'Sides my share as skipper at say fifty dollars a trip, or a thousand dollars for th' season."

While the room became befogged with tobacco smoke, uncle and nephew wrestled with problems of insurance, overhauls, expenses for dories, depreciation, wear-and-tear of gear and sails, and possible accidents. They figured up profits on salt fishing and halibuting trips, and at the end of it all, when sheet after sheet of paper had become filled with figures and Shorty's brain was a-whirl, the fishing skipper expressed himself satisfied.

"You're my boy, Frank," he said slapping the stocky

youngster on the back. "Consarn me, but ye figure a dern sight better'n that ol' white-haired book-keeper down to Cullahan's Wharf in Gloucester—an' he kinsiders himself no small beans. That joker kin git th' hail of a trip when th' vessel swings in th' dock end, an' by th' time she's tied up he hez th' share checks all ready for th' gang t' git an' draw. Let's git in an' see what th' cook's got, Frank. I hear yer ma rattlin' them dishes, an' I cal'late we'll go an' see what she means by it."

The Captain remained in Long Cove until August, and Shorty went with Long Dick in the dory. Though he had been out often before, yet this time it was different. He was through school now, and working for his living, and things began to appear in a different light. There is a mighty difference between hauling a trawl for fun and hauling it day after day in all kinds of weather for a living.

He had to turn out at all hours, according to the state of the tide, and with Long Dick he cut herring bait, and baited up his tub of three hundred fathom trawl with its seven hundred gangins and hooks. Then they launched their dory, and, sailing or pulling, they made their sets from two to three miles off-shore. Long Dick generally did the rowing while Shorty hove the baited trawl into the water in whirling coils after the end line had been anchored to the bottom. When the set of two or three tubs had been made they hung on to their dory anchor and Shorty reverently produced "Omoo" or "Two Years before the Mast" from the pocket of his coat and read aloud to Long Dick, lazily smoking and listening in the bow of the boat.

After a spell of twenty to forty minutes, Long Dick would regretfully buckle on his broad leather belt, and, slipping the woollen nippers over his hands, proceed to get the anchor up and haul in the lengthy trawl. Shorty, as a rule, coiled down the line as Dick hove it in, and in silence, broken only by the schloop and flop of the hake and pollock whirled into the dory bottom and the vicious slats on the dory gunwale when the fisherman knocked the dogfish and sculpins off the hooks, they hauled and coiled and collected the harvest of the sea. When the gear had been hauled they made for the shore, and, pitching out their fish on the wharf, wheeled it to the shed where they dressed and cleaned them.

Some of their fares were bought by Jud Morrell or Zeke Ring, who salted and dried them, and afterwards sold them to a big fish company in Anchorville; and sometimes, when the wind was fair and prices right, they ran the dory right to Anchorville and sold their fish fresh and direct to the company.

Thus the summer passed. Mornings when Shorty saw the sun rising over the pine-clad hills to the eastward while he was toiling with Long Dick out on the waters of the Bay. Days of oily calm when Fundy's waters stretched like a mirror of glass along the western horizon and the blazing sun was reflected in them and scorched the faces of the fishermen to an Indian bronze; when the lumber and gypsum ships from the Basin of Minas and Chebucto Bay lay rolling in the swells with chafing sails and creaking yards, and the trawlers sweated as they hauled the squirming fish over the roller. And the evenings! Were there ever such as those on the Bay shore? When the whole western sky radiated flame, when the sun dropped like a blood-red ball beneath the silent sea, and the lisping waters stretched before the Cove like a vast sheet of molten metal. And behind, the gaunt spruces reared their greenery tinged to a sanguinary gold in the westering sun, the shadows deepened in the thickets or stretched inky black across the sward, and the window-panes of the houses glowed in lambent fire from the reflection of the sunset. Gradually the light faded, and the soft azure of the night replaced the yellow and purple of the short twilight, and the stars twinkled overhead in myriads and danced in the reflecting pool of the quiet sea. Occasionally a porpoise would break water, and the noise would come rolling in like the splashings of mermaids in a hidden rock-pool, while ever and anon on those wind-free nights the sonorous clang of some big ship's bell marking off the hours could be heard vibrating on the drowsy air.

There were other days too, and every bit as grand, when under a strong breeze, sunshine, and fleecy clouds the Fundy combers would race in foam-laced battalions and burst in acres of white water upon the rock-girt shore. These were the days when the big ships whirled down the Bay in all their pride of billowy canvas; when, with topgallantsails and royals drawing, they careened to the breeze and displayed their lumber-laden decks with lee water sluicing over the high to'gallant rail. Many a time Shorty watched them as they passed him in the dory, and as they stormed along he sighed for the romance of blue water and the storied lands to which they were bound.

The fall fitting-out season came in due time. The haying was over once more, and the men began to get ready to join their vessels. Shorty had put in a good summer with Long Dick, and though he was hardly big enough or strong enough to do his full share in a dory, yet he "was worth his salt," as Long Dick expressed it. He could rig the trawl gear, hitch gangins, and hook up as nimbly as the most expert, as well as bait and overhaul the lines after a set. For his size and weight he handled a dory as good as the best, and could take his stand at the dress tables and "dress down" either as a throater, gutter, or splitter.

"Now, son," said Dick, "you kin go a-bankin' naow as good as any o' them. I've l'arned ye all I know 'cept sailin' a vessel an' findin' fish. Ye kin splice an' knot; ye kin rig trawl gear an' make tubs outer flour bar'ls; ye kin rig a buoy kag in proper Bank fashion an' heave a trawl 'thout snarlin' it all up. Ye kin hook an' bait up, overhaul an' comb, throat, gut, an' split like any ol' shacker, an' all ye've got t' l'arn now in th' fishin' line is to stand in the bow an' haul a four-tub set on a hard bottom, snarled up an' tide settin' agin ye; git adrift for a week in a dory with nawthin' to eat; swear in three langwidges—Portygee, Judique, an' T Dock Irish; an' pick up a skipper what is a high-liner. When ye kin do that, ye're a blooded Banker an' ready t' become a second Clayton Morrissey. You git along with yer uncle for a spell an' I'll guarantee ye'll be runnin' a vessel o' yer own afore ye're a man's age.''

At supper that night his uncle spoke the long-hoped-for words. "Frank, git yer duds ready. Ye'll ship as spare hand with me this fall.'' And Shorty felt that he had at last crossed the rubicon of his dearest desire.

CHAPTER FOUR

> There's th' men who set on Georges,
> On th' Channel an' Cape Shore,
> From th' Quero down to Cashes,
> An' th' Peak to Labrador;
> There's seiners, shackers, salters,
> But where'er a vessel steers,
> They'll tell you fishin's hardest
> In th' first hundred years.

SHORTY AND HIS UNCLE BOARDED THE LITTLE PACKET schooner on a misty August morning, and, in company with many other Long Covers bound for the Bank fishing, they waved their farewells to the little knot of women on the wharf. While his uncle and the other men were assisting Cap'en Bill Daley to "hang out th' patch," Frank Westhaver stood on the schooner's quarter and listened dutifully to his mother's advice. His feelings were varied by pleasurable anticipation at the life before him and regret at leaving home. A boy's leave-taking sorrow does not last long, however, and Shorty nodded bravely to his mother's admonitions, while his eyes roved up on the brow of the hill where a white-frocked figure was waving a handkerchief.

Shorty had gone through a valedictory hour with Carrie Dexter the evening previous, and in his canvas dunnage bag there reposed a little token of her friendship in the shape of a pair of red woollen wristlets.

"You won't forget me, Frankie?" she had asked, and Shorty swore by all his boyhood gods that it was impossible.

"There's lots of girls in Gloucester, I hear," she ventured.

"There may be," replied Shorty emphatically, "but they ain't up to your class, Carrie, so don't worry. I'll write you whenever I git a chanst, an' don't you forgit t' do th' same."

The schooner's sails filled to the light breeze and swung the little craft out from the wharf. "Good-bye, Frankie," cried Mrs. Westhaver, with a quaver in her voice. "Don't forget to say your prayers and change your clothes when they're wet."

"So long, Shorty," rumbled Long Dick. "Show them Glo'ster townies that ye're a Novy what kin bait small an' catch large. Th' first hundred years o' fishin is th' hardest, son!" And with their farewells echoing in his ears, he waved his cap until the morning fog blotted the wharf and schooner from each other's sight.

As they glided down the coast in the mist he began to feel very forlorn and lonely. Joe Small was at the wheel steering, and his Uncle Jerry and the other passengers were seated around the main hatch gossiping and smoking. It was only then that Shorty realized the heart-gripping sensations of leaving home for the first time, but, boy-like, he soon forgot his feelings when the fog lifted and the glorious August sunshine flooded the sea and landscape with golden effulgence.

By noon they shot alongside Anchorville pier, and, shouldering his bag, he trailed in his uncle's wake and boarded the train for Yarmouth. It was Shorty's first time on a train, and the journey to the seaport was a wonderful revelation to the boy, who feasted his eyes on the panorama of farms, forests, and rivers which flashed past. And what a man the brass-bound conductor seemed! Shorty felt that such a position might well be envied, and he regarded the pompous dignity of the uniformed official with reverential awe. As he collected the tickets from the trawlers and drummers who crowded the smoking-car he carried such an air of dignity with him that almost caused the boy to gasp when his uncle addressed the conductor with the familiarity of old acquaintance.

"Hullo, thar', Ben Simpson! How's she headin' this trip?"

The conductor's official mask relaxed into a beaming smile. "Howdy, Cap'en Clark. Off for th' fishin' agen? More high-line trips an' big stocks to ye! Two tickets, eh? Your boy, Cap'en? Your nephew, eh? Not Cap'en Frank Westhaver's youngster, is he? You don't say! Goin' a-fishin' are ye, son? Waal, here's hopin' ye steer a close wake to yer uncle, sonny." And while Shorty acknowledged the advice in blushing pleasure, the man of tickets passed down the aisle.

The train journey opened Frank's eyes as to his uncle's importance. Everybody appeared to know him, and the smoking-car seemed to have become Jerry Clark's reception-room. Sun-bronzed trawlers lurched up the aisle and respectfully begged for "a chance" to sail with him; old shipmates flopped into the seat alongside and exchanged yarns and notes, and all who passed through the car seemed to have a hail for Cap'en Clark. Shorty divided his attention between the passing scenery and the boisterous gossip of his uncle's friends, and by the time the train pulled into Yarmouth, Frank had a new conception of his Uncle Jerry's importance, and the conductor's job began to pale into insignificance beside that of the "high-line" Bank skipper.

They disembarked at the flourishing Nova Scotian town —then in the zenith of its greatness as a mighty shipbuilding and shipowning port—and boarded the waiting Boston steamer. The voyage across the Gulf of Maine to the big American city constituted another memorable experience to Shorty, and it was late that night ere he turned into his state-room bunk. While his uncle yarned and gossiped in the smoking-room the boy paced the steamship's deck and watched the loom of the Nova Scotia coast sinking into the evening mist until the whirling flash of Cape Forchu light alone remained to mark the existence of the land. The second engineer—a friend of his uncle—took him in hand then and conducted him down to view the racing arms of steel which whirled in their guides with hissings, and clankings, and purrings as they drove the steamer through the sea at a twelve-knot gait. Altogether it had been a day of days to the boy, and when he turned in at last it was but to dream over the memory of the things he had seen.

Next morning his uncle roused him. "Look through th' port, Frankie," he said, his newly washed face shining like the sun in a Bank fog. "Thar's ol' Cape Ann away off thar'. Ye'll see it often after this, I hope. Glo'ster's jest inside thar', an' by th' week-end we sh'd hev the old *Kastalia* a-pokin' her horn outside o' Ten Pound Island. Eastern P'int lays a little t' th' west'ard o' th' Cape, an' I cal'late afore ye're much older ye'll git t' love th' sight o' them ol' rocks."

Breakfast was over when they passed the Lightship, and through a sea smooth as glass and glittering in the sun they swung up Boston Bay. What a morning it was! To Shorty, the steamer trip had the train ride beaten hollow, and the passage up to Boston on that glorious August morning was a perfect delight. Off the Lightship they passed a Yankee man-o'-war—yacht-like in white and buff, with brass a-glitter and the Stars and Stripes floating proudly from the stern pole. Near the Graves they saw a splendid clipper ship towing out to sea—a black-hulled dream of a ship with sky-raking masts and yards braced faultlessly square. Shorty was absorbed in the contemplation of her nautical loveliness when his uncle leaned over the rail. "What a beautiful vessel," said Frank in admiration of the deep-laden windjammer.

His uncle was not so enthusiastic. "Yankee hell-ship," he growled. "Cape Horner, with bullies aft and an all-nation gang o' shanghaied scrubs for'ard. Ye'll notice there ain't none o' her crew on deck. Riggers a-takin' her out—crew in their bunks sleepin' off th' knock-out rum they swigged last night. Aye, Frankie—they're beautiful ships t' look at, but floatin' hell t' sail in. That's th'

Martha Starbuck—a proper Cape Horn blood boat—three skys'ls an' monkey's allowance for th' forem'st crowd. Now look over t' port here an' see what I call a vessel. She's a T Dock marketman from Georges with a trip o' fish. Ain't that a beauty for ye now?"

On their beam lay a beautiful schooner under all sail, and making but bare steerage-way in the light breeze. The gang of men lounging around her quarter stared at the Boston steamer with a sort of contempt, although it must have annoyed them exceedingly to see the advantage of steam over sail on such a morning.

"She's th' *Mannie G. Irving*—a Burgess model. There's her skipper at th' wheel—Stormalong Joe Evans—a pow'ful hard driver an' a mighty good fisherman. But wait, Frankie, till ye see th' *Kastalia*. Smartest vessel out o' Glo'ster—sails like a steamboat. Now we're comin' in among the islands. Boston's dead ahead. D'ye see th' smoke of it? Here's a big Atlantic liner a-comin'—boun' for Liverpool, I cal'late. Some size vessel, sonny, eh?"

A long two-funnelled, four-masted liner glided majestically past. Shorty could see the uniformed officers on her bridge and the white-haired master pacing the starboard wing. A tug was trailing astern, swinging the huge bulk as it threaded the channel, and the long promenade deck was thronged with passengers.

"What a monster!" ejaculated Shorty almost breathlessly. "I reckon she must be th' biggest vessel afloat."

Uncle Jerry laughed. "Not by a long way, Frankie. Thar's hundreds o' bigger ships than her. Wait till ye git up on Grand Bank or off Sable Island. Ye'll see them New York packets a-flyin' past at twenty knots, an' as big as two o' them put t'gether, an', sonny, ye'll pray hard ye don't get anywheres near them in thick weather. I like t' see them in a dock best, an' not when we're on th' grounds with fog shuttin' down an' liners tearin' through it at a hell-for-leather clip. Look at th' forts, Frank. See th' guns a-stickin' out? Thar's Deer Island—it's a prison. Great raft o' islands 'round here. Thar's Bug Light. Won't be long now afore we step ashore. Go git yer dunnage, Frank—th' customs'll be overhaulin' yer kit soon."

They came alongside the wharf at last, and Shorty and his uncle were cross-examined by an official, who passed them with a laugh and a joke. "You're 'most a United States citizen, Cap'en Clark," he said.

" 'Most, but not quite," replied the other. "We Nova Scotians seem t' be in every country but our own."

The immigration officer laughed. "That's true, Cap," he returned. "My ol' dad was proper Bluenose himself. Your son, Cap?" He indicated Frank with his pencil.

"No! my nevvy."

"Aha! lickin' another young cub inter shape. Waal, waal, I dunno what Glo'ster 'ud do for fishermen ef you Nova Scotiamen didn't come travellin' over. Good day, Cap, an' good luck t' ye." And the officer turned away, while the custom's inspector came forward. "No diamonds in yer dunnage, Cap?" he enquired jokingly.

Uncle Jerry smiled. "Waal now, I don't know but what they might be. I was thinkin' o' decoratin' my vessel's figure-head with a few jooals, an' I'd take a look aroun' ef I was you."

The inspector made a cabalistic mark upon the bags and passed on, while a teamster hustled them on to his waggon. When the inspection was over uncle and nephew passed out to see the city.

"A bigger place than Anchorville," remarked Captain Clark as they strolled around. "See th' buildings, Frank! Some height, eh? An' that Elevated an' th' 'lectric cars. Ye never saw th' like o' them afore."

Shorty never had, and he was impressed with the immensity of it all. What sights his unaccustomed eyes had feasted upon that day! The bustling crowds, the whirling Elevated, the buildings and stores with their wonderful wares. Mingled in his brain were memories of the gold-domed State House, the Common, and the thronged alleys of commerce down around Washington, State, and Milk Streets. Of course, being fishermen, they took in T Wharf, and Frank was bewildered with the maze of vessels which herded within the dock, and he had confused recollections of shaking hands with numerous fishing skippers, of boarding many vessels, of listening to the forty-fathom talk of fish and fish prices, and the relations of wild races for market in windy weather. When they left the odoriferous precincts of the fish wharf Captain Clark commenced a biographical comment upon the men he had met, and Shorty listened with awe and respect. "Th' little stocky man ye met on th' *Valhalla* is Jeb Wessel—a Lunenburg Dutchman an' a reg'lar devil t' carry sail. Ran from Portland t' th' Lurcher once in seventeen hours—blowin' a gale an' thick o' snow. Tom Brand—th' big man what was with him, ye mind—was run down by a steamer on Quero 'bout two months ago an' jest got clear o' his vessel afore she sunk on him. They were two days and nights in th' dories afore they were picked up. Th' dark man with th' gold wire in his ears is a Portygee—Manuel De Costa—good Georges fisherman—owns a fine vessel—nice, quiet man." And so on.

The time passed quickly—so quickly that Shorty felt loath to leave Boston for Gloucester. With reluctance he followed his uncle to the station, and there entrained for the famous Massachusetts fishing port. It was dark when they arrived, and tired out with the events of the day, the boy was soon fast asleep between the sheets of the hotel bed.

Next morning he breakfasted in company with a collarless, bewhiskered crowd of vessel masters, who talked fish and discussed the merits of every vessel in the port; who prophesied the outcome of the season, argued over the price of bait, and incidentally ate up everything in sight. The pick of Gloucester's fishing skippers were assembled around that board, and Shorty felt honoured whenever one of these great men deigned to address him.

"Had enough to eat, Frank?" queried his uncle.

Shorty nodded.

"Waal, then, we'll git down aboard. Cook came this morning, an' I cal'late th' gang is 'most all here. Go git yer bag an' we'll hev th' porter carry it down for us.''

And leaving the hotel, they bore up for the water-front. There were many vessels in port, and around their decks sat the gangs rigging gear. Here and there were vessels being overhauled, and the tap-tap of caulking mallets echoed among the alleys of fish sheds. Everybody seemed busy. Here was a man painting dories, there another was making trawl tubs, aboard the vessels the various gangs were working with trawl-splicer or hook-set rigging new gear or overhauling old, and the wharves seemed to hum with life. Stacks of salt fish were wheeled in and out of the sheds, an Italian barque was discharging Trapani salt by means of a tub and mainyard tackle, a three-masted schooner was loading salt cod for the West Indies—everything was fish or in connection with fish. Gloucester's wealth lay in the shoal waters of the open Atlantic, as also many of her sons.

Captain Clark pointed to a schooner which lay at the end of a wharf. ''Thar's th' *Kastalia*, Frank,'' he said proudly. ''How's she look to you?''

Shorty regarded the vessel with ill-concealed admiration, and he breathed his approval. ''Ain't she a dandy, Uncle! A reg'lar yacht she looks.''

''Aye, Frankie,'' assented the other, ''an' she's jest as good as she looks. We put a lot o' money into that vessel—sixteen thousand dollars she cost t' build—but she's one o' th' finest fishermen that ever left th' ways of an Essex yard. Burgess designed her, an' he never made a better tooth-pick in his life. She's hardwood built—every plank of her is American oak, an' she's full o' hangin' knees an' ironed in every place whar' strength is needed—an' she's proved her strength many a time.''

Shorty gazed over the shining black hull of the schooner, noted the well-stayed topmasts, the long varnished main-boom stretching over the taffrail, and the graceful fore-and-aft sheer which swept in a glorious curve from the break of the quarter to terminate in the scroll-work of a carved figure-head crowning the sweet clipper bow which distinguished a type of fishing schooner seldom designed nowadays. She was a ninety-five tonner carrying ten double-trawl dories nested in fives amidships, and as she swam in the clear green water of the dock she looked a queen among the rusty-hulled salt Bankers crowding the berths.

Uncle and nephew scrambled aboard at last, and the latter found himself among many friends, as most of the *Kastalia's* crew were Bay Shore men who had followed their skipper to Gloucester vessels. Indeed, there are more Nova Scotians and Newfoundlanders in Gloucester than there are Americans—a peculiar condition of affairs which is, nevertheless, a fact.

"Come below, Frank," said the Captain, and both entered the cabin. It was an oak-panelled apartment with a stove in the centre of it which took up most of the room. Lockers ran all around, and double bunks were set, cave-like, into the walls on both sides, and still more cave-like aft of the companion-ladder, where the sleeping-places stretched up into the run between counter and deck. A miscellaneous heap of tarred cotton trawl line littered the floor, dunnage bags and suit-cases were hove carelessly into the bunks, and the place smelt strongly of tar, tobacco, and new oilskins.

Uncle Jerry indicated a starboard bunk filled with an old hawser and lanyard rope. "That'll be yours, Frank," he said. "When that porter brings down yer bag ye'd better change yer clothes an' clean this cabin up. You're spare hand on th' *Kastalia* now, an' I cal'late ye'd better take hold an' start right in on yer job."

For the next two days Shorty worked around the vessel. A balloon jib was bent on—the boy scrambling up the slender foretopmast and reeving the halliard without experiencing the trepidation of the green hand at his first scramble aloft—and Uncle Jerry, who watched him clawing his way up the foregaff-top-sail halliards with more fear than was felt by his nephew, was secretly pleased. Then, with a pot of paint, Frank essayed his artistic abilities upon trawl tubs, pen boards, and other gear around decks, coming in for a great deal of rough chaff from the gang rigging their trawls around the sun-flooded quarter and waist of the schooner.

"Reg'lar bird, that noo spare hand of our'n," remarked an old trawler, addressing nobody in particular.

"Yep! he's a dog," said another slyly. "Goin' t' work hard an' git a vessel soon so's he kin hitch up with that Dexter girl back to Long Cove."

Shorty, assiduously painting a trawl tub, heard, and blushed consciously.

"Got a girl has he?" queried another man splicing a tub becket. "He's a devil of a feller that new spare hand, ain't he?"

And during the day Shorty had to stand for all his private affairs being aired, discussed, and criticized by a gang of gossip-loving fishermen who took a secret pleasure in roasting him. They made a great mistake, however, and those who knew the Shorty Westhaver of Long Cove should have been wiser by experience. Jack Hanson and Johnny Leblanc, two dory-mates who had been doing most of the chaffing, found their best shore-going boots floating around in a butt of fish oil that evening, and when turning in about midnight discovered a good gross of Arthur James number seventeen fish-hooks scattered liberally in their bunk blankets. When they crawled cursefully aft to have it out with the perpetrator they found him sleeping peacefully, with but his tousled, sandy head appearing above the blanket. Aboard a fishing vessel a man's sleep is always respected, and Shorty escaped a rope's ending more from this than from his apparently innocent appearance, and the victims clattered for'ard again to comb the fish-hooks out of each other.

Next day all hands turned to in double gangs getting the salt aboard and loaded into the bins in the hold, and Shorty spent the day on the wharf tallying the salt and stores as they came down. And he carried out his duties well—so well that when his uncle glanced over the neat entries in the notebook he smiled in pleasure.

"Fine, fine," he chuckled. " 'Tis better than old Clancy, th' clerk in the office, c'd ha' done it. Ye'll keep th' run o' all th' bills for me, Frankie, after this, an' I'll give ye charge o' all th' store tallyin' an' th' fishin' when we make th' grounds. Now shoot up to th' store an' ask them t' let ye have their account, an' see ef they jibe with yer tally."

Shorty procured the store's account, checked it over, and discovered a few discrepancies in the prices of certain commodities. "Look here, Uncle," he said. "This feller has one hundred pounds o' butter at twenty and one-half cents a pound charged up as twenty-five dollars, an' it sh'd only come to twenty dollars fifty cents—four dollars fifty cents too much. He's got one dozen o' pickles at twelve and a half cents a bottle charged up as one dollar seventy-five cents, when it ought t' be one dollar fifty cents. Almost every item hez an overcharge of a few cents——"

"But they gimme a discount, Frank, 'cause I allus pay cash afore I sail 'stead o' settlin' at the end o' th' trip."

Shorty was not satisfied. "Yes, an' they take their discount out o' you by these overcharges. Did you ever check up these bills afore?"

"Waal," replied the skipper hesitantly, "I tallied th' stuff as it came down, but I niver bothered t' check th' bill. I allus cal'lated they was honest."

His nephew smiled grimly. "Let's walk up to this store, Uncle. We'll hev a palaver with them."

Into the store they went, and Captain Clark was greeted effusively by the proprietor. Shorty, as a common boy on a fisherman, was ignored.

"About my bill——" began Uncle Jerry.

"Ah, yes, Captain. Just step into my office!" The storekeeper rubbed his fat hands together and smiled ingratiatingly.

Captain Clark wasn't looking pleased, and he turned to Shorty. "Frank, jest go in an' settle up with this feller. Whatever it is, I'll pay."

The other gazed upon the grimy little figure in jersey and sea-boots.

"Who's this kid, Captain?" he asked in surprise.

"My nevvy," replied the skipper shortly. "He'll go over th' bill with ye an' show ye a few things." And he did.

The account was a long one, and Shorty went over every item, pointing out mistakes until the storekeeper was furious. It was very seldom that fishermen bothered checking up his figures, and the ignorant Jerry Clark was the last man he ever expected to doubt his honesty. When it was finished and Shorty had brought the bill down to some fourteen dollars less than originally charged, Captain Clark had his say.

"Now, sir, I've bin a-buyin' stores from you fur a consid'rable time, an' I've allus paid cash afore sailin'. I took ye fur an honest man, an' now I find ye ain't. Ye knew I warn't much o' a hand at figgerin', an' ye've bin takin' advantage of it. I'll pay ye this bill, but no more business will ye git from me, an' I'll take dam' good care ye don't get a good many more vessel's bills. A word from me about this will queer you with 'most every skipper out o' Gloucester, I cal'late. Frank, here's some money. Pay him, an' let's go."

The man was abject in his apologies and pleaded various excuses to account for the overcharges, but Captain Jerry was adamant. "Don't talk t' me," he rumbled. "Tell it to th' boy. He does all my business for me now."

They left the store at last, with the proprietor apologizing to the door. On their way down to the wharf Uncle Jerry spoke: "Now, Frank, that'll jest show ye how much good eddication does a man. Look at th' hundreds o' dollars I must ha' bin swindled out of, 'count of not bein' able t' keep track o' things. Ye did fine, my son, an' 'twas a proud man I was when I saw ye givin' that longshore shark his proper soundin's——"

Shorty strutted along proudly, and he winked knowingly up at his uncle as he handed over the remainder of the money. "Yes, Uncle, an' I drew some o' th' shark's blood too! I made him gimme a discount o' fifteen per cent off th' bill 'stead o' ten."

The big fishing skipper burst into a laugh. "Ye did? Waal, you little runt, ef you ain't th' limit! Ye Jewed him down, an' then took fifteen per cent discount off'n him. Ha! ha! Oh, but you're a dog, Frank! A man'll need keep a-grippin' t' work t' wind'ard o' you afore ye're much older. Ha! ha! ha!" And Uncle Jerry chuckled all the way along the wharf.

That evening all the stores and gear were gotten aboard. The dories, refitted with thwarts, thole-pins, pen-boards, bow and stern beckets, painters, and oars, were brought alongside and nested upon the decks. After supper the gang, with but one or two exceptions, dressed themselves in their shore toggery and went up-town for a last "look around" and gossip before starting out on their long trip to the eastern Banks. Shorty wrote three letters—one to his mother, one to Miss Dexter, and one to Lem Ring—and, in company with his uncle, went up to the post office and mailed them. The balance of the evening was spent listening to a band concert in East Gloucester, and Shorty strolled among the crowds thoroughly enraptured with the beauty of the night. The soft wind from the sea, the moonlight, the gaily dressed summer visitors, laughing and chattering, and the stirring strains from the regimental band made an impression upon him which he dreamed over with subconscious pleasure as he lay in his bunk in the *Kastalia's* cabin. Since he had left Long Cove his eyes had seen many strange things, and as he turned them over in his retrospective mind he began to feel that life was good and well worth living.

CHAPTER FIVE

Hey! Tally on! Aft an' walk away with her!
  Handsome to the cathead now! O! tally on the fall!
Stop, seize, an' fish, and easy on the davit guy.
  Up well the fluke of her, and inboard haul!
For it's well, ah, fare you well! The Channel wind's took hold of us.
  Choking down our voices as we snatch the gaskets free—
And it's blowing up for night, and she's dropping light on light,
  For she's snorting under bonnets for a breath of open sea!
                                                        KIPLING.

SHORTY WAS IN THE MIDST OF A DELIGHTFUL DREAM, wherein he had got command of a vessel like the *Kastalia*, and he was taking the admiring Miss Dexter down to have a look at her when the pleasant fancy was rudely disturbed by the roar of his uncle's voice. "Tumble out, all hands! Get underwa-a-ay! Come on now, fellers! Show a leg! Shake a stockin'!"

In the light from the cabin lamps the gang emerged yawning from their bunks and proceeded to don coats and sea-boots. Blinking at the clock, Shorty noted the hour—half-past three—and he pulled on rubber boots, coat, cap, and mittens and joined the mob shivering on deck. It was a dark morning; the moon had gone down, but the stars were shining, and a light breeze was ruffling the waters of Gloucester harbour. Captain Clark was standing upon the dock, and when the crowd mustered he gave the word. "Get her down to the end o' th' wharf. Slack away yer starn-lines. Haul away for'ard."

Warping the vessel down to the wharf end, they tugged and strained at the hawsers until she was far enough. The skipper then jumped aboard. "That'll do," he said. "Up on yer mains'l now!" Shorty cast the stops off, and when the great roll of canvas had dropped on to the cabin house the whole gang of twenty men tallied on to the peak and throat halliards. "Now then, up she goes!" And with three men fore-all to each halliard, the rest strung along the quarter alleys and hauled in unison to the encouraging shouts of some of their number. The mighty sail slowly climbed the mast to the creaking of blocks and the panting barks of "Walk her up now, bullies!" "Give it to her, fellers!" "Heave an' walk away with her!" While Captain Clark stood well aft and directed the operation with a "Hold yer throat, an' up on yer peak!" "Hold yer peak, an' up th' throat!" until the big mainsail was hoisted as taut as the halliards would take it.

"Come up yer slack!" cried the gang at the fife-rail. The fore-all trio held on while the pin-man took a turn and belayed, then all straightened up for a breather after the haul.

"All right," cried the skipper. "Jig her up now!" The jigs or peak and throat halliard purchases were manned, and they took up all the slack until the mainsail luff rope set up "bar taut" and the great canvas was stretched until the wrinkles ran from peak to tack.

"Well yer mains'l. Come up on yer lift now. Unship th' crotch an' tend th' sheet, some o' you!" On the order the fisherman's topping lift, which belays on the boom, was manned and the boom topped up and out of the crotch.

"Well th' lift. Up on yer fores'l now, fellers!" The foresail was soon hoisted and jigged, then the skipper sung out, "Up on yer jumbo, boys! Make th' tail-rope fast t' wind'ard. Let go bow-line!" The forestay sail or jumbo was quickly hauled up and the tail-rope—an auxiliary sheet —was made fast to windward, and the *Kastalia's* bow swung out into the stream. Captain Clark took the wheel and spun the spokes over. "Cast off yer starn-line! H'ist yer jib! Draw away yer jumbo!" The stern-line was cast off the bollard by a dock lumper, the tail-rope was slacked away, and the jib hoisted. Under her four lowers the

Kastalia worked her way out the harbour with the fresh morning breeze in her sails.

Shorty had been busy tailing on to halliards and casting off stops, and, as spare hand, it was his duty to pick up the gaskets, strops, heaver, and boom guys and stow them away until called for again. When he had put them in the cabin lockers he came on deck and looked back at the town fading into the half-darkness astern.

"Waal, son," said a man, slapping him on the back, "you're in for it naow. No seein' Glo'ster agin 'til th' salt's wet an' th' hold's full, so pray like blazes for full decks an' fishin' weather."

Up to the present Shorty had no idea where they were going, and neither his uncle nor the men had volunteered any information. Captain Clark made it a point of never telling anybody his intentions, and the men never asked him. If they did, his invariable reply was, "To the east'ard!" The successful Bank skipper is the one who keeps ears and eyes open, but mouth shut, and Jerry Clark was one of the successful ones.

With a breeze freshening with the dawn they rounded Eastern Point and passed the twin towers of Thatcher's Island, when the cook's whistle sounded for the "first half" to go down for breakfast. Shorty was among this gang, and regretfully he left the deck to take his place at the triangular fo'c'sle table, which had its base at the foremast and its apex at the pawl-post, both of which timbers had their massive sides festooned with beckets for the sauce, vinegar, pepper, and salt bottles. The "grub" was placed upon the oilcloth in great enamel-ware pots, and armed with knife, fork, spoon, plate, and mug, each man "dug in" until hunger was satiated.

It was a strange sea-picture. The dim-lit fo'c'sle ranged on either side with two tiers of bunks which ran behind the pawl-post up into the dark recess of the peak; the narrow table, piled with steaming pots of potatoes, boiled beef, cabbage, and beans, bread, doughnuts, and stewed cranberries; the aproned cook standing by his stove at the after end of the fo'c'sle ladling out mugs of coffee to those who called for the beverage; the tousled bunks littered with suit-cases, ditty-bags, and vari-coloured counterpanes and blankets; the oil skins hanging like dead men upon the bulkheads; and lastly, the men themselves, ruddy-faced and loud of speech, clad in odds and ends, sea-booted and rough-looking, all piling in to the food, while the whole apartment creaked and swayed to the rising lift of the sea under the *Kastalia's* forefoot.

A glance at the vessel's crew then would have confirmed a landsman in the belief that they were a gang of pirates. Gone were the nice table manners of the shore; gone were the trim clothes, collars and ties, shirts of linen, and natty shoes; and gone also were the niceties of speech. Men passed their remarks cursefully, and conversation became painfully free and highly charged with the red-blooded talk of the sea. The environment had changed it all, and the kick of the surge underfoot had dissipated the shams and foibles of the land. At sea a man comes out in his true colours and he speaks as he thinks, and Shorty himself began to feel he had taken his place as a man and no longer as a fourteen-year-old boy.

When he came on deck again it was to see Cape Ann astern and the *Kastalia* scudding along and curtseying to the swell. The sun had risen clear of the sea to the eastward, and the day was sunshine and clouds with a fresh sou'-westerly breeze blowing. As soon as the first table gang emerged the skipper sung out sharply, "Set th' light sails." Spying his nephew, he called him. "Kin ye steer, Frank?"

"Sure thing," answered the boy. "I kin steer Cap'en Daley's packet."

Uncle Jerry laughed. "Huh! Waal, ef ye kin steer that barge I cal'late ye kin steer anythin'. Take th' wheel. East-no'th-east th' course!"

"East-no'th-east, sir!" repeated Shorty, and he grasped the spokes, while his uncle went forward for breakfast.

If ever a boy felt proud it was Shorty that morning.

Standing at the wheel of the schooner he kept a vigilant eye on the compass and aloft at the gaff-topsail which was set. There was a spanking breeze blowing, and when the gang piled on the "kites" the *Kastalia* careened to the weight of the wind in them and buried her lee scuppers in a boiling of froth. Up went the great balloon jib, and the men swaying on the halliards were drenched in spray when she hefted the sail. "Hey yi! Sheet her down!" And six brine-drenched fishermen laid their weight on the lee sheet and belayed it taut as a wire backstay.

The fisherman's staysail or maintopmast-staysail was sent aloft next and set to leeward, and then, having "dressed" the vessel with all the "patch" of four lowers, two topsails, balloon, and staysails, the gang trooped aft.

"Thar' now, son," cried a man, addressing Shorty. "We've hung out all her rags for ye. See ef ye kin tear th' patch off'n her. Drive her, son, drive her!"

The skipper came up from below with a polished brass instrument.

"See this, Frank," he said.

The other, intent on steering, nodded.

"This is a patent log. I'm a-goin' t' put it over now. We take our departure from here—five miles off Cape Ann and jest seven o'clock. Remember that, Frank."

"All right, sir. Five miles off Cape Ann an' seven o'clock."

Heaving the log over the stern, the skipper watched it for a few minutes, and then with a sigh of contentment lit up his pipe and began pacing the weather quarter. The gang were laying around in sunny places overhauling and rigging trawl gear, while some who had finished their work were lolling in their bunks below. After the sail is put on her there is very little work to be done on a fishing vessel except steer and keep a look-out.

The loom of the land faded from a streak of green, brown, and black into a silhouette of blue, and when they hauled the log at nine and found they had made twenty-two knots the vessel was alone on a sunlit circle of rolling blue sea. They were out on open water at last; the land had sunk below the horizon, and Shorty, as he steered, sniffed at the salt-laden air and glanced at the stretch of surrounding ocean with gladsome eyes. The long roll of the Atlantic could be felt now, and the *Kastalia* would rise easily over a hill of blue water and descend the slope with a crash of spray and the slat and slam of sails and booms.

From the wheel the boy took in everything with his eyes. Ahead, the long, black bowsprit poked far out over the water—the standing gaskets upon it streaming out in the wind—and it seemed to be describing a continual seesaw with sea and sky, while from under the sharp forefoot came a ripping and tearing as the bows sheared through the water. Little steam-like clouds of spray came whisking up, and the windlass gear, anchors, and foredeck dripped and gleamed wet in the sunshine. The vast stretches of canvas reared silently aloft, full with the wind and quietly doing their work with but a cheeping of mast hoops, the grinding of boom jaws, and the clink of sheet blocks fetching up against shackles when the vessel bowed to a surge. Amidships sat a few of the men overhauling trawls, and their voices floated aft in a growling monotone, while the rattle and clink of pans sounded from the fo'c'sle interjected by snatches of song from the cook.

With the letters "E.N.E." for ever before his eyes, Shorty was yet able to day-dream a little as he twirled the spokes to the swinging of the needle around the lubber mark, and his fancy pictured himself as a modern embodiment of Amyas Leigh steering on his mission of revenge to the Spanish Main. It was a delightful fancy, and the boy's imagination took a dreamer's licence and wove the ancient story into a more modern conception, with Carrie Dexter as Rose Salterne and Bob Morrissey as the hated Don Guzman. Not that Shorty hated Bob as much as all that, but Bob was forced to take the part owing to the lack of a better, or worse, rival. At the wheel of his ship Shorty was steering to rescue his lady-love, and he had got to where he was hanging the wretched Bob from the cross-trees when his uncle stopped in his weather-alley pacing and sung out in the peculiar long-drawn shout common to all seafarers, "H-e-y thar'! Sheet in an' jig up!" And when the men turned out to sweat up on the slackened halliards he relieved Shorty at the wheel.

"Git all th' gang aft here, Frank," he said. "We'll set th' watches at noon." When the men were haled out from fo'c'sle, hold, and cabin he tossed a piece of chalk to John Ross, the oldest fisherman aboard. "Mark th' baitin' places, John," he said, and the man went around the house and kid marking the baiting positions.

Everything aboard a fisherman is drawn for at the beginning of the voyage, and by this means there is no squabbling afterwards, as each will stand by what he draws for. The top of the cabin house is capped around its edge by planks, upon which the men cut their bait, but there is not enough room for all the twenty men to cut bait and bait their trawls around these bait-boards, so some have to bait on the gurry kid—a huge box just forward of the cabin house—and down in the hold. Thus the reason why the favoured spots are drawn for.

After this apportionment was satisfactorily carried out the skipper asked, "Who drawed Number One dory?" Two men answered. "All right, boys. Set th' watch at twelve noon. One hour an' twelve minutes to watch." The positions for the fishing work were also portioned out, and the men were detailed off into "splitting gangs" consisting of a "throater," "gutter," and "splitter," while the best and oldest salt fishermen aboard were selected for the salting and "kenching" work in the hold. Shorty, as spare hand, was given no definite place, but he was competent enough to join a splitting gang if necessary, although he did not understand the science of salting fish. He did not have a watch to stand, but he was supposed to give a hand to anyone who wanted him.

The day passed quietly, and the schooner sped along at a steady eleven-knot clip. Hourly the log was hauled and the reading mounted by eleven sea miles on every sight.

It was good going, the breeze was steady, the barometer "set fair," and the gang surmised that they'd be up with the "Cape" at daylight next morning. Even though the skipper had not told them, yet they all knew that the E.N.E. course would take them to Cape Sable, Nova Scotia —the point where most Eastern Bank-bound fishermen make for on their journey to the "grounds." Where the skipper was going to after that none knew, though in the fo'c'sle various surmises were made. Some said Halifax, others said Canso, and some ventured on the Magdalens or the Treaty Shore of Newfoundland, for the bait had yet to be procured ere they could start fishing.

Shorty turned in that night with all the sea noises acting as his lullaby, and the easy rise and swing of the vessel tearing over the dark-swathed sea cradled him into the forty-fathom slumber of blue water. When he awoke next morning at four the wheelman pointed with a mittened hand to a light gleaming over the port bow. "Cape Sable!" he said, and Shorty stared once more at the land of his birth until the sun quenched the flare of the lantern and illuminated the low-lying sandy shore, fringed with the dark green of spruce, past which they were tearing.

All day long they stood up the coast of Nova Scotia, dropping the land into a blue streak towards nightfall, when another light gleamed, star-like, in the darkness off the bow. "That's Ironbound," said the skipper in reply to his nephew's enquiry. "Th' next one jest barely showin' above th' horizon is Sambro Head at the entrance to Halifax harbour. We'll see th' lights all night long as we travel up th' coast. That is, ef it don't shut in thick o' fog."

When Sambro Head was passed Shorty turned in and fell asleep with his uncle's admonitions to the watch ringing in his ears. "Keep a good look-out an' call me ef it shuts in thick or th' wind shifts." It seemed but a few minutes ago that his uncle had spoken when the boy was awakened by the skipper's voice. "All out below! Git th' light sails in!" and he crawled on deck to find the vessel driving through a steaming wall of fog. The breeze had freshened and the *Kastalia* was driving ahead in lurching dives, while from out the gloom for'ard came the drone of a horn.

The crowd were all up and mustered aft—their oilskins gleaming in the wet of the mist. "All right," cried the skipper, taking the wheel. "Clew up yer tops'ls an' tie them up. Down balloon an' stays'l!"

The topsails were quickly clewed up into a ball of canvas and a man nudged Shorty in the ribs. "Up you go, youngster! There's a nice little job for you. Tie th' maintops'l up. Ye'll find the gasket coiled an' stopped on th' springstay." And Shorty, nothing loath, scrambled up the mainrigging to where the stays converged and prevented rattlins; so booted and oilskinned, the lad grasped the shrouds and shinned up until he could get a grip on the spreader and haul himself bodily upon them. Tying up the gaff-topsail was quite a job for a beginner to tackle. The sail was full of wind, and fluttered and slattered about, while the slender topmast and spreaders jerked to the thunderous flaps of the staysail; but Shorty managed it, and aloft upon the spreaders, ninety feet above the deck and in the darkness, he beat the wind out of the sail, rode it down, and lashed it securely to the masthead. Panting from his exertions, he had a chance to look around. Below him, the gleaming length of the maingaff thrust up into the gloom, but the deck and sea were shrouded in vapour, out of which could be heard the shouts of the men working on deck. Very far away it seemed, and the boy, standing on the spreader, could imagine himself to be floating upon air, unsupported save for the spar, which seemed to vanish within six feet of his vision. Somewhere a horn was droning—in fact two horns were droning. Was it the echo? Shorty listened intently. Zzzz-z-z-ah! It appeared to come from astern—no, ahead —no, on the port bow. He strained his eyes around. What was that? A vessel's topmasts sticking up out of the mist? No—yes, it was! And Shorty yelled, "Oh, below! Vessel on port bow! Wa-a-a-tch out!"

As he clung with fingers tightly gripping the topmast

stays he could hear the excited shouts from the deck and feel the mast jerking to the slatting mainsail as the wheel was put hard down. Crash! The vessels shuddered to the shock of collision and he was almost thrown from his precarious perch. Torches cast a luminous glare in the pall below; the other vessel backed off and could be discerned stealing away in the fog, while stentorian cursing filtered up from the deck.

"You infernal dam' coaster!" he could hear his uncle shouting. "Clumsy four-eyed swine. . . . Any damage thar'? . . ." Shorty clambered gingerly below—a little nervous from the fright he had received, and as he jumped off the shearpole to the rail the skipper spied him in the glare of the smoking kerosene torches. "That you, Frank? Where were you? Aloft tyin' th' tops'l? Who th' devil sent ye up thar'? Some lazy beachcomber too lazy t' go himself——"

"No, sir. I jest went up on my own hook."

"Was that you what hailed?"

"Yes, sir. I c'd jest make out his topm'sts a-comin' through th' fog."

"Waal, your young eyes hez saved us a bad mix-up. Run away an' turn in—ye've done yer share, boy."

"Did he damage us?"

"No, nawthin' t' speak of. Hit us a glancin' blow on th' bluff of th' bow. Scraped th' paint—that's all. Go'n finish yer sleep, Frank, we're all right now." But Frank decided that sleep was not to be wooed without something to eat, so he stumbled down for'ard for a "mug up" at the shack locker in the fo'c'sle. It was two in the morning, and a number of the gang were busy eating at the fisherman's quick lunch, but when Shorty clambered down the ladder they hailed him with a shout.

"Here he comes, th' dog! Make a place for th' lad, you trawlers! What'll ye have, son? Mug o' coffee an' a slice o' pie, eh?"

Shorty nodded, and a man handed over the victuals. The fisherman who had sent the boy aloft was solicitous and friendly. "I h'ard th' skipper raisin' hades 'bout me sendin' ye up——"

"Oh, that's all right," replied Shorty. "I'd ha' gone up anyway. I want t' be worth my salt aboard here, y'know."

"So ye are, son. No fear o' you. Ye're th' son o' yer dad—ivery little inch o' ye, an' when ye git a bit more muscle in them little arms an' back o' your'n you an' me'll go dory-mates. Ye're 'most as good naow as thet big lunk I got——"

The "big lunk" referred to rolled off a locker and seized his mate with a pair of mighty hands. "What's that ye said, Jud Haskins? Big lunk am I? Naow I jest cal'late I'll pick you up in my teeth an' jump overboard with ye! Fancy you askin' th' lad t' go dory-mates with ye! You that kin hardly haul seven shots o' trawl 'thout pantin' fur breath. Cook, pass me the axe till I open up his thick skull an' see ef he has anythin' but bazoo an' rum notions in it."

After the meal all hands turned in again, and Shorty made his way aft to his bunk, where, in a few minutes, he was sound asleep. The fog still held when he turned out for breakfast next morning and found his uncle on deck. Somewhere in the gloom a fog-whistle was hooting, and the schooner, under four lowers, was slipping along easily through the smother. "What whistle is that, Uncle?" enquired the boy.

"Cranberry Island, sonny. We're shootin' in to Canso now." The skipper paced the quarter, smoking, and every now and again peering into the mist and into the binnacle.

"Let her come up," he said to the helmsman. "Mainsheet here! Trim her down! So! Stand by, all of ye. Some of ye get for'ard an' stand by th' jib an' jumbo!"

Through the wreathing mist they crawled with the horn blowing and all hands standing by. A bell buoy clanged somewhere to port, and the skipper's voice came rolling through the vapour. "Hard a-lee! Hold yer jumbo! Light up yer jib! Ma-a-insheet!" The vessel came around on her heel; the jib fluttered and flapped as the sheets were let go; the booms started to come inboard, and while the jumbo tail-rope was hauled to windward the vessel payed off on the other tack.

"All right! Draw away an' sheet down!"

Three or four times they tacked until finally they shot in among a shadowy fleet of vessels at anchor. "Get a range over th' windlass an' get ready to anchor!"

"All ready for'ard?"

"All ready, sir!"

"Light up yer jib! Down jib! Down jumbo! Down fores'l!" The schooner shot up into the wind and with a rattle of hanks and rings the down-hauls were manned, the headsails hauled down, and the vessel lost her way.

"Let go yer hook!" The shank-painter and ring-stopper were cast off, and with the shoe the anchor flukes were prised clear of the rail. Splash! the anchor plunged to the bottom with the chain roaring through the hawse pipe. Crash! the cable fetched up on the windlass barrel and the vessel strained until the flukes bit the bottom.

"Aft here and tie up yer mains'l! Ease off yer jigs an' lower away!"

In a few minutes the *Kastalia* was denuded of her canvas and lay snugly anchored in Canso harbour among a fleet of invisible vessels. At noon the skipper ordered a dory hoisted over, and jumping into her, the dory-mates pulled him ashore. A scant twenty minutes later a tug came puffing out of the mist and ranged alongside. A head thrust itself out of the pilot-house. "*Kastalia* ahoy?"

"Aye, what d'ye want?"

"Make fast my lines to yer fore an' main bitts an' get yer hook up. Cap'en Clark said I was t' shoot ye in t' th' wharf."

"All right." The fisherman turned and roared down the fo'c'sle scuttle. "All ha-a-nds up anchor aho-o-y!" And within a minute the links were coming in to the clink and clank of the pawls as the men hove down on the brakes.

"Anchor's broke out!" The tow-boat man pulled a bell and tooted his whistle, and while the gang were heaving the anchor to the rail the vessel was edged in past the anchored schooners alongside a wharf.

Captain Clark was standing on the string-piece. "All right, fellers. Git yer hatches off an' stand by t' take ice an' bait aboard!"

The work of loading the ice and the barrels of herring bait did not take long, and when it was finished the skipper jumped aboard. "Now git underway. Git yer stops off, Frank."

The tow-boat gave them a haul out into the channel and clear of the fleet at anchor, and in the fog they hoisted sail again and stood out to sea.

"Waal, son, an' what d'ye think o' Canso?" enquired a man facetiously.

"Canso?" ejaculated Shorty, picking up the furling gear. "Some place is Canso. Yes, from what I c'd see of it, it sure must be some town— when th' fog lifts. I cal'late th' folks in that town must hang cow-bells 'round their necks an' steer by compass in order t' keep from gittin' astray. Yes, I like Canso."

When they swung clear of the fog that afternoon the land had disappeared and they were once more out upon the vast expanse of the Atlantic. With ice and bait aboard they were all ready for fishing, and when the skipper made a favourite berth somewhere upon Canso Bank he passed the word which told every man aboard that they were upon the grounds at last. "Unbend yer balloon an' stow it away! Tie up yer topsails and stow away th' stays'l! See yer fishin' hawser shackled to the anchor! Make th' tail-rope fast an' sweat in th' mainsheet!"

By making the jumbo fast to windward and heaving the helm hard down the vessel was thrown into a semi-hove-to condition known in fisherman's parlance as "jogging." The schooner carries but little way on her, coming up and falling off as she does, and in this condition she will look after herself without anyone tending the wheel.

The barometer stood steady, and the skipper looked for a day's fishing on the morrow, so all hands turned in early to catch up on sleep. At three in the morning Captain Clark turned out of his bunk and glanced at the glass, and clambering the companion, scrutinized the sky and sea. The inspection must have satisfied him, for he sung out in a long-drawn roar, "Wake, you sleepers! Bait up!"

Three o'clock in the morning is a most unearthly hour to begin work, but fishermen take no account of hours when upon the grounds. In five minutes from the time the skipper hailed, the gangs were on deck, oilskin-clad and long-booted, and in the glare of kerosene torches they started a tattoo with the bait-knives upon the bait-boards around the house, kid, and down in the hold. Gleaming herrings were chopped into small pieces and swept into buckets, and when each man had cut his share he proceeded to bait the six hundred odd hooks which go to a tub of trawl line. Hour after hour they worked, knocking off to wolf a steaming breakfast of meat stew at four. At sunrise all the trawls were baited and the men retired below for a smoke and a stretch while the skipper drew away and made for a likely spot. Frank was steering when his uncle buttered the bottom of the lead—the fisherman's third eye— and spoke. "Come to, Frank!" The lead was cast, and motioning to Shorty to haul it in again, Captain Clark took the wheel and gave the shout. "Get ready! Lower way top dory!"

The two mates who owned the top dory on each nest overhauled their oars, placed the plug in position, also thwarts and pen-boards, and with roller, gurdy winch, gaff, pew or pitchfork, shack-knife, water-jar, and bailer installed they hooked the dory tackles dependent from the fore and main shrouds into the rope beckets in the bow and stern of the dory, and, manning the falls, hoisted the little eighteen-foot boat over the rail. As it splashed into the water, Frank, as spare hand, held the painter while the tackles were detached ready for the hoisting out and lowering of the next dory. The dory-mates hove the two trawl buoys, lines, and anchors in, and one of them, jumping in himself, caught the tubs of baited trawl handed to him by his partner. As soon as this was done the other man leaped over the rail, while Frank or the cook allowed the dory to drift astern, when the painter was belayed to a pin in the taffrail.

The successive dories were prepared and launched in a similar manner, but when they swept astern the first dory painter was handed down to them and made fast to their stern becket, while theirs was belayed to the vessel's taffrail until another dory was launched. Thus in twenty minutes there were two strings of five dories each towing from the port and starboard quarters of the vessel, and Frank was mopping the perspiration from his face. A man has to be sprightly on his feet and quick with his fingers to handle dory painters with the schooner sailing at a five knot clip.

"Let go!" cried the skipper. The last dory in the starboard string hove their buoy over, and while the line was running out made one end of the baited trawl fast to the anchor. When the anchor and buoy-line had run its length, the dory-mate tending the trawl sung out, "Cast off!" And the dory painter was unfastened from the stern of the dory ahead of them, while the schooner towed the rest of the string on.

In this manner—a flying set—the whole string of ten dories were scattered over some four miles of sea and left to set their baited trawls into the waters of the Bank. When the last dory had been left, the schooner was put about, the tail-rope belayed to windward, and the vessel jogged to leeward of the string.

"Now, Frank," said his uncle when the cook had left deck to attend to his culinary duties below, "ship th' penboards an' git th' pews out. Then ye'd better give th' cook a hand an' fill his lamps. Lots o' work for spare hand aboard a fisherman." And while his uncle steered up and down the line of dories Shorty busied himself shipping the penboards, which form the divisions on deck into which the fish are pitched; getting out the forks or "pews," cleaning up the remains of the herring-bait cutting, and filling and cleaning the cook's lamps fore and aft.

BLUE WATER 81

Thus the days passed as they wandered from berth to berth and Bank to Bank. It was good fishing weather; fish were striking good, and evenings saw the pens piled with gleaming cod and a sprinkling of haddock, hake, and pollock. Sometimes they fished in "flying sets" as described, and at other times they anchored with the big eight-inch manila fishing hawser over the bows, and the dories rowed out from the vessel and fished in positions with the schooner as a common centre. It was hard work. Roused out before sunrise to bait up the trawls, setting tub and tub all day long, pitching out the fish, and in the evenings "dressing down," "salting," and "kenching" by the light of lamp and kerosene torch until the wearied body almost dropped from sheer physical exhaustion.

Shorty took his share with the crowd. He tended dories, shipped pen-boards, cleared up decks, and oiled lamps, and when the loaded boats came alongside he held the painters and helped hoist them aboard when the fish had been pitchforked out. In dressing down the fare he prepared the dress keelers or gutting tables, filled the wash-tubs, and saw to it that the gutting and shacking knives were sharp. He kept a tally of the "count"—all the dory-mates counted the fish they caught—and checked up the "kenched" or piled salted fish in the hold pens. Incidentally he learned the correct way to salt and stack the cleaned fish, and learned the evils of "slack" salting and bad piling. It was a hard daily grind, but the men were well fed, ate like horses, and slept like dead men, and the boy could feel his muscles hardening under the work.

Captain Clark was a "driver," and much of his success was due to this characteristic. While the fine weather lasted he turned his gang out at four in the morning and had them setting out all day long, and when they returned aboard at dusk it was to clean and salt the fish until midnight. Men snatched sleep when they could, wolfed food in "mug-ups," and lived their waking hours in oilskins and jack-boots, with the skipper in a bantering, but insistent, way driving them to the limit of human endurance. Unshaven, faces sunburnt, encrusted with salt, and smeared with torch smoke, the fishermen appeared a rough and desperate-looking crew, but in spite of their weary bodies they kept up an incessant round of chaff and jokes while they prosecuted their monotonous daily grind.

Then came a day when the "hold" man announced that the bait was done, and those who heard murmured their relief at the intelligence. "All right, bullies," cried the skipper. "Git the anchor aboard! Take in th' ridin' sail an' set th' patch! Swing her off sou'-west for Canso!" And when the sail was put on her the men, except the two on watch, retired to their bunks to catch up on sleep.

It was clear when they arrived off Cranberry Island and negotiated the channel into the harbour, tenanted, as usual, by a fleet of fishing vessels. There were many Gloucester men among them, and as the *Kastalia* swept in the crews shouted rough greetings and enquired of the prospects outside.

"What are all these vessels in here for?" enquired Shorty of a fisherman.

"Waal, some are waitin' for bait, I cal'late, an' others are laid up, an' others are jest spendin' their time loafin' here 'til th' cod comes crawlin' aboard."

"How is it that we kin git our bait 'thout waitin' like these fellers for it?"

"How? Waal, sonny, it's 'cause you hev an uncle what hez a long head on him, an' makes his arrangements t' git a supply long before. Yer uncle hez a good name among th' trap fellers ashore here, an' they'll oblige him afore anyone else—'sides that he allus pays a little more'n the other feller, an' it pays in th' long run."

Shorty nodded. "Tell me," he asked after a pause, "how is it that an American vessel like we are kin come inter a Canadian port an' git supplies? I thought American vessels couldn't enter a Canadian port unless it was for shelter or water, or to refit after damages."

The oracle bit off a quid before replying. "Neither they can, son. An American vessel hez no right t' enter a Cana-

BLUE WATER 83

dian port onless, as you say, to git necessary supplies or shelter, but an American vessel kin git bait, ice, an' stores ef she takes out a Mody Veevendy (*Modus Vivendi*) licence by payin' th' Canadian Government a dollar'n half a ton on th' vessel's registered tonnage every year. She's entitled to them special privileges ef she takes out th' Mody Veevendy, an' this craft hez one o' them things."

When they came to an anchor Shorty went ashore with his uncle in a dory, and while the skipper was arranging for a supply of ice and bait the boy wandered off to look at a dingy-looking French brigantine lying at the end of the wharf. She was a wonderfully ancient craft, seemingly manned by a huge crowd of swart-skinned Breton fishermen. Her masts seemed stayed anyhow, the foremast had a decided rake over the bows, while the mainmast canted aft, and both spars were hung with rigging which looked positively ragged with frayed Irish pennants and chafing gear. Upon the foremast there hung four scandalized yards with the sails tied slovenly upon them, while the shrouds sagged for want of setting up, and the braces and running rigging streamed from aloft in unsightly bights. A line of ragged washing was strung across the deck between the masts, a few dried cod hung in the rigging, while over the stern depended a string of what Shorty deduced were skate fins. Rust and dirt predominated, and the boy contrasted this lumbering French hulk with the trim, yacht-like American fisherman upon which he was sailing.

While he was staring down upon the dory-littered maindeck there was a sound of someone shrieking in the forecastle, and a little boy came running out on deck hotly pursued by a man, who beat him unmercifully about the body with a rope. The lad cowered down in a corner endeavouring to shield his face with his arms, while the great brute beating him threw down the rope and started in to use his sea-booted feet. The sickening thuds as the man drove his heavy boots into the little body roused all Shorty's anger, and before he was aware of it he found himself on the deck of the brigantine and rushing for the tormentor.

"You big swab!" yelled Shorty, and picking up a belaying pin from the rail, he caught the astonished Frenchman a stunning blow on the side of the head which dropped him to the deck.

"Come on, kid!" he shouted to the boy cowering and crying on the deck. "Cut an' run!" And grasping the lad by the arm, he hauled him to his feet and hustled him over on to the wharf.

An excited jabber arose from the brigantine as the boys jumped on to the dock, and in a trice a mob of tatterdemalion St. Malo toughs came running up the wharf after them.

"Run, Frenchy, run!" cried Frank, dragging his frightened companion by the arm, and both lads legged it up the wharf as hard as they could go. The French boy was too sick, or too frightened, to run fast, and when Shorty glanced behind he could see the pursuers gaining upon them. "Go to it, Frenchy," he panted. "They're hard after us! 'Round th' corner here, quick!"

As they turned a shed they almost collided with a number of fishermen leisurely strolling down to the dock. "Hey thar', Frank!" cried someone in astonishment as the boy cannoned into a bulky figure. "Where'n tophet are ye goin'?" Shorty looked up, panting, and recognized Jud Haskins with four of the *Kastalia's* gang and two strange American fishermen.

"Frenchies—knockin' this kid about—kickin' him. I—laid out th' feller an' told—kid—t' run. Frenchies a-comin' after us!"

He had barely gasped the words out before the St. Malo men came swinging around the corner and into the group. Instantly Haskins dropped his parcel, and with a growling "Who th' 'tarnal blazes are ye shovin'?" he hauled off and smashed a Frenchman between the eyes with his fist. This was the signal for a general mix-up, and with whoops of delight the other American fishermen sailed in. It was not long before the sounds of battle attracted a crowd, while the excited yells of the Frenchmen brought the whole crew of the brigantine to the scene. "Trawlers! trawlers!" roared a voice. "A scrap! a scrap!"

Upon the hail every American, Canadian, and Newfoundland fisherman upon Canso wharves rushed hot-foot to the fray, and the fight developed into a proper beach battle between some forty of the brigantine's crew and a good twenty or thirty Anglo-Saxons, who, carried away by the excitement of the mêlée, shouted and roared with deep-water oaths and kicked and smashed their opponents with hairy fists and heavy sea-booted feet. "Look out for their knives!" bawled a man whose hand was dripping blood from an ugly slash, and Shorty saw him drive his boot into the face of the man who had cut him. "Take that, ye dhirty, knifin' swine!" he growled, and turning, he smashed another Frenchman on the mouth with his bleeding fist.

The little French boy cowered into the doorway of a shed and looked on with frightened eyes, while Shorty ducked in and out of the tussling mob and struck wherever he could see a swarthy face.

It was but the affair of a minute before the Frenchmen wavered and ran, and the Anglo-Saxons, who had been reinforced by a gang of Judique men—great six-foot Scotchmen, who had seen the fight from their vessel and pulled ashore in order to participate—followed the retreating St. Malo men in a roaring, vengeful mob. Over the rail of the brigantine they piled—McTavishes, McDonalds, and McCallums in the lead and thirsting for French blood, and it only ceased when the vanquished barricaded themselves in the forecastle and refused to come out.

Rory McTavish—a huge Judique fisherman, six feet four and broad in proportion—pleaded pitifully for the Frenchmen to come and renew the combat, but his entreaties fell upon ears which heeded not. "No? Ye wullna come?" he growled. "Well, lads, ah cal'late we'll hae tae burst in th' fo'c'sle door an' pull them oot! Stand back, some o' ye! Ah'll juist knock this wee bittie door in!" And with a lunge of his powerful shoulder he caused the barricade to split from top to bottom. "Anither wee bit dunt 'ull dae th' trick! Stand by tae clip them as a throw them oot tae ye!" And gathering his breath he made another onslaught on the door and disappeared with a splintering crash of planks into the yelling mob inside.

The Frenchmen must have thought that the red-headed McTavish was the devil himself. They cowered away from the grasp of his enormous hands, and, ludicrous as it may seem, he grabbed them like so many children and hove them out on deck. As they came staggering through the door the Canadians, Newfoundlanders, and Americans laid violent hands upon them and beat them unmercifully, an to the accompaniment of many objurgations—"Take that, you infernal skate-eater!" "You little boy bullies!" "You soft-hook men!" "Fish hogs!" "Stay on yer own side o' th' water an' don't be pokin' 'round on aour grounds!" And so on.

After the Judique men had satisfied themselves that not a man of the brigantine's huge crew would stand up to them they tore up all the deck fittings and piled on to the wharf again, the big McTavish putting a finish on "a graund fecht" by casting off the vessel's mooring ropes and letting her drift out into the harbour. Here the brigantine let go her anchor, and the men scattered to their several vessels to yarn and gossip over the "finest fracas that ever happened in Canso."

When Shorty saw his uncle some time later the latter looked at him with a severe frown on his brow and a twinkle in his eyes. "Waal," he said, as he scrutinized the stocky, sun-burnt youngster in front of him, "ef you ain't jest bound t' raise hades whar'ever ye go."

"It warn't my fault, Uncle Jerry," pleaded Shorty. "I saw that big brute of a Frenchman kickin' th' boy aboard th' vessel, so I jest clips him over th' head with a pin an' brings th' lad ashore with me——"

"Aye," interrupted the other, "an' raises th' biggest fight in Canso at th' same time. Oh, Frank, but ye're a dog! An' whar's th' kid ye were fightin' about?"

"He's down for'ard, sir."

"Down for'ard is he? An' what are ye goin' t' do about him?"

"Take him along with us," answered Shorty without any hesitation.

"Oh, ye are, are ye? An' whar' do I come in? Ain't I got no say in the matter? What am I goin' t' do with two kids aboard this craft?"

"Oh, he'll be useful, Uncle. Do let him stay. They'd kill him ef he was t' go back to th' Frenchy; an' he wouldn't go anyway. He's a nice boy, even ef he is a Frenchy!"

Uncle Jerry pondered and broke into a laugh. "All right, Frank. Have it your own way. Go git th' gang up an' get under way. We'll git our ice an' bait an' swing out."

CHAPTER SIX

SHORTY'S FRENCH FRIEND PROVED TO BE A BRIGHT LITTLE twelve-year-old Paimpol boy. He could not speak a word of English and seemed rather afraid of the *Kastalia's* crowd at first, until one of the gang, Johnny Leblanc—a French Canadian—took him in hand. The lad's delight at being addressed in his native tongue was evident, and, surrounded by a curious gang of kind-hearted trawlers, Leblanc acted as interpreter to the questionings of the men.

"He has no father nor mother," said Johnny. "Said his father was drowned at sea by the capsizing of a boat, and when his mother died an uncle took him to the Grand Banks on the Miquelon craft. He says his uncle was very cruel to him—look at th' marks on his face an' arms, will ye? Look how thin he is? Take off your shirt, sonny, and let me see where they beat and kicked you." The latter command was spoken in French, and the boy hastened to obey. A low growl of rage went up from the crowd when they viewed the great bruises and red welts upon the little fellow's pinched body, and it would have boded ill with any Frenchman who fell foul of them then. Though originally of French descent himself, Johnny Leblanc regarded the old-country Frenchmen as being foreigners, and he was as loud in his condemnation as anyone. "*Sacré!* look at dat!" he growled. "Mo' Dieu! I'd like to have bin in dat fight ashore! *Asseyez-vous là, mon petit garçon.* I will rub the bruises with some medicine. Whar's that liniment, fellers?"

A dozen bottles of Fisherman's Painkiller were routed out from under bunk mattresses, and, selecting one, Leblanc tenderly rubbed the ugly bruises and welts with his horny fist; and after drawing on his shirt, the little French waif was placed into a bunk and told to sleep.

"Sleep as long as you have a mind to, sonny," said Leblanc, "and if you feel hungry ask the cook here and he'll give you all you want. I cal'late we'll put some fat on them little bones o' your'n afore ye're much older. In a day or so you an' that other imp what pulled you aboard 'ull be plaguin' th' life outer us."

Leblanc's words were prophetic. Under the good treatment of the American and Canadian trawlers and the ministrations of the cook little Jules Galarneau frisked up and put on flesh visibly. He adored the aggressive, swaggering Shorty Westhaver, and jumped about to do him favours, and the latter in turn looked upon the French boy as his especial property. Shorty taught him English—taking him around the vessel and naming each article he pointed to, and the French boy, repeating after him, soon picked up a number of words. The men, of course, thought it was their privilege to teach the boy to swear, but Frank tabooed Jules's learning from anybody but himself; and, contrary to the usual manner, little Sabot, as the men called him, picked up a conversational English without profanity.

As they made their berths and fished on Canso, Quero, Sable Island, and up to the southern edge of St. Peter's Bank during the shortening September days Shorty and his companion worked around the vessel together, and each learned many things. Little Sabot made himself useful in a hundred ways. He could hook up, bait, and overhaul trawl as good as Shorty, and helped the men out in many ways by overhauling their gear for them, cutting bait, sharpening knives, as well as relieving the overworked and harassed cook from the job of tending dories. Shorty relieved his uncle at the wheel when the dories were out and gave the worthy skipper a chance to snatch a nap before they came alongside again. He also learned the use of the lead—that wonderful fisherman's instrument by which they feel the bottom and determine their position upon the shoaling Atlantic waters, and in off moments he studied the charts and gained an idea of how the courses were laid out upon it.

His tally sheet was mounting up when, at the end of September, they shot into Canso for a last baiting. Down in the hold pens a good fifteen hundred quintals of fish were stacked, and the men, as they checked up the count, smiled with satisfaction and calculated the future share that would be coming to them. Another five hundred quintals and then they would swing off for home.

It was a fine fall, and they had had no bad weather to speak of. A little fog and a bit of a twelve-hour westerly blow, but good fishing weather all round; and out on Banquereau they set their trawls for the last few sets, each man spitting on his bait for luck. Then came a morning when the sun rose upon a sea of oily calm, and when the gang had been turned out to bait up for the set, one of the dory-mates found he had a poisoned hand, which prevented him from going out in the dory. Though it could not be helped, yet the skipper regretted the loss of a dory during the last hauls, and as he dressed the man's swollen fingers he said so.

"I don't see how th' dickens, Asa, how you sh'd go'n git p'izened jest about now. Th' bad weather'll be comin' along 'most any minute now, an' ef we're goin' t' git a trip at all we need every dory out. However, boy, don't think I'm sore on ye 'cause o' somethin' ye can't help. I wouldn't ask any man t' haul trawls with a hand like that——"

Shorty came out from the shack locker, where he had been stuffing himself with cranberry pie—a specialty of the cook's and a favourite with the boys. "Waal, Uncle," he said. "How about me? How about yer spare hand? Let me'n Sabot take Asa's dory. We'll make th' set——"

Sabot crawled out, licking his lips. "Yaas, *m'sieu Capitan!* Frankee an' me make de set *très bon. Bon pêcheur,* Frankee an' me. I lak to go in doree."

The big skipper laughed. "Will ye look at th' trawlers!" he guffawed. "A couple o' minims! Both o' them c'd be stowed in a trawl tub. Ha! ha!"

Shorty frowned with disapproval upon his uncle's unseemly mirth. "Huh" he snorted. "We may be small, but it ain't allus th' big fisherman that makes th' big sets. Let me'n Sabot take th' dory, an' Asa's dory-mate kin take a spell at shippin' pen-boards an' catchin' painters. I'm sick o' that work."

Captain Clark pondered for a moment. "All right, Frank," he said finally. "Bait up a couple of tubs, an' set them one at a time. It'll be as much as yer little backs kin stand haulin', I cal'late. Off ye go, now!"

With a whoop of delight, both boys scrambled up on deck and proceeded to cut bait for two tubs of trawl. With deft fingers each boy garnished the six hundred odd hooks of the seven-shot trawl with a portion of bait, and when the baiting-up was finished they got the dory ready for launching.

"Give us th' water an' th' bearings!" cried Shorty, as he hooked the dory tackles into the bow and stern beckets.

"Forty-five fathom," replied the skipper. "Make yer set t' wind'ard thar'—just atween Jim Rolston an' Westley Carson. Hev ye got all th' gear in? Gurdy winch? Ye might need that t' wind yer trawl in, ha! ha! All right, swing her up!" And tallying on to the dory tackles, the dory was quickly swung over into the water.

The boys jumped in, while Captain Clark handed the two tubs of trawl down to them. "Away ye go, now," he said, "an' see'n come back high dory. Look out ye don't git over th' side!"

Shipping the oars, the boys pulled away from the anchored schooner in the direction indicated. How beautiful the vessel looked as she rode lazily over the sunlit swell! The long bowsprit, clipper bow, slender topmasts scraped and varnished with their gilded trucks and coloured windvanes or "highflyers" fluttering lazily in the morning air, the beautiful run and sheer of the black hull—riding deeper now with the weight of the fish below—all served in a distinctive way to enhance the trim appearance of the able Bank schooner. The sea itself was like glass, and dotted around the horizon by the tiny dories which strung around the circle of blank ocean like the rim of a wheel with the vessel as a common centre. Far away to the south the sails of another schooner could be discerned, while a smudge of smoke to the north betokened the presence of some ocean liner ploughing her appointed course. Impressed with the beauty of it all—the immensity of the ocean and the frailness of their tiny eighteen-foot dory, the boys pulled silently, with the ripple of their passage and the working of the oars against the thole-pins alone breaking the quiet of the sleeping sea. About a mile from the vessel Shorty unshipped his oars. "''Vast rowin'!" he grunted. Jules backwatered, and the dory floated motionless.

"Gimme the end line o' that first tub!"

Jules cast the tub becket adrift and handed the looped end of the baited and coiled trawl to his companion, who proceeded to make it fast to the small buoy anchor.

"All right, Sabot. Ship yer oars an' pull down to'ards Westley Carson thar'." And Shorty hove the buoy, with its black ball inserted, over into the water, while, as Jules rowed, the buoy-line was paid out. When the line had snaked over the gunwale and the buoy floated, black ball upraised, far astern, Frank hove the anchor out, and, standing with the tub before him, he threw the baited line into the sea by means of a heaving stick—the baited hooks and their dependent gangins coming clear of the main or back line as he dexterously whirled the line out of the coil in the tub. With the adept manner of an old trawler, Shorty hove the gear out without a single snarl—twenty-one hundred feet of line with six hundred and seventy hooks on gangins or snoods spliced into it requires some skill to handle—and when at last the gear had been "shot," he grunted a "''vast rowin'" to his dory-mate and made the "tub end" of the trawl fast to the second anchor and threw it over.

Riding to the roding of the last anchor, they lazed away the time for twenty minutes in order to give the fish prowling over the bottom, two hundred and seventy feet below, a chance to sample the succulent herring and squid bait, which, oily, tasty, and glittering, was well calculated to lure any ordinary cod to bite. Jules and Shorty, with the ease and abandon of hardened trawlers, stretched themselves out in the bow and stern of the dory and lit up their pipes.

Jules, lolling over the bow, was the first to speak. "O-ah, Shortee!" he cried suddenly. "*Regardez le requin! Oh, le gros requin!*" And he pointed into the cool green depths below them.

"What?" ejaculated the other. "Rekin? What th' deuce is that? Oh, yes, a shark. Gee, ain't he a brute!"

A long, rakish black body, fully eight feet in length, floated in the water just below the dory. The dorsal and tail fins quivered slightly, and a wicked blue eye winked as the boys looked over the dory gunwale.

"Look at th' blighter winkin'," cried Shorty. "He's awaitin' 'til we start a-haulin' th' trawl, then he'll make a snap for a fish. Gimme th' fork an' I'll poke him, th' dirty blue dog!"

The pew, or pitchfork, was handed over, and Shorty poised it for a lunge. "Steady now, not a word!" hissed the boy, and his arm drove down like lightning.

Bang! There came a smack on the dory bottom which almost stove the thin planks, and the water swirled in foam as the shark, with the fork imbedded in his eye, lashed around. Shorty yanked the pew clear, and Mister Shark sunk down into the depths below. "That got him," growled the harpooner jubilantly. The French lad laughed nervously. He didn't like sharks, and said so.

"I no lak dem *requin*. One man I know trawl in doree got hand bit off by *requin* one tam. Me much afraid."

Shorty spat contemptuously. "Tcha! they ain't no 'count. I've caught 'em on th' trawl plenty o' times up th' Bay Shore. Me'n Long Dick hez sprits'lyarded them lots o' times. Yank their jaws open an' jam a piece o' wood 'cross their mouth so's they can't shut it. They're a pest —gittin' in among yer gear an' cuttin' it all t' pieces. Me'n

Dick lost three tubs o' trawl one afternoon 'count o' sharks."

Sh-h-u-u-uh! A great black bulk broke water a scant cable's length away, and a jet of steam-like vapour shot into the air. "Whale!" cried Shorty. "*Baleine!*" piped Jules, and they watched the huge mammal up-end with a lazy roll and sound for the depths again after striking the water a resounding smack with his enormous tail. Sh-h-u-u-u-uh! Another huge black head appeared, blew a jet of vapour, and sounded, and almost instantly a whole school of a dozen or more broke the glassy mirror of the sea.

"Look! a hull fleet o' them!" shouted Shorty excitedly. "Gosh! Warn't that a monster! Geewhillikins! they're in among th' gear. Look at Westley shoutin' an' wavin' his oars! Thar's Jud Haskins doin' th' same. They're foul o' his gear. Look at his dory! Look at him tearin' through th' water! Ah, he's swampin'—no, he's cut adrift——"

The gambolling school were breaking water all round, and the men were standing up in the dories shouting and yelling. Jud Haskins was fouled, sure enough, and to save being towed under by the entangled leviathan he had cut his trawl. With the shouting and yelling the huge mammals, more frightened than the men were, plunged for the depths, and when they broke water again the school were far to windward and well clear. It was but the happening of a minute, and all that remained as evidence of the incident was the sight of Haskins and his dory-mate rowing up to the weather buoy to pick up the end of their parted trawl.

"Waal, ain't this a day, Sabot?" ejaculated Shorty. "Sharks an' then whales. Wonder what'll happen next?" He gravely stowed his pipe away, and shipped the gurdy winch across the bow gunwales of the dory. "Cal'late we'll haul th' gear now, Sabot. I'll gurdy up the anchor an' you coil th' line as it comes in."

The anchor line, wound up by the little hand-winch,

came in quickly, and in a few minutes the anchor with the end line of the trawl showed at the rail.

"Ketch holt!" The boy unshipped the winch and placed the hardwood pulley or roller into the dory gunwale, and while Jules hung on to the trawl, he slipped the woollen circlets or "nippers" over his hands and grasped the line. "Now for th' haul! Git yer anchor out th' way, Sabot, an' bring th' tub over here an' coil th' gear as I haul it in. Savvy?"

"I savvy," answered the other, obeying the commands.

"Now!" And Shorty commenced heaving the twenty-one hundred foot length of heavy trawl over the roller, while Jules, immediately aft of him, coiled the gear back in the tub again.

A good hundred feet of the line was hauled in, and the first dozen hooks came up with the baits still on them. "Good sign," grunted Shorty. "Allus more on th' trawl than comes up on th' first shot o' gear. Ah, here he comes! We ain't skunk dory, anyway. Stand by t' gaff any that falls off. Uh!" And a huge cod came limply up to the gunwale. Grasping the line off the roller, the boy swung the fish inboard by a dexterous turn of the wrist, and the jerk caused the hook to break free, while the fish flopped into the pen prepared for it in the bottom of the dory.

Hauling steadily with the old fisherman's pull, Shorty braced his feet firmly, and grasping the wet, hard cotton line with his nippered hands, pulled the trawl over the clacking *lignum-vitæ* wheel with but a momentary pause when he lifted an extra heavy fish over the gunwale and snapped it off into the pen. Jules, behind him, coiled deftly, and broke off only to gaff an escaping fish or to twist the hook out of a cod with the gob-stick when it proved too much for his mate to slat clear.

It took the boys a good hour and a half to haul the gear, and when they brought the last buoy aboard Shorty was dripping perspiration with his exertions. The sky had become overcast in the meantime and the dory rolled over a great swell, which tossed them upon its crest and then dropped them into a valley of limpid green. Shorty loosened his oilskin coat and glanced over the fish in the dory bottom. "Cal'late we ain't done so bad for our first set Bankin'. Thar's a good eighty or a hundred large fish thar'. Now for th' second tub. Sling the other gear out th' way, an' gimme a drink from th' dory jar beside you."

Jules understood hardly a word of what his companion was saying, yet with wonderful boyish intuition he knew almost exactly what he was asked to do.

"Cast th' tub becket off now an' heave out that gear, Sabot. I'll row this time——"

Bang! The report came from the schooner, and a gunny sack fluttered from the signal halliards at the topmasthead.

"What's dat?" cried Jules.

"Th' queer thing's h'isted!" replied the other. "Tie up yer tub again an' ship yer oars. We're wanted back aboard."

From all the points of the compass the dories could be seen pulling towards the schooner, and when the boys ranged alongside in the swell they were greeted with shouts and jests from the men already aboard and those in the dories waiting to lay alongside and pitch out their fish. "How many d'ye git, Shorty?" "High dory, I cal'late!" "Ain't no slinks or skate among that set o' your'n, is they?" "Back achin'?" And so on.

When it came their turn to pitch out, Jules hove the painter up to the cook, and they lurched alongside the rolling vessel, while Shorty hove the tubs of trawl up to the men aboard. Uncle Jerry glanced down into their dory. "Good boys," he said. "You got quite a little haul thar'. Mighty good for one tub." And both youngsters felt proud.

It takes quite a bit of strength and dexterity to stand in a lurching dory and pitchfork heavy fish over the rail of a schooner rolling and diving in a seaway, but Shorty and his small dory-mate did the job quite creditably. When the work was finished they threw their forks aboard, and, watching their chance when the dory rose on a swell, they leaped for the rail and tumbled aboard, while the men hauled their dory forward to the midship rail and hove it up into the nest.

Removing the pen-boards, thwarts, buoys, anchors, and gurdy winch, they pulled out the plug and sluiced the boat with a few buckets of water. "Thar' now," observed Shorty when the dory had been drained and the gear stowed away, "that's th' way you fellers ought t' go a-fishin'. Ninety-eight fish for one tub, an' all runnin' large; th' gear nicely coiled, an' th' dory drained clean. Ef some o' you lazy shackers 'ud take a lesson from Sabot an' me, ye'd become good fishermen in time. As it is, ye're a very ornery bunch o' trawl-haulers. Jud Haskins and Joe Milligan especially. Cod ain't big enough for them—they must go a-settin' for whales!"

There was a roar of laughter from the group, and the indignant Haskins reached for a stray piece of buoy-line. "Infernal imps!" he growled. "I'll tan ye, my sons."

"Let th' boys be, Jud, or th' fust thing you know they'll be cuttin' ye down to yer boot-straps. Ha! ha! That's a good one. Settin' for whales! Ho! ho!" And Haskins, though vexed over the loss of a tub of gear, laughed with the rest.

The skipper's voice rolled from aft. "Heave short on th' cable! Frank and Jules! Come aft here an' git th' stops off th' mains'l!"

The boys obeyed the call. "What's goin' on, Uncle?" asked Shorty, as he stepped into the cabin with an armful of stops. Captain Clark was regarding the barometer attentively.

"See here, Frank." The boy stepped forward. "Look at th' glass. D'ye see what it says?"

"Yes," answered the youngster. "Twenty-nine an' three-tenths. Very low, Uncle——"

"Yes, it is," assented the other, "an' when ye git a big swell runnin' up from th' south-east an' a greasy, dirty-lookin' sky, what would you opine?"

"Dirty weather, Uncle."

"Yes, dirty weather; an' it's liable t' come quick an' sudden. That's why I called th' dories back afore they started making another set. We've hed fine weather all September, an' when ye carry it well inter October ye're 'most bound t' git a snorter t' make up for't. Th' Western Ocean never gives ye too much of a good thing. Go up on deck now an' take a sound afore we break the anchor out."

Shorty was back in a few minutes to find his uncle poring over a chart.

"Well?" he interrogated.

"Forty-seven fathom—fine sand an' small stones."

"Huh! Come over here an' look on this chart. D'ye know whar' ye are?"

Shorty glanced over the soiled, pencil-marked ocean map. "Lemme see," he muttered, opening a pair of dividers, "we made our first berth after leavin' Canso last time jest on this spot here. Then we hauled out a bit more th' next set an' made a berth twenty-five miles to th' southeast o' that; then forty miles to th' no'th-east there, and another twenty to the east'ard o' that, which puts us twenty miles to th' no'th'ard o' Sable Island. Fifteen miles east o' that puts us on Quero here, an' forty-seven fathom fine sand an' small stones 'ud put us here, I cal'late. Am I right?"

The skipper nodded. "Ye're quite right, Frank, that's exactly whar' we are. Now fetch yer tally sheets. How much have we got in th' pens in th' hold?"

"'Bout nineteen hundred an' fifty quintal—more or less, an' there's ten thousand o' fish to be dressed yet."

"Um!" The skipper nodded. "All right, Frank. Go'n give a hand in gittin' sail on her. Th' swell's kickin' up more'n ever. H'ist th' mains'l!"

Shorty jumped on deck. "H'ist th' mains'l, he says!" And the gang, lolling over the windlass brakes, came trooping aft.

"Is he swingin' off, Shorty?" enquired a dozen men.

"Don't know," replied the boy. "He ain't told me yet

what he's a-goin' t' do. When he does, I'll let ye know!"
And he winked saucily at the crowd.

"Listen to th' shrimp!" cried a man. "Lord Harry! ye'd think he owned th' vessel by the airs o' him."

"Ef I owned her, Tom Cantley, I wouldn't carry you for ballast." And in the roar of laughter which followed, Tom Cantley looked foolish and shook his fist at the saucy, freckled youngster lolling lazily over the spokes of the wheel.

"Come on thar'! Git that mains'l up, you loafers!" he shouted. "Me'n Sabot ain't a-goin' t' wait all day on ye——"

"Shorty's in a hurry t' git back to that girl o' his up th' Bay Shore. What's her name, fellers?"

"Carrie Dexter, I cal'late," answered Cantley, smiling at the blushing Frank.

"Oh, yes, Carrie Dexter, that's th' name! Nice girl— too good fer sich a hard-drinkin', drivin' dog like Shorty. I cal'late he's a-going t' git spliced as soon as he draws th' share for that dory load o' cod he cotched this mornin'. Ha! ha!" And the men, heaving on the halliards, roared with laughter, while Shorty glowered at them under pent brows.

Frank Westhaver was too quick-witted a boy to be "strung" for any length of time, and it was not long before he had turned the laugh upon some other member of the *Kastalia's* gang. Upon a fishing vessel, joking and chaffing predominate in the conversation, and the foibles and idiosyncrasies of each person aboard, except the skipper and the cook, are made the topic for banter and fun. A stout man is made aware of the fact that he is fleshy in almost everything he does, and the lean ones are ragged in turn. Any person afflicted with a huge appetite for sleep soon hears about it; while the escapades, scrapes, and amours of every man aboard becomes a topic for general conversation. Idle talk is peculiar to fishermen—"scandalizin'" being a fine source for fo'c'sle gossip. It is harmless though, and rarely carried ashore, as most fishermen when their feet are on the dry land cut themselves adrift from the rough-talking crudity of their sea life and change their manners with their environment.

Getting the anchor aboard, they hoisted sail and lurched into the long swell under four lowers. There was very little wind, and during the afternoon, while the men dressed and salted the fish of the morning set, the schooner wallowed and rolled with the slatting of sails and the thunderous crashing of booms fetching up on the tackles. The sky became obscured with a greyish pall which could be seen scudding athwart the heavens before some air motion in the upper strata of atmosphere. Around the horizon the sea-line stretched in an undefinable circle of slaty mist, while the southerly swell rolled up in ever-increasing undulations.

The last fish had been stacked away, and the men had retired below for a lay-off, when the skipper's voice hailed from the deck. "Oh, below! All up an' stand by for squalls!"

The south-eastern sky had taken on a darker hue; a feeling of sultriness pervaded the air, and the oilskinned gang, coming out of fo'c'sle and cabin, cast apprehensive glances to the south'ard. The skipper stood on the weather quarter staring at the leaden pall to windward; the men lounged around the house aft, smoking and talking in low tones, while the vessel rolled and pitched thunderously into the almost windless swell.

"Stand by!" cried the skipper. A low hissing was heard; the murk to windward changed to a light grey, while the horizon stretched as a black line under it. A blast of heated air struck the vessel—a mere puff which bellied the listless sails for an instant.

"Did ye feel that?" growled a man. "Jest like openin' a furnace door—— Ah, here she comes!"

Another puff, sharp, sudden, and strong, struck the schooner and she rolled down until the lee rail went under. The wind whined in the rigging, and as the vessel gathered way upon her she headed close-hauled into the puffs and drove the spray over her bow in steam-like clouds.

"This ain't nawthin'," ejaculated a fisherman. "Th' real dirt'll come in a minute." He had hardly spoken before sea and sky were blotted out in a whirl of white, which hissed and roared as it rushed across the water. Instantly the vessel was headed into it—a wild, howling inferno of wind and hail. Hail which slashed like shot upon the decks and caused the men to cower and hide their faces from its stinging lash, and wind—what a wind! The schooner rolled her lee deck under, while all hands hung on the rail to windward. The head-sails flapped in thunderous reports, the foresail slatted and fetched up on the tackles with nerve-rending shocks, while the sea pounded on the bluff of the bow and burst over the vessel in sight-defying clouds of spray.

Captain Clark was standing by the man at the wheel, his hat gone, and his face red with the sting of the hail. Shorty and Jules were clinging, bat-like, to the weather main rigging, while the rest of the gang clung to the house, mainmast, or by the weather dories. For several minutes the squall lasted, then came a lull which allowed the vessel to lift her deluged lee-rail.

"Wa-a-a-tch aout!" bawled the skipper. Crash! Swish! An enormous cresting sea came thundering over the bows, and it swashed aft, submerging the oilskinned figures which hung to rail, gear, bait-boards, and pins. Jules was coughing and sputtering after it had passed.

"What's th' matter?" asked Shorty, flicking the water out of his eyes.

"My mout' was open——"

"Wa-a-a-tch aout!" Men turned apprehensively and tightened their grip when they glanced at the curling wall of water lifting above the rail. Crash! All hands held their breath; the water roared in their ears; it plucked at their bodies and caused the arms to crack with the strain of resisting the pull; then it sluiced away, and the skipper roared in a voice which sounded above the shriek of the wind and the hissing crashes of the rapidly rising and cresting sea! "Take in th' mains'l!"

Detaching themselves from the gear to which they were hanging, the gang staggered aft along the reeling, sea-washed decks and laid hold of the mainsheet while the skipper eased the wheel down. "Now then! Heave her in!" shouted the mob as they snatched up all the slack in the fluttering, slatting sail. "Walk away with her!" "Bring her aboard, th' rag!" The boom was sheeted aboard as far as it would come with the sail full of wind, the crotch was shipped, and the boom tackles hooked in.

"Lower away peak an' throat!" cried the skipper. "Man yer gaft downhaul. Steady now!"

Getting that mainsail in—six hundred odd square yards of canvas with a seventy-foot boom—was quite a job, even for twenty men. The wind was blowing so hard that it filled the sail like a balloon, and when lowered it trailed all over the lee quarter. The men, hanging on to the gaff, jumped and stamped on the refractory canvas with their heavily booted feet, but they were absolutely unable to make an impression upon it. For the present the mainsail had "taken charge."

"Never mind her jest now," said the skipper. "Hook on yer boom guys an' belay that gaft downhaul. Get th' jib in an' sing out when ye're ready t' roll her up!"

For'ard went the gang, and, ducking their heads to the spray, they slacked away the jib halliards and manned the downhaul. "Now! drag her down!" The jib came reluctantly down the stay, and in a whirling, flapping bundle it slashed around, thumping the bowsprit with the heavy chain-sheets.

"Run her off, skipper!" The vessel was driving her bowsprit into the seas, and it would have been as much as a man's life was worth to have attempted to roll up the jib while the schooner was close-hauled.

Someone started the foresheet, and the schooner sped before the fury of the blast, lurching and diving as she overran the seas. In a veil of spray the men clambered out on the foot-ropes of the bowsprit and laid hold of the slatting jib. With growls and oaths they fisted the wind out of it, while a tiny oilskinned figure, growling as loudly as the rest, clambered up the jib-stay and stamped the hanks down with his feet.

"Waal, look who's here!" cried a man. "Here's th' spare hand workin' like a son-of-a-gun. Look out, boy, one o' them flaps don't knock ye over."

The vessel reared on a sea, her bowsprit poked sky-high, and as she descended, the men on the spar gave a yell. "God Almighty! hang on, boys!"

Under a creaming crest went the bowsprit, while jib and the yellow figures tying it up disappeared from view. Knightheads, windlass, and fo'c'sle scuttle dived from sight in a yeasty boiling of solid green sea, while those out on the bowsprit hung to the gear like limpets and waited for the vessel to rise with lungs which expanded to bursting. After a seemingly interminable period they emerged, red-faced, dripping, and cursefully indignant. Shorty, jammed up in the eyes of the bowsprit gear, was panting for breath.

"Come on, sonny," cried the man next to him. "Pass that stop an' let's git out o' this. Another o' them dives 'ull about cook our goose, boy."

When they came in the skipper was waiting for them. "Tackle yer mains'l now," he said. "Stand by yer fores'l! Hook on th' jibin' tackle—I'll jibe her over an' spill th' wind out o' this mains'l. Ready?"

"Ready, sir!"

Captain Clark put the helm hard up; the foresail gave a savage flap, and then the boom whirled over, fetching up on the relieving tackle with a crash and shock which almost started the decks. The mainsail, which had been sailing over the quarter full of wind and water, collapsed limply, and the men quickly hauled it in and rolled it up.

The squall had settled down into a proper Western Ocean buster; the wind blew a whole gale from the southeast, accompanied by rain and a rapidly rising sea; and when the long fall night set in the storm-wrack was flying athwart the sky with express speed. The barometer still continued low, so, after figuring up his position, the skipper decided that the best thing to do would be to heave her to for the night, or until the wind hauled more favourable. This was done under the foresail and jumbo, sheeted well in; and wheel lashed hard down, and staggering, lurching, and rearing over the roaring foam-laced surges, the *Kastalia* rode out the fury of the storm as easily as a gull resting on the billows.

After supper the gang, except the two on watch, turned into their bunks and yarned and gossiped. In the cabin an argument was in full swing, and loud-voiced opinions were shouted across the reeling apartment from the bunks. Shorty was in his bunk reading a book by the light of a candle stuck in a sticking-tommy. Jules was in back of him playing with the cat. It was a proper "lay-off" scene common to the vessels of the Banking fleets. Outside, the gale howled and shrieked in the rigging, the decks sluiced water, and the racing seas curled their foam-crested heads in sibilant roarings, while the vessel under the foresail and jumbo, side-stepped, cavorted, plunged, and curtseyed to the heaving, wind-whipped undulations. Below decks, the flickering lamps smoked and flared, blue tobacco reek wreathed from out the bunks, the stoves glowed lambently red through the haze of ship's plug and odoriferous bilge emanating from the hold below, the oilskins hanging on the bulkheads swayed in pendulous arcs to the roll of the vessel, while boots and buckets slid noisily from starboard to port. The men, rolled in quilt and blanket, lolled upon their straw-filled ticks in muscle-relaxed luxury, hanging into their narrow bed-places by the exercise of that peculiar adhesive quality possessed only by shell-fish and seafarers in small craft.

"What are ye readin', Shorty?" A man, tired of argument—fishermen's arguments consist of all hands talking and nobody listening—asked the question.

"I ain't readin'," answered the boy. "I'm only tryin' t' read, an' now that you fellers hev quit shoutin' all ye don't know about th' history o' th' United States an' whether it was George Washington or Abe Lincoln what signed th' Declaration of Independence I'll maybe git a chanst t' read——"

"Read it out to us," came a chorus of voices.

"It might not interest ye in th' least——"

"Yes, it will. Go ahead, let's hear it whatever it is."

"It's a French book written by one o' Sabot's countrymen called Dumas," explained Shorty before reading. "Th' yarn is about things what happened a couple hundred years ago in France—Sabot's country—so, ef ye've a mind t' listen, I'll read ye th' yarn from the beginning."

Silently the gang listened to the roistering story of the "Three Musketeers," as read aloud by the boy in a clear, fluent voice. The snore of the wind came down through the half-drawn slide; the vessel creaked and groaned in all her oaken timbers, the muffled thunder of seas could be heard, but it was the rollicking, sword-flashing D'Artagnan and his three companions who dominated the *Kastalia's* cabin that night. Though a subject utterly strange to those Nova Scotian Bank fishermen, yet they were able to follow and appreciate the yarn with just as much pleasure as if they had been educated to it.

The oilskinned head and shoulders of the watch on deck appeared in the scuttle for an instant, and a raucous voice, unaware of the reading below, bawled for the time. The rasping curses hurled at him upon asking such a simple question led him to wonder what was happening in the cabin, and he clattered noisily down the brass-shod steps.

"Get t' hell out o' here, you clumsy-footed swab!" barked a man. "Kain't ye see th' lad's readin' to us? Go ahead, Shorty. Let's hear how th' dooal came out with them Athos, Porthos, an' Aramis guys."

The news leaked down for'ard that a cracking good yarn was being read out by Shorty in the cabin, and in twos and threes the men turned out and "cal'lated they'd go down aft an' hear it." Before the first chapter had been read the cabin was crowded with some twenty listening trawlers, and when the cook came crawling down, the skipper looked out of his bunk. "Say, for th' land's sake! D'ye think this cabin is a blame' theayter for all you for'ard gang t' roost in an' squirt t'backer juice all over our stove? Sink me! th' blame vessel'll be down by th' starn with all this gang aft—an' will ye look at th' watch that's supposed t' be keepin' a look-out on deck! Aground on their beefbones in th' gangway, by th' Lord Harry, an' leavin' th'vessel t' look after herself. Get up on deck, you watchmates! This ain't in harbour, remember. There's steamers a-runnin' 'crost this here Bank. Go on, Frank— let's hear some more."

Shorty read on, while the minutes passed, and the gang listened with rapt attention—smoke wreathing around their heads, and bodies inclined to catch the sentences.

"Oh, below thar'! Steamer bearin' down!" The hail came from the deck, and the crowd below jumped as if electrified. Shorty hove the book down and grabbed his boots, Captain Clark jumped out of his berth and leaped for the companion, while the whole mob streamed on deck.

"See her?" The watchman pointed to a triangle of lights on their port quarter. Red and green at the base and white at the apex—a steamer's port, starboard, and masthead lights.

"Git up torches!" yelled the skipper. "Ring th' bell! Blow th' horn! They's jest as liable t' run ye down as not. Holy sailor! He's makin' slap-bang for us!"

The triangle of lights were coming up fast; the loom of a large steamer could be seen through the blackness of the rain-swept night, and the men perspired, despite the cold.

"For Christ's sake, look alive with them torches!" bawled the skipper. "He'll be into us in a jiffy! Hey, th' steamer, ahoy!" But his voice, powerful and all as it was, sounded but faintly above the roar of the gale.

The steamer held her course, and while the watchers stood petrified on the schooner's decks, someone up in the port fore-rigging snatched the lantern out of the light-bracket and waved it. The officers on the steamer's bridge must have seen it; the helm of the liner was starboarded at the critical moment, and with torches aflare on her decks the *Kastalia* scraped the liner's steel plates with her long bowsprit. Far overhead towered the long, white-painted rails, davits, and life-boats of the steamer; two huge funnels belched smoke; someone shouted meaningless phrases; the lighted ports flashed past; there was a churning of white water as the stern glided away from them, and while the frightened fishermen staggered upon the slippery decks as the schooner rolled in the wash, the blinking stern light alone remained to tell them of their escape.

Captain Clark wiped the sweat off his forehead with the back of his hand. "How was it ye c'dn't git a torch alight, some o' yez? Lord Harry! we'd all ha' bin drowned ef we ha' waited on torches. All in th' kid, I suppose, an' no ile in any o' them. Who was up th' fore-riggin' wavin' that lantern?"

"Me!" piped a boyish voice from the depths of the mob, and the men fell apart to disclose Shorty.

"Waal, I be goshswizzled!" ejaculated the skipper "Blamed ef th' kid ain't the only one aboard that can keep his wits about him. Fancy thinkin' o' that white lantern in th' sidelights! It was a close shave—a pow'ful close shave! I c'd feel her scrapin' that vessel's hull with her bowsprit. Let's git out o' this. Turn to thar' an' reef th' mains'l! Put th' muslin on her an' we'll git home." And he stepped below to change his soaking stockings. Shorty, shivering and wet, followed him, and the boy could see that his uncle had been given a bad shake.

"By th' Lord, Frank, that was a close call. I don't remember ever havin' been in sich a nip-an'-tuck place afore. D'ye remember what I was a-tellin' ye in Boston when we passed that steamer?"

"Yes," answered the other, "and I understand. I don't want t' see any more o' them onless they're in dock. Gee! I was frightened up in th' riggin' thar'. I sure thought she was comin' slam inter us."

"Thank th' Lord ye warn't so frightened but what ye knew what ye were doin' when ye swung that lantern. They never saw our red light on that steamer, an' a half a minute more an' we'd ha' been at th' bottom o'th' sea——"

"Mains'ls reefed, skipper!" shouted a voice on deck.

"Then h'ist away an' shoot her off sou'-west. We'll slam her for Gloucester as hard as she kin clip." And the gang on deck heard the news.

"Homeward bound, bullies! Sheet in that mains'l! Sou'-west th' course, an' drive her, you!"

CHAPTER SEVEN

THEY WERE DRIVING HER! CAPE SABLE HAD BLINKED at them in the dark of an October night, and when it had flickered into nothingness astern Captain Clark turned the gangs out fore and aft to hang the whole patch upon her. "Jig up an' sheet down!" he commanded. "This old gal never made a slow trip from the east'ard in her life. Give that lee balloon sheet a pull! Start that stays'l a grind! Take up th' slack in them two tops'l halliards! So! Now, drive her!"

Storming along on the wings of the wind, with all her sail set, the *Kastalia* pointed her long bowsprit for Cape Ann and sheared through the black waters with a dull, sonorous roaring at her forefoot. The forecastle resounded to the low thunder of racing seas, and the timbers of the staunch schooner creaked and groaned with the load of canvas she was lugging along. It was grand! A very poem of motion! Not a listless, sentimental idyll, but a shouting, surging, storming song—a booming anthem accompanied by the whine and snore of a breeze of wind in the taut rigging and crashing, bellowing, deep-toned shout of resisting, out-flung sea. Rising grandly to a full-bodied wave, the *Kastalia* drove down the succeeding trough with a creaming yeast of foam which bubbled and hissed clean to the rail. Up she would go again; bowsprit soaring sky-high and copper-painted underbody showing clear aft to the heel of the fore-mast. It was an ocean see-saw, when vessel and elements played and flirted with each other, but, despite the waltzing and curtseying, the sharp bows were held to a defined seapath, and the trailing log astern was clicking up the traverse of watery miles.

Jules and Shorty lounged over the weather dories and

watched the scenes around them. "Waal, Sabot, ol' man, we're hoofin' it for home. Homeward bound—d'ye know? D'ye understand?"

The little French lad stared hard at the sea for a space. "I have no home," he said sadly. "W'en we git to Glo'ster, I no know w'at to do——"

Shorty raised a threatening hand. "Jules Sabot!" he said severely. "As sure as my name is Frank Westhaver, I'll bat ye on the ear ef I hear ye talkin' thataways ag'in! When I'm goin' home, you're goin' home, see? You ain't a Frenchy any longer, are ye?"

"No, no," replied the youngster emphatically. "Me no French no more. No want go back. No like France or Frenchy peoples—'cept Johnny Leblanc——"

"He's a Canadian—a Nova Scotian," interrupted Shorty.

"*Oui!* Nova Scozian—dat's what I be!"

"That's just what you are, Sabot. You're a Nova Scotian—a Bluenose—an' you'n me's goin' dory-mates next year. You keep pickin' up English th' way you're doin' an' ye'll pass for a white man any day." Shorty spat deftly over the rail, and the little Breton fisher-boy regarded him with eyes of admiration.

"You dam' fine fellow, Shortee," he said.

"Bah, Sabot! Cut out th' soft soap. Let's go'n hev a mug-up. Cook's bin makin' doughnuts. I'll talk to him, an' you hook a few."

Into Gloucester harbour they shot in the dark of a late October morning, and the old New England fishing town was scarce awake before the news went around the breakfast tables that the *Kastalia* was in with a high-line trip. They discharged their fish—Frank acting as tally-man—and the out-turn was better than they expected, and with good prices the gang each drew a share check for a respectable sum.

"Now," said Captain Clark when the men had been paid, "I suppose my spare hand'll be wantin' his wages? Waal, ye've bin a very handy, useful boy, an' I'm very pleased with ye—very pleased indeed. Here's fifty dollars t' ye. Now, call your dory-mate.''

Jules came down at the hail and stood apprehensively before the skipper. Though Shorty had assured him that he would never be cast adrift, yet the lad was afraid that the Captain would send him on shore.

"Waal, sonny. I cal'late you need a riggin' o' new clothes. Here's twenty dollars. Go with Frank here, an' he'll see t' ye. You kin stay by th' vessel—we'll be makin' another trip fresh-fishin' in a week after we git them topmasts down—an' I reckon you'll go along with us. Clear out now, th' pair o' ye, an' don't go out on a time like some o' yer shipmates.''

Before the boys went up-town Frank opened a little bundle of letters. One was from his mother—a proper motherly epistle, cautioning the youngster against wearing wet clothes and eating too much. "Change your clothes every time you get wet or damp," it read, "and do not stand around in the rain. Stay in the cabin when the storms come, etc." Shorty smiled. What would his mother have thought if she had seen him hanging on to the main-rigging and being deluged in the seas and soaked to the skin; of being "run under" on a bowsprit; of living continually in wet clothing? Poor mothers! What they don't know won't hurt them, and it is just as well for their peace of mind. A number of short letters from Carrie Dexter occupied his attention next—letters full of girlish chatter: of the minister, of teas, dances, weddings, and dress, and concluding with a line of crosses which made the boy smack reminiscent lips. The last was an ill-written scrawl from Lem Ring—unpunctuated, uncapitalized, and bristling with "Well Shorty's." In it Long Dick sent his regards, and wanted to know how his "Depitty" fared a-Banking; Jud Morrell wished to be kindly remembered; and the epistle ended with a mournful hope that Shorty would come back soon.

With the roll of bills in their pockets and feeling at peace with the world, the boys swaggered into a Fisherman's Emporium and Jules invested his money in a new rig-out of clothes. With all the eagerness of a child he scurried back aboard the vessel to put them on, and ready-made and ill-fitting as they were, the boy strutted around the fo'c'sle, showing off to the laughing fishermen, as proud as a dog with two tails.

Within ten days of their return from the salt Banking trip the *Kastalia*, denuded of her long topmasts, and rigged with her winter backstays and gear, poked her long horn outside Ten Pound Island bound on a fresh-fishing, or "haddocking," voyage to the Nova Scotia coast. They carried no salt this time—the hold pens being filled with some twenty-five tons of ice—and with frozen herring bait aboard they made a fast "run-off" to the Seal Island, and made their first set some twelve miles south of Cape Forchu.

The weather continued fine, and working over the grounds from the Cape to the Lurcher Lightship, they had a trip of eighty thousand prime haddock, cod, hake, pollock, and cusk on the ice within eight days of leaving port. The method of fishing was practically the same: Shorty and Jules tended dories and worked around the deck, but while the former learned little from his physical labour, yet he acquired hard muscles and began to grow.

Uncle Jerry, with consummate skill, kept the boy under his lee, and taught him many things without letting his nephew know that he was being instructed. He kept him at the wheel for many hours steering by the wind and by compass; he had him keeping an unceasing tab upon the rise and fall of the barometer, and practically all the casting of the lead was done by Shorty. Every move of the vessel from berth to berth was traced upon the chart by the boy; he kept the "count," or fish tally; as "hold boss" he reported daily upon the supply of ice and bait left after each set; and while his stocky frame was toughening and stretching his brain was expanding also. Among the men he was a great favourite. He read to them in the short hour before turning in, and while he was improving the

BLUE WATER

intellectual side of his mind by the reading of good, instructive literature he was making many staunch friends. There was no denying it. The fishermen he sailed with adored the boy and would have done anything for him in their rough, simple, kindly way, and when they left for their homes at Christmas it was their entreaties which prevailed upon the skipper to bring his nephew back fishing for the balance of the season.

They marketed their fresh fish in Boston, running into T Dock and herding with the crowd of able marketmen which ranked two and three deep at the wharf. Here Frank met many men and learned many things. He kept tally of the "out-turn" when unloading their catch, and saw how the fish were graded by the eagle-eyed cullers standing by the scales on the dock. He learned to distinguish the various grades of fish—the large-sized cod and hake classed as "steak" and put upon the market for the purpose of slicing; the fat, full-fleshed "mediums"; the smaller "snappers" and "scrod." He also saw the difference in the class of fish caught by the "hand-liners," who fish from the schooners with hand-lines upon Georges Bank; he talked with the crews of "rip fishermen," who fished by hand-lines from the deck of their vessel while she drifted among the whirling tide eddies of Nantucket Shoals; and a visit aboard of a newly arrived "halibuter" from the Labrador coast opened his eyes to a new and fascinating phase of the fishing business.

It was a great college for the boy, this rollicking sea town collected for a short space from the various shoal-water "spots" of the Western Ocean. From the ice-piled beaches of the desolate, rockbound Labrador they came; from the traffic-ploughed waters of the "Channel" and the tide-rips of Nantucket Shoals; the treacherous Banks of Georges; the ledge-strewn Cape Shore of Nova Scotia; and the misty, tide-ruled waters of the Bay of Fundy. With Newfoundlanders, silent, rough, and hairy; Portuguese from Lisbon and the Azores, swarthy, ear-ringed, black-haired, and volatile; Boston Irish, ruddy, ready-tongued, and strong with the burr of the Galway and Connemara brogue; and a strong sprinkling of Nova Scotians from Shelburne, Yarmouth, and Digby counties, the various crews constituted a cosmopolitan gang who talked and yarned in their varied dialects upon one common topic— the forty-fathom gossip of the great sea-world of fish.

The city of Boston held a mighty attraction for the country-bred Nova Scotia boy, and uncle and nephew strolled around the thronged, bustling streets viewing the wonders displayed in the store windows, watching the traffic and admiring the tall buildings, with little Sabot trotting open-eyed and silent in their wake.

They spent Christmas at home up on the Bay Shore— a genuine, Christmassy Christmas with frost in the air and snow on the ground. And what a time Shorty had! The little packet schooner had scarce ranged alongside the Long Cove wharf before Long Dick, Lem Ring, and Jud Morrell had sprung aboard and were wringing the boy's hand off and slapping him upon the back until he coughed again. Can anyone describe Dick Jennings's pleasure when he surveyed the stocky, sea-bronzed youngster he had trained, noted the erect breadth of the boy's shoulders, felt the grip of his hardened hand, and gazed into the cool grey-blue confidence of his eyes. "You're a dog, Shorty!" he ejaculated. "Yep!—a proper rip-roarin' dog! An' this is th' little French kid ye started th' scrap up in Canso over eh? Shake a mitt, son! 'Tis a Novy we'll be makin' of ye afore long, an' ye'll soon forgit ye ever were a blame' parley-voo! Tell us of that fight, Shorty! Tell me about that close call ye hed with th' liner—th' tearin' vessel-sinkin' scum!" And the worthy fisherman volleyed questions and made comments in the same breath, while little Jules opened his brown eyes wide and gazed in pleasure upon the hearty greetings showered upon his friend.

Mrs. Westhaver was standing in the porch when uncle, nephew, and Jules trudged through the snow up to the door. Who can express the motherly admiration which filled the good lady's eyes as she greeted her boy back from his first voyage on deep water; the huggings and kissings, the incoherent greetings and laughter, and the joy of the homecoming. Shorty felt that it was worth while, felt that it was good to be alive and to be home again. He surveyed the old familiar furnishings of the cozy house with a sense of pleasure he had never felt before, and in the ecstasy of the greetings he forgot the little sea-waif lingering in the hall.

"Ho, mother!" he cried after the first flush of the salutations were past. "I 'most forgot little Sabot! Here, Jules—come an' meet ma! This is the little chap I was tellin' you about in my letter. Jules Galarneau is his name——"

The tears came into the French boy's brown eyes when he received a kiss and a hug from the sympathetic Mrs. Westhaver. "You poor child," she said in a voice tender with compassion for the little foreign orphan. "Come up an' set ye by th' fire. I'm glad Frankie brought ye with him——"

"Why, t' be sure, ma," interrupted Shorty. "I wouldn't leave Sabot behind in Gloucester not for anythin'. Me'n Sabot's goin' dory-mates later on——"

"Aye, an' 'tis a handful any skipper'll have with you two in his gang," laughed Uncle Jerry. "But never mind, boys, you ain't so very bad. Draw to, Jules an' Frank! Here's some grub that wants punishin', an' I cal'late we're th' boys what kin do it. Eh Jules?"

And Jules, the runaway Breton fisher-boy, hospitably treated on every hand, and solicitously waited upon by the kindly widow, felt that his cup of joy was overflowing. "*Merci, merci, madame,*" he murmured. "*Je suis très heureux*—ver' happy, ver' please'—t'ank you ver' kind."

Christmas morning broke clear, cold, and sunny, and the boys were astir early overhauling their presents — little Jules especially being in transports of delight with the little things he received. Dancing around the bedroom in his bare feet, he produced each article with whoops of pleasure —leather wool-lined mittens, a pair of fancy braces, a silk muffler, and a box of maple-syrup candy giving him as much gratification as if they had been worth twenty times their value. "Ohé, le bon Noël!" he cried. "Frankee, I am please'. Regardez le gant—il est très bon—n'est ce pas? No, I mus' speak Engleesh—no more Français. I say Meree Chris'mas, Frankee!" And with shouts and yells the two boys scampered all over the house until Uncle Jerry, disturbed in his slumbers, drove them back to their room.

The week passed in a round of visits and festivities, and every house from Port Stanton to Long Cove was an open "Liberty Hall" to all who entered. Jules was introduced to Lem Ring, and as a friend of the redoubtable Shorty the French lad was a friend of Lem's also. And Carrie Dexter? Well, she constituted the prime reason for the various occasions on which Jules had to look after himself. When Shorty brushed his hair with extra care, donned his best tie, and scrubbed his hands, then Jules knew that he was bound off upon a visit, when he—Jules—was invariably told "to knock aroun' an' enjoy himself for a spell." These were daily occasions too, and Sabot wondered if they were part of some religious rite until he stumbled upon the pair one evening while walking up from the Rings' house.

Shorty blushed very red and he shuffled under Jules open-eyed stare. "Er—Sabot—I mean Jules—'low me t' make ye acquainted with Miss Dexter—Mister Galarneau."

Jules—always the Frenchman in politeness—bowed. "I have ze plaisir de votre connaissance, Mees Dexter." And the trio strolled and chatted together on their way to the Dexter home.

"What d'ye think o' my girl, Sabot?" queried Shorty after they left.

"Ver' nice, ver' pretty girl, Frankee," replied the other. "Dat girl you goin' marry sometime?"

Frank blushed. "No, confound you, Sabot! Who said anythin' 'bout gittin' married?"

Jules pondered. "Well," he said slowly, "I hear men 'board vessel say dat Shortee git married to Carrie Dexter soon——''

"Aw, they're only jawin', Sabot," interrupted the other. "She's my friend, same as you'n Lem Ring."

"Yes?" Jules spoke quietly. "S'pose some oder boy come an' be ver' great frien' wit' Mees Dexter—you lak dat, eh?"

Frank's brows wrinkled. "No," he said. "I wouldn't like that——"

"Den you love her ver' much——"

"Waal——"

"You love her, Shortee?"

"Waal——"

Jules laughed. "Of course you do! I see dat right away. You love her ver' much. I love you, Shortee, but I no t'ink dat girl for you——"

"What?" growled the other.

Jules repeated. "I no t'ink dat girl for you, Shortee—"

Shorty was indignant. "Oh, shut up, Sabot. What do you know about it? Let's run for home. Mother made some lemon pies to-day, an' I cal'late I know whar she hid them."

They left for Gloucester again during the first week of the new year, and after a couple more haddocking trips they fitted out for the long spring salt Banking trip. On this voyage they only carried an eight-dory gang—sixteen men, cook, skipper, and the two boys. Nine dories were taken along, and during the fine, smooth days upon the grounds Shorty and Jules manned the extra dory and made the set, and by the time they had "wet the salt" and swung off for home both lads were competent to go in the dory and haul the gear the same as graduated fishermen. With a record trip of twenty-four hundred quintals they shot into Gloucester one blowy July morning after five months out from port. They did not keep the sea all that time, as many days were spent lying to anchor in the bait ports of Canso, Souris, the Magdalen Islands, St. Pierre in Miquelon, and various coves on the Treaty Coast of Newfoundland, but the long spell from home had the effect of making a man out of Frank; his muscles hardened, and his stocky frame knit solidly, until at sixteen years of age he was as strong as an ox. His books travelled with him, and his young mind absorbed and pondered over the printed thoughts of clever men, and the cultivation of his intellect was unspoiled by the trash of newspaper supplements, light novels, wishy-washy flim-flam, dissipations and distractions of shore life in a city. Out on the broad waters of the Atlantic in the lay-offs between the work of fishing a brainy man thinks, while a stupid one sleeps. There are always the two types to be met with upon the vessels of the fishing fleets, and belonging to the former class one may meet quiet-spoken, horny-handed trawlers who, though blessed with very little education, are able to converse in an intelligent manner upon many subjects, and in their level-headed, even conversation one can detect the well-balanced thoughts and reasonings of the thinking man. The sea gets very near to the heart of the pensive toiler upon its breast; he becomes impressed by its immensity, by its power and beauty in storm and calm, by the myriad life it contains and the strange natural laws by which it is controlled. Such impressions leave their mark upon a man; he welcomes the silent hours of his watch on deck to commune with his thoughts; he can lighten the monotonous labour of the fishery by retrospection and reflection, and in the "lay-offs" or watch below he is invariably the one who, with pipe and book, can pleasantly while away the hours when others of his shipmates will be drowsing or indulging in loud-voiced, useless argument and altercation.

Of such a meditative turn of mind was Westhaver. Not that he was unsociable, serious, or a dreamer of dreams, for a man can be a reader and thinker without losing all the attributes of a good shipmate. Westhaver was a good shipmate and a good fisherman. He sang, laughed, and joked more than any of them, yet, as his uncle said, he had "more brains than th' whole ship's company."

The years passed rapidly for the boy, and before he was fully aware of it he reached man's estate—small in stature, but broad, strong of muscle and will, and good-looking in features. Under his uncle, his education had been a thorough one both as regards his chosen vocation and his intellectual accomplishments, and at twenty-one years of age Frank Westhaver was a man singularly endowed.

They were upon Grand Bank when Frank's birthday came along, and the uncle, pacing the quarter, glanced proudly over the manly form of his nephew steering. "Thar's nawthin' mean about that boy," he murmured. "Look at th' shoulders on him! Short he may be, but height don't allus make a man, an' Frank ain't so very short either. So he's twenty-one to-day! Eh, eh, but th' time passes quick. It seems but a year or so ago when he was runnin' aroun' th' Bay Shore gittin' inter trouble an' raisin' a rumpus gen'ly. Eh, eh, but th' years soon go!"

Back in Gloucester again, Uncle Jerry spoke what had been on his mind for many weeks, aye, months. They were sitting upon an old topmast lying on the sunny side of the wharf—Frank, cool of eye, healthy-skinned and powerful, with life before him, and the uncle, stout, grey-haired, and jogging easily down the shady side of earthly existence. "Now, Frank, you're a man!" Uncle Jerry paused for a moment to gaze into his nephew's clear eyes. "Aye, you're a man now, boy, an' it's drawin' away on yer own course ye'll have t' be after this, for I have no hold upon ye now. I've brought ye up as a father. I've trained ye up as a fisherman and a sailor. You kin handle a vessel an' navigate better'n I kin, and in th' dory there are none can show ye anythin'. Now I must leave ye t' work out yer own traverse. You can make or break yerself from now on—I have no say in th' matter, but I kin still advise ef ye care t' listen. Now ye've bin sailin' with me for six years, but I don't want men t' say that Frank Westhaver was his uncle's pet an' only worth his salt while his uncle was behind him. No! that would never do, an' I cal'late you wouldn't like t' hev sich things said, so I want t' give ye my advice. Leave me for a season—you an' Jules—an' ship with another skipper. Make a trip or so with a driver so that men can say that Westhaver hez gone through th' mill an' come out ground. They can't scare you, Frank for you kin keep yer end up with any o' them. What d'ye think? Will you an' Jules ship with Tom Watson in th' *Fannie B. Carson* this next trip?

Frank kicked at the planking of the wharf. "Ship with Tom Watson?" he repeated slowly. "Waal, he's got a kinder hard name, but I cal'late he kain't eat me. Yes! I reckon me'n Jules'll ship, Uncle. Now suppose you'n me git rigged out in our shore rags an' take a shoot up to Boston. We'll take in a good show at a theayter an' sit down to a white man's meal afterwards. Even though we hev t' live like hogs at sea, we kin live like gentlemen ashore. What d'ye say, Uncle?"

The stout skipper laughed. "Lordy, Frank, I'm afraid this book-readin' o' yours is a-goin' t' kill ye as a fisherman. Ye'll be allus hankerin' t' git clear o' th' stink o' gurry an' bilge. Theaytres an' resterongs ain't exactly in my line, Frank, but I will admit—yes—that your way o' livin' 'ull shape up th' best in th' long run. Rum an' th' dance hall was good enough for th' ol' trawlers o' my day, but I cal'late things are diff'rent now, an' 'tis better so—aye, far better."

CHAPTER EIGHT

IT WAS A BRIGHT, YET COLD, JANUARY MORNING, AND Shorty and Jules were engaged rigging up trawl gear upon the deck of the Boston marketman *Fannie B. Carson,* then lying to anchor inside Provincetown harbour. Jules, the runaway, and the "Little Sabot" of the old *Kastalia,* could no longer be identified as the shrinking, brown-eyed Paimpol fisher-boy, for he towered head and shoulders over his stocky dory-mate. He had grown and stretched and broadened under the kindly treatment and wholesome fare of the American fishermen, until at nineteen years of age he stood six feet in his socks; broad and strong in proportion, and to all but Frank Westhaver he was known as "Big Frenchy." To Shorty he was always "Sabot," or Jules, and the friendship of their boyhood days had cemented firmer with the years.

Captain Tom Watson of the *Carson* was, in fishermen's parlance, "a dog of a feller," and a hard driver with gangs, and it was only hard gangs that sailed with him. Wharfside gossip had it that he'd have the dories out when gulls couldn't fly to windward, and with Watson a fisherman had to turn out on the shout of "Get ready!" and prepare to make sets without cessation, day and night, until the weather or the finished bait declared a stop. While the *Carson* was on the grounds sleep was not to be thought of, and crews were kept relentlessly at work until they almost dropped from sheer physical exhaustion. But it paid them in the long run when the share checks were distributed. The *Fannie Carson* was never long at sea, and her fresh-fishing trips were invariably "high-line," while the T Dock fish-buyers in their estimates and sales always counted on a trip from "Driver Tom," no matter what the state of the weather might be.

When the pair shipped aboard the *Carson* in Boston a trip previous, the stout, saturnine Watson looked them over critically and said bluntly, "I'll ship yez, but let me tell yez somethin' afore we start. I'm a driver, first, last, an' all th' time. Thar's no lay-offs on this peddler. When I sing out—you jump, see? Ye'll keep yer gear in A1 order —no rusty hooks or ol' gangins. We go by th' count, an' th' man what comes low dory too often packs his kit for th' dock when we hit in, see?" And he dismissed them.

Men made big money with Tom Watson, but they earned it, and the fisherman who had hung out a season with him was entitled to some consideration. Jules and Shorty, strong and hardy young bloods, made an ideal pair in a dory, and when they completed their first trip after eight days on Georges, the skipper had paid them with a grunt of approval.

On this sunny January morning, the pair overhauled their tubs of gear on deck in a corner remote from the other men, and chatted as they snipped off rusty hooks and stuck fresh gangins. It was Jules who was speaking.

"Well, Shortee, your girl ess in Boston, you say?"

"Yep!" grunted the other, straightening out a bent hook upon the set-block placed on the lip of the tub. "Jest got a letter yestiddy. Says she's takin' up nursin' an' goin' inter th' hospital as a probationer."

"O-ah, yes. Dat's good t'ing for girl. *Sœur de merci dans l'hôpital*—ver' good. You kin see her ver' often now, Shortee——?"

"Waal, no, I kain't. Ye see, she's only got one night a week free, but she says I kin come up an' see her at th' hospital certain days when she's off duty. Still, I'll see her oftener than ef she was livin' up in Long Cove. Did ye see th' little bracelet thing I sent her last trip?"

"Yes; dat was ver' pretty t'ing. I mus' send one lak dat to Mamselle Leblanc up Long Cove——"

"Ha, ha, Sabot," laughed Frank. "So Johnny Leblanc's sister hez got you hooked! Waal, ef this don't beat all my goin' a-fishin'. Got'ny letters from her? Ye hev? Let's read them——''

"O-ah, yes. Ef you let me read yours——'' And the two sniggered and chuckled happily.

"W'at news from Captain Jerry, Shortee?"

"Got a card from Noof'nland t'other day written by Jud Haskins. Says they're loadin' frozen herrin' up in Bonne Bay, an' swingin' off in a day or so. Should be 'most back to Gloucester now.''

"How's your mamma, Shortee?"

"Oh, ma's pretty fit," replied the other, working away. "Wants me t' come home an' fish out of Anchorville in Canadian vessels. Maybe, I will some day, when I git a vessel of my own. I wouldn't fish out o' there in th' dory though. Ain't enough money in it."

"W'at's Lem Ring doing?"

"Dryin' fish, I cal'late. His ol' man hez started a kinder business up to th' Cove an' Zeke an' Lem are runnin' th' store end of it. They buy fish from th' boat fishermen an' dry them. Cal'late they're makin' a good thing out of it. Saw an old friend o' me'n Lem's last trip— feller called Morrissey——"

"O-ah, yes. Th' feller you fight so mooch wit' at school?"

"Yep! He's mate of a big three-master runnin' to th' West Indies outer Boston. Got on purty well, he says, an' cal'lates gittin' skipper soon. We didn't palaver much. He don't like me, an' I don't think he forgets 'bout th' scraps we useter have. I ain't got nawthin' 'gainst him. He's a decent enough feller."

For a space both busied themselves with their work, and with pipes going and arms a-whirl they coiled fathom after fathom of the tarred cotton trawl down into the tubs. The crisp cold of the January air encouraged exertion, and the groups scattered around the deck blew on their numb fingers and cursed the idiosyncrasies of a skipper who forbade any man overhauling his gear in the genial warmth of cabin or forecastle. The *Carson's* gang was an extra good one, as far as their hardiness, daring, and fishing abilities went, but otherwise their characters were aptly designated by the term "hard bitten." Rough Newfoundlanders; Highland Scotch from Arichat and Judique in Cape Breton—great, sandy, raw-boned men who jabbered in Gaelic and spoke English with a sibilant lisp delightful to hear; one or two Boston Irishmen—good shipmates and fishermen, but pugnacious and quarrelsome with a skinful of rum; and the usual crowd of Nova Scotians from the southern part of the province. Good shipmates and fishermen while at sea, but a crowd to avoid when the dollars were in their pockets and an Atlantic Avenue saloon under their lee.

"W'at made Mees Dexter come to Boston for learn nursing?" queried Jules quietly. Jules had a queer way of pondering over things and springing unusual questions.

Frank paused in his trawl coiling. "What made her come t' Boston an' take up nursin'?" reiterated he in surprise. "Why—I don't rightly know. I cal'late she wanted to, an' 'sides that her mother hez married agen. Carrie hez bin livin' with an uncle an' aunt up to Lynn somewheres—they're purty well fixed—an' I s'pose 'twas them what wanted th' girl to take it up. Carrie's uncle is a manager up in one o' th' mills, an' as he ain't got no children of his own he kinder takes t' th' girl. I figger out 'twas them what put the idea into her head. Why?

"Well——" Jules paused. "You goin' to marry that girl?" he asked suddenly.

Shorty blushed visibly under his tan. "Er—ah—waal, I ain't prepared t' say," he stammered. We hev a kinder understandin' between us, but I ain't given her a ring or nawthin'. She give me to understand that I'd hev t' git a vessel o' my own first afore I broached sich a question—but thar's plenty o' time for that. I ain't for hookin' up yet awhile."

The skipper came upon deck at this juncture and the subject dropped. "Git yer anchor!" he cried. "Git under way!" And the gang stowed their gear away to heave up and stand out.

It was on their return from Georges that the dock postman handed Shorty a letter of the size and bluish hue of paper much affected by young girls. *"Billet-doux!"* murmured Jules when he saw it, and Frank rolled into his bunk for the privacy of reading such a sacred epistle. It was from Miss Dexter—he knew that before he opened it— and it smelt faintly of perfume. "Dear Frank," it ran, "My free night will be Fridays, and I shall expect you this week if you are in town. It is deadly dull here in the hospital, and I think we might take in a show. There is a dandy play on at the ——. Try and get seats for it if you can. I am putting in a fairly good time here—the work is hard but the doctors are awfully nice. Hoping to see you soon, I remain, with lots of love, your friend, Carrie."

They had scarce knocked off unloading the fish before Frank was down in the fo'c'sle "sprucing up," and Jules, as he glanced at his dory-mate's radiant face, knew that he would be left to kick his heels alone for another evening.

"I'm a-goin' up t' see th' girl," confided Shorty. "Buck aroun' taown a bit, ol' sock, an' pick out a nice bracelet for Jenny Leblanc." And dressing under difficulties among the shouting, laughing, half-drunken mob in the forecastle, he hove his suit-case into his bunk and leaped up the ladder.

Procuring theatre tickets on his way up-town, Frank, looking undeniably handsome and well-built in his neat blue-serge shore toggery, stepped gingerly up the broad steps of the hospital. "Nurse Dexter!" he whispered to the door-keeper, and a white-clad orderly piloted him along interminable corridors which smelt strongly of iodoform and disinfectant until they reached the nurses' quarters.

Here he was ushered into a waiting-room, glaring in the whiteness of the unpapered walls and severe in the scantiness of its furniture. A matronly lady, ruddy of complexion and white of hair, approached him. *"Captain* Westhaver?" she enquired politely.

Shorty was taken aback at the title. "Er—ah—Frank

Westhaver, ma'am," he replied. "I'm callin' for Miss Dexter."

"Oh, yes," replied the matron. "She said that Captain Westhaver would be calling for her—here she is." And Carrie Dexter, petite, rosy-cheeked and strikingly pretty in her neat street costume, stepped lightly into the room.

"Hullo, Frank!" she cried, her blue eyes a-sparkle with pleasure and the warm blood mounting to her cheeks. "When did you arrive in? This morning? Well, well, I'm glad to see you. This is Mrs. Kenealy—Captain Westhaver." And wondering at the uncalled-for title, Frank acknowledged the introduction gracefully. They chatted for a few minutes, until Carrie opened the door. "We are going to the show, Mrs. Kenealy. We won't be late——"

The matron laughed. "All right," she said. "I'll take your word for it, but we've all been young once. See'n enjoy yourselves now. Good-bye, Captain."

Out in the street, Frank overcame his mystification enough to ask Carrie a question. "Why th' dickens d'ye call me 'Captain,' Carrie? I ain't no skipper yet—nawthin' but a common trawler."

Carrie's pretty face clouded. "I know that, Frank; but I couldn't tell them that up to the hospital or the girls would drive me crazy. They've all heard about you and seen your letters, and when they asked me who you were I said you were captain of a schooner——"

"Captain of a double-trawl dory 'ud be more like it, Carrie," laughed Frank. "But ef it pleases you, why, clap on th' handle, though I'd sooner you wouldn't."

"Why?" Miss Dexter was not pleased at his attitude in regard to the matter. Most men would have been highly flattered, but Frank Westhaver was too open-minded and honest to masquerade under false colours. "You should be a captain by now, anyway. You've been a common fisherman long enough. Why don't you get a vessel? You don't expect me to tell my friends that my gentleman friend is a common fisherman——"

"And why not?" remonstrated the other gently. "A

fisherman earns his living honestly and by the sweat of his brow——''

"Oh, Frank," interrupted the girl, "do leave out that 'sweat of the brow' business. It's not genteel; it's common and seems like talking about labourers—no gentleman earns his living by the 'sweat of his brow,' as you call it."

"Oh, they don't, eh?" returned Frank, slightly nettled. "Then God save me from being a gentleman, if that's th' way they're rated. I'd far sooner bunk in with Jack Muck an' share his quilt an' his pipe than palaver an' truck around with any lily-fingered swab what thinks hard work's beneath him. But here, girlie! Let's step inside an' git a box o'chocolates. Thar's a fine-lookin' box in th' winder for two dollars. Let's go'n git it."

Forgetting her annoyance with the present, the pretty little Nova Scotia lassie made herself agreeable and entertaining during their walk to the theatre; the play was a good one, which both enjoyed mightily; and when they came out at the conclusion of the piece, Frank piloted his young lady to an exclusive after-theatre restaurant for supper. Here they chatted and talked upon subjects of absolutely no interest to any person but themselves, and the young fisherman, drinking in the pretty features of the girl with his eyes alight with admiration, felt that he was indeed a lucky man.

When they left the café for the hospital, Frank's attention was arrested for a moment by the sight of a big, loudly dressed fellow who swaggered past with a showy-looking girl hanging to his arm. The man had his hard hat cocked over his head at a rakish angle, and a cigar protruded from between his lips. As he passed them he whisked his hat off with an elaborate bow. Shorty thought the face looked familiar.

"Who th' dickens is that, Carrie?" he enquired. "Looks as if he knew us, an' I know him too. Who is he, d'ye know?"

The girl hesitated. "Why, surely, Frank, you remember him? That was Bob Morrissey!"

Shorty grunted. "Huh! that's him sure enough. Might ha' known it too, for I saw him last trip aboard a three-master. Now, how d'ye like this hospital work?"

Miss Dexter's face was suspiciously red when she entered her dormitory, and the great bronze figures which guarded the hospital gates might have told a little tale were they but endowed with human attributes. Well, Frank had insisted on a kiss—one it was to be—but Frank was too good a fisherman and too much of a sailor to be content with a single osculatory embrace—and Miss Dexter was just as much of a girl to make no really strenuous objection to the caresses of such a strapping, well-built, handsome young man as Frank Westhaver.

Whistling happily, Shorty caught an elevated car, which landed him at Rowe's Wharf on Atlantic Avenue, and stepping out briskly, he soon swung down to the odoriferous confines of T Dock. The *Carson* was lying outside of another vessel, and Frank no sooner put his foot on her rail before he was aware of a "shine" in the forecastle. "Drunk as pigs, I cal'late, an' raisin' sulphur all night. Lordy, I don't wonder at Carrie tarrin' me with a full brush when Boston folks draw their judgments o' fishermen on them Atlantic Avenue rot-gut soakers." And he clattered down into the forecastle.

It was just as he surmised. The gang had drawn their money and were having the worth of it. A quarrelling, cursing card game was in progress, and a number of the men lolling around on the lockers were full to the bung and argumentative. Jules, with others of the quieter men, were sleeping, or trying to, in their bunks, but the din—the singing, shouting, and swearing—made a perfect bedlam.

A lumbering Newfoundlander — quiet enough when sober, but noisy and dangerous when drunk—was evidently trying to "boss" the forecastle, and when Shorty came down the ladder he became offensively rude and maudlinly hospitable.

"Here you, Westhaver — you sawed-off, shore-rangin'

dude! Hev a touch on me! Bes' drink y'ever put yer tongue to, I cal'late——'' and he broke off to sing:—

> "Oh, blow ye winds, heigh oh!
> Blow down from old Increau!
> For thar' fish an' gold, so I've bin told,
> On th' Banks off th' Baccalhao!

Good song that, m'son. Hev a drink, Westhaver, you ol' dog! You bin' 'shore somewheres lally-gaggin' an' gum-suckin' wit' some blame' Bluenose slavey up t' East Boston, I cal'late. Hev a drink, I say!''

Shorty took no notice of him, but busied himself folding his clothes and putting them away in his suit-case. The other became more offensive, and the drunks around knocked off arguing to watch developments. Westhaver was a "kid" to them; he wasn't in their class and never fraternized with them ashore, and they resented it in their simple, touchy way.

"Ain't you goin' t' hev a nip, son?" The man proffered a bottle of Kentucky red-eye, and on Frank's negative, he drew back as if offended. "Oh!" he grunted. "Ye kinsider yerself too good t' drink with honest fish'man! Ain't fancy 'nough for you, eh? Ye won't drink, maybe ye won't fight, eh?"

"Aw, stow yer jaw!" growled a man from a peak bunk. "Go'n turn in, you crazy cod-hauler, an' give people a chanst t' sleep."

The other took no notice. He was spoiling for a fight, and wouldn't be satisfied until he had started something. Shorty knew what was coming and calmly unbuttoned his collar and shirt.

The Newfoundlander returned to the charge. "Say, Westhaver, you're a damned stuck-up long-shore pup! Ye won't drink with honest fish'man. . . . Say, I c'd lick ye out yer boot-straps!"

Frank had his collar, tie, and shirt folded and stowed away in the suit-case, and quickly divested himself of his shore trousers. Pulling on his old fearnought pants, he buckled his belt and waited for what he knew was going to happen. The men lounging around sensed something, and they watched quietly without interfering. The bellicose one straightened up to his full height—he was a big man of thirty, hairy, be-whiskered, and stupid. "Say, you Westhaver, y'ain't lis'nin' t' what I'm tellin' ye! I'm sayin' ye're a sneakin', oil-an'-shine, Novy—a dam'——"

Frank hove the suit-case into his bunk. "Go'n turn in, Jake," he said quietly. "I don't drink with ye 'cause I don't tech liquor——"

"Naw, ye don't," sneered the other, lurching forward aggressively. " 'Tis a little milk ye want——"

"Go'n turn in!"

"I'll see you in blazes first!" growled the fellow, raising a huge fist. It was a bad move on his part, for as quick as a flash, Frank caught him on the peak of the jaw—a tremendous drive with all the strength of his arm and the weight of his stocky body behind it, and the Newfoundlander crashed back among his shipmates completely knocked out.

"I cal'late that jarred him some!" commented Frank calmly as the men lifted the inert body up. "Heave him inter his bunk, fellers. He'll come to in a little while."

The men were very much impressed, and Frank saw it. It was a good punch—a punch which Long Dick had taught him and which his instructor had said "would knock a man cold with one drive." And Shorty knew it; knew that a heavy lunge on the chin would jar a man's vertebræ and numb the brain. The occasion was a good one to define his standing with this rough and tough crowd, and with the fearless intuition which makes born leaders out of very few men, he spoke.

"I'm a-goin' t' turn in now an' I don't want t' sp'ile yer fun. Go ahead an' raise all th' rumpus ye like, *but steer clear o' me*, for by th' Great Trawl Hook, I'll finish any man what tries t' take a shine out-a this chicken!"

And he tumbled into his bunk with the crowd visibly respectful.

They did not bother him after that, and next morning the Newfoundlander, sober and quiet, reached across the fo'c'sle table with a hairy paw. "By th' Lord, son, that was an awful wipe ye guv me last night. Shake, Westhaver; I'm sorry t' ha' bothered ye, but ye know what th' rum is." And Shorty grasped the man's hand and respected him accordingly.

The dock tug shoved them out that morning, and hoisting the patch of four lowers, they shot across Massachusetts Bay and dropped Race Point light astern in the evening as they steered an E.S.E. course for Georges Shoals. After clearing the low, sandy spit of Cape Cod, the *Fannie B. Carson* smashed into a breeze of wind from the south'ard, and during the night the vessel performed some wild antics in the sea running, flooding her decks full to the rail with every dive and shooting cataracts of chilly green sea down into forecastle and cabin.

They made the grounds without putting a tuck in a sail —Skipper Watson never reefed or took a sail in if he could possibly help it—and on a bitter, sunless February morning the skipper passed the word to get ready and lower away dories for the set. Jules and Frank had their trawl all baited up, but when they came to hoist their dory out—she was the bottom dory on the starboard nest—they found that her side was stove in.

"Look at dat, Frank!" said Sabot in disgust. "Some feller have brought one o' dem big meat rock for sling-ding aboard an' she's bin drive against de bilge of doree las' night!" And he exhibited a large stone with a fleshy sea-growth adhering to it and which often attach themselves to the trawl.

While the two dory-mates were examining the damage, the skipper, impatient at the delay in getting the dory over, sung out from the wheel: "Naow thar', you number five dory! Why'n sheol don't ye h'ist her aout? D'ye think I'm a-goin' t' wait all day for yez?"

"Dory's stove, sir!" replied Frank.

The stout, saturnine Watson slipped the wheel in the becket and came lumbering for'ard. "What's that you say?" he snapped. "Dory's stove? How did that happen, eh? Why did ye let her git stove?"

"Waal," answered Shorty respectfully, "I cal'late it ain't our fault. Some feller must ha' left this rock kickin' 'round in th' scuppers, n' in them dives las' night th' blame' thing hez bin bangin' agin' our dory——"

"Aw, hell!" rasped the skipper savagely. "A dory out-a business with yer cursed carelessness. Some o' you guinneys need a blame' nurse t' look after ye! Kain't ye patch her up? Don't stand an' goggle at it!"

Frank reddened. "Why, skipper, you kin see for yerself that nawthin' kin fix that. Th' whole plank is smashed——"

Watson turned on him in a blaze of temper. "Ye don't want t' make th' set, eh?"

"How kin we in a stove dory?"

"Waal, stay aboard then, snarled the skipper. "Stay aboard, but devil th' share ye'll draw when we git in——"

"All right, sir," replied Frank coolly; "an' devil th' hand's turn o' work we'll do aboard here ef that's th' way ye look at it. Come on, Jules, let's turn in!" And both left the stout skipper stamping and cursing with rage.

Frank knew that Watson would calm down in a day or so. He was a very short-tempered, irascible man, with nerves always on edge with the big chances he was forever taking, and much given to bursts of unaccountable fury over trifles.

"Well," remarked Jules when they entered the fo'c'sle, "I'll catch up on sleep, I t'ink——"

"An' I'll do a little readin'," said Frank. "I bought some books in Boston last time an' I ain't even looked them over yet." And they rolled into their bunks—Jules to sleep, and Frank to forget his troubles with the exploits of John Ridd in "Lorna Doone."

The skipper carried his temper for the whole six days they were on the grounds. He never spoke to them, nor would he look at them. As far as he was concerned, Jules and Shorty were not aboard. This state of affairs continued until one night, when, with a nor'-wester making up, they were lying-to.

It was after midnight, and Frank was rudely awakened by one of the men who bunked aft in the cabin. "Westhaver! Westhaver!" he said, and his voice was shrill with fright. "Skipper's taken bad in his berth an' is askin' fur ye. Hurry! for I think he's 'most gone!"

Frank was out in an instant and pulling on his boots. "What's th' matter with him? What happened?"

The man answered and the heads craning out of the tiers of bunks listened for his reply in half fear: "Bust somethin' in his innards. I woke up t' hear him gaspin' in his berth an' th' blood was pourin' out his mouth an' nose. Hurry, Frank! He was jest gaspin' your name when I left him t' come for'ard."

In less time than it takes to relate Frank was elbowing his way through the silent crowd of fishermen standing in the cabin. A candle inserted in a sticking-tommy was burning inside the skipper's partitioned-off berth, and by its feeble glimmer Frank could see the old man lying upon a huddle of blood-stained blankets and breathing heavily. Kneeling down beside the bunk, he took the skipper's limp hand in his. "Skipper," he said quietly, "here I am—Westhaver."

The laboured breathing stopped for a space. "Westhaver—bust—blood-vessel in chest—goin' out soon—I cal'late. The dying man paused and breathed heavily. "Are ye thar', Westhaver?—can't see, y'know"—the words came in gasps—"git vessel home—Boston ef ye kin—no'-wester comin'—be careful—shoal t' loo'ard——" He broke off in a spasm of coughing and blood oozed from the corners of his lips. "Git vessel an' me home—tell wife it got me—so long, boys!" And, with a sailor's valediction, the soul of Tom Watson—"Driver Tom"— the hardiest and most daring skipper from Grand to Georges—went out to his long home.

"He's gone, boys!" said Frank, rising to his feet. It was a simple sentence, but it meant much, and the words caused strong, hard-bitten men to sob like children. It was a strange scene. Outside the wind whined in the mainmast rigging; the roar of the sea dominated all other sounds, and the vessel lurched and dived over the cresting surges. In the reeling cabin were collected a mob of rough-looking, sea-bronzed fishermen, and the flickering light from the lamps swinging in their gimbals illuminated their tense faces as they gazed in on the silent body outlined in the feeble glow of the candle stuck into the bulkhead.

"Gimme a blanket, some o' you!" whispered Frank. "I'll cover him up."

After he had closed the staring eyes and covered the silent form Westhaver felt the weight of responsibility resting upon his shoulders. Watson, knowing that Westhaver was probably the only man aboard competent to navigate the vessel home, had saddled him with the charge. But what a charge for an untried boy! A February nor'-wester brewing; the wind blowing stronger and colder every minute; the shoal water of Georges to leeward; while twenty-two men, relieved at having no responsibility, were looking to him for orders.

Westhaver pulled out the chart-drawer and glanced over the grimy, brine-stained sheet. "Take a cast, one of you!" he whispered, and when a man had quietly hailed the water he pricked off the position and paralleled off a course for Cape Cod.

Closing the drawer, he drew the door of the skipper's berth and staggered along the ice-scaled deck to the forecastle; he went down and donned his oilskins. "I'm a-goin' t' have a night of it," he murmured. "Yes!—a night of it." And with a determined glint in his grey-blue eyes and a grim set to jaw and mouth he swung on deck. "Reef th' mains'l an' set it!" he roared to the gang gathered in the cabin. The dead was forgotten in the old familiar sea-

shout, and with minds dwelling only upon the present exigency, they piled up on deck to wrestle with frozen canvas, haul out earrings upon precarious boom foot-ropes, and tie, with many anathemas and objurgations, reef-points stiff as steel wire.

"Mains'ls reefed, skipper!" Frank gave a start at the title.

"All right!" he bawled in order to make himself heard above the din of wind and sea. "H'ist away easy now! Get th' bonnet off th' jib an' stand by t' set it when I sing out. Ready?"

"All ready!" came a voice out of the darkness. And it was dark—black dark. Men felt one another's presence by sense of touch. They groped for the halliards by blind instinct, and strung along the brine-drenched alleys they heaved upon the ice-filmed ropes, while the sail went up with a snapping of canvas and banging of sheet blocks.

"Hold yer jumbo! H'ist yer jib! Draw away!" And Westhaver spun the wheel over while the schooner sidewiped a cresting surge into a burst of spray and rolled down to the pressure of the breeze. "One hundred good miles t' Race P'int," he muttered as he checked the plunging schooner until the compass needle wavered at north; "an' it'll be tack, tack, tack all th' way with this blame' no'-wester blowin' dead in our teeth." Aloud he shouted. "Aft here to th' wheel, someone! John Simms, you better take her for a spell while I wind th' log and put it over. Keep her close-hauled—she'll look up 'bout no'th with a good full."

The tardy daylight came at last and revealed a chilly expanse of wind-lashed black-green sea. Streaked and laced with foam, the Western Ocean combers creamed in white-watered crests and the wind whipped the wave-lips away in a whisk of frozen, hail-like shot, which slashed across the staggering schooner like the whip of a slave-driver. And there is no lash which bites like the sting of a winter wind—a wind laden with particles of frozen spray which cuts the face until the blood starts, and which the men in their work have to butt into, glancing for their own safety at the cresting billows under the sou'-wester thatch or the upraised arm.

The cold was cruel, and men stamped below with the icicles forming on beard and moustache, and their fingers and toes numb with the chill of the frost. The sanctity of the cabin, with its silent dead, was ignored in the living misery of the frost-nipped men who clattered cursefully down into the apartment to thaw out frozen mittens and warm their chilled feet. There was no let-up in the gale, and Westhaver, red-eyed and blue-lipped, struggled at the wheel and bullied the gang into keeping the vessel clear of the ice which was forming on her decks and rigging.

A snow squall carried away the jib, and in a trice but a few ribbon-like rags fluttered from the stay. Then the mainsail proved too much for her in the weight of the wind blowing, and Frank called the gang together for a tussle with the ice-filmed, slatting devil.

"Take in yer mains'l! Set th' ridin' sail! Aft here, all hands!" And tugging with the strength of desperation at the main-sheet, the oilskinned mob dragged the big boom aboard and snapped the crotch and iron turn-buckle guys in place, while the young commander at the wheel watched sea, vessel, and men with eyes which snapped alert and wakeful through their swollen, red-rimmed lids.

It was big Jules who proved Shorty's most valuable lieutenant during the wild, man-killing passage to T Dock. It was Jules who hovered jealously around his old dory-mate, ready to give a hand at the bucking wheel, or to execute an order. It was the Frenchman who hurled himself on the bellying, thunderously slatting mainsail, and with wild oaths and whirling fists set the example to the back-weary, listless men. "Git her in, de defil!" he yelled. "Come on, boys, beat de hell out of heem!" And they rolled that heavy, ice-coated sail up in record time.

Under the triangular riding sail, whole foresail and jumbo, they came about somewhere off Cape Ann, and in the whirling snow-squalls the *Fannie B. Carson* dragged her lee rail under as she swung off on a long slant for Boston Light. Men lolled in their bunks, oiled up and sea-booted ready for a call. Sleep was snatched in fitful dozes, and they wolfed their meals and drank huge mugs of steaming coffee standing up at the shack locker in the forecastle. Ice formed quickly over the spray-drenched bows. The cable box, fishing hawser, windlass and bowsprit were shrouded in a solid mass; the lower portions of the sails scaled and crackled like sheet-iron with every slat, and the rigging and blocks were festooned clear to the cross-trees.

Standing upon bags and scattered ashes from the galley stove, watch and watch pounded the brittle film away with hammer, axe, and iron belaying pin, while Shorty hung to the wheel, coaxing the wallowing schooner through the seas—leaving it but to warm his chilled blood with scalding tea or coffee.

The red flash of Eastern Point blinked at them in the small hours of the morning, and it had scarce been blotted out in the whirling snow before the schooner was struck by a sea which boarded the whole length of her. Men were catapulted out of their bunks clean across th fo'c'sle; the stoves scattered their glowing embers into the gloom, and everything fetched adrift and drove to leeward. Then came the sea—frigid, hissing brine which streamed down the half-opened slides, skylights and ventilators, and, swashing around the stoves, enveloped them in steam. The lamps flickered and went out, while men struggled and cursed in wild, meaningless oaths as they extricated themselves from the tangle splashing around to leeward.

The slides were hauled back. "All right below thar'?" came a muffled hail above the roar of the wind and sea.

"All right be damned!" was the invariable answer fore and aft. "Blame' near drowned. Cook's knocked stiff by a bar'l hitting him, an' every blame' one of us was hove out our bunks. What a gory mess!"

Westhaver was now at the wheel—it was another man who had allowed her to be knocked down—and he shouted down the cabin gangway. "Open th' door—skipper's berth —see how he is!"

A ghastly face peered above the slide. "He's fetched adrift in his berth—washin' 'round in water—gang says you'd better come down—scared stiff!"

"Oh, Sabot! Take her for a moment!" And Jules grasped the spokes while Westhaver entered the deluged cabin and lifted the heavy body of the dead skipper from out of the water, boots, caps, charts, and buckets sluicing around the lee side of the place.

"Come on here, bear a hand, blast you!" he snarled at the frightened mob huddling as far aft as they could get. "D'ye think I kin handle him alone? Come here, Simms, an' help me lash him into his bunk." And with the perspiration pouring off his face with the ardour of his gruesome task, Shorty lifted the corpse reverently back and shored it fast with pillows and lashings.

They put it hard to her after that, and when morning broke, bitter cold but clear, they were sliding in past the Bug Light, while the crews of the barges and anchored coasters turned out to stare at the iced-up fisherman coming in from outside.

"Th' flag," croaked Westhaver dully. "H'ist it—half-mast!" And when the tug ranged alongside them off the dock, the curious crowd of fishermen and spectators wondered whom it was for.

When they passed their lines ashore and let the sails drop in stiff, unmanageable sheets, Westhaver left the wheel and turned to meet the crowd jumping aboard for news. They pressed around him—reporters with notebooks and pencils poised; fishermen from other vessels, salesmen, buyers, and loafers, and all pointed to the flag fluttering idly half-way up the main-rigging. "Who's gone?"

"Skipper died suddenly at sea—that's all!" And the weary, sea-tired boy staggered on to the wharf to report at the owner's office, while the hardy, sun and wind bronzed trawlers nodded sympathetically and murmured their requiem. "Waal, ol' Driver Tom hez shot in for his last port. May God be good to him!"

CHAPTER NINE

FRANK WESTHAVER, CLEAN-SHAVED AND RIGGED OUT IN his shore clothes, was sitting in the waiting-room at the hospital. The matron had spoken to him for a few minutes, and had retired to call Carrie Dexter from the dormitory.

"Oh, Frank," she cried as she burst anxiously into the room, "how are you? How do you feel after the awful experience you had?" And she scrutinized his face with eyes of concern.

"Why, I'm fine an' fit, Carrie," he replied; "but how did you git to know that we hed any experiences? I've never said nawthin'——"

Miss Dexter's blue eyes opened wide. "Haven't you seen the paper to-night? Oh, Frank, but you've got me into a mess with the girls—— Here, wait and I'll bring the 'Post' to you."

She was back in a few seconds, and, handing the paper to him, he read:

AWFUL VOYAGE OF GEORGES FISHERMEN
CAPTAIN OF SCHOONER DIES AT SEA
VESSEL BROUGHT INTO PORT BY ONE OF THE CREW AFTER TERRIBLE WINTER TRIP
ICED UP IN NORTH-WEST GALE

The Boston fishing schooner *Fannie B. Carson* arrived at T Wharf yesterday with her flag at half-mast for her master, Captain Thomas Watson of Essex. The Captain burst a blood-vessel while the schooner was upon Georges Bank, and succumbed while handing the care of the *Carson* over to Francis

Westhaver—a young Nova Scotian who was one of the crew.

Westhaver, who is a mere boy, brought the schooner in from the Banks to Boston during the heavy north-west gale which raged here on Wednesday and Thursday, and it was evident from her ice-coated decks and sails that the young fisherman and his crew had a hard time.

When interviewed by our reporter, members of the schooner's crew told tales of incredible hardship while on the passage to this port. For fifty hours they fought the bitter cold and savage snow squalls, pounding off ice continually during the whole time.

In the height of the gale the schooner's jib was blown away, and at one time she was hove on her beam ends by a terrific sea which caused havoc in the cabin and forecastle. The body of the deceased master was thrown out of the bunk in which it was lying, and the cook was knocked unconscious by being struck by a flour barrel which was hurled at him by the impact of the sea.

Westhaver, who remained on deck at the wheel the whole trip from Georges, is a Nova Scotian hailing from Long Cove, N.S., and is but twenty-two years of age.

The *Carson* hailed for a fare of 78,000 pounds of mixed fish, haddock, hake, and cod, and was an unlooked-for yet welcome arrival owing to the scarcity of fresh ground-fish.

Frank laid the paper down with a grunt of disapproval. "Huh!" he said. "Wonder who they got all that yarn from——"

Carrie sat down in the chair beside him. "Oh, Frank," she lamented. "That isn't the worst——"

"How's that, sweetheart?" queried Frank in surprise.

"The girls here—the newspaper, you know. It has given me away. The girls saw the account and they've been jollying me about my *Captain* Westhaver all day long. I'll never be able to look them in the face again."

The young fisherman laughed. "Waal, Carrie, that's what ye git for lyin'—they allus hit back some time or other."

The girl pouted indignantly. "I wasn't lying," she protested. "I was only doing it for your sake, and you don't seem to appreciate it."

"My dear girl," hastily replied Frank, "I—I appreciate it all right, but still I'd rather you hadn't called me Captain before those people. It might get round, an' I'd be th' laughin'-stock o' th' fleet."

Carrie drew on her gloves. "Well, Frank, it's up to you to make my words good. You should get a vessel now."

"So I will, girlie. I'm goin' to ask th' *Carson's* owners for her to-morrow morning. I kin handle her, an' ef I git a chanst I kin catch fish. Now what d'ye say to a little stroll out Franklin Park way whar' 'tis quiet?"

Miss Dexter's eyes fell. "Why not a theatre, Frank? There's nothing to see out at Franklin Park——"

Frank was slightly taken aback. After the experiences he had gone through he wished for quietness and the delights of Carrie's company *à la solitaire*. Theatres did not appeal to him then, and before he replied to the suggestion his mind went back to the heart-searching scenes he had witnessed but a few hours before. The night on Georges; the dying skipper with his farewell of "So long, boys!" muttered through blood-smeared lips; the sobbing of strong men; the nor'-wester; the night off Eastern Point when, alone, he had picked the body out of the debris-littered water in the cabin; and lastly, the taking ashore of Tom Watson's body and the weeping old lady who knelt over the disordered sea-swilled bunk and kissed her dead. . . . His reply was quiet and determined. "No, girlie. I don't fancy a theatre to-night. I'm lookin' for a little quiet whar' I kin talk with ye, Carrie. Lord, girlie, ef ye only knew how I've bin longin' t' see ye. 'Twas th' thoughts of you that nerved me for th' tussle out yonder. . . . Let's go somewhere whar' 'tis quiet."

The girl assented with reluctance, and they strolled out to Dorchester, and forgetful of the hum, bustle, and lights of the big city, they wandered back in reminiscent memory to their childhood days on the Bay Shore when Shorty

Westhaver was the plague of the place and the admiration of his companions.

"And do you remember, Frank, how you used to read us that story of the Spanish Main and Amyas Leigh and poor Rose Salterne——?"

"Aye, to be sure I do. That was 'Westward Ho!'—a great book—a grand book. I've read it over a dozen times since, an' th' whole o' th' *Kastalia's* gang know it off by heart. Jud Haskins useter grip a shack-knife an' cut slices out th' cabin lockers when I read about the Inquisition. I cal'late Jud 'ud ha' bin fer cuttin' that Guzman feller inter trawl bait ef he c'd ha' laid hands on him. An' 'Treasure Island'—d'ye remember that? 'Fifteen men on a dead man's chest'; Long John Silver, an' ol' Pew, an' Israel Hands——"

Carrie nodded. "But, Frank, you should see the dandy books we get at the hospital—Charles Garvice, Bertha M. Clay, an' Mrs. Georgie Sheldon—great stories, an' all about poor girls who end up by marrying lords and millionaires. You should read some of them. They are paperbacks, and you can get a whole pile for a dollar 'most anywhere——"

"Um!" Shorty had run across a few kicking around in fishermen's bunks, and they had not impressed him. But he was no judge, and what suited him wouldn't suit everybody. "Yes, I cal'late they'll be good yarns for them that likes them. Kinder slushy, an' too much lovey-dovey for my taste——"

"Oh, Frank," interrupted the girl. "How can you say that! I'm sure they're simply splendid. The heroine always rises above her station and marries someone great——"

"Why sh'd she want t' do that?" asked Frank, who had an intuitive feeling that Miss Dexter's nature pandered a little to romances of this type. "Why don't they ever hitch up with some honest feller what earns a good living? Lords an' millionaires ain't everything." Then jocularly he continued, "Why, Carrie, ye'll be for throwin' me over 'count o' bein' nawthin' but a common trawler what spends half his time in ileskins an' rubber boots, gurry an' bilge——''

The allusion did not please Carrie, although she laughed nervously and answered chidingly: "How can you talk that way? You're not going to be a common trawler all your life, I hope. You'll be captain soon—though it seems to me that captain of a fishing schooner, isn't much of a position after all——"

"How d'ye mean, girlie?"

"Well—I don't know——" she stammered in her reply. Frank had a brusque way of taking her up on the things she said which was decidedly awkward. "There's no position to it—no society like doctors, or office managers, or even captains on steamers and big coasters. It's a dirty life when you come to think of it. Fish! Ugh!" And she made a grimace.

"Um!" Frank was silent for a space. "I don't see how ye kin think thataway. How about Captain Ring up to Long Cove? Ain't he got a fine home? Look at his daughter—goin' t' th' Seminary at Wolfville, allus well-dressed an' a perfect lady. They got a fine piano in their house, an' Melissy Ring gits all th' latest music sent acrost from Boston every month. Look at Captain Conover's place on Anchorville Bay—ain't his wife an' girls no-end swells with their buggies an' teams an' tennis courts? Take yer doctors! D'ye cal'late Doctor Smiley in Anchorville earns more'n these two skippers? Waal, I guess not! An' look at us common trawlers! Thar's that dandified clerk in the owner's office with his fancy ties an' his cigars an' his coloured socks—him what pays us our share checks, an' many's th' time he's told me that we fellers earned more in a ten-day trip than he did in a month. It's a dirty life at sea all right, but a decent fisherman don't carry his dirt ashore with him. Take Jules—my dory-mate, whom you know—he's an ignorant Frenchman unable to read or write hardly, but see him when he goes ashore! Why thar's blame few folks ashore dress better'n th' same Jules with his thirty-dollar suits an' his silk shirts an' his patent-leather boots—an' thar's plenty more good, decent-livin' fellers like him. No, girlie, I think ye're a little bit off yer course when ye git talkin' 'bout us fishermen. Thar's gentlemen in all professions, an' plenty o' fellers what calls themselves gentlemen and ain't by a long chalk.''

Frank left Carrie at the hospital that night and made his way to the vessel absorbed in thought. It seemed to him upon retrospection that the girl had ideas which differed materially from his own and the Carrie Dexter of the Bay Shore days.

"Aye," he soliloquized, "she's gittin' queer notions in her head these days, but still, I may, jest as bad. A girl is not to be blamed for wishin' t' better herself in th' world, an' I cal'late she hez t' stand a lot o' jollyin' from her friends at the hospital 'count of her young man bein' a common fisherman. She's a fine girl, anyway, an' ef I git command o' th' *Carson,* I'll be for buyin' her th' best ring I kin afford. So ho! here's T wharf, an' I cal'late th' gang 'ull be full to th' bung after their trip, even though they ain't drawed their shares yet.''

It was even as he had said. The *Carson's* crowd, liberally supplied with liquor by the touts which swarm aboard vessels just arrived, were enjoying a Bacchanalian revel in the fo'c'sle. There was nobody aft in the cabin—the memory of the dead was still strong enough in superstitious minds to keep any of the gang from having a time there, and as a result the wedge-shaped fo'c'sle was crammed. When Westhaver entered he was greeted with a joyous shout.

"Ho, thar', skipper! Yo're jest th' man we was a-talkin' about. Come over here!" The spokesman was the Newfoundlander who, the voyage previous, had felt the heft of Shorty's fist.

"Waal," Frank laughed, "I hope ye warn't a-scandalizin' me——"

"No, no, skipper!" protested a score of voices.

The Newfoundland man rose to his feet and banged the table with a heavy fist. "Belay jawin'!" he said. "I wanter tell th' skipper what we've bin a-talkin' over. Now, Frank, me'n th' gang hev bin a-thinkin'—you bein' a good head an' a navigator belike—that see'n poor ol' Tom Watson's gone, you'd be th' very man t' take this vessel out a-fishin'. Ain't that right, fellers?"

An affirmative roar came from the mob. Westhaver felt pleased.

"Boys," he said, "I thank ye kindly for what ye've said, an' I may tell ye that I've decided to ask the owners for this vessel t'morrer. Ye've taken an awful load off my mind, as I was afraid ef even I got this hooker that you fellers 'ud refuse t' ship with a green skipper who'd never brought a trip o' fish in. Ef I do git her, I wouldn' wish t' hev a better gang than you fellers, for I cal'late thar' ain't a vessel out o' Boston or any other port for that matter what kin beat this crowd a-fishin'———"

Big Jules rolled out of his bunk. "Boys!" he said, glancing with eyes of admiration at his dory-mate, "Frankee Westhaver has bin dory-mate wit' me for many a year. We been shipmate togedder since we was no bigger'n trawl tub, an' he's darn good feller. He pull me out of Frenchy boat up in Canso many year ago, an' he make good Canadian out of me. I know him ver' well, an' I say he make good skipper. Dis gang mighty good gang—fine fellers—but dey be bes' gang out of Boston wit' Shorty Westhaver as skipper———"

"Right ye arre, Fr-r-enchy!" burred a red-haired Judique Scotchman. "An' 'tis ta pr roud man I will pe when she sings out for-r ta pait up. Will she pe for takin' a leetle touch wae me, skipper? 'Tis mysel' t'at will pe pr-roud tae trink a dr-ram wae ye!"

This was a question which Frank knew would inevitably crop up, and knowing the touchiness of the crowd he was handling, he stepped among them and spoke.

"Boys," he said, and the earnest note in his voice compelled attention, "I would willingly have a drink with any of ye, but I don't tech liquor, an' ef I'm goin' as skipper ye'll need a man what ain't swillin' booze all th' time.

Now some o' you hev known o' th' loss o' th' *Grace Westhaver* on Sable Island many years ago. Her skipper was drunk when he piled her up an' lost his own life an' ten o' his gang. Boys! That skipper was Frank Westhaver, an' my father . . ." He paused, and in the silence that ensued a pin might have been heard if dropped on the floor.

The red-haired Judique man rose and stretched out a huge hand. "I will pe for askin' your par-r-don, skipper. I tid not know!"

With a wild whoop of applause the men surged about, and half-seas-over as most of them were, they appreciated the sentiment and liked him all the better for it. Before Frank's explanation many of them were under the impression that Shorty's refusal to share their bottles was from priggishness, but now that they were aware of the true reason, they respected him more than ever.

Frank spoke once more. "Though I don't drink anythin' hard myself, yet I would never hinder any of you from havin' a good time ef it suits ye, an' t' show that thar' ain't no ill-feelin' atween us I'll stand th' cigars for th' crowd. Jack, here's five dollars. Would ye mind shootin' up to th' head o' th' dock an' gittin' a couple boxes." And while the maudlin mob wrung his hand, slapped him on the back, and declared that "he was a dog of a feller," Frank gave a wink to Jules and discreetly left them to continue a carouse which lasted until five in the morning.

Sleeping at a near-by hotel that night, Shorty dressed with extreme care next morning, and at ten o'clock walked into the office of the Zigler Fish Company.

The dandified clerk nodded to him affably. "Good morning, Westhaver," he chirruped. "Great screed they gave you in th' papers. Must have had an awful time——"

"Pretty so-so," replied Frank. "Mr. Zigler in?"

Mr. Zigler was in, and on Shorty's name being given him, the clerk motioned for the young fisherman to step inside the private office.

The vessel owner—a perky-looking man of Dutch extraction—was engaged in conversation with a heavily built, rough-looking fellow who chewed tobacco and expectorated deftly into a heavy brass cuspidor.

"Ah, Westhaver?" The little man raised his eyebrows questioningly. "You want your share checks?"

"No, sir," replied Frank respectfully. "I jest dropped in t' see ye about something."

"Ah?" The vessel owner blotted a signed letter and wheeled in his chair. "What is it, my man?"

Westhaver glanced at the stout man masticating the quid. He did not want to tell his business before strangers.

"Can't I speak to you in private?" he said. "I'm sure this gentleman'll excuse me for a minute."

"Pouf!" Mr. Zigler made a gesture of impatience, while the stranger chewed calmly on without making an effort to move. "What can you have to say in private? Speak out, my good fellow. I'm busy."

There was nothing for it but to take the bull by the horns and go right at it. "Well, sir, I've come to ask you for the *Carson*. I cal'late I kin take her out an' git a trip."

Mr. Zigler laughed—a nerve-shaking falsetto spasm which jarred on Westhaver's ear—while the stranger straightened up in his chair and stopped the motion of his jaws for an instant.

"Te-he-he!" The owner gave a final bleat and spoke. "This is too funny, Westhaver. You want command of my vessel because you took her in from the grounds when Watson died? You—a mere boy, inexperienced and a perfect stranger to me—expect me to entrust you with an investment of twelve thousand dollars? Te-he-he! Very ambitious! Plenty of nerve! But allow me to introduce you to the *Carson's* new master—Captain Hiram Jessy——" The stout man nodded curtly without proffering his hand, and Frank felt his heart thumping like a trip hammer as the owner continued. "No, my man! You'll need to get a great deal more experience than you have before you take command of a vessel. Good day, my man!" And he made a gesture of dismissal with a scrawny, yellow hand.

Crestfallen, Frank turned to go, when the stranger emitted an arresting grunt. "Say, you," he drawled, "better git yer dunnage ashore or I'll niver git'ny peace with ye. I don't want'ny swell-headed younkers along o' me that'll be fer shovin' me over th' side t' git my berth."

Westhaver swung around, his face blazing. "What's that?" he rapped out. "Why, damn my eyes, I'll turn-to an' ram yer words down yer throat, you narrow-minded scum! What d'ye mean by 'swell-headed younker'? What d'ye mean by accusin' me of a desire t' shove ye over th' side? I came here as a gentleman with a perfectly reasonable request, an' you must go out o' yer way to insult me with your nasty remarks! By the old Judas! I'll take off my coat an' knock flames out of you ef you've enough sand in ye t' step on to th' dock!"

There was a shuffle of heavily booted feet outside in the outer office—the gang were in for their money—and a hoarse voice with a Judique accent rolled over the glass partition.

"T'at's right, skipper! Trag him out here an' 'tis mysel' t'at will pull ta ears an' nose off t'at Hime Jessy—ta pig pounce!"

"Slam him in th' mug, Shorty!" "Give him a poke in th' jaw!" "Knock his eye out, skipper!" The voices came in a roar, and while Frank stood looking down at the now perturbed Jessy and the more concerned Zigler, the glass partition creaked with the hustle of heavy bodies lounging against it.

"Call the police!" bleated Zigler, pale with fright, and Jessy croaked thickly. "Aw, man, 'twas only my jokin'. Don't start a shine here. Go back to th' vessel, m'lad, an' we'll say no more about it."

Frank put on his hat and gazed at Jessy with ill-concealed contempt. "Yes," he said disdainfully, "you're haulin' in yer horns now. Back to th' vessel I'll go, but it's t' git my gear. I wouldn't sail with a swab like you." And he strode out among the delighted gang, who had overheard every word.

"Wull we stert in an' wreck ta place, poys?" anxiously asked the McCallum from Judique.

"No, no," hastily commanded Westhaver. "Don't do anything like that or 'tis a jail we will be fetchin' up in——"

"An' what do I car-re for-r a chail?" rumbled McCallum. "I've peen in chail for-r ta fun of ta thing mony times afore this——"

Shorty grasped the pugnacious Highlander by the arm. "No, no, Mac, ol' son. Let's go'n leave them without a fracas. We kin show them that fishermen can behave themselves if they like. Come on, fellers!" And McCallum, after giving the clerk a look which almost petrified him, clattered noisily outside.

While he was packing up his clothes aboard the vessel Jules and the Newfoundlander, Jake Simms, came clattering below. Jules's face was aglow with pleasure, and he almost pounced upon his chum. "Frankee! Frankee! Leave your stuff an' go an' see Captain Hoolahan! Says he wants to see you. He's owner of de *Mabel Kinsella* lyin' over to Glo'ster. Hurree, Frankee!" And with the gang helping him on with his coat and flicking the dust off his hat, he jumped up the ladder and up the wharf, with Jules and Jake Simms piloting him to where Hoolahan was waiting in the rear room of a fishermen's outfitter.

The skipper was an old man with snapping grey eyes, and when Westhaver was ushered in he overran him with exacting scrutiny. "Westhaver?" he enquired cordially. They sat down, and the old fisherman began. "That was quite a tussle you had last trip? Poor old Tom Watson —he went out quick. An' ol' dory-mate o' mine in the old days. . . ." He paused for a moment in reflection. "Waal, waal," he resumed, "that warn't what I wanted t' see ye 'bout. Th' boys here war tellin' me that ye wanted a chanst t' take a vessel. So?"

Frank nodded, while Hoolahan continued. "Now, I've a proposition t' make t' ye, an' ye kin think it over. I own a smart little craft over t' Gloucester—th' *Mabel Kinsella* her name is—an' a well-built, handy craft—seventy tonner, hardwood toothpick. She ain't noways new—bein' nigh twenty year old, but she's able an' sound as a bell. I don't go a-fishin' any more—I've done my time at it—an' I'll 'low 'tain't everbody as cares t' take out an' ol' vessel with all them new-fangled knockabouts an' sem-eye knockabouts floatin' aroun', but ef ye care t' take her over, ye kin have th' skipperin' of her. I knew yer father well—fine man—an' I know yer uncle still better, an' I cal'late ef you're o' th' same blood as them you'll git along all right. Now here's my proposition. She needs a noo mains'l an' noo jumbo an' jib. Th' fores'l an' th' light sails are all right. Ef you take her, ye'll need t' buy them sails for her—that'll cost ye 'round five hundred dollars. Now, I'll value her purty low, an' what money you pay on her fittin' out will go as yer share o' th' vessel. Say I put her value as three thousand five hundred dollars—an' she's worth more'n that—an' you put six hundred dollars o' noo gear in her, I'll give ye a six-hundred-dollar interest on my thirty-five hundred, which'll mean 'bout one-sixth. You'll own a sixth of her an' I'll hold the other five-sixths, an' say th' vessel takes a quarter share o' th' stock on each trip, you'll git yer sixth share o' that 'sides yer stock as skipper. Ef ye're a smart man, ye sh'd do well."

Frank nodded. Six hundred dollars was a lot of money —seven hundred was the amount he had in the bank—but he knew that if he required five times the amount he could get it from his Uncle Jerry. It was a good proposition, and he was quite taken with it. What would his uncle say? What would Carrie and his mother think? As he thought it over he smiled in pleasure. He would not tell his uncle until the transaction was completed, and he pictured his worthy relative's surprise when he did tell him.

"I'll go over to Gloucester this afternoon, Captain, and, have a look at her. Can you go? Good! Then ef we make a deal I'll git her sails made an' hunt up a gang. See you later, Captain!" And humming a song Frank strode back to the vessel.

There was a mob of eager fishermen awaiting him when he swung aboard. "How d'ye come out?" "Hev ye got a vessel?" "What did ol' Mike Hoolahan say?" The questions were volleyed at him.

"Any o' you fellers know this *Mabel Kinsella?*" Frank put the question to the crowd at large.

"Sure!" shouted someone. "I've fished a season in her. Is that th' craft ye're gittin'?"

"Waal, I ain't decided yet. I kin have her ef I put some new gear on her——"

"She's all right, Frank. A little small nowadays, but able an' strong. Old Mike allus took good care o' her."

"She's in good shape, is she?" enquired Shorty. "Handle well under sail? Yes, eh? Waal, then, thar's every chance that I do take her—that is ef I kin git a gang t' ship with me in that little craft."

"Git a gang?" bawled the Newfoundlander. "*Why, we're all goin' with ye!* 'Twas you gittin' a vessel what worried us most!"

Westhaver staggered up against the foremast scarce able to believe his ears. Here was a crowd of the roughest, toughest, and best fishermen out of T Dock ready to leave a sure thing and ship with him—an untried skipper—in a small, old vessel. As a fisherman himself, he realized what these fellows were giving up. All of them were men any skipper would take on the word: men whom many vessel masters would discharge less competent fishermen to make a place for them; men who could stand for the hardest driving with the certainty of making good money. It was a big sacrifice on their part, and Westhaver appreciated it to the full.

"Fellows!" he said, his heart almost too full for steady utterance of the thanks on his lips, "you don't know how much pleasure it gives me t' hear ye say what ye hev said. I wish t' thank ye heartily one and all, an' ef good luck goes with me, we'll git fish. I'm goin' t' Glo'ster this afternoon, an' I'll git that vessel. Th' sails'll be made right away, an' though I haven't talked it over with Captain

Hoolahan yet, I cal'late we'll go haddockin' an' run our trips to th' market what suits us best.''

"Go ahead, skipper," they said in unison. "Git th' vessel. We'll show up in Gloucester towards the end o' th' week, never fear. Now, fellers, let's pack up an' quit this scurvy tub an' her scurvy skipper."

Westhaver had departed on his joyous way to Gloucester when Captain Hime Jessy swung down into the *Carson's* fo'c'sle. The men were engaged stowing their gear away in dunnage bags and suit-cases when he entered, and with no little surprise he addressed them. "Hullo, boys, what's this? Y'ain't goin' away, are ye?"

"None o' yer infernal business!" growled a voice.

Jessy was nonplussed. "Why—why, what's th' matter? Ain't ye goin' t' make a trip this week with me?"

"Wit' you?" exclaimed Jules, pulling on his silk shirt. "Why, I would not sail in de East Boston ferry-boat wit' you!"

"'N I wouldn't mug-up at th' same cupboard with you, you big bluff!" ejaculated another man, while from the gloom of the peak came a wild Hieland screech. "Is t'at t'at Cheesy chiel? Wait a meenut, and I will pe for pullin' ta fat head off her shoulders!"

Captain Jessy ascended the ladder. "Are ye all leavin'?" he asked in bitter mortification.

"Yes, we're all leavin', dearie!" piped a voice. "So sorry t' go, y'know——"

"Who're ye goin' with?"

"A better man nor you, lovey!" drawled the same voice. "Captain Frank Westhaver—th' feller what was a-goin' t' knock yer block off in the office this mornin'——"

Cursing under his breath with rage, the fishing skipper jumped on to the wharf and burst unceremoniously into Zigler's office. "Th' *Fannie B. Carson*'ll not go out this week, nor next week, nor maybe th' next again. Her whole gang hez quit, an' they're follerin' that Westhaver feller. He must ha' got a vessel somewheres, for they're packin' their kit t' jine him; an', believe me, Mr. Zigler, it's goin' t' be one hoot of a job t' git another crowd."

When he had gone, the vessel owner dented at the blotter with a pen. "I made a mistake," he muttered. "I should have given that Westhaver a chance. Now the vessel'll be lying idle, and the Lent markets comin' on. Yes, I'm some fool when it comes to handling such queer cattle as these fishermen." And inwardly recriminating himself, he went out to bully the dandified clerk.

CHAPTER TEN

THE *MABLE KINSELLA*, UPON EXAMINATION, PROVED AN even better vessel than Westhaver expected, and the deal between Hoolahan and himself was quickly consummated. In less than an hour, Frank had been aboard the schooner, and given orders for the new gear, while a professional rigger was to start work on the morrow and turn in and set up the rigging and reeve off new running gear.

Coming back to Boston by an early train, Frank dived into a telephone booth at the station and immediately communicated his good fortune to Carrie Dexter at the hospital.

"I'll try an' git a chanst t' see ye afore we swing out, but ef I don't, ye kin look for me back in about ten or fourteen days. Wish me good luck, sweetheart, an' ef it comes, I'll hev somethin' t' give ye." And humming a song to himself, he proceeded down to the boarding-house where Jules was staying.

Next day he drew all his money out of the bank, and in company with the jubilant Frenchman he took train for Gloucester. The schooner was examined by Jules and favourably commented upon, and for the balance of the week, the two worked around the vessel assisting the rigger. The masts were scraped; new bait-boards fitted around the house; a little paint was expended around the decks; and in addition to new mainsail, jumbo, and jib, Westhaver added two new dories to the eight already belonging to the vessel. Feeling not a little anxious as to whether the *Carson's* old gang would keep their promise with him, Frank was relieved to run across Jake Simms—the Newfoundlander—lurching down the wharf, dishevelled and very drunk.

"Yesh, they're all a-comin', skip, ol' son," answered the man to Shorty's enquiry. "We've bin havin' awful time to Boston—awful time. I think McCallum an' Davy Baird hev bin run-in for fightin'. Awful time, skip, but they'll all be down by t'night's train."

When the sailmaker's bill had been paid, Frank found that he was reduced in monetary assets to fifty dollars. With ice, bait, stores, and dock charges to pay for yet, and some probable advances to be made his gang for gear and outfits, Westhaver had still some financing to do.

"Cal'late I'll hev t' git credit on th' trip from some o' th' stores for that stuff, an' I don't care t' do that. Uncle Jerry allus paid cash for everythin' he got. I wish he were only here now—he'd help me out."

He was down in the cabin making up a list of necessities, when Jules clattered below.

"How ees she comin', Frankee?" enquired the tall Frenchman, mopping the perspiration off his forehead.

"Pretty so-so," answered the other, sucking away at the end of the pencil. "Awful lot o' things t' git yet."

Jules nodded. "I guess you pretty well strapped after pay for sails an' rigger an' dorees?"

Frank nodded absently—his brow corrugated in thought. Jules grunted and went to his bunk. Returning, he slammed a roll of bills on the locker.

"What th'—what's this, Sabot?" ejaculated Frank in surprise, as he fingered the money.

Sabot laughed. "Leetle advance, skipper. You take dat for get stores for vessel."

"Why, thar's three hundred dollars in this wad, Jules. I—I couldn't think o' takin' it——"

The other frowned. "You take dat, skipper. No good to me—good for you jest now. Pay me back when you like——"

Westhaver shook his head. "No, no, Sabot! We might not make a trip at all, an' I don't want t' let ye in for a loss ef I don't make good. Thanks, ol' man, but I'd rather not take it——"

The Frenchman straightened up his full six feet. "Frankee Westhaver!" he growled, "ef you don't take dat money I'll t'row it into th' dock. You'n me been doree-mate for years, an' good doree-mate share up wit' his partner all tam'. You're my skipper now, Frankee, but still my doree-mate. You help me a lot. You make man of me. You take me to home up de Bay Shore. You make for thrash me one tam' in *Kastalia* because I say I got no home. I make for thrash you ef you don't take dat money. Dere!"

Shorty laughed. "Waal, waal, Sabot, I ain't a-goin' t' let ye git at me with them big hands o' yours, so I'll use th' money. Now, Sabot, you big whale, I want t' take a shoot up t' Boston this afternoon. Will you stay by th' vessel an' check th' stores? An' th' gang'll be comin' down t' night. Git them aboard ef ye kin an' hev th' cook here for t' make breakfast t'morrer. I want t' swing out with th' morning's tide. Here's Lent a'most on us, an' ef we're a-goin' t' make any money out this packet, we'll need t' be on th' grounds mighty soon."

Frank spent a delightful evening with Miss Dexter. Never had he known her to look so pretty, and the enthusiasm she displayed in his accounts of the *Mabel Kinsella* and his prospects made him declare that she was the finest little girl in the world.

"I'll be for changing her name, sweetheart. Th' *Carrie Dexter* is what she'll be called ef I kin git Hoolahan to assent. Ye've allus brought me luck, girlie, an' any vessel what is called by your name couldn't but help bein' high-line. Next trip I'll be for buyin' th' best ring I kin git in Boston. Oh, Carrie, but 'tis th' happy man I am this night." And the young fisherman and the pretty Nova Scotia lassie sped the fleeting hours with the talk of those who love.

Frank was humming a little song to himself when next morning he stood on the string-piece of Gloucester wharf, waiting for his crew. Some were aboard and overhauling their gear, but a number of the rougher and tougher characters were up in town having a last carouse. It was a

BLUE WATER

cold, dull March morning, and the schooner was at the dock-end ready to cast off, but Frank was happy—supremely happy, and as he stamped his rubber-booted feet to warm them, he crooned a little love song—a fisherman's love song:

> "Then when I come home from sea again,
> I shall happy be.
> For I shall see my own true love
> Sit a-smiling on my knee."

He waited around for some time, and when the missing members failed to show up, he glanced at his watch and sung out for Jules.

The love thoughts dissipated before the needs of the present, and there was another and different tone in his voice when he spoke to his friend. "Sabot, I cal'late I'll hev t' git up t' Jack Rooney's an' haul some o' them jokers out. Ef any comes down, git them aboard an' keep them aboard. Don't let any feller go ashore t' buy ileskins, as they gen'ly git *wet* ones, an' I cal'late most o' them hez enough *wet oil-clothes* t' last them th' whole season."

Yes, the gang were up in Jack Rooney's bar, celebrating, and among the quarrelling, drunken mob who crowded the tobacco-laden room, Westhaver picked out the members of his crew and coaxed, cajoled, and wheedled them away. And it required a great deal of tact and diplomacy upon his part; diplomacy which necessitated a blindness to obvious insult and enough "toughness" to ward off interference from strangers. All of the gang but McCallum were on their maudlin way down to the vessel, and after seeing them on to the wharf, Frank had to enter the saloon again for the red-haired Judique man.

McCallum was very drunk, and in the state where he jabbered in Gaelic and commented insultingly upon every person in the bar. He had quite a lot of money left, and a number of the wharf-side loafers were slobbering leech-like around him and assenting to everything he said. It was from these parasites that Westhaver had to drag his man, and knowing the breed, he prepared himself for trouble.

Elbowing his way through the mob, he clasped the big fisherman by the arm. "Come on, Mac! Let's git aboard. We're goin' out in a few minutes."

"Al'righ', skipper, I will pe with you chust in a meenut."

"No, no, Mac. Never mind another drink. Come along, or I won't wait for ye!"

"Chust anither bit tram o' whusky, skipper?"

"No, Mac, ye've hed enough. Come on!"

A low-browed dock rat of the genus "thug" lurched aggressively forward. "Why'n blazes don't ye leave th' man alone? Curse me, you kid skippers seem t' think yer gory men need a nurse. Let him be!"

Westhaver looked up at the fellow coolly. "Suppose you mind your own blame business. I'll look after mine——"

Before Frank had a chance to defend himself, the man shot out a grimy fist and smashed him between the eyes. Shorty reeled to the floor, but was up in an instant and making for his adversary with his eyes blazing.

Tables and chairs were hurled to one side as the occupants of the bar cleared the way for the combatants, and in less time than it takes to relate, Frank was in the centre of a hard-eyed, drunken crowd of fishermen and loafers, engaged in a hammer-and-tongs fight with the hulking wharf bully. Sock! a hard smack on the jaw jarred Shorty's whole frame. Smack! another wallop caught him on the ear and made his head buzz. Westhaver was feeling groggy when Long Dick's words flashed through his mind. "A hard drive on the chin would knock a man cold with one blow!" Yes! that was the thing—he would watch his chance. Smack! another blow on the head from the loafer and Shorty saw his opportunity. The man had lowered his guard and drawn his other arm back for a swing, and Westhaver gathered all his energy and strength together. His shoulders hunched; muscles stiffened. Now! Sock! His fist shot out—all his hardened sinews and stocky body behind it—and the terrific up-drive landed on the peak of the loafer's stubbly, tobacco-stained jaw. Ouf! the man's teeth clicked together with an audible snap; his head jerked back with a wrenching of muscles and jarred vertebrae, and he reeled backwards among the mob and lay on the dirty floor with eyes staring and the breath hissing between his lips.

Frank had but a moment's breathing space before the loafer's friends took a hand; the protesting bar-tender was swept aside, and the young skipper found himself jammed against the wall warding off the blows of two lumpish brutes who lunged at him, swearing horribly. He had a memory of receiving a severe blow on the temple; stars floated and danced before his eyes; and when he recovered himself, it was to hear a wild Hieland shriek, a roar in Gaelic, and a huge red-headed figure was whirling the leg of a table over his head and bringing it down on the bodies of struggling men with fearful thumps.

"Ah'll gie it tae ye, ma chiels!" he yelled. "Ye'll pe kennin' ta heft o' ta McCallum's arrm this tay! Ye'll pe chostlin' ta skipper, wull ye? T'at forr you—an' you—an' you!" And the table leg came down with every word.

In an incredibly short space of time, the saloon was empty and Shorty dragged the almost berserk Highlander outside and down to the vessel. "Grab him, some o' you!" he commanded, and McCallum, still grasping the table leg, rolled over the rail.

It was with a sigh of relief that Frank saw Gloucester harbour slipping astern, as, under four lowers, the *Mabel Kinsella* lifted to the roll of the open sea. Jules was at the wheel—the others had hoisted sail more by instinct than comprehension, and they were all down for'ard listening in drunken admiration to McCallum's account of the "graund fecht t'at herself an' ta' skipper had up to Rooney's saloon."

"Ant you should chust ha' keeked at ta skipper, poys!" he was saying in language almost incomprehensible. "By ta Cross of ta Chrinahanish! she was simply creat—chust creat! Laid t'at pig loafer out cold—chust wit' one punch —chust so, ant aal py hersel' too. T'en I panged them ower their heids wae ma claymore an' cleant ta place out—chust so!'' And while the forecastle creaked with the swing of the off-shore sea the hard-bitten trawlers chattered and sang, while two of their number essayed doleful music upon a mouth-organ and fiddle.

Shorty walked the quarter—his face swollen and bruised—and when the twin towers of Thatcher's Island lifted over the taffrail he reset the log and hove into the wake.

"Bring her up east b' south, Jules!"

"East by sout' it is, sir!"

Haulin a few feet of the mainsheet aboard, Frank resumed his pacing and listened to the strains of merriment and music floating up the fo'c'sle hatch.

"Got much rum thar' for'ard?" he asked of Jules.

"'Most every man has a long-neck," replied the other.

"Humph!" Westhaver grunted, and continued his weather-alley tramp. "What a rough life this fishin' is," he ruminated. "Wonder what Carrie would say ef she knew what I've hed t' buck up against in th' last few hours? Handlin' drunks an' humourin' them. Luggin' them out o' saloons an' gittin' inter a bar-room fight with a crowd o' wharf rats.—Humph! I'm glad we're at sea—yes, mighty glad. I'd never want t' go ashore 'cept t' see ye, Carrie girl. Now, I cal'late that gang down for'ard'll git good an' drunk in a while an' they'll turn in an' sleep it off. There'll be no gittin' them on deck t' take a watch or handle sail this night, an' that means poor Jules an' me 'ull hev a long spell—yes, a long spell, an' its 'most likely we'll hev some wind afore long.''

As Frank had prophesied, the gang, worn out with their week's dissipation and stupid with the doubtful whisky they had been imbibing, soon rolled into their bunks, and throughout the afternoon and evening Shorty and Jules spelled one another at wheel and look-out. As they hauled off the land there was a spiteful heft in the westerly wind, and when the night shut down, dark and cold, the schooner was lurching and diving over a breaking sea.

"Glass is down to twenty-nine six," remarked Westhaver, coming up from the cabin at midnight. "I tried t' rouse some of these fellers out, but they're dead to the world. Whew! she's breezin' up!" Lighting his pipe, he took the wheel, while Jules walked the waist and peered into the blackness ahead.

There is a feeling indescribably grand and awe-inspiring in the sight of a schooner tearing through the night with all her sail set. Everything appears an opaque wall, broken only by the Rembrandtesque illumination of the oilskinned figure straining at the wheel in the yellow light of the binnacle lamp, the hazy loom of the sails towering into the blackness aloft, and the phosphorescent gleaming of the churning bow wave streaming aft to merge with the ghostly irradiancy of the creaming wake. Schooner and sea were hidden and absorbed in the dark of a cloudy, starless night, and the only indication of the presence of a human being upon the deck was the glow of a pipe or a wind-blown spark. No tramp of sea-booted feet could be heard above the hum and whir of the wind in sails and rigging; the hissing drone of the racing foam and the sullen crash of the seas on the bow—the darkness was palpable and a shipmate's nearness to one was acknowledged by an intuitive feeling and not by sight.

The *Mabel Kinsella* stormed thus until the increasing weight of the wind compelled a clipping of her wings. Two or three big seas had piled aboard, and Westhaver, bearing in mind that this was his first trip, and having no desire to lose the fragile dories nested on the deck, handed the wheel to Jules and went down to call the gang.

"Up belo-o-w! Reef th' mains'l an' trice up yer jib! Come on, fellers, all out!" Then he staggered for'ard through the flying spray. "Turn out, fellers!" he roared. "Reef th' mains'l—take in th' jib!"

It was evident by the prone forms snoring in the bunks that the cry fell upon deaf ears. Westhaver noticed the fact and jumped below.

"Come on thar'!" he bawled, grasping the occupant of the nearest bunk by the arm. "Reef th' mains'l! D'ye hear me!" And he dragged him out protesting feebly. Along all the line of bunks he went, and in every case he was compelled to pull the stupified men out with a none too gentle hand. Seated upon the lockers, they blinked owlishly at the light, and cursed the mainsail and the vessel with lurid oaths.

Westhaver's voice boomed down the ladder. "Come up thar' now or I'll come down an' drag ye up. Look smart!" And recognizing the snap of authority and command in the young skipper's voice, they reached for their boots and oilskins.

The cabin crowd were trundled out in a similar manner, and when all had mustered on the spray-drenched, lurching deck, the skipper took the wheel. "All right now, fellers! M-a-i-n-sheet! Git her in!"

In the solid blackness of the March night, the *Kinsella's* hard-bitten gang lowered the sail and tussled cursefully with the reef points, while out on the boom foot-ropes three men barked and hauled out the ear-ring. The schooner was lying to the wind and making but little headway, when a shout came from the boom-end, and the men aft of the wheel-box yelled, "Man overboard!"

Westhaver jumped and glanced around, and wheeling he grabbed a shack knife from a becket and groped for the lead-line tub. "Git up torches!" he almost screamed; "an' grab a-holt o' this line!" In a flash he had cut the lead adrift and knotted the stout cord around his waist, and while the frightened mob were grasping at it, he leaped over the taffrail into the sea.

Clad in his oilskins and rubber boots, Westhaver hit the chilly water with a splash which filled his nose and mouth, but snorting like a grampus, he struck out manfully to the spot but a few feet ahead of him where a faintly discernible bundle was paddling and bawling with the lustiness of fear. "Don't grab at me!" gasped Shorty as he came up to the floundering fisherman. The other was too frightened to heed the warning, and as Westhaver drew alongside him he clutched him round the neck. "Heave in!" yelled the skipper, and with the other man hanging to him frenziedly, both went under.

Down, down, down, they seemed to go, and Frank's feet groped for an imaginary bottom while his lungs filled to bursting with the awful pressure. A sensation of fearful pain pressed upon his temples; his eyes seemed like lead in their sockets and his ears were filled with a mighty thunder. Then came a feeling of peacefulness; he thought of Carrie Dexter, his mother, and Uncle Jerry, and, forgetful of the position he was in, he felt supremely happy, while a curious fancy ran through his mind. "Who would take the *Kinsella* home?"

The cold air beat upon his face again and interrupted the lightning-like trend of his thoughts, and a strong hand clutched at his collar and dragged him into something which heaved up and down and made him sick. Yes, he could remember being sick—fearfully sick, and when the fit passed, he was standing on his own deck with the lead-line around his waist and a jostling, shouting crowd of men who seemed to leer at him in the flickering glare of the torches. Then he was sick again, and must have gone to sleep for when he awoke it was broad daylight, and Charley Costa, the cook, was forcing hot soup between his lips.

"What's th' matter, steward?" he croaked, and his voice seemed strangely weak.

"Hah! skeepper. You're come 'round again. Sup up this leetle bit soup an' you'll be all right."

Frank sipped at the brew and full consciousness came back to him.

"Who was that I went after?"

"Jake Simms."

"Is—is he gone?"

"Not a bit of it. He's in his bunk for'ard 'most frighten to death."

Hearing the conversation a troop of men gathered around the door of the berth. "How d'ye feel, skipper?" they cried, crowding into the narrow apartment. "Lord, that was a nervy thing you did last night, boy!"

"Where's Jules?"

"Here I am, Frankee." And the big Frenchman pressed forward with the light of adoration in his eyes. "Oh, Frankee boy, but I was 'fraid you was gone——"

"Yes," interrupted a man, "I sure cal'lated that Big Frenchy had gone crazy after ye jumped over th' rail. He had a dory over an' after you 'fore a man c'd say knife——"

Frank looked up. "Then it was you Sabot, what hauled me out. I hev a kinder recollection o' bein' in a dory. Sick, wasn't I ?"

"Yes," Jules replied. "You lay in bottom of doree an' vomit de salt water you swallow. Dat dam' Newf'nlan' bear had you 'round de neck. I had to hit heem wid de bailer to make heem leave go—me'n McCallum——"

"Was McCallum with you?"

"Yes! When I come roun' stern in doree, he jump from de boom into de doree an' help pull you in——"

"Humph!" The skipper nodded, and sensing the peculiar lurching of the vessel, he enquired: "What hev ye done with th' vessel. She ain't under way."

"No, skipper," answered Jules. "It come on heavy after we got you aboard, and I hove her to. She's on de starboard tack under de fores'l, an' it ees blow hard wit' snow from sout'-east——"

"Hove-to, is she?" Westhaver rolled out of his bunk aching and sore all over his stocky body. Looking down at his sodden clothing, he exclaimed: "Waal, ef you ain't a rough bunch o' skates t' heave a man inter his bunk with all his wet clothes on. Ain't that th' limit——"

"We rolled ye up in all th' blankets we c'd lay a-holt of," pleaded a man in extenuation.

"T' be sure ye did," laughed Shorty, "an' look at my bunk—jest swillin'. Clear out now 'til I git some dry rags on."

Endowed with the iron constitution common to most of the deep-sea fishermen, and being a temperate man, Westhaver did not take long to recover from his experience

BLUE WATER

of the night. With dry clothes on, and Charley Costa's hot soup under his belt, he felt himself again, but when he glanced in the cabin mirror and saw the reflection of his bruised and cut face, with the stubby growth on his chin and the brine-matted hair plastered over his forehead, he was fain to remark, "What a hard-lookin' case you are, Frank Westhaver! Ef Carrie c'd but see ye now, she'd throw a fit."

On deck he found the vessel taking care of herself lying-to under the foresail with the wheel lashed. It was snowing hard and the sleety flakes drove athwart the grey sky and tumbling black-green sea like chaff from a blower. There was no one on deck—Jules had turned in, exhausted with his all-night spell, and the others were nursing sore heads and caring little whether the vessel floated or sunk. Shorty knew how they were feeling, and he knew the best way to work the drink aftermath out of them.

Down the fo'c'sle scuttle he shouted: "Up on deck, all of you, an' make sail! Come on, now! Look sharp!"

Forgetful of their feelings, the gang turned out with alacrity. "Holy Trawler!" said someone, "ain't that beggar a dog? Gee! he's worse'n ol' Tom Watson for drivin'. By the Lord Harry! Thar's some ginger in that boy——"

"Ant it pe a creat pleasure for me to sail with her—so it pe!" declared McCallum, passing a red paw over an aching head. "She's chust ta smartest skipper t'at I effer met. What a fery sore heid I haf, to pe sure!"

And with the admiration of hardy, rough men for those hardier and more daring than themselves, they hauled on their boots and oil-clothes with exceedingly profane, yet heart-felt, compliments to their young skipper.

They put the reefed mainsail and jumbo on her, and, setting the watch, they swung off on their easterly course again. The shore and its orgies were forgotten, and with the lift of blue water under their feet the rough Western Ocean trawlers settled down to the regular routine of the sea. The sea! The great stretches of clear, clean water rolling tireless and ever changing under the lash of the great untrammelled winds. Always beautiful; ever mysterious; charged with the compelling grandeur of the gale; languorous with the calm and the soft zephyrs of summer, and sublime, yet fearful, in the storm. Swept with the winds of heaven, which, laden with brine, fill the lungs with their cleansing purity and clear the brain befuddled with the vice and dissipations of the land, the mighty watery wastes purge body and soul and rejuvenate the jaded mind. The nerve-shattered, stupefied inebriate who rolls aboard his vessel at the port feels the influence as soon as the forefoot rises and snores to the heave of open water. The brine-laden air is drawn into his lungs; the heart, harassed by alcohol, resumes its normal functions; the eyes snap and sparkle with life, and the liquor-benumbed brain emerges through the mist of stupefaction and lends itself to the cleaner thoughts induced by the great, clean ocean around. As the great rejuvenator, it eradicates the dregs of vice and bestiality hereditary to the land, and makes men of those who fare their lives upon its mighty breast.

With the schooner heading on her course for Brown's Bank, Westhaver, secure in the knowledge that the men could now be trusted to carry out their duty, stretched himself on a locker and whiled away the hours with a book. It was poetry—Longfellow—and he enjoyed the verses with all the love of a man who dwells upon noble thoughts in the privacy of his mind. The schooner was driving through a March snowstorm with a south-easter slamming her along; she lurched and dived, storming and roaring through a tumbling sea, but Westhaver was thinking little of it, though there were passages in his reading which made him appreciate the beauty of the words.

> Then comes with an awful roar,
> Gathering and sounding on,
> The storm-wind from the Labrador,
> The wind Euroclydon,
> The storm-wind!

"Great! Simply great!" he murmured. "Now, here's 'Evangeline'—somethin' right in my own country. 'This is th' forest primeval. Th' murmurin' pines an' th' hemlocks. . . . !'" And he read the words to himself with pleasure.

At midnight, with the push of the strong breeze, they made the western edge of the Bank, and they hove-to till daylight. At four, the south-easter had blown itself out and hauled to the nor'west—the breeze coming away puffy and cold. Swinging off again, Westhaver fetched her up when they sounded on the north-eastern edge of Brown's in forty-seven fathoms, and after breakfast at five he shouted out his first hail as a Banking skipper: "Bait up!"

The day was cloudy and cold, but the sea had gone down enough for a set to be made, and at nine Shorty had the whole ten dories strung out on a flying set with three tubs each.

"Set one tub at a time, fellers," he cautioned them, "an' haul yer gear ef I h'ist th' 'queer' thing. Barometer don't look too good."

With only the cook and himself aboard, he patrolled the string of dories, and waited impatiently for the men to haul the gear.

"Wonder what we'll git?" he muttered to himself a dozen times, and as he lurched past the tumbling dories he scanned them with boyish eagerness.

"Thar's Mac pullin' in his trawl—ain't much on th' first shot—ah, there they go—haddock—runnin' large too. Ye-e-s," he murmured slowly. "By th' looks o' things I'm a-goin' t' git a deck, anyway." And almost unconsciously he repeated the Fisherman's Prayer:

> "Lord! Let me get a deck of fish,
> So large, that even I,
> When tellin' of it afterwards,
> Will have no cause to lie."

Whistling and singing, he spun the wheel and scrutinized the scattered dories, until the last tub was hauled and they came pulling down to him.

"Good set, skipper!" shouted the first dory-mates alongside, and, slipping the wheel into the bucket, he looked over into the dory-load of gleaming haddock, cod, cusk, and hake, and grabbed the tubs of trawl as they were handed up. The flop of the fish as they were pitchforked into the deck-pens, and the monotonous count of the men, sounded like music in his ears.

"Three hunder an' eighty-eight! Number four dory!"

"Good work for a beginnin'," remarked Frank as he noted the count on the tally board. "Hope it'll only keep up. Thar's McCallum comin'. He-e-y, cook! Dory on th' port!" And while the cook attended to their painter, Shorty looked after the starboard nesters coming along.

For a green skipper, he struck luck, and after eight days on the north and north-eastern edge of Brown's Bank he found that he had a good hundred thousand pounds of haddock, cod, cusk, pollock, and a few hake and halibut upon the ice below. They did not fish every day, as the weather was not of the best, but whenever there was a momentary let-up in the vicious March squalls, the dories were over and the set made.

Frank was delighted with his good luck. "That's the best o' havin' them tough gangs. They'll stand anythin' an' work 'til they drop, an' ye kin drive them all ye hev a mind to. 'Tis th' lucky man I am—aye, mighty lucky. Now for Boston market!"

CHAPTER ELEVEN

THEY PUT THE WHOLE PATCH OF FOUR LOWERS ON her as soon as the last fish was hove into the hold pens, and while the *Mabel Kinsella's* long bowsprit headed on a west-by-north course the gang turned to with draw-bucket and corn broom to clean up the gurry-littered decks. It was a cloudy night with but a light southerly breeze blowing, and Westhaver, as he glanced at the low barometer, speculated on the outcome of the weather, and set the glass at the last reading—twenty-nine and seven-tenths.

"Glass fallin'?" queried a man, cutting a fill for his pipe.

"Yes," answered the young skipper with a sigh. "More dirt, I'm afraid. I only hope it'll hold fair 'til we make Boston. It can blow all it likes afterwards. We've got jest two hundred and fifty miles t' make t' th' Lightship, an' ef this southerly wind 'ud only stiffen a bit or haul t' th' east'ard we'll make port inside thirty hours." And, pulling on his mittens, he clambered up on deck.

At midnight the wind dropped and left the schooner wallowing her gunwales under in a heavy southerly swell. The sails flapped thunderously with the patter of reef-points and the slap of gaff downhauls, boom jaws groaned and chafed against the masts, the jib chain sheets screeched across the fore-stay, while the booms fetched up on the tackles, travellers, and jibing gear with terrifying shocks. It was a "howling calm" in every sense of the word, and the gang essaying sleep in their swaying bedplaces anathematized the noise with lurid oaths, while the skipper gazed with anxious eyes at the steadily falling barometer.

At three in the morning the glass was down to twenty-nine—a quick drop—and Westhaver had just re-set the pointer when the watch on deck hailed him.

"Wind a-comin' from th' sou'-west, skipper!"

"Call the gang down for'ard! All out, you cabin crowd, an' stand by for squalls!" And so saying, the young skipper leaped on deck.

The wind came away in light puffs at first and then in bursts of savage fury which necessitated heading the schooner into it until the spite was passed. For two hours they jockeyed with the wind, heading into the squalls as they drove down on them, and paying off when they eased up. Then would come intervals of calm, during which time the vessel would wallow from side to side and almost roll the masts out of her, while the gang, oiled-up and ready for anything, would lounge around the decks smoking and dodging the sweeping booms.

"He-e-re she comes!" wailed a voice out of the gloom for'ard. Shorty strained his eyes into the darkness and made out a cloud or haze of audibly hissing whiteness coming up on the starboard bow.

He glanced at the compass. "Um! from th' west'ard," he muttered, and when the *Kinsella's* sails filled with the advance of the air motion he jammed the helm down just as the blast struck them.

Instantly the air became grey-white with flying sleet, and the schooner laid down to the weight of the wind with her lee-rail under and her head-sails flapping thunderously. The roar of the wind and the hiss of the sleet striking the water drowned all other sounds, and the schooner trembled to the slats of the jib and jumbo and the short, savage shocks of the seas on the bow. While the initial force of the squall lasted the sea was flattened with the press of the wind, and the gang on the almost beam-ended schooner clung to the rigging and cowered under the slash of the sleet and the flying spray.

Dory-sails lashed up in the rigging were blown to tatters in an instant, and many men had the oil hats torn from their heads. It was a blow, and no mistake, and Westhaver, spinning the wheel, never remembered having encountered a squall like it. When the fury passed the sea arose terribly, and the deep-laden schooner filled her decks to the rail. "She can't stand this," said Frank, as he clung to the spokes and a seething grey-back sluiced over the quarter. "In mains'l an' jib!" He shouted the words into Jules' ear, and the order was passed along the gang, mouth to ear, as they hung to the gear around the decks.

Taking in the sails that wild March morning was a strenuous job, and Westhaver was in deadly fear that he would lose some of the men, and when they were out on the bowsprit tricing up the jib his heart was in his mouth every time she made a 'scend. But the *Kinsella's* crowd were sober this time, and being a hard, tough bunch, they thought but little of being run under on a bowsprit. They were used to incidents of that sort, having sailed with driving skippers who carried their sail until the last minute and only took it in when they were forced to. Taking in the mainsail was a good thirty minutes' superhuman struggle with hard, new canvas, and when they finally got the stops passed around it, it was with the peak halliards foul of the spreaders and all hands almost exhausted.

Under the foresail and jumbo they hove her to on the port tack with the wheel lashed and two men on deck— one between the dories and the other standing on the cabin house—peering through the blinding whirl of snow which limited the range of vision to within a scant hundred feet of the vessel.

At some time or other in the winter season there comes what fishermen call "the big breeze," and when it comes it is a case of "look up and stand from under!" The vessels in the vicinity of a harbour run for it and remain there until it has blown itself out, and those who find themselves jammed down on a bad coast stand out to sea again and lay-to. Then under the foresail, or foresail and jumbo, they will ride out the worst Western Ocean winter gale in comparative safety—the only hazard being the liners driving ahead on schedule time and hidden by the snow or rain; the helpless fisherman becomes an easy prey to the carelessness of a steamer's look-out.

The *Mabel Kinsella* had struck the "big breeze," and Westhaver knew it. The thought was not a pleasant one, as with a trip of fish under hatches he had no desire to keep the sea any longer than he could possibly help with Boston market waiting for their catch.

Patience is a virtue which all fishermen possess. They have to, or they would not go a-fishing. But it is a patience which is sorely trying to the temper; a patience which eats the heart out of a man with worry, and as the long hours go by with the wind and sea prohibiting the slightest forward move on his part, he is forced to see the dollars slipping through his fingers. Westhaver was worried, and throughout the long day he scanned the glass and the sea for a let-up in the wild inferno raging upon the waters. The wind blew with fearful velocity at times, and the schooner, deep-laden and with only her strong double nought foresail hoisted, was often pressed lee rail under with the weight of the breeze.

Below decks the men, with muscles aching with the jolting and knocking about, hung into their bunks—jammed in with rolled-up clothes, mattress, and pillow—and smoked plug after plug of tobacco until forecastle and cabin became opaque with the blue reek. Oil-clothes swung like pendulums from the hooks on the bulkheads, and boots and buckets clattered and rolled across the floors. Charley Costa—the Portuguese cook—worked around his stove in momentary danger of being hurled against it, and he prepared meals after a fashion. The bilge-water in the vessel's bottom swashed among the ballast, and the fumes made the lamps burn blue and blackened the fresh-painted woodwork lining of the cabin and forecastle, besides making many of the men sea-sick with the nauseating odour. Creaking and groaning in every beam, knee, and plank, the schooner wallowed, lurched, reared, and flung herself over the roaring crests with all the twists and lunges of an unbroken broncho.

BLUE WATER

For four long and apparently interminable days the gale continued, and the *Kinsella*, hove-to all that time, drifted away to the eastward. "So far," as one of the gang remarked, "that it 'ud need a dollar's worth o' postage stamps on a post-card t' reach us." Needless to say, his joke was not appreciated by the scowling fishermen in the adjacent bunks.

With the dawn on the morning of the fourth day came signs that the storm was breaking. The snow had ceased, and the cold glint of a cloud-enshrouded sun illuminated a waste of tumbling grey-blue sea, foam-streaked and rearing white-capped heads in sullen fury. The sky was lightening up to windward, and when the ragged clouds, racing like smoke athwart the heavens, opened up a faint patch of blue, the watch hailed the news with delight. "Weather's liftin', skipper. Thar's a streak o' blue sky showin' now!"

All hands tumbled up to see it—a common, ordinary and unimportant sight to a landsman—but as beautiful as the sight of home to the sea-weary men with eyes jaded by the monotonous vista of restless sea and sullen, depressing snow-filled sky. They watched it spread as the strong nor'-wester drove the fleecy storm-wrack away, and when the sun broke clear, the watery waste reflected the cobalt of the western heavens. Blue water! It was good to see it once again, and the whole aspect of things changed with the colour, and Westhaver gave a joyous shout. "Come on thar', bullies. Put th' double-reefed mains'l on her! H'ist th' jumbo!" And while the men ran to execute his commands he hove the lead over for a sound.

"Gee whittaker!" he said as the coils flaked out and he was forced to belay. "No bottom at a hundred fathoms! Cal'late we must ha' blown away outside th' hundred-fathom curve. Now, ef I only had a sextant an' knew how t' use it I'd know whar' I was. As it is, I'll hev t' slam her to th' west'ard until we raise somethin' or git a position from another vessel."

A huge two-funnelled Atlantic liner overhauled them as they swooped to the westward under their scanty canvas, and the crowds thronging her spacious promenade decks crowded to the rails to gaze at the tiny "fish boat" plunging like a sea-bird in among the great rollers.

"Hev a look, consarn ye!" bawled a fisherman, unimpressed by the majesty of the rolling ocean palace towering above them. "Yer blame skipper hez shifted his course t' let ye see us. Ef it was thick he wouldn't shift his ruddy course an inch ef we was under yer bows." And carried away with the hereditary hatred of the Banks, he shook his fist at the wondering spectators on the liner's decks.

Westhaver, steering, glanced into the binnacle as she hauled ahead. "Now that craft's a New Yorker, that's evident, an' a New York boat on th' course she's steerin' means that we're south o' forty-two, so we'll jest haul th' *Mabel* a little more no'therly." And on this slight deduction the young skipper shifted the course. Aye! shifted more than the vessel's course—but there are some who will contend that the God of Luck has controlled the destinies of many lives; and a turn of Fate's wheel has upset the thrones of kings, the powers of empires, and while showering wealth on the beggar it has beggared the wealthy. Is it blind luck, chance, destiny, or fortune? Or is it the hand of God—a God who sees all and knows all, and who holds the lives, the fortunes, and the destinies of all men in the hollow of his hand?

It was McCallum who roared the intelligence down into the cabin where Westhaver was reading. "Oh, skipper! T'ere's a park or a t'ree-master town to loo'ard looking fery distressful, sir. Wull ye pe for looking at her, skipper?"

It was a barque, and, as McCallum had said, she was "looking very distressful." The foretopgallant mast was gone, and she was evidently lying-to under a goose-winged lower maintopsail with the lee clew hauled out and a small rag of a mizzen staysail. The furled-up sails on the yards had broken free of the gaskets in many places and were bellying out in balloon-like knobs; the hull rode very low in the water, and it appeared that some of the seas were making a complete breach over her. As the *Mabel Kinsella* neared her a string of flags ran up to her spanker gaff, fluttered for an instant, and vanished.

"What's th' use of him flyin' International Code hoists to a fisherman," said Westhaver. "We don't know what they are, 'though I cal'late that was N.C. what went up— Thar' now! He's talkin' English." The British merchant ensign, union down, broke out half-way up the signal halliards. It had streamed out like a sheet of tin for but a few seconds when the wind whiffed it into nothingness.

"He's in distress," cried Frank to the crowd lounging aft, "stand by the mainsheet, some o' you! Make th' tail-rope fast as I put th' wheel over! Ready? Helm's a'lee!" And jogging to windward of the loggy, sea-washed barque, the fishing schooner tumbled and rolled in the swells. The gang trooped aft while Westhaver scrutinized the barque with his binoculars.

"Humph!" he muttered as he laid them down. "She's a small craft loaded with deals. Thar's all her gang aft on top of the house. Whole main-deck's a-wash. Waal, I cal'late we kin git them. Off with th' gripes on yer lee nest an' put three dories over. I'll pick ye up down t' loo'ard——" The words were scarce out of his mouth before a rush was made by the whole crew for the dories nested amidships.

"Say!" shouted Westhaver, "I said th' lee dories— three o' them only. Come aft here, you other fellers what ain't asked t' go——"

They came aft, protesting and pleading. "Let me go!" "An' me!" "Jim Hudson kain't handle a dory like I kin!" " 'Tis my dory usually goes on that lee nest—I sh'd go by rights." "Three dories ain't enough, skipper." And so on, but Frank was firm.

"Three's enough," he said. "Belay yer jaw now an' help them git them over 'thout stavin' them on th' rail." Westhaver went forward. "Now, you rescue fellers," he said. "Be careful goin' 'longside that hulk an' see she don't roll down on ye. Round up t' her lee quarter an' git her people off, an' make them lay in th' bottom o' th' dory. Be careful, fellers!'' And in a minute they were clear of the schooner and reeling over the creaming, wind-lashed waves.

It was blowing very strong from the nor'-west, and there was a heavy sea running, and if the rescue had been carried out from a steamer with similar conditions existing there would have been a call for volunteers—single men preferred—and they would have pulled away in the same spirit as a forlorn hope, while the steamer would have manœuvred to windward of the thirty-foot lifeboat with oil dripping from the latrines to break the sea.

With the men of the deep-sea fishing fleets there were no such preparations. They are used to handling boats in rough water and heavy winds, and the six dory-mates from the *Mabel Kinsella* pulled away in their eighteen-foot dories with the supreme confidence of men who know what their boats can stand—for the dory, those ugly, cranky, flat-bottomed bronchos of the sea, will ride out a howling gale if not overloaded and improperly handled.

While the boats were rounding up under the barque's counter Westhaver drew away on the jumbo, started his sheets, and swung down to leeward, where he rolled with wild swoops among the debris-littered combers, while the gang lined the rail and watched the work of rescue with anxious eyes.

There were ten all told taken from the water-logged barque, and when the first dory pulled alongside the schooner willing hands lifted the benumbed members of the wind-jammer's crew over the rail. A boyish figure, slight in build but beautiful in the alabaster paleness of his features, dressed in seamen's oilskins, was lifted aboard by Westhaver, and when he glanced at the face in curious wonder, Jake Simms in the dory confirmed his suspicions. "Git her below, skipper! She's fainted——"

A girl! Westhaver leaped for the cabin gangway with the burden resting in his strong arms as lightly as a feather. "Git th' cook aft here!" he roared. "Tell him t' bring along coffee—tea—soup—anythin' hot. Jump, some o' yez!"

Clattering below, he laid the still form of the girl on a locker, and for a moment he pondered as to what he had better do to revive her. "Now I'll be hanged ef I know what t' do?" he muttered, when a grizzled old man clad in a long black oilskin coat stepped down the ladder.

"Is she all right?" he queried, giving Westhaver a piercing, anxious glance.

"Waal, I reckon she's jest fainted," returned the young skipper. "I've sent for th' cook t' come aft with somethin' hot—here he is now. What ye got thar', Charley? Coffee? I cal'late ye'd better git some of it atween her lips——"

"Yes," said the old man, bending over the faintly breathing form. "Wait, an' I'll git them oil-clothes off'n her. Got a bunk, sir?"

Shorty jumped to his own berth. "She kin hev my berth," he said eagerly. "Jest a couple o' shakes 'til I fix it up." And he hove old newspapers, pipes, mittens, tobacco plugs, dirty collars, and old socks out of the coffin-like hole and smoothed out the sodden bilge-reeking pillow and blanket with a blush of shame for the hoggishness of his sea life.

"Put her in here, mister," he said when he had kicked the rubbish to one side, and between them they laid the sodden, girlish body into the bunk and rolled her up in the blankets.

"All aboard, skipper!" shouted someone down the hatch. Westhaver left the berth. "Th' steward here'll git ye anythin' ye want for her, sir," he said. "I'll hev t' leave ye for a few minutes."

On deck he saw the water-logged barque a good mile to windward; the rescuers had returned safely, and the dories were nested and the gripes over them.

"Draw away yer jumbo! Aft here to the wheel whoever's on watch. Same course as before. Where's them other fellers ye took off?"

"Down for'ard muggin' up, skipper. They're all right——"

The grey-headed stranger appeared from the cabin and addressed Westhaver. "You're skipper aboard here, I take it? That was my vessel—my name's Denton, an' th' young lady below is my daughter Lillian. She's had a tough time aboard that hulk and ain't comin' 'round very quick. Any whisky aboard?"

Westhaver gave a shout. "Any you fellers got'ny whisky?—Lord Harry! we were floatin' in it when we left Gloucester! What? You got a drop, Westley? Good boy! It's a blame' miracle! Here you are, Cap'en but I won't vouch for th' brand." And jumping below, the barque's captain forced a spoonful of genuine "forty-fathom" joy-water between the ashen lips of his daughter. As the fiery liquid drained between her pearly teeth she gasped at the pungency of the spirit, and a pair of large brown eyes opened and stared at Westhaver, who was holding the gorgeously labelled bottle.

"That's th' style, lassie!" exclaimed the old skipper. "Now, jest take another sip o' this——"

The girl turned her head away, and Frank noted the beautiful small ear which peeped from under the wealth of brine-sodden brown hair streaming over his grimy pillow. "No, no, father," she said in a whisper. "I'm all right now, but oh, so cold—so cold."

Shorty turned and grabbed the steaming mug of coffee out of the cook's hand. "Gimme that, Charley! Away down for'ard an' attend to the other fellers. Here y'are, Cap'en, give her some o' this. It'll warm her up." The coffee was poured into a spoon, and the exhausted girl sipped at it until the chilled blood in her veins revived under the warming influence, and she fell back on to the pillow breathing regularly.

Westhaver went around every bunk in the cabin collecting blankets, and he came into the berth with a pile of them. "Heave these a-top of her, Cap'en. Ye'll take some o' th' wet clothes off her first? All right, sir! I'll leave ye for a spell." And he clambered up the ladder and drew the companion slide.

"None o' you go down in th' cabin 'til I give ye leave," he said to the gang lounging aft.

"How is she?" asked a dozen voices.

"Comin' 'round nicely," replied Shorty.

"That was my whisky that did th' trick," exclaimed Westley. "Good stuff, that was——"

"Good swash!" growled Shorty. "Why, she hed but one sniff o' that T Dock rot-gut o' your'n an' wouldn't take another. Lord Harry! that nose-paint 'ud revive a corpse."

"Say, skipper," remarked another man who was a bit of a gay Lothario when ashore, "she's a peach, that girl, an' I wouldn't mind makin' a date with her when we got ashore——"

Westhaver's brows lowered ominously. "An' I wouldn't mind knockin' blazes out o' you ef ye dare talk thataway when I'm around. Kain't a girl come aboard a vessel 'thout you shore-rangin' dock-head sports makin' remarks——"

"Aw, skipper," said the man, "don't git so hot about it. Sure I didn't mean anythin'——"

"All right then," replied Frank, "keep a stopper on yer jaw when she's aboard, an' turn-to, th' crowd o' ye, an' git th' mains'l on her!"

They shook the reefs out and set the jib, but at midnight the wind came away so heavy from the north'ard that it compelled Westhaver to give orders to reef down and trice up the jib again. Under the double-tucked mainsail, whole foresail, and jumbo they lurched along close-hauled to the bitter wind. The barque's crew were quartered in the forecastle bunks, while aft in the cabin the *Kinsella's* for'ard gang stretched on the lockers and floor and spoke in whispers. In the skipper's berth lay the girl, and her father dozed upon Frank's sea-chest, oblivious to the swings and lurches of the schooner.

"Wind, she's come away strong again, Frankee," remarked Jules, as he struggled at the wheel.

The skipper grunted. "Lord! I'm afraid we'll never git to home. Five days now sence we left th' Bank, an' we're away t' blaze-an'-gone out on the Atlantic somewheres at least two hundred an' fifty miles east o' Highland light. Holy Trawler! It's great weather for a green skipper. Sh'dn't blame th' gang ef they left me for a hoodoo when we do hit in, an' us with sich a good trip o' fish aboard." And stamping his feet, he paced the quarter, thinking until a welter of sea came toppling over the rail and forced him to jump for the safety of the main-rigging.

"Let her fall off easy, Jules!" he commanded.

Crash! another comber swashed aboard, and everything for'ard went under.

"Nurse her, Jules!" roared Westhaver anxiously. The wind was heeling the little vessel over on her rail now, and she was making some hair-raising dives, while Jules at the wheel was exercising every trick he knew to ease the plunging schooner.

"Wa-a-tch aout!" It was the look-out standing between the dories who cried. The vessel wavered for an instant in the trough of a mighty wave, then, as she rose, her sails filled with the full strength of the breeze and she literally smashed through the whole top of the sea. Crash! The whole deck disappeared from sight with but the masts, sails, and the top dory on the weather nest visible above the froth. When the gallant little vessel lifted her decks clear, Westhaver was shouting down to the gang swashing around in the flooded cabin.

"All up an' git th' mains'l in!" And the crowd for'ard, rescued and all, floated out of the lee bunks, came on deck without being called.

Under the foresail they hove her to once more. "By the ol' Judas! Ef this ain't weather I don't know what is!" growled Shorty. "Dana talks about Cape Horn, but Lord Harry! it kain't be worse'n th' Western Ocean in winter time. Oh, I'm a dog, I am, when thar's any dirt a-flyin'— I'm sure t' git it. Now, ef this was only th' *Kastalia* or th' *Fannie Carson* we c'd drag our sail all right, but this is a small craft for winter weather—too small. I don't wonder that Hoolahan was glad for me t' take her. I wonder how th' girl is?"

She was awake and talking to her father when Frank stepped below. "Weather too much for ye, Cap'en?" queried Denton as Frank staggered over to the berth.

"Aye," answered Shorty, whisking off his dripping sou'-wester. "It's breezin' up again. Had t' heave her to after she shipped that last load. How is the young lady?"

Captain Denton looked at his daughter. "Well, Lily, how d'ye feel now? This is the captain of this vessel, my dear. Captain——?"

"Westhaver, sir," answered Frank.

The girl turned in the bunk, and Shorty thought he had never seen anyone look so beautiful—except his own Carrie. The pallor of exhaustion had faded from her cheeks, and they were suffused with a rich warm colour which contrasted well with her large brown eyes and silky hair. The rough, evil-smelling blankets were thrown back from her shoulders and revealed a glimpse of a full, rounded throat white as marble and lovely in its curves. She extended a small well-shaped hand, and the glimpse of pearly teeth which Frank caught in her smile caused his boyish heart to flutter strangely.

"I'm sure we owe a lot to you, Captain Westhaver," she said in a voice which fell like music on his ear. "You and your brave men."

"Oh, miss, that was nawthin'," replied Shorty, blushing a little as he clasped her hand in his heavy paw. "I'm more'n glad I fell in with you, an' if it warn't for one o' them liners I'd never ha' altered my course in your direction." And he explained the circumstances to the old shipmaster.

The girl spoke, "What a wonderful thing!" she exclaimed. "Do you know where we are now, Captain?"

"Waal," replied Frank, "I hev a kinder idea. 'Bout two hundred an' fifty miles east o' Cape Cod, I cal'late. What d'ye think, Captain?"

The other nodded. "I guess you're about right. I never got a sight for three days after leaving Yarmouth."

"Are you from Yarmouth, Captain?" queried Westhaver.

"Yes," he replied. "My home is there, and I was born in the country. That barque was my own vessel, and I was bound for Cuba with a load of spruce deals stowed by some four-eyed St. John wharf rat what called himself a stevedore. We caught that westerly th' day after we towed out, and her deck-load started to work so much that I had to heave her to. Then she started a butt somewhere, and with a big sea she shipped smashing her up about the decks, she filled, and we couldn't free her with the pumps. Then we hung to the mizzen gear the whole of a night and day until you hove in sight and took us off. She was a fine little barque—a fine able little craft wrecked by the bad stowage of a bum stevedore." And he sighed.

"Were you just makin' a voyage for pleasure?" asked Frank of Miss Denton.

"Yes," she replied. "I was just through college and feeling pretty well done up after the examinations, when papa suggested taking me with him to the West Indies. Of course, I was immensely taken with the idea, and this is how it has turned out. But we are lucky—very lucky, and I have to thank God for His mercy in bringing your vessel in our direction. By what little insignificant acts are our lives controlled! If you had not changed your course after the steamer passed we would have perished in the gale that is raging now."

"Aye, Lily," said her father, "that's th' way of the sea, and it is the little things which have to be reckoned with. A degree of error in a compass will put a vessel on the rocks. But—where are you sleeping to-night, Cap'en Westhaver?"

"Oh, I won't turn in until th' weather eases up an' I git her under way again. I'll git all day t'morrer for sleepin'. D'ye fancy anythin' t' eat, miss?"

"No, Captain," she replied. "Your steward has attended to us, and your men have been very kind—very kind indeed, and I don't know how father and I will reward you for the trouble you have taken to make us comfortable——"

"Sh! don't say a word!" exclaimed Frank. "I'm only sorry we haven't better accommodation to offer you, but fishermen are not strong on comfort at sea. We sleep in our clothes all the time, an' only change when we go ashore——"

"It's a hard but courageous life you live, Captain," she said. "Out in all this wild winter weather in these tiny schooners. Oh, it must be awful sometimes."

Frank laughed, and Miss Denton remarked to herself that he had nice even teeth and fine grey-blue eyes. "We don't mind th' weather much in these craft, Miss Denton. They're well built, able an' strong——"

"Weather's easin' off a bit, skipper!" came Jules's voice from the deck.

Frank buttoned on his sou'-wester. "Excuse me, miss. I hope ye'll git a bit o' sleep. Cap'en, turn in on th' lee locker ef ye feel like it." And whistling to himself, Shorty jumped on deck.

Miss Denton looked over at her father. "Isn't he a fine young fellow for a fisherman. I always thought fishermen were rude, uncouth, half-civilized creatures."

Her father smiled. "Good land, no," he replied. "They're mostly all Nova Scotians aboard here, an' just th' same as any of the farming folk up around home. That young skipper comes from up Anchorville way, an' they're gen'ly very decent people."

It was two in the morning when Frank roused the gang out and set the riding sail—that strong triangular piece of stormy-weather canvas which is set on the mainmast above the furled mainsail by means of detachable hoops and the throat halliards for a hoist—and when it was sheeted down to leeward he swung the vessel on to her course again.

"Now," he remarked to the gang, "slap it to her! Th' barometer's steadyin' down, an' th' first rise after low blow is past. I'm for havin' a bit of a snooze. Call me when it moderates!" And after a mug-up down for'ard he hove his weary body down on a galley tank-top and slept like a dead man.

It moderated before daylight, and Jules and McCallum took the responsibility of setting the whole mainsail and jib without calling him, and when he came on deck he was thankful for their thoughtfulness. After breakfast, at five, he went aft and saw the shipwrecked skipper and his daughter.

"How's things lookin' this mornin'?" he greeted them cheerily, and Miss Denton laughed with a flash of teeth and dancing brown eyes.

"I'm feeling fine," she answered, "but I'll have to remain in your bunk, Captain Westhaver, until we get to port, as I have not a dry stitch to wear. Isn't that an awful situation to be in?"

Old Denton's leathery face creased in a deep-water guffaw. "Ha, ha! If you were an ol' sailor now, Lily, we'd turn ye out, clothes or no. Eh, Westhaver?" And Shorty blushed at the suggestion.

"I'm afraid it's goin' t' be kinder dull for ye, Miss Denton," he said, "but I've some books in my chest here that may help pass th' time away—that is, ef ye care for readin'——"

"Why, certainly," answered the girl, vaguely wondering what kind of books a fisherman could possibly have. She was prepared for a tattered collection of Diamond Dicks and Buffalo Bills; but when Frank handed her Herman Melville's "Omoo," Hugo's "Toilers of the Sea," and Longfellow's Poems she almost exclaimed in her surprise.

"These are pretty good yarns," said Frank as he handed them to her. "That 'Omoo' is a dandy, an' th' poetry is mighty fine."

"Are these your books?" she ventured to ask.

"Yes," answered Frank. "I'm kinder fond o' good stuff. Melville is a great favourite o' mine, an' I kin recommend him. I've read 'Typee,' but his 'Moby Dick' is kinder too strong for me. He flies too high for my understanding."

She took the proffered volumes with thanks, and made another mental note upon the characters of fishermen, while Shorty returned to his duty on deck.

All day long they "put it to her," as fishermen say, and as wheel after wheel came aft for his trick it was—"West-no'-west, an' drive her, you!"

In the afternoon Frank called a few of the cabin gang on deck. "See here, you fellers," he said. "Git a broom an' some water an' scrub out that cabin—it's like a pig's-sty, an' smells like one. Git that dirty ol' bucket out o' there an' quit shootin' yer quids into th' stove while th' girl's aboard. Don't let her think like what ol' Skys'l John Summers useter say when he came down inter his cabin——"

"An' what did he say, skipper?"

Frank laughed. "He useter look aroun' th' old baits, papers, an' rags kickin' about, an' he'd remark, 'Boys, a fisherman is th' dirtiest, G—d dam' hog what's made!' So! Go to it an' clean her out!" And they did.

While the old deep-water skipper was taking a "constitutional" on the schooner's narrow quarter alley, Frank and Miss Denton spent an entrancing hour with the world of books. She was a clever and remarkably well-read young woman, and her tastes were strangely similar to the young fisherman's. From Charles Kingsley and his "Westward Ho!" to Stevenson's "Ebb Tide" and "Wrecker"; Dumas' "Three Musketeers" and Longfellow's Poetry; Clark Russell and that prince of Nova Scotian humorists— "Sam Slick"—they travelled in their conversation, and when Frank left for his oil-clothes and the deck again Miss Denton's estimation of the young fisherman was of the highest, while her surprise at finding such a man upon a foul-smelling schooner and engaged in such a hard, rough life was profound.

Shorty kept on deck all night, pacing from the wheel to the windlass and peering every now and again into the darkness. It was a clear, starlight night with a cold easterly wind blowing, and the *Mabel Kinsella* was reeling off the knots at the rate of ten and twelve an hour. Two hundred and thirty-five were registered on the log dial when it was hauled at 3 a.m., and Frank, knowing that they must be nearing the land, clambered to the main cross-trees and caught the glimmer of a flashlight over the port bow. "Now I wonder what light that is?" he muttered as he sat astride the spreaders. "'Tain't Cape Ann, 'cause ye'd see th' twin lights o' Thatcher's Island, an' they're visible 'most twenty mile on a clear night like this, an' 'tain't Eastern P'int, 'cause that's a red flash. It may be Highlands on Cape Cod, an' it may be Minot's Ledge. We'll soon see. He-e-y, below! Take a cast o' th' lead!"

The spreaders trembled as the vessel laid to the wind, and as she swung off again a voice rolled up from the deck—seventy feet below: "Thirty-eight fathom, skipper!"

"That's Minot's," ejaculated Westhaver. "Ef it was Highlands at this distance off we'd be gittin' over fifty fathom o' water. Gee! what a lucky shoot for dead reck'nin'. Blame' wonder I didn't fetch up below th' Cape." And as he clambered down the weather rigging he whistled a song.

His reckoning was confirmed when they picked up the lightship just before dawn, and at nine in the morning they swung in on the wings of the easterly and dropped their sails off T Dock.

Hoolahan was standing on the string-piece as they warped in, and his face betrayed his anxiety. "What d'ye git, skipper?" he roared.

"'Bout a hundred thousand an' a shipwrecked crew!" answered the young skipper.

Hoolahan was off like a shot, and returned in a minute with two or three buyers trailing in his wake.

"What have ye got, Cap'en?" asked one of them.

"'Bout seventy thousand o' haddock an' thirty thousand o' shack."

"Where d'ye git 'em?"

"On Brown's."

"How old's yer last fish?"

Westhaver faltered for an instant. His fish was a trifle old to sell fresh, but the weather had been cold and the market was sure to be a strong one and not too particular at Lent. He replied truthfully. "'Bout seven days ago!"

"Were you out in that westerly?"

"Yes, sir!"

"Hove-to?"

"Lyin'-to for four days an' part of a night!"

The buyer waved his hand. "Ye needn't take yer hatches off, Cap! That fish o' your'n ain't no good here after th' bucketin' about you must 've had in that small vessel. They're all ground t' gurry by now. Sorry, Cap; hard luck!"

Here was a blow to all his hopes! Yes, the buyer was right enough. After the tumbling about which they had been doing the fish must have been grinding on the powdered ice, and as market fresh fish they were unsalable. It was an unfortunate trip all round, and nothing would be coming to them for their man-killing labour. The men lounging around cursed vigorously, and Westhaver stood as a man dazed until Captain Hoolahan hailed him with a shout.

"Git away up t' Vinal Haven, Cap'en, with that fish! Some of it 'ull be all right for saltin'. I'm telegraphin' John Cameron. Away ye go now, an' make yer next trip out o' Portland ef ye're settin' on Brown's!"

Westhaver jumped, and as he turned he was greeted by Captain Denton and his daughter. The young lady was dressed in a long overcoat which hid her sea-drenched clothes, and there was a cab awaiting them on the dock.

"I've just h'ard what you're up against, Westhaver, said Denton, "but never fear, you'll come out all right, boy. I have your address, an' I'll fix up this obligation of mine later. Good-bye, and on behalf of myself, daughter, an' crew I thank you for what you have done for us." And he grasped the young skipper's hand with true heartiness.

Lillian Denton's beautiful eyes expressed more than her lips could utter, and as Westhaver gazed into them he felt a strange thrill. Holding out her hand, she grasped his and said softly, "I won't say good-bye, but I'll look for you in Yarmouth when you go home. God go with you!"

Frank watched them go, and then he remembered Carrie Dexter.

"Poor girl," he muttered. "There's no engagement ring this trip an' no time for an hour with her. I'll git her on th' 'phone!"

Unfortunately, Nurse Dexter was engaged, and with Hoolahan dancing at his heels, Shorty swung aboard the schooner again and within a quarter of an hour was hoisting his mainsail for a one hundred and fifty mile shoot up the coast to Vinal Haven in the State of Maine.

With a fair wind in the shape of a roaring south-easter over the starboard quarter the *Mabel Kinsella* showed her heels, and the skipper, as he brooded over his misfortunes, felt an alleviating pleasure in two thoughts. The first of which was that it was blowing hard and driving him on his way to a market, and the other consisted of entrancing recollections of the beautiful creature whom he had saved from a terrible death on the face of the waters.

"Aye," he muttered, "Long Dick says th' first hundred years o' fishin' is th' hardest—after that it comes easy. But she was a fine, clever girl an' worth losin' a trip over." Then, glancing at the boiling scuppers, he growled to McCallum at the wheel, "Give it to her, Mac! Keep her off, an' drive her, you!"

CHAPTER TWELVE

THE *MABLE KINSELLA* WAS ON BROWN'S BANK AGAIN on her second trip, and Westhaver was at the wheel, while the vessel was jogging to the string of dories. The day was sunshine and fleecy clouds with but a light westerly breeze and a smooth sea, and the gang out on the water were making a four-tub set.

As he spun the wheel, Frank sang a little song to himself and indulged in day-dreams for the future. They had sold their fish in Vinal Haven at a price which just cleared their expenses for the trip and no more, and after procuring their bait and ice at the little Maine port they shot across the Gulf of Maine for the Bank again, with telegraphic instructions from Captain Hoolahan to sell their trip to a firm in Portland.

The latter instruction did not quite fall in with Frank's wishes. He wanted to get back to Boston and Carrie, but fishermen and sailors are a class that have to obey orders "even if they break owners," and Shorty's personal desires were not to be considered in business. At Vinal Haven he had written her a letter telling of his ill-luck on his first trip, and in it he had asked her to wait in patience until he had made good. "And, dearie," he had said, "I hope to get back to Boston before the vessel is hauled up in June. Then I'll have the ring to place on your finger, sweetheart; and later on, when the *Mabel Kinsella* pays for herself, I'll be for taking my little girl back to the Bay Shore as Mrs. Frank Westhaver. Write me to Portland Post Office as soon as you get this, for I'm hungry to hear from you."

As he steered to leeward of the string of dories, his fancy turned to thoughts of love, and he planned out the delights of a future with Carrie as his wife. "We'll git th' house up in Long Cove fixed up for ye, girlie, an' when I'm away at sea, th' mother an' you kin keep each other company. Then I'll take out a Modus Vivendi licence for the ol' *Mabel Kinsella* an' I kin always shoot up an' see ye when we drop in a handy Nova Scotian port for bait an' supplies. An' later on' maybe, Uncle Jerry an' me'll be for buildin' a vessel of our own—a Canadian craft—an' I'll fish out of Anchorville an' be close to home." And musing on these pleasant thoughts, Frank felt strangely happy.

With fine weather on the grounds and a good trip aboard he shot into Portland and made a good sale of his fish— the high dory, Jules and McCallum, drawing ninety dollars for ten days' work. If the gang had any doubts of his ability before, they swore by him now, and it is doubtful if a fishing skipper had a more loyal crowd than what Westhaver had in his rough and tough Georgesmen. In a long letter he had from Uncle Jerry—written by proxy—the old skipper gave word to his fears in that respect. "You've got an awful hard crowd with you, Frank, and I'm afraid they'll be for taking charge of you if you ain't careful. Men like them are used to hard-driving skippers like Evans and Watson, and if you don't strike fish and make good stocks they're liable to leave you quick. They're the best of fishermen, but very rough and quarrelsome when they get rum. I heard about the fight you had in Gloucester here, and they're talking about it yet. They think you are a holy terror, and every old trawler around the wharves has been yarning over that scrap for the last two weeks. I met Mike Hoolahan and he told me how you and him came to a deal. Why didn't you let me put some money into that craft? I'm awfully proud and pleased with you, Frank, and I'm glad to see you standing on your own legs. That was a great piece of work you did in bringing the *Carson* from Georges in that nor'-wester. I met a fellow called Jessy up here looking for a gang for the *Carson*. He didn't know who I was, and we was up at the Master Mariner's Club together with some other skippers. He said that you had swiped his gang away from him. I gave him a few hot shots and he went away. The *Carson* has no gang yet, and I think it will be some time before Jessy gets one, as they are all down on him. Hoolahan told me about you being out in that westerly blow and spoiling your fish. That was too bad, Frank, but you'll find out that these things will happen to anybody. I was just on Quero when it hit in, and I had quite a tussle in the old *Kastalia*. I saw something in the paper about your picking up the crew of the barque *Santa Ana* of Yarmouth. Hoolahan said something about it. He tells me you are fishing on Brown's. It's a good winter ground. Try the hole on the N. edge in 51 to 55 fathoms. I've made some good sets there. Little La Have to the N.E. is sometimes good for a few sets——" And the letter concluded with tips on likely "spots" and advice regarding "tide sets," which only interest a fisherman.

Shorty folded the letter back in the envelope. "Good old Uncle Jerry," he mused. "Waal, I cal'late he don't need t' worry about my gang—tough an' all as they are, they're th' best trawlers anywhere aroun' these waters. They'll put th' dories over in half a gale an' they'll set an' set an' bait up an' dress down 'till th' cows come home." A letter from his mother and one from Lem Ring occupied his attention next. The mother's was maternal in every respect, and the admonitions of his boyhood days were not omitted; but the pride at his command evinced in her epistle caused the tears to well in Shorty's grey-blue eyes. "Poor ol' ma," he murmured. "She's tickled to death to think I got skipper o' this ol' peddler. I cal'late she thinks it's a second *Grace Westhaver*. Waal, waal, an' what has that ol' flake bird, Lem, got t' say?" "Hear you're rushin' Carrie Dexter mighty strong these days an' that you're skipper of a vessel—Um!—Our ol' friend Morrissey hez bin home visitin' his uncle, Cap'en Asa Crawford. No end of a sport—says he's got skipper of a big four-masted coaster runnin' coal outer Boston. Cal'late he's stickin' aroun' Cap'en Asa for his money. Ol' man's kinder shaky now— was askin' after ye—Um!—Met a fine girl to Anchorville

—am rushin' her strong. When are ye comin' home?" Shorty laughed. "So Lem's settin' trawls for th' girls too. Ha, ha! Poor ol' Lem."

There was no note from Carrie, but Frank excused her on the ground that possibly she did not know where to reach him, and with a board across his knees in the *Kinsella's* cabin, he sent her a four-page letter, in which he described his trip, fare, stock, and future prospects, winding up with hopes of an early meeting and a line of crosses. "There now," he said when his correspondence had been answered. "I cal'late I've written them all th' news. I'll up now an' post these, then git th' gang out o' them prohibition rumshops an' h'ist away!"

Shorty's third trip on the *Kinsella* he was wont to call his "engagement-ring set." On this voyage he planned making enough money to buy Carrie's ring, and never did a rough and tough crowd of Nigger Cape Bluenosers, Judique men, Boston Irish, and Bonne Bay cod-haulers work so hard for the purpose of purchasing a golden circlet for a girl's dainty finger as the *Kinsella's* gang did those April days on Brown's Bank.

The cook turned them out at half-past three for breakfast; they baited up and made the early-morning set by torchlight, and at night they crawled aching and tired over the rail to dress down "full decks" of glittering, slimy fish.

From windlass aft to mainsheet bitts, the decks were littered with haddock, cod, pollock, cusk and halibut, and when the dress keelers were shipped athwart the pens, the men took their stations with ripping-knife in hand and canvas gutting-gloves on, and for hours they worked in the glare of the smoking kerosene torches, cleaning the catch and stowing it away upon the ice in the hold pens. It was hard work—very hard work—and though the men cursed the stocky, tireless young skipper who was driving them, yet they carried out the work with a certain amount of satisfaction in the thought that there was money in it.

Westhaver spared neither himself nor his men. He helped them bait up their trawls; cut bait and pitched fish, besides tending to dories and handling the schooner. He was everywhere, and the men could not help but see it. One minute he was at the wheel; a second later he would be hauling in the mainsheet; then, splashing through the pens of fish, he would be for'ard belaying the jumbo tail-rope. Another glance would find him, pitchfork in hand, heaving the dressed haddock down into the hold or out of the dress tub; and when the perspiring men at the keelers sung out for "Water!" he would be down to the tanks for'ard with a dory-jar and handing it around to the thirsty men a few seconds after the cry. The hours passed—twelve midnight, one o'clock, two o'clock—and the tired men hove the last fish below and commenced cleaning up the gurry-littered decks.

"Go below an' turn in fellers!" Westhaver would say. "Ye'll git an hour'n half o' sleep, anyway." And they would leave him on deck steering the vessel to a fresh berth; and when they turned out again later, it would be to see him red-eyed and grim astride the wheel-box.

"Don't that young dog plan on sleepin' at all when we're on th' grounds?" the men would say. "Lord Harry! I'm all in, an' I only wish it 'ud blow a gale an' keep us aboard for a spell."

"Talk about yer Tom Watson!" remarked McCallum, looking redder and more uncivilized than ever. "Py ta creat McCallum More! she's ta hardest skipper I efer saw —chust t'at! Man, put it's too pad she was not from Chudique an' Hielan'. She would pe chust grand then!"

"An' is it from that God-forsaken Judique ye'd have th' lad come?" growled a Pubnico Bluenose. "Lord save us! Ye'd be for makin' a blame 'oatmeal-scoffin' Scotchie out of a man what is worth any ten o' yer red-headed Cape Bretoners——"

"An' wull she pe for insultin' th' McCallum?" roared he of the clan. "You tam Nigger Cape push wacker——"

"Bait up!" Westhaver's voice rolled down the hatch, and the incident was forgotten.

Five days on the grounds and eight days out, the *Kin*

sella swashed past Cape Elizabeth and round Spring Point with her scuppers shooting lee and weather water across the decks, and a trip of one hundred and thirty thousand below in the pens. It was the biggest fare the *Mabel Kinsella* had ever brought into a port, and when Shorty telegraphed the stock to Captain Hoolahan that old fisherman celebrated the event in Gloucester by going on a spree for two days. And he was not the only one, for when the share checks were made out, the gang, with but the exception of Jules, who did not drink, vanished completely, and Shorty and the big Frenchman caught only occasional vistas of them reeling from one blind pig to another.

Westhaver knew that it would be at least three days before he would get his gang together again, so he left the vessel in charge of the faithful Sabot and took train for Boston.

Landing at the North Station, he immediately proceeded to a jeweller's, where he bought a magnificent diamond solitaire ring. As he gazed at the glittering bauble, he remarked to the smiling clerk who waited upon him, "Ye think that'll be a good one, eh? Good for an engagement ring, eh? I don't know nawthin' 'bout them gadgets an' I'll hev t' take *your* word for it."

The clerk laughed. "Captain," he said, "that is a mighty fine stone, and any girl, no matter who she is, would go crazy over a ring like that. Besides, in buying a diamond, you can always get value for it if the girl should go back on you."

Shorty smiled. "No fear o' that," he said confidently; and counting out the money, he put the ring into his pocket, while the salesman, who was a philosopher in his own way, wondered what there would be in a jewelry business without the tender passion and the vanity of women.

With light steps and a heart fluttering with expectant joy, Frank walked into the hospital and found himself in the same severe waiting-room. It was a Friday evening— Carrie's off night—and Frank pictured her surprise at his unexpected visit. "'Tis nigh eight weeks sence I saw her last an' I'm 'most crazy t' see th' rosy cheeks an' blue eyes of her once more. An' this ring! Wait 'til I spring that on her. Wonder how she'll take it?" And he communed with pleasant thoughts until the door opened and the matron, Mrs. Kenealy, entered.

"Why, how do you do, Captain?" she greeted him. "It's such a long time since *you've* been here."

Frank acknowledged the salutation with a confused murmur. He had expected Carrie and not the garrulous old matron.

"Miss Dexter?" he asked. "Is she around?"

"No," answered the other with some little hesitation. "She's out to-night."

Westhaver's heart fell. "Oh?" he managed to ejaculate. "Hez she gone t' visit friends? I cal'late she didn't expect me?"

The matron flopped down in a chair before replying. "Well," she said slowly, "I don't know whether she went to visit friends or not, but a cousin of hers called, and she's gone somewhere with him."

"*Him?*" exclaimed Frank. "A cousin? From Lynn, was he?"

"N—no," answered the lady doubtfully. "He is a seafaring man——"

"What was his name?"

"Morris, I think——"

Frank almost jumped in his seat. "Morris?" he growled in surprise. "A cousin? She ain't got no Morrises relations o' hers." Then a thought struck him. "'Twarn't Morrissey, was it? Surely not!"

The matron smiled. "That's the name—Morrissey—Captain Morrissey! She introduced him to me as her cousin——"

"That's a lie!" quietly returned the young fisherman. "He's absolutely no relation. An' how often hez Captain Morrissey bin callin'?"

The matron felt that she had hit upon something which was likely to prove interesting, and being a woman with a very enquiring turn of mind and with a penchant for anything approaching scandal, she made no bones about answering the perplexed Westhaver's questions. It would, at least, be something to gossip over in the dormitories.

"Well, now," she replied, "I don't rightly know. He's been in Boston for a long time—his ship is being overhauled—and I've seen him here twice or three times. Once he came on one of her on-duty nights, and they sat in here for quite a while. She's been getting flowers and presents from him, I know. She's an awfully pretty girl, y'know, and she's got lots of admirers. Some of the students who come here are 'most crazy over her, and she's an awful little flirt"—Frank grunted, while the matron continued—"and she has a host of admirers among the patients who have been here."

Shorty listened in a daze and fingered the brim of his hat nervously. "Gone out with Bob Morrissey, had she? A great hulking slob with nothing to recommend him but his bounce and fancy airs!" He gripped the hat in his fingers and almost wrenched the brim off with the emotion of the thought.

The matron watched him, and there was something of sympathy in her voice when she asked a little hesitantly, "Are you engaged to Miss Dexter, Captain? Excuse me for asking such a question, but I'm a kind of mother to all the girls here, and I generally keep tab on them as a mother should."

The young skipper's eyes fell and he blushed. "Waal— I ain't quite prepared t' say, though I cal'late some 'ud say I was. Ye see, we've known each other sence we were kids an'—yes, we kinder hev an understandin'."

The old lady nodded. "Well, Captain, I'll tell her you called. Will you be in Boston long?"

"I'll be here all day to-morrow. I was plannin' t' leave for Portland th' nex' mornin'."

Mrs. Kenealy rose as a bell rang. "I'll tell you what to do. Ring her up to-morrow morning, and if you want to go out with her to-morrow night, I'll let her off to go with you. You'll have to excuse me—that's my bell. Good night, Captain."

Outside the hospital gates Shorty crammed his hat on his head savagely. "Bob Morrissey, eh? Awful little flirt—lots o' presents an' flowers—humph!" And striding to his hotel, he went to his room and threw himself fully dressed upon the bed to commune with his thoughts. After deliberating over things, his fit of resentment passed, and he began to look at things in a more favorable light. "I'm jealous, that's what I am," he murmured. "Why shouldn't she hev a good time? I wouldn't want her t' tie herself up from havin' any fun 'cause o' me. She's only a girl, an' girls like t' hev a good time, while I'm only an ol' fish trawler what takes no pleasure out o' life but chewing th' rag with a gang o' rough-necks what swear a lot an' spin nasty yarns. Yes, I'm no judge o' women, that's evident—but what gits me, is why she sh'd call that slob Morrissey her cousin? Cal'late she's tryin' t' bluff them at th' hospital. However, I'll sleep on it, an' ring her up fust thing in th' mornin'." And, like the hearty, clear-minded young blood that he was, Frank slept like a log.

After breakfast he went into a telephone booth and rang up the hospital.

"Nurse Dexter there?"

"Who's speaking?" queried a voice at the other end of the line.

"Er—Cap'en Westhaver."

There was a silence for a few seconds, and the voice replied:

"Sorry, Captain. She's busy just now!"

"Well, when'll she be through?"

"Don't know — may be all day. Important case, y'know."

"I'll ring up again." Shorty hung the receiver up with a perplexed face.

"Didn't know them probationers hed anythin' t' do with important cases," he muttered, "onless scrubbin' floors an' washin' folks be called important cases. However, I'll take a round turn an' ring up again later."

Three times he got the hospital on the 'phone, and in each case Miss Dexter was engaged. The last time Frank began to suspect something which greatly disturbed his equanimity, and after a moment's thought he went to a telegraph office and wrote out a telegram.

"Miss Carrie Dexter,
——— Hospital,
Boston.

Can I see you to-night and where? Reply care Lomax Hotel.—FRANK."

"An' I'll prepay a reply t' make sure," he said to the operator as he handed the form over.

All afternoon he remained in the rotunda of the hotel smoking and keeping a vigilant eye upon the desk and the messenger boys who scurried around. There were bell boys with telegrams, who called various names, but no falsetto shout of "Westhaver!" greeted his ears, and the desk clerk looked hard at the stocky, sun-bronzed young man who came to him every half-hour with the question, "Any wire for Westhaver—Cap'en Westhaver?"

When five o'clock came and no answer, Frank strode down to the telegraph office and saw the operator.

"Say!" he said anxiously, "ye remember that prepaid wire I sent this afternoon? Kin ye tell ef it was delivered? Will ye find out?"

The girl rang up the suburban office and Frank loafed around impatiently awaiting her reply.

"Yes," she said. "It was delivered at four-fifteen and the messenger's slip is signed 'C. Dexter.' He said that the reply was not given to him."

"Thank ye kindly," answered Frank, and he went out into the street like a man dazed.

"What'll I do now?" he pondered. And he stood on the pavement while the hurrying crowds jostled him as they passed. "Humph!" He squared his shoulders and strode back to the hotel. "Anythin' for me yet?" he asked the clerk.

"Nothing, Cap'en!"

Frank turned away, and there was a determined gleam in his grey-blue eyes and an ominous set to lips and jaw. "Up to the hospital I'll go this night, an' know th' reason of all this."

With his determination strong in mind, he strode up to the porter's office. "Kin I see Nurse Dexter—Probationer Dexter?"

The uniformed official glanced up quickly at Westhaver's set face, gazing at him through the glass partition.

Pretending to glance at a book, he replied, "Er—Miss Dexter's engaged t'night. She's on duty——"

"That don't matter," returned Frank harshly. "Kain't I see her in th' waitin'-room for a minute?"

The man was perplexed. He was evidently making a "bluff" and Westhaver knew it—sensed it instantly with the acute perception of a jealous lover.

"Git her on yer phone!" commanded Frank, with something of the Banking-skipper ring in his voice, and the man obeyed.

"Hullo! Yes! Ward K, please! Dexter! Yes!"

Frank listened with straining ears.

"Hullo Miss Dexter? Gen'elman—Cap'en Westhaver —wants t' see you a moment. Can't, eh? Busy? Oh, ah, I see! All right!"

Shorty was at him ere he put the receiver up. "What's that? What did she say?" he snapped.

"Very busy to-night, Cap'en," answered the man glibly. "Can't possibly leave the ward to-night——"

"Is that all she said?"

"Yes, sir!"

"Humph!" Frank leaned through the wicket. "Say!" he said quietly, and fixing the man with his eyes, "is it usual for probationers to be kept on duty like this? Ain't it possible t' see them?"

The porter shook his head. "The laws of a hospital are

very strict," he said assertively. "Nurses can't do as they like, and if you want to see Miss Dexter, you'll have to come around on her off-night——"

"But th' matron, Mrs. Kenealy, told me that I c'd see her t'night ef I wanted to. She said she'd arrange t' let her off. Get her down here an' I'll talk to her. Go ahead, now!"

Impressed by the young skipper's authoritative manner, the porter pressed a button, and while Frank waited for an apparently interminable minute, during which time he scrutinized the face of every nurse who passed along the corridors, the stout, red-faced matron came over to him.

"Walk over here, Captain," she said as soon as she saw him. He followed her to a seat in the entrance hall.

"Do you really want to see Miss Dexter?" she enquired.

"Do I really want t' see her?" reiterated the other. "Good heavens, lady, I've come all th' way from Portland t' see her! I 'phoned th' hospital a dozen times an' even sent telegrams. Is this a prison?"

The matron sighed. "I don't know what to do," she said quietly and with something of motherly sympathy in her voice for the distraught young man by her side. "Miss Dexter says she don't want to see you."

"*Don't want t' see me?*" repeated Westhaver dazedly. "An' why, Mrs. Kenealy?"

The old lady evidently had something on her mind and it was distasteful to her to give it utterance. Frank sensed it, and asked abruptly, "You've got somethin' t' say, Mrs. Kenealy! Out with it!"

The matron paused for a moment and then placing her hand upon the young skipper's arm in motherly fashion, she spoke: "Captain! we women are very peculiar and you'll probably think so too after what I tell you. I saw Miss Dexter last night when she came in with that Morrissey man, and I gave it to her pretty strong. She cried a bit— in fact she cried nearly all night—but I got a pretty clear confession from her. Captain! she never really cared for you——"

Frank gave a start, and while he remained silent the matron continued in sentences which seared his soul.

"She is a very vain and selfish girl, Captain, and she lives in an atmosphere of high ideas entirely unbecoming to her station. We see a lot of that in a hospital where there are girls of high and low degree engaged in nursing, and none know their characters better than I do who have had thirty years' experience with them. When Miss Dexter came here first she seemed a very quiet and demure young woman, but being pretty, she soon became a favourite with the students and internes who come around here. They flattered her a lot and sent her chocolates and flowers until she began to develop what is vulgarly known as a 'swelled head,' and the girls did not like it. She always referred to you as her 'Captain' when you were sailing out of this port, and the girls heard no end of talk about you. Then came that paragraph in the Boston paper about that very brave thing you did last winter in bringing in that vessel, and, of course, the other girls got hold of the fact that you were an ordinary fisherman, and they made Carrie's life pretty miserable, I can assure you. It rankled in her mind quite a lot, and the others up in the dormitories did not spare her. They'd be asking her all about fish; telling her that she'd have to live on fish when she got married, and so on, and they made out that a fisherman was a degraded profession. Now, Captain, I don't think that for a minute, and many's the time I've told her so. Those who earn their bread as you do—out on the stormy waters winter and summer—are to my mind every bit as respectable and even entitled to more consideration than those who work in commonplace pursuits ashore. Our Saviour Himself showed His judgment of men when He chose for His disciples the men who hauled their nets on Galilee. However, my arguments had but little effect upon her giddy mind, and when this Morrissey man came around— and that has been the case even when you were going with her—she's been writing him and telling the girls that he was the 'Captain' to whom she was referring, and not you at all. I asked her what she meant by her conduct when she came in last night, and she practically told me that she liked Morrissey better than you. She said that if she were to marry you she'd have to live up in some lonely village in Nova Scotia, and she hated the idea intensely. Then she said that your prospects were poor and that you'd be captain of a fishing boat all your life, and in her mind that was a very poor and mean profession. She'd have to live in an atmosphere of fish and hear nothing but fish all her days, and she hates the very mention of the word. This Morrissey man will be sailing out of Boston all the time, and if she marries him she can either stay in the city here or go to sea with him, and he makes a lot of money—enough to keep her supplied with all the fancy clothes and things that she likes——"

"I c'd do that too," interrupted Frank brokenly. "She c'd live in Boston as well. I c'd git a vessel an' sail out o' 'T Dock."

The matron nodded. "Yes, that's so, but it is your profession that she objects to, and I think you'd be foolish to change it and ruin your career for a girl who is really not worth it. Captain, she is vain, extravagant, and giddy. There is nothing in her head but dress, good times, theatres, and fellows. You don't know her like I do, and I think you are too good a boy to be tied up to a girl of that sort. Forget her, my son——"

"How can I?" groaned the other. "Good God, woman! I've lived for that girl! I've toiled an' slaved an' risked men's lives for her sake! She has been the only thing what made life worth while! God! if you only knew what I've had to go through in order t' make her happy! An' now? It's all gone—all gone for nawthin'. My schemes, my hopes, an' my ambitions! All gone—all gone!" And he clasped his head in his hands with the mental agony which was consuming him.

The matron's eyes filled with tears—she, who had gazed on many travails; the last bitter moments of the dying—and she rose to go.

"Never mind, my boy. You're made of sterner stuff

than to break up over the unfaithfulness of a flighty girl. You're too good for her. Go, my son, and may God help you to forget. Good-bye!"

Like a man in a dream, Frank came away, and still in a daze he collected his clothes and took train for Portland, where he arrived early on a fine June morning.

Walking down Commercial Street, he met the runner for the ship's store people who supplied him, and the man greeted him effusively. "Your stuff's all aboard, Captain," he said. "Will ye come an' hev a touch, eh?"

"No!" growled the other savagely, and changing his mind, he said, "Yes, I will. Heave ahead!" And, for the first time since he was a boy, Frank Westhaver allowed strong drink to pass between his lips.

CHAPTER THIRTEEN

JULES HAD SHEPHERDED THE *KINSELLA'S* GANG ABOARD THE vessel without much trouble. Their money was nearly all gone, and sick and miserable with the aftermath of a "big drunk," most of them were glad to crawl into their bunks to sleep it off.

Shorty showed up around ten in the morning, and Jules noted in no little surprise that the skipper had been drinking. "Why, Frankee," he said, as his old friend lurched along the deck towards the cabin gangway, "where have you been?"

Frank took no notice of the question. "Are all th' gang aboard?" he growled instead.

"All aboard, Frankee, an' all veree dronk."

"Humph!" The young skipper grunted and swayed slightly on his feet, while his old dory-mate regarded him with eyes of consternation.

"Why—what's de matter, Frankee? Ain't you well?"

Shorty laughed—a harsh, grating laugh. "Oh, well enough, Sabot! Well enough!"

The other nodded doubtfully, and reaching into his pocket produced a letter. "Here's somet'ing which come for you after you left for Boston."

Frank grabbed at it, and scanning the address on the envelope, he gave a start of surprise. "From Carrie?" he murmured thickly. "Le's see what she has t' say." He sat upon the cabin-house and read it. It wasn't a long communication, but if he had any doubt of her feelings towards him before, the letter and subsequent events dissipated any hopes he might have entertained.

"Dear Frank"—it ran—"In order to save you and me

a lot of pain and trouble I'm writing this to make clear to you the impossibility of my ever becoming your wife. I have been anylising my feelings, and I find that I do not love you, though I like you very much. Do not come to the Hospital again. I am sorry this has to be, but hope you will forget and forgive. Beleive me always your friend—
Caroline Dexter."

"Huh," growled Frank when he had read it. " 'Anylizin' ' her feelin's—look how she spells 'analysing' an' 'believe'! Th' wench! Tcha!" And with a gesture of disgust, he crumpled the letter up and threw it on the deck.

When he had clattered below, the astonished Jules picked the note up to find out what it had to do with Shorty's complete change of manner, and though he could scarcely read it, yet he understood the full significance of the communication.

"Poor Frankee!" he said with a sigh as he hove the letter over the side. *"Mon pauvre ami*—an' I was afraid so—veree mooch afraid. Dat girl she was no good. Frankee too good for her!"

There were sounds of protest emanating from the gloom of the cabin and Jules could hear Shorty cursing. "Come out-a my bunk, you scurvy swine!" he was saying. "Come on! Heave out, th' lot o' ye, an' git under way! D'ye hear? All out an' git under way!"

Jules shook his head. "Frankee's bit off, I'm afraid. Bad t'ing to get outside to-day. Blowin' veree hard outside."

The skipper's head appeared above the companion. "Go for'ard, Sabot, an' turn th' gang out t' make sail. Git her down to the end o' th' dock."

Sabot, whatever his thoughts were, never disregarded an order of Frank's, and he gave the shout down the fo'c'sle scuttle. As may be surmised, there was very little heed given to the command—a chorus of stertorous snores and groans being the only evidence of the tenancy of the tiers of bunks. "D'ye hear me!" bawled Jules. "Skipper says to git under way! Turn out!"

Frank's savage face appeared in the scuttle. "Are they turnin' out, Sabot? No? By the ol' Judas! I'll turn them out!" And jumping down into the gloomy apartment, he started in hauling the intoxicated men out of the bunks and rolling them out on floor or locker. Have you noticed a telephone switch-board operator at work? Well, Shorty, savage, dangerous in his present state of mind, and half-drunk himself, pulled the men out just as a switch-board girl would pull out a succession of plugs, and inside of a minute the gang were extricating themselves from their quilts and blankets and cursing the whims of the skipper in the lurid and flowery oaths peculiar to the rougher type of deep-sea fishermen.

When they emerged on deck—each man a living paradox to the efficacy of the Prohibition Laws of the State of Maine—Frank bullied them into warping the schooner down to the tongue of the wharf, and sullenly they laid hold of the hawsers and walked the schooner down the dock. A small tow-boat puffed up, and the man in her pilot-house hailed, "Give ye a pull outside? Only three dollars, Cap!"

"Naw!" growled Frank. "Ef I couldn't git out o' this harbour 'thout a tug I'd give up fishin'. Sheer off now! I don't want ye t' scrape th' paint off my vessel's top-sides with yer ol' steam-pot!"

The tow-boat skipper gave a sarcastic laugh. "Too much Portland rum," he murmured. "Give him a wipe for his jaw." And with some skilful work on his part he turned his tug short around and managed to give the *Kinsella* a bang with his stern as he did so.

"You clumsy swab!" bawled Shorty, and he was about to say something more when his better nature predominated for an instant and he let the incident pass.

They hoisted the four lowers and stood out through the Peak's Island channel, and as soon as the sails were jigged and sheeted to the skipper's critical satisfaction the gang hove the coiled halliards over the pins and retired below to their bunks again.

Frank at the wheel and Jules clearing up the gear were the only two on deck when the schooner passed out by Cape Elizabeth, and when the latter came aft he spoke. "'Nother hard tam, Frankee. 'Spose we steer de vessel all day an' all night, you'n me. Blow lak hell off-shore wit' dis sout'-westerly win'——"

The skipper interrupted him with a grunt. "I don't care two pins whether they come up for their watches or not. Thar's a good breeze a-blowin' an' I'll sober them all up afore I'm through."

The big Frenchman nodded slowly and gazed furtively at the young skipper, who, dressed in his shore clothes with collar, tie, and Derby hat on, sat on the wheel-box and steered. His face was flushed, and there was a hard look in his grey-blue eyes—an expression which Jules did not like to see.

Eh—ah—wat's de matter wit' you dis mornin', Frankee?" asked the other after a pause.

Frank looked up and laughed in an absent manner. It was another of the strident laughs which had jarred on the Frenchman's ear earlier in the day. "Matter?" reiterated Shorty. "Why, nawthin's th' matter. Why? What d'ye think's th' matter, anyway?"

The other played with a bait-knife and cut a notch in the bait-board before he replied. Frank's present state of mind was one which resented sympathy—Jules could see that in his eyes. "Dat Dexter girl?" began he.

"Aye? That Dexter girl? What about her?"

"She play mean trick on you? She turn you down?"

The young skipper's mouth hardened. He knew that Jules had been his confidant, and to his memory at that moment came a recollection of the Frenchman's opinion of Carrie Dexter. Westhaver was very sensitive. He had worshipped an idol with all the strength of his strong nature, and it had proved false. Well! He wished to keep his troubles to himself and brood over them alone. He wanted no sympathy. He had been a fool, he knew that, but he resented others thinking so. No, not even Jules, and when he thought over what his old dory-mate did know about his affairs he mentally castigated himself for having been so free with his confidences. Jules had listened to his rapturous ambitions and his hopes and Jules would be sure to sympathize, and sympathy of the kind he abhorred—what all wilful men abhor—that of the "Poor fellow! I told you so!" variety, was what he feared that his friend would give utterance to. When he replied, there was an aggressive, resentful ring in his voice.

"Suppose you mind your own business, Jules, an' I'll mind mine!"

The Frenchman's swarthy face reddened. "All right, sir!" he said quietly, and walked away for'ard.

Frank regretted his answer almost as soon as he had said it, but the liquor he had consumed and the chaos of spite, injured pride, and unrequited love which possessed his brain swamped his better nature under, and he came to look upon Jules's enquiries as an impertinent interference into his affairs.

When Ram Island Ledge passed on the port quarter the schooner began to feel the wind and to lurch and lift to the rising off-shore sea. It was blowing a sou'-west gale, but the schooner, running before it, did not feel the real weight of the breeze until they left Sequin astern. The day was sunny with a clear blue sky flecked with fleecy clouds, and under the impetus of the sou'-wester the sea was breaking into foam-capped crests which hissed, roared, and sparkled in the sunlight. Here was blue water in all its glory! Sunshine, blue sky, clouds, and a rip-roaring breeze. The sea—that huge, uncontrollable element which mirrors the skies and stirs to the lash of the wind—had absorbed the azure of the firmament above, and the great undulations reared their serried tops, which gleamed evanescently emerald with the sun-glare behind, and curling, broke into tons of seething foam, which showed dazzling white against the background of dark blue ocean. The sprays, torn from the ragged wavetops by the lick of the breeze, glittered like myriad diamonds in the solar effulgence and slashed across the deck of the plunging schooner like fine rain until everything dripped water.

The little vessel herself became as a creature of the sea. She leaped the hills and dales of wind-harried brine with sails full and bellying to the wind, and under her sharp clipper bows stormed and creamed a welter of white water which surged to the knightheads as she drove down the declivities into the troughs of the waves. The anchor-stock tore up a furrow of spray which flared over the rail in miniature rainbows and drenched the straining jibs. From the lee bow raced a tossing, hissing chaos of foam which seemed to stream overhead as the vessel rolled her lee rail under, and while the eye drank in the rugged grandeur of this storming along a veritable pæan of the sea was sung in the sonorous roaring of the fighting water, the hissing of the froth, the low thunder of the wind in the sails, and the Æolian minstrelsy of the breeze in the tautened rigging. It was a day expressed beautifully in the tenor of Thomas Fleming Day's song of the "Trade Wind":

> How I laugh when a wave leaps over the head,
> And the jibs through the spray-bow shine,
> While an acre of foam is scattered and spread,
> As she shoulders and tosses the brine.

And with the glory of it all— the supreme freedom and grandeur of Old Ocean in one of her loveliest and most impressive moods—the gallant little schooner, like a faithful horse, responded to the touch of a man who saw no beauty in the day—a man who looked upon life through dark glasses and felt in the tumult of wind and sea but a reflection of the war in his soul.

"Lay aft here, Jules, an' take th' wheel!" he growled to the figure leaning over the dories. The Frenchman obeyed, while the other dropped below into the cabin.

Glancing around the dirt-littered floor—the broken bottle glass, the miscellaneous heaps of clothing scattered about, and the snoring figures in the bunks—Westhaver felt no feeling of disgust. No, they were happy, the dogs!

They had nothing to worry them, and if drink could render such oblivion to torment of mind, well there were some uses for drink. So he reasoned, and, proceeding to his berth, he produced a bottle and drank.

When he came on deck later Jules saw what he had been doing, and he was troubled. "You been drinkin', Frankee," he said with something of reproach in the tone of his voice.

"Waal, what ef I have?" growled the other. "Cal'late it don't need bother you any."

The big Frenchman took no notice, but continued as if he had not heard. "Will you put de log over now?" he said. "Dere's Monhegan astern."

"I'll put it over when I'm good an' ready," snapped the skipper, lounging against the house and looking at the tossing wake.

Jules took no notice again.

"Ain't you goin' to set de course, Frankee?" he asked after a lengthy pause. "Eas'-by-sout'-half-sout' ain't de course for de grounds."

Westhaver turned around savagely. "Gimme that wheel, you!" he rasped out. "An' get away t' blaze-an'-gone out o' this. I'm runnin' this vessel—not you!"

The Frenchman made no effort to relinquish the spokes. Westhaver's face went white. "Did ye hear me?"

"Yes, Frankee!"

"Damn yer eyes! Don't Frankee me! Gimme th' wheel!" And he made to elbow Jules off the wheel-box, but the latter refused to be budged from his place.

"Blast you!" Frank exerted his strength, and tore the wheel out of the big Frenchman's grasp, and the latter in surprise at his old comrade's childishness stood to one side regarding the surly look on his face.

"Who are ye star-gazin' at, you big gawk?" snapped Westhaver.

Jules strode forward, and laying his hand upon the skipper's shoulder, he said gently, "Frank, go below, ol' man, an' let me take her. You ain't veree well."

In answer, the other, puffed up with rage and blind to

everything right and reasonable, knocked the Frenchman's hand off his shoulder and snarled, "Git away an' leave me alone!"

Jules hesitated for a moment, and then grasped a spoke of the wheel. "Frank!" he commanded. "Go below!"

With a growl of suppressed fury, Westhaver let the wheel go and drove his fist into his old dory-mate's chest. Taken unawares by the unexpectedness of the blow, Jules staggered back, his heels fetched up against the wash-board of the cabin companion-way, and he fell head first down the brass-shod steps.

"Now, maybe, ye'll mind yer own business!" And Westhaver grasped the wheel again and steered the schooner on her plunging course without giving his action a moment's thought.

In his fall Jules had struck his head on a corner of the stove, and for a minute he lay half-stunned. Then he got up and sat down upon a locker thinking, until a trickle of blood ran down his face.

"Huh! Mus' have cut myself—uh? Dat feller ees crazy sure! But he no treat me right for ol' doree-mate. I'll speak to him." And with a scowl on his dark features he ascended the ladder and faced the skipper.

Westhaver noticed the blood on his face and gave a perceptible start, but said nothing. Jules looked hard at him for a few seconds and spoke quietly—very quietly. "Frankee, you hit me! Struck your ol' doree-mate! I t'ink of dat, or I would break you up. I big 'nough to t'rash you, but you're my fr'en' still. Steer de vessel yourself—I leave you w'en we get to port." And with the other glaring balefully at him for the threats, Jules went below and turned into his bunk.

With the fall of night the wind came away stronger and the westering sun gilded a huge expanse of tumbling, wind-tossed sea. Westhaver, dressed in his shore clothes, was still at the wheel. He had left it but for a moment to go below in the cabin and bring up his bottle of whisky, and with it sticking out of his coat pocket, he sat astride the wheel-box and steered the rearing schooner. The sun, in a great ball of fire, dropped below the serrated sea-line; the sky flushed from nadir to zenith in delicately blended tints from the crimson of the west, the orange and gold of the mid-altitude to the night azure of the zenith and the starlit dark of the eastern heavens. It was a night for the gods! Nature's painting of a June sunset in all the gorgeous colours and tints of her incomparable palette; the twinkling, diamond-like stars set in the deep nocturnal blue of the firmament overhead and to the east, and the blackness of the raging waters, wind-hounded and breaking in livid crests which caught the sanguinary glare and appeared like foaming waves of blood.

Drenched in the spray which slashed across the decks, and drinking from the bottle at intervals, the lone man at the spokes of the *Kinsella's* wheel found a fit setting for his torment of soul in the wildness of the night, and as he strained at the wheel, wild-eyed, hatless, and with hair tossing in the wind he roared strange songs which were snatched up by the breeze. He had drunk so much of the vile Kentucky whisky by now that he was maddened with it—mad, reckless, and defiant, and Jules, offended and sulky, lay in his bunk below and sensed the wilder plunges of the straining vessel and listened to the snatches of song which came from the skipper.

"Morrissey, eh? Morrissey—Bob Morrissey—he's th' lucky man! Ha! ha!" And he broke off to sing.

> "Oh, th' carts will creak in th' lanes to-night,
> An' th' girls will dance to th' band.
> But wo'll be out with th' sails to fist,
> An' th' tops'l sheets to hand!"

"Go it—you ol' peddler! Slam your ol' horn inter them greybacks! Drive, you ol' barge, or I'll tear th' patch off ye! Ha! ha!

BLUE WATER

> Hilo town is far away!
> John's gone to Hilo!
> Hilo town is in Haw-way!
> 'Way down Santy Anna!
> 'Way down—'way down, I tell you!
> John's gone—Hilo!
> 'Way down—you Mobile hoosier!
> 'Way down Santy Anna!"

Shouting his roistering old sea chanteys—picked up in his boyhood days from the sing-songs and concerts of the Bay Shore, where men who had learned them in packet ship and Cape Horner were wont to croak their weird melodies for the edification of the stay-at-homes—he talked to himself and felt a keen delight in the manner in which the brave little vessel was swooping over the shouting seas. There was something in it which appealed to him, and when the tide began to back against the wind and the schooner commenced wilder antics he roared in pleasure at the sight. Crash! The little craft staggered against a tide-backed surge, and with the weight of the wind behind her she burst the solid water into a vast cloud of harmless spray which drenched the laughing and singing madman at the wheel.

"Morrissey, eh? God, I wish I had ye here, you dog! Ha, ha! The infernal cat that she was——

> Oh, th' hog-eye men are all th' go,
> When they come down to San Francis-co!
> Now, who's bin here sence I bin gone——
> Oh, a railroad nigger with his sea-boots on——
> A hog-eye railroad nigger with his hog-eye.
> Row th' boat ashore with a hog-eye oh!
> For she wants her hog-eye man!

Ha, ha! That's a good one! Up she goes! Look out!" Crash! Over the quarter slammed a sea which filled the whole after-part of her. Westhaver hung to the spokes with the water swirling up to his knees, and as it drained off over the taffrail as she lifted to the next wave he laughed in savage glee.

"'On th' first of August, bullies, we did set sail,
An' th' wind from th' no'th'ard was blowin' a gale.
To Sable Island our vessel did steer,
With Cap'en John Viver in th' *Spencer F. Beer* . . .

Ha! Tide's on th' turn. Up! Oh!" Crash! the *Kinsella's* whole bow, windlass, and fo'c'sle hatch went under a frothing surge, the great mainsail strained at the sheet, the rigging stretched and creaked with the dead weight of water resisting the push of the gale in the canvas, and hissing and creaming, the schooner stormed her bows clear and shook the water from her like an amphibious animal. Then came another plunge even worse than the previous one, and the drunks in the fo'c'sle, drenched by the chilly brine which poured down on them, began to wake up.

"What th' hell is he doin'? Who's at th' wheel?" growled someone.

"Go'n hev a squint." A man hauled himself out of his bunk, stretched himself with a yawn, and clambered up the ladder. Crash! Swish! A sea met him as he peered out through the half-drawn slide and in a torrent of chilly brine he was driven into the fo'c'sle again.

"Holy Trawler! It's blowin' ol' blazes outside!" he growled as he wrung the water out of his soaked trousers. Crash! Another boarding sea which thumped thunderously upon the deck above and streamed down scuttle, ventilator, and through the cracks where foremast and pawl-post came through the deck.

"Py ta Cross o' Chrinahanish!" grunted McCallum, rolling out of his bunk. "She's runnin' ta vessel under, so she is." The men began to turn out, and staggering and slipping around the drenched forecastle, they changed their clothes for their sea toggery and oiled up, while the schooner 'scended and swamped herself in the tide-whipped sea.

"Feel her tremblin', fellers? Lord, he's got th' whole patch on her!"

They lolled on the lockers, oilskin-clad and waiting for the call which they knew must come soon. In such a breeze and sea she should be down to her foresail—whole four lowers was too much for a vessel like the *Mabel Kinsella,* and the manner in which her staunch timbers were creaking and groaning told of the awful strain to which she was being subjected.

"Wonder why th' skipper ain't given us a call?" shouted someone above the din. "Never knew him t' carry sail like this afore——"

Thump! The vessel staggered with a trembling in every plank and beam; the men jumped to their feet in apprehension, and then, with a sullen roaring above their heads, the forecastle seemed to turn upside-down. The lamps flared and went out. Men were flung bodily to leeward, and while the sea poured down upon them, they struggled, yelled, and cursed in their fright.

"God Almighty!" screamed a man. "She's runnin' herself under! Aft ye git an' make th' skipper take th' mains'l in! He must be crazy!"

McCallum leaped up the ladder and glanced out. He was only up a few seconds before he slammed the slide and jumped below again. Crash! Another sea. The men cannoned against one another in the Stygian darkness, and all rolled in a heap to leeward. "Skipper's gone daft!" bawled McCallum. "Ta tories are gone from off ta deck——"

"Who's at th' wheel? Who's at th' wheel——?"

"All out, fellers! We'll go aft an' see what's th' matter.—Holy sailor! be careful or we'll be washed off!"

Westhaver was still at the wheel, talking and singing to himself, and when he saw the men scrambling along the swept decks—the dories had been carried away—he laughed and shouted, "Lord Harry! I knew I c'd bring ye out! I'm soberin' ye, my bullies—— Eh? What d'ye want aft here?"

"Cal'late ye sh'd be takin' th' sail off'n her. It's hell down for'ard!" The man had to shout into his ear to make himself heard, and Shorty pushed him away.

"Clear out," he shouted aggressively. "I'm handlin' her, an' I'll take in sail when I feel like it." And taking the bottle from his pocket with one hand, he drew the cork with his teeth and indulged in a nip before the astonished men congregated aft.

"So t'at's what iss ta matter," said McCallum. "She's peen trinkin', so she has——"

"Git below, th' lot o' ye!" The stocky figure at the wheel bawled the command, and the men hesitated for an instant and went down into the cabin.

"She's crazy trunk!" said McCallum. "She'll pe for runnin' ta vessel under wae aal this sail on her—Chules! what iss ta matter with ta skipper hersel'?"

The Frenchman, lying in his bunk, shook his head. "I don't know an' I don't care!"

"But we care!" shouted a man. "Lord Harry! I ain't a-goin' t' be drowned by no crazy skipper, an' I cal'late we'll jest hev t' take charge o' th' vessel ourselves."

And while the crowd below were arguing over the question, Westhaver's madness began to pass off and he began to awake to a realization of what he was doing. He was feeling the cold now, and he shivered in his dripping clothes. Another nip would warm him, and he reached for the bottle. Oh, how his head throbbed! The wind in the rigging sang weird tunes to his ears—tunes which set his brain whirling like the incantations of the savage. His body felt like ice, but his head burned like fire, and his whole being seemed to be rocking and wheeling in space. The stars were sweeping past him in great circles. What was it that was dragging the arms off him? Oh, yes! There he was hanging on to the tail of a comet—was it a comet?—and they went so fast that everything roared in his ears and the stars flashed past with express speed. What a curious thing! He felt that the strain of holding on was becoming too much. He couldn't hold on any longer—it was killing him. He held his breath and let go. Instantly there came a great peace to his soul. His head cooled, and when the mist cleared from his eyes he was at the wheel of a plunging, storming schooner. What vessel was it? Not the *Kinsella*—it was too big a vessel for that, and—most curious of all—it was snowing. Snowing on a June night in the Bay of Fundy! And it was blowing hard too—very hard. Lord! what a night—black, howling, and thick of snow, which made the sea appear blacker against the grey-white of the sky. It was hard steering, but someone—huge, and clad in gleaming oilskins—was standing by the wheel. Who was that? Not Jules, nor McCallum, nor Simms. Who then? Westhaver could feel the snowflakes melting on his face, yet he didn't feel the cold. The big figure alongside of him turned and laid his hands on the spokes of the wheel. Frank could feel his strength, but he was putting the wheel hard down? He didn't want the vessel to come up. "Keep her off!" he yelled savagely, and he strained at the spokes with all his strength. The stranger appeared not to hear him. And Frank felt the wheel being dragged away from him. Damn the man! What did he mean? In a burst of fury he laid all his weight on the gear, and the pull of the other was arrested. Then he turned and gazed into Frank's face. It was but a fleeting glance, but the young skipper gazed under the other's dripping sou'-wester into eyes which shone into his without malice. It was a dead-white face, but the expression in mouth and eyes was of tenderness and sympathy. Who was he? What did he mean? Frank asked himself these questions, conscious that the wheel was being dragged out of his hands in spite of his resistance. "Speak! speak!" cried Westhaver. "What is the matter?" Still hanging on to the spokes, his arms were being hauled over by the fearful strength of the stranger; he could feel the strain of his muscles, and the joints cracked. The other was too strong for him. He would have to let go! He did so, and as the wheel spun to the pull of the oilskinned figure, a voice roared in Shorty's ear:

"*Sable Island North-East Bar—an' dead ahead!*"

The words sang in the young skipper's brain, and a great flood of recollection swamped him all of a sudden. "Sable Island No'th-East Bar?" The *Grace Westhaver* ... his father. . . .

"Lord God! there's th' Lurcher dead ahead!"

Someone screamed the intelligence, and Frank swung the helm hard down. A chaos of seething sea broke over him as the vessel swept up into the wind; he felt something give inside his chest; men were shouting and yelling in the roar of the storm. He heard himself calmly giving orders to a great bulk standing alongside him. "Mainsheet! Scandalize yer mains'l—lower away yer peak!" Another sea burst over him, and when it drained off he was blind—stone blind. He groped for a hold somewhere. There came a thunderous slattering to his ears, shouts and curses, then a fearful crash. He saw a myriad of stars dancing in blackness, and then came forgetfulness.

. . . .

When consciousness returned to him again he found himself lying in a swash of water on the lee side of the cabin floor. The vessel was bucking and plunging in a fearful manner; spray was splashing across the deck above his head, and above the whine and snore of wind and sea he could hear the shouts of the men on deck. As recollection returned to him, he picked himself up painfully. One of his arms seemed useless—he was afraid it was broken—and he almost screamed with the grinding pain in shoulder and chest. "I'm stove up," he muttered between set teeth, and white-faced and dishevelled he dropped upon a lee locker.

"For God Almighty's sake, get the skipper up here!" shouted someone. "Thar's nawthin' but white water an' breakers all 'round this hell-roarin' pond."

Westhaver heard, and crawled with gasps of agony to the companion. He was sober now, and as he clutched the gangway bulkhead with his right hand, he shouted up the open hatch into the square of star-sprinkled darkness, "Come below here an' gimme a hand!"

McCallum and another man stepped over the washboard.

"Carry me up—so! Lord Harry! what pain! Easy now—oh! All right, I'll stand in here. Where's th' mains'l?"

"Gone!" roared a man. "Went with th' blame' mast

a while ago—when ye put th' brute about. She's under fores'l now. For th' Lord's sake, tell us what t' do. Thar's nawthin' but breakers all 'round, an' we've jibed her over twice——''

Westhaver glanced around. A terrible sea was running and tossing in livid, foaming crests, and the schooner, with mainmast gone, was plunging and burying her bows in the seething turmoil.

"Where's th' Lightship?" queried Frank.

"'Bout two miles t' wind'ard thar'—sou'-west from here." Westhaver did some rapid thinking. "We're in th' shoal water, I cal'late, an' between th' one'n half an' five-fathom spots—thar's breakers on either side of us——" Aloud he spoke. "How's she headin' now?"

Jules's voice answered, "East-no'th-east!"

With excruciating pain at every articulation, he spoke to the man standing by him. "Jibe her over carefully—an' head her—south-east-half-east. D'ye hear?—south-east-half-east—an' hold on that course 'til ye git Cape Forchu abeam. Be careful in jibin' or ye'll jump th' foremast out o' her. Oh, Lord, how my side pains!"

The jibing tackles were hooked into the foreboom, and on the hail from for'ard Jules put the helm up. Crash! The boom flew over and fetched up against the tackles with a fearful shock, and the men gathered in the sea-swept waist looked anxiously at the mast.

"What a wonder it didn't go," muttered Frank, and when the gang came aft, he called to them. "Git a hawser fast to the forem'sthead an' set it up well aft on th' starboard side here with th' boom tackle——"

"Breakers ahead!" The men jumped, and Jules shouted to the skipper.

"All right—don't worry," cried Frank. "That's jest a tide rip. We're past the real shoal spot—ye kin hear th' whistlin' buoy well t' wind'ard. Keep her on that course, an' set up that preventer backstay. Let me know when Yarmouth Cape shows up."

He limped painfully down the ladder just as the vessel

made a wild plunge in the rip; a frightful pain shot through his side, and with a groan he dropped to the floor and slid like a log into the water and debris to leeward. "Heavens! what pain I'm in," he murmured, and, afraid to move, he lay in the sluicing water until Jules, exhausted with his spell at the wheel, came below and found him groaning.

"*Mon pauvre ami!*" The big Frenchman came over to him, and, lifting the limp body of the skipper as gently as he would a sleeping child, he laid him into his bunk.

"Oh, Frankee, Frankee," he said with heartfelt commiseration in the tone of his voice. "'Tis a bitter day an' night you've been spend dis day——"

Frank moaned. "Oh, Jules—my ol' dory-mate—get some pillows an' wedge me in. Git a doctor aboard as soon's ye git in. I'm all stove up, an' th' pain's killin' me every time she rolls—Ah!" And the broken body, taxed to the limit of human endurance, collapsed in a dead faint.

CHAPTER FOURTEEN

"WHAT A WONDERFUL CONSTITUTION THE MAN must have!" It was the doctor who was speaking. His collar-bone is fractured; three of his ribs and his arm broken in two places—and you say he was able to attend to his duties? Well, well! How did it happen?"

Jules answered, "A sea hove him down on de wheel an' de spokes mus' have hit him in de chest, den when de mainm'st go, it fall over de quarter an' knock him to de deck. I cal'late he broke shoulder an' arm dat way——"

"Does he drink?"

"No, sir."

"Well, I smell liquor on him."

"Dat's w'at I give him when he faint," lied Jules.

"Oh, ah." The doctor nodded and opened his instrument-case. "Can you get me some hot water and a towel? Get me some small pieces of wood for splints to set his arm—then he'll be in shape to go ashore to the hospital."

Frank listened with closed eyes, and when the doctor ripped the wet clothes off him and commenced to set the broken bones he fainted again. When he awoke to full possession of his faculties he found himself between snow-white sheets and in an atmosphere which seemed strangely familiar. His body seemed to be unusually stiff and rigid, and when he made a movement it was accompanied by a slight twinge of pain. Then recollection came to him, and his eyes roved around the plainly furnished room.

"Oh, yes . . . th' smell . . . hospital," he murmured. "I'm all bandaged up. Wonder what I broke . . . arm, I cal'late." There was a swish of skirts, and a young woman in nurse's uniform came over to him. "How do you feel now, sir?"

"Not bad—not bad," replied Frank with a wan smile. "What's all my damages?"

The nurse laughed. "Oh, nothing very much, Captain. Broke an arm or so. We'll soon have you up and about. The doctor will be here soon, so let me fix you up a bit. So! That's all right now."

The doctor came, made his examination, expressed himself satisfied and was about to leave when the nurse stopped him. "Oh, doctor! There's a number of fishermen from that dismasted vessel off there who've been around wanting to see him. I wouldn't let them in until you gave me instructions——"

The man of medicine was about to make a negative answer, when Westhaver called him. "Doctor! Let them come up. I want t' see them, an' I cal'late it ain't a-goin' t' hurt me any to have a talk with my gang——"

"Well, now, Captain, I'm not so sure about that. It won't hurt your arm, but it might not do your other injuries any good. Quiet, rest, and perfect stillness are essential to your quick recovery, but I'll let them come for a few minutes. Nurse, see that he doesn't talk too much."

For over an hour he lay and watched the play of the shadows on the wall. A few flies buzzed around the room, but everything was quiet save for the occasional blast of a tow-boat's whistle in the harbour outside. Then came a shuffling of heavily booted feet at the door, and the nurse entered followed by McCallum, Simms, and a couple more of the *Kinsella's* gang.

"Here's some people to see you, Captain," said the nurse. "There's about a dozen more outside, but I would only let four come up."

"An' how wull she pe feelin' to-day, skipper?" The great red head of McCallum bent over him.

"Not so bad, Mac. Not so bad. How's everything?"

"Aal right, skipper. Ta vessel's lyin' snug in ta back channel an' she's no sae pad after aal. She'll pe needin' a new mainmast an' new dories. Ta mains'l an' poom an' ta gaft was picked up this mornin' py a shore fisherman py Port Maitland, ant Chules has claimed it."

Glancing around at the nurse, who was gazing out the window, the Judiquer leaned over and whispered: "I hev a pottle of ta real whusky in ma pocket. If ye wull pe for havin' a wee tram——?"

A look of fear passed across Frank's face. "No, no, Mac! My God, no! I'll never drink liquor again after what I've come through——"

McCallum nodded sagely. "Maype yoursel' wull pe right, skipper—chust so, an' I'm not offented at aal, at aal. It is goot for some folks an' fery pad for others."

"Look now, Mac," said Frank. "I'll 'most likely be hauled up here for some time, an' th' *Kinsella* needs a new mast an' other gear. What kin I do for you fellows? Ye've no trip to draw on, an' it's my fault that you're stranded over here——"

"It's all fixed up, skipper," interrupted Simms. "Jules has fixed it all up. He's sent up to Long Cove for yer uncle, an' he's comin' down by to-morrer's train from Anchorville. We'll live aboard th' vessel as long as th' cook an' th' stores hang out, so don't worry. Jules has got th' mains'l an' booms, an' he's ordered a new mainm'st——"

"Jules—ordered—a—new—mast?" Westhaver spoke in slow surprise. "Where is he now?"

"I dunno," answered the Newfoundlander. "He went ashore this mornin' all spruced up. Cal'late he's maybe gone up to th' Bay Shore——"

"Without comin' t' see me?" There was a plaintive note in Frank's voice, and as he thought of the events of the previous day, of the way in which he had treated his old dory-mate, of striking him . . . Jules's words as he stood before him with the blood trickling down his head, "Steer de vessel yourself. . . . I leave you when we get to port!" came to his mind. . . . Well, he could hardly blame him for not coming.

"What happened outside thar'?" asked the injured

man. "I have nawthin' but a jumble a-runnin' in my head about it. I kin remember seein' th' Lurcher Shoal breakin' an' th' Lightship——"

"Then you guv a yell what brought us all on deck, an' ye were heavin' th' wheel hard down when she shipped a sea which threw ye on th' spokes. We were heavin' in on th' mainsheet, an' you sings out t' scandalize th' mains'l. She started slattin' in that breeze, an' th' sea sluggin' over her somethin' savage; we had a blaze's own job t' stand on deck. We lowered away on th' peak halliards an' was a-h'istin' up when she guv a whoop of a slat an' parts th' spring stay—then she jest comes tumblin' down an' th' boom hits you at th' wheel. Jules an' Mac here lugs you from under th' wreckage an' lays you down in th' cabin, an' we gits busy an' cuts th' gear adrift. After that, we started runnin' in among th' breakers an' rips, which blame near scared us t' death until you comes up an' gits us out o' them again. Lord Harry! I never thought we come out o' that place alive. Th' place was breakin' water for miles in that sou'-wester . . . hell of a night we had.— Excuse me, miss." The nurse had come forward.

"Now, men, you must go," she said; and promising to call on the morrow, they left Frank alone with his thoughts.

If ever a man received a castigation from his own conscience, it was Westhaver, and his mental flagellation gave him more pain than did his injuries. Luckily he was spared the additional lash of a wounded heart. The ordeal he had gone through had somehow put the affair in a different light, and his mind ceased to be haunted with disturbing visions of the girl who had driven him to the actions of his madness. She was a memory of the past—an unpleasant memory, but one, which, like a nightmarish dream, could easily be dismissed from recollection. No! He did not care about her now. The scales had fallen from his eyes and he had become critical—cruelly so—and her sayings and actions he had analysed mentally until he had weighed her in the balance and found her wanting. He had known her for many years, and yet, upon cool reflection, he began to doubt the fact that he had really loved her. He had longed to possess, yet having possession he was not sure that he would have been entirely satisfied. It would be like a man who coveted a jewel, and when he finally owned it would put it away in a case without giving it a further thought. It was not love which had prompted him in his mad rage, but rather a sense of wounded pride at the success of a rival—a realization of having failed in his efforts to own and control, and being a strong, self-willed man, he was uncontrollable in his frenzy at failure. So he had reasoned—even while he was at the wheel of the schooner —and mature reflection had purged his mind. But it was the madness of his actions which seared his soul; and as he thought of the gamble with Death, the near sacrifice of twenty-one souls upon the altar of his insensate fury, he trembled and broke into a sweat of fear. The roar of the hungry breakers sounded in his ears; the scream of the wind mingled with it, and a vision of the galehounded vessel, staggering, plunging, and storming through that awful inferno of shoal water, wind and tide whipped, flashed persistently through his mental retrospection. *What if he had struck?* The thought almost caused him to groan with the agony of the conception, and a strange illusion haunted him. *Who was the oilskinned man at the wheel of the "Kinsella" that night?* The man who had torn the spokes from his grasp and gazed at him with eyes of tender commiseration, and who seemed to have exercised a power over him which saved him from striking the Shoal? *"Sable Island North-East Bar dead ahead!"* Frank shivered. He knew now, and the thought frightened him. The father had come to warn the son—to save him from himself; and as he turned it over in his mind he felt all the terror and reverence for the supernatural. And yet why should he be afraid? The child is not afraid of the mother who lifts it from the floor to which it has fallen. Why should he be afraid of the spirit of his father?

In their sequence came other disturbing reflections. Jules! The man who had been his shadow for years; who had been his confidant and his dearest friend. Jules, who had advanced him money for the furtherance of his ambitions, and who was content to follow him without thinking of himself. Jules, who had proved sterling and of the best—true-hearted, trustworthy, and honest. How had he treated him? He had not been so drunk but what he remembered, and memory at his callous conduct made him weep bitter tears into his pillow. He would repay him as soon as he got better—if it were not too late. Then came the thought of his gang—the rough and tough, but staunch and warm-hearted fellows who had thrown in their fortunes with his. What had he done for them? Dragged them out to sea in a gale of wind and would have thrown their lives away in his blind rage had not a greater Power intervened and saved him from being a wholesale murderer. *Murderer!* What an awful conception! And yet they forgave him without a murmur; sympathized with him, and wished him well. And he had risked their lives but the night before and deprived them of a possible livelihood for a month at least! And Hoolahan! What about him? Had he not played fast and loose with the old man's property and lost him money? The vessel was only insured under a policy which covered total loss only, and a new spar and dories would have to come out of his and Westhaver's pocket—each in his proportionate share. Truly, in his review of events the young fishing skipper was flayed by conscience; conscience which touched him on the raw, and seared his soul until the scalding tears dropped from his eyes at the recollections of his ungratefulness. But he would pay it all back. He was blind, blind, blind, but he had tried himself before the harshest of all judges and had promised to atone.

The golden glory of the sunset was flooding the room when he became aware of someone entering. The nurse came over and looked down upon him. "Yes, he's awake. Some people to see you, Captain." And he turned his eyes to look up at Jules and Miss Denton!

"Miss Denton! Sabot!" he gasped in delighted surprise.

"How—how did you know I was here?"

Miss Denton sat down beside the cot. "Oh, Captain Westhaver," she said sympathetically, "if I had only known sooner, I would have had you taken up home instead of to this lonely place. And how do you feel?"

Frank laughed in pleasure. "Oh, not so bad, miss. We trawlers are hard t' kill. An' how are you yourself? How's your father? None th' worse o' th' wreck, I hope?"

The girl smiled, and Frank thought he had never seen such a pleasing smile in his life. "Dad is all right. He told me to tell you that he'd come to-morrow and have you out in—in—what was the expression, Mr. Galarneau?"

Jules was smiling all over his swarthy face. "Two shakes of a brace-block, Miss Denton."

She laughed—a silvery trill which came like a ray of sunshine into Frank's jaded heart. "Yes, that's it! 'Two shakes of a brace-block!' That's one of Dad's nautical expressions. He gets me absolutely bewildered sometimes by the way he talks. Are you in any pain?"

"No, I don't feel anythin' at all. They've got me all parcelled, served, and fished like a sprung spar, until I can't move hand or foot for fear of startin' a lashin'."

Miss Denton laughed again. "More nauticalisms! Good gracious! What is a poor woman to do to understand you sailormen. Now, see what I've brought for you. Don't they smell sweet?" And she thrust a bunch of flowers under Frank's nose.

"Ah!" He drank in the fragrance. "Oh, but they're beautiful—and you are so kind—so kind. They're lovely!"

"Now, I'll just put them in this vase alongside your cot. Flowers *do* make one feel good sometimes, and I simply love them." And while she was busying herself arranging them, Frank looked over at his old dory-mate with a questioning, half-fearful look in his eyes.

It was Jules who spoke first, and there was nothing but friendliness in his eyes. "Well, Frankee, ol' boy, an' how you feel now? I t'ink you was thinkin' I was never come to see you, but I was here wit' you w'en we brought you ashore in de doree dis mornin'. You were faint den, so I go back to de vessel an' dress up. Den I make deal for new mainmast—she's bein' made now—an' I get de sail an' boom an' de oder gear from shore fisherman. De vessel will be all ready in a week, an' I send message up to your uncle at Long Cove to come down. Maybe he take her for one trip until you get well again.''

Frank nodded. "Good ol' Jules. You done jest right, an' I'll never be able t' pay ye for what ye've done. An' th' way I treated you——"

Jules frowned. "Say nawt'ing. I forget." And with his answer Frank's heart felt lighter.

Miss Denton had finished arranging the flowers, and the nurse was bringing in some supper. "Well, Captain, I'm afraid your nurse will forbid our staying longer. Now, you're to make up your mind to get well as quick as possible, or Mr. Galarneau and I will have something to say in the matter. Papa and I will see Doctor Willis about having you moved up to our place, and your friend and I will call and see you to-morrow. Now, be good 'til then. *Au revoir!*"

"So long, Frankee, 'til to-morrow. I see you then." And Jules, dressed like a gentleman in his shore clothes, escorted Miss Denton out.

After being fed like a baby, he dropped into a refreshing sleep, with a mind strangely free from the harass of care. He had gone through the mill of recrimination and emerged to find his old friend by his bedside and still his friend, and his heart was cheered also by the visit of a girl whom he had almost forgotten, but whose very presence seemed to linger with as much fragrance to his mind as the flowers she had brought.

Frank held a big levee next day, and his visitors came in a perfect stream. First came McCallum and Simms, and then his mother and Uncle Jerry. Frank had seen neither of the latter since the New Year, and the greetings were affectionate in the extreme. It was his uncle whom he wanted to see most of all, as the tangled skein of his affairs would have to be taken up by his avuncular relative.

"Now, Uncle," he said, "about th' vessel. Jules has ordered a new mainmast an' gear an' dories, so that she sh'd be ready in a week or two. The ice an' bait are aboard, an' th' gang is waitin' for someone to take her——"

Uncle Jerry nodded. "Is she sound, that vessel?"

"Sound as a bell. All hard wood, an' don't leak a drop."

"What's her length, depth, an' tonnage?"

" 'Bout seventy-eight feet in length; draws eight feet, an' registers 'bout fifty-eight tons an' carries a good seventy."

The other nodded again. "All right, Frank. Don't worry about her, but I won't take her out a-fishin' now. Most vessels are haulin' up aroun' this time——"

"But what about my gang?" interrupted Frank.

"Waal, I'll sell the ice an' bait an' I'll fix up with them an' send them back to Boston. That's th' best thing t' do, an' they won't hev any trouble shippin' again. There's a friend o' mine just launched a new semi-knockabout hundred-ton Banker, an' he'll snap up your gang in a minute ef I say th' word."

"Yes, but how about me?" said Westhaver. "I'm goin' a-fishin' again as soon as I git fixed up, an' where'll my men be then?"

"You don't want them any more, Frank. I've got some schemes on hand which I want ye to help me out on."

"Yes?"

"Aye, Frank. I'm gittin' too old for Bankin' now, an' I'm for stayin' 'round home an' startin' a little bit of a fish business. Your mother doesn't want you to go off in them American vessels—she wants ye t' be nigh home, an' between us we're plannin' t' buy th' *Kinsella* an' put her under Canadian registry an' use her for hakin' in th' Bay an' shackin' 'round th' Cape Shore. You c'd handle her, an' I'll look after th' shore end up to Long Cove."

Frank's eyes opened wide in surprise. "Waal, that's a good scheme," he said; "but ain't th' *Kinsella* too big for Long Cove wharf?"

"She was," replied the other, "but she ain't now. Cap'en Ring an' me hev got a grant from th' Government t' build a hundred-foot addition to th' present wharf, an' also another one on th' north side. We're goin' t' make a harbour there, an' a vessel kin lie up inside them wharves as safe as a house even though it's blowin' a westerly gale dead on th' shore."

"By th' Lord Harry! but that's news t' me!" cried Westhaver. "A harbour at Long Cove? Waal, waal! Now I know that, I ain't for sailin' an American vessel any more. That's simply great." He was lost in contemplation for a moment, and after a pause he spoke. "Who owns th' land by them wharves?"

"Cap'en Ring owns th' strip on th' north side, whar' th' new wharf is bein' built, an' Cap'en Asa Crawford owns th' strip whar' the old one is."

"Kin ye buy Asa's land, Uncle?"

Uncle Jerry shook his head. "I'm afraid not. Asa's gittin' awful cranky these days an' ye kain't do nawthin' with him. He's suspicious all th' time that somebody is after him for his money. Bob Morrissey"—Frank winced —"hez bin up hangin' after him, an' the ol' man seemed glad t' see him, so I cal'late he plans leavin' his property to him."

Frank grunted. "Um!" After a pause he continued, "Waal, Uncle, I'll go 'n see him as soon as I git out o' this. Maybe I kin dicker with him."

Mother, uncle, and son conversed for a considerable time, but when the doctor came they were forced to leave. "Too many visitors are not conducive to a quick recovery," he remarked professionally.

"Oh, come away, Doctor," said Westhaver with a smile. "I feel better every time someone comes in an' talks to me. How would you like t' be shut up in this lonesome place all day long?"

The medico laughed non-committally. "Well, Captain, I suppose you have some logic in your desire, and we might strain a point. How is it to-day? No pain there? Or there? Ah!" And after his examination he left the injured man to the solitude and his own thoughts.

After dinner Jules and Miss Denton came up, and Frank thought she looked irresistibly beautiful in her neat white blouse, cut away just enough at the neck to reveal a glimpse of her fine-moulded throat. Yes, she was pretty, there was no denying it. Her face was well-proportioned and regular in the contour of nose, eyes, and mouth, and when she smiled or laughed the dark brown eyes seemed to dance with mirth under their long lashes and the ivory of her teeth gleamed through the cherry lips like sunshine through a summer cloud. She wore a soft West Indian grass hat trimmed with a simple fluff of chiffon, and her hair streamed from under it in a fascinating tangle of silky brown revealing but a glimpse of pink ears half hidden. Her skin was soft and tanned to a becoming colour by the summer sun, and the warm blood mantling with all the health of young, strong life in her cheeks added an additional glow to a countenance which would cause an observer to look twice.

As she walked around his cot with the lithe grace of an athletic and out-of-doors young woman, Frank thought that the slim lines of her figure were just perfect, and he compared them to the lines of a beautiful vessel—a vessel with the graceful run and sheer, entrance and delivery, which catches the eye of a sailorman and holds him in a spell of admiration; and when he turns away it is with a feeling of reluctance and a desire to go back and look again. Carrie Dexter was pretty, but Carrie had not the grace of form and carriage possessed by Miss Denton, and when Carrie spoke it detracted a little from the flush of admiration in first impressions.

"And how is our sick man today?" she enquired with a sunny smile which kept Frank's eyes riveted on her face.

"Comin' along, miss. Comin' along nicely."

She sat down beside him. "Look," she said. "More flowers. Aren't they nice?"

"They're glorious," murmured Frank, sniffing at the

sweetness of the blooms. "Simply glorious—an' they smell so sweet. I never really appreciated flowers afore, but now I do, an' it is kind an' thoughtful of you to bring them—very kind." There was a suspicion of mistiness in his eyes when he concluded, and his voice ended in a tone of plaintive longing. Flowers! The sun was shining outside; a vista of blue sky could be seen through the window, and by the little cloud flecks passing by he could imagine he was out in the fields up in his Bay Shore home, with the great smiling waters in front of him and the odour of spruce and wild rose, raspberry and apple blossom wafting to his nostrils. He was brought back from his day-dreams by the musical voice of his visitor.

"Papa and I saw the doctor, but he said you were not to be moved. Father would have been up to see you, but he is troubled very bad with rheumatism, so he sends his best wishes and hopes to get along here perhaps to-morrow. Can you read at all?"

"No," answered Frank. "I have to lay on my back, and I can't move a hand to hold a book. If I could read a bit I wouldn't feel so lonesome."

"That's just what I thought," she said, "so I got permission from the doctor to bring along a book and read a bit to you——"

"That's very kind of you indeed," murmured Frank gratefully. "It's too good of you to go to all this trouble over me. I've done nawthin' to deserve——"

"Oh, no," she interrupted with a laugh. "You've done nothing at all except save my life, my father's, and his crew, and if you think that is nothing, well—I shall have to believe that you value *me* at a very low estimate indeed. Picking shipwrecked people off wrecks in stormy weather doesn't amount to anything——"

"Oh, I didn't mean that," said Frank hastily, and blushing to the roots of his sandy hair in confusion. "I—I meant what we did was only th' right thing, an' what any other man 'ud do."

Miss Denton smiled—a tantalizing smile, which caused

Westhaver to wonder what she was driving at. As he gazed at her healthy, laughing, dimpled face, his memory went back to the time when he held a limp, sea-drenched figure in his arms. How white and wan she looked then!

"Now, I've brought along a book called 'Lorna Doone,' which I think you said was a great favourite of yours——"

"So it is! I'm very fond of it."

Miss Denton nodded. "You and I have similar tastes. I've been over in that country, you know."

"Is that so?"

"Three years ago I was with papa over in Bristol, and while the ship was unloading we took a tour down through the Exmoor Valley to Taunton, Bridgwater, Lynmouth, and all these places. They have a coach which goes right through the Doone Valley, and they point out all the places mentioned in this book. We also went to Ilfracombe and Barnstaple and saw the pebble ridge at Clovelly——"

"That's in 'Westward Ho!' " interrupted Frank.

"Yes, it's the country of both books. Lynton and Lynmouth are such lovely places. I was sorry to leave them. They're so romantic and so picturesque, with their straw-thatched cottages winding up beside the steep road from the sea and all covered with creepers and ivy. Every time I read the books I think of those places. As I read to you, I'll tell you about the things I saw." And Frank listened with delight to her soft, even voice; and Jules himself sat quiet and attentive during the short hour of the reading.

Thus passed the long weeks while the young skipper lay in the hospital. The gang came and wished him good-bye, and left for Boston to join a new vessel, but before they went McCallum expressed the views of the crowd. "When she'll pe ready for ta fishin' again, she'll chust give a call an' we'll aal pe for comin' pack again. Chust so. Coot pye, skipper." And they were gone. A hard, tough crowd they were, but theirs was not the toughness of the alley thug or bar-room lounger. They drank hard, swore hard, and lived hard, but there was nothing of hardness in their hearts.

Sea-children, with their faults begotten of the ports only, they went their ways, and Frank felt regret at their going.

Mrs. Westhaver stayed for a week in Yarmouth, and finding that her son was coming around all right, she left for home. Uncle Jerry and Jules had the *Kinsella* overhauled, and after fixing up a deal with Hoolahan Captain Clark sold out his interest in the *Kastalia* and invested it in the smaller boat. Application was made for a change of registry, and after the vessel was repaired they sailed her up the coast and anchored her in Anchorville Bay. Jules and Captain Clark went up to Long Cove, where they busied themselves in preparing fish flakes for the contemplated business.

Thus Frank was left, but with Miss Denton visiting him daily, he was by no means lonely, although he yearned to be up and about again. Sometimes he had his blue moods during which the future looked black; but as soon as Lillian Denton came they vanished like fog before the sun. Daily he looked forward to her coming, and when she failed to arrive one afternoon he had a feeling as if something had gone out of his life.

It is not to be supposed that reading was the only subject which occupied the time. Some days there were when the girl would lay the book down after the recital of a few paragraphs, and they would wander away from the romance of the Doone Valley to the nearer romance of home. She was a lover of the water, of the open spaces and the beauty of nature, and in Frank Westhaver she found a man who had seen and done many things. Unlike the majority of seafarers, he retained the impressions of what his eyes had gazed upon, and had a faculty of simple description which held Miss Denton entranced for many a pleasant hour. His life upon the Banks, the work of the fishery, and tales of the rollicking, dare-devil gangs who manned the vessels of the off-shore fleets, were to her as something entirely new in spite of the fact that she was a Nova Scotian girl and bred in a seaport town. A strange paradox this, but one which is universal. People refuse to see the romance right at their own doors until a stranger comes and opens their eyes.

By the remarks which she was in the habit of letting fall during these talks, Frank wondered how she came to know so much about his history. He had never told her of his trip in from Georges in the *Fannie B. Carson*, yet she seemed to know all about it; the rescue of Jake Simms; the happenings of his first voyage as skipper, even to the incident of Jules's escape from a St. Malo fisherman, were betrayed by her in casual references to the events. When she left, he was in the habit of pondering over their conversations, and the interest she evinced in his past, and in the ambitions of his future, led him to ask her a question.

"Miss Denton, tell me how you came to know so much about things I've done? I don't remember sayin' anythin' 'bout them?"

She laughed in her usual sunny way. "Ah, so I've let the cat out of the bag, have I? And I thought I was so diplomatic, too! Captain, it's a fine thing to have good friends—friends who will stand to you like old Salvation Yeo did to Amyas Leigh——"

"That's ol' Sabot—Jules!" exclaimed Frank. "So he's th' dog!"

"He's a sterling fellow, Captain," she said. "And he thinks the world of you——"

Frank nodded, and with a puzzled look in his grey-blue eyes, he asked, "Excuse me, but how did you git t' know I was in hospital here? I never rightly knew how that came about."

"Jules again, Captain," she replied. "He had no sooner got you in here before he was up to our house."

"He was, was he?" Frank was still perplexed. "I wonder what put it into his head t' go an' bother you about my affairs? You were a'most a stranger t' me. . . . An' it's been him what has been spinnin' ye all these yarns? Poor ol' Jules."

He paused for a few seconds and then gazed into the brown eyes of the girl beside him. "Did he say anythin' about what happened outside thar'?" He hesitated as he saw the embarrassed flush on her cheeks. "How I came t' git inter this scrape?"

For a space she turned her gaze away. "Yes," she answered softly. "He told me all."

Westhaver remained silent for a long time thinking. He wondered why his old dory-mate should have told these things. What was his object? Jules had a curious trait of turning things over in his mind and springing unusual questions, and the remarks he sometimes made had impressed Frank many times with their strange truthfulness.

"You know about that—that girl?" he asked at length.

"Yes," she replied. "Your friend told me all."

For some minutes neither spoke. Frank was gazing hard out at the vista of blue sky showing through the window, and the girl stole a glance at him in his reveries. She remembered the day she first saw him as oilskin clad and ruggedly strong he stood in the door of the berth and looked down upon her. She remembered hearing the tones of his masterful voice as he sung out to the gang while the vessel was lurching and plunging in a Western Ocean gale. How frightened she was then! The roar of the wind and sea; the thunderous crashes of the water on deck; the straining of the little schooner's fabric as she tumbled into the seaway; the water pouring down into the cabin; and lastly she retained a vivid impression of his dripping figure as he came below that night. "Yes . . . breezin' up again. . . . Had t' heave her to after she shipped that last load. . . ." How confident and strong he looked! The sun bronze had faded from his face now, but it glowed with the clear pink of health, and the well arm which lay over the white sheets was muscular and powerful. How wistful and gentle his eyes were at that moment! The strong chin, determined mouth, well-shaped nose, and high forehead with the silky brown auburn hair streaking across it made up the features of just such a man as she would imagine had done the things she had heard, and a man who would be no quitter in the face of danger. And he was no common man with but the endowments of strength and iron nerve to commend him. She knew him better than that, and in their many conversations she was able, from the standpoint of a well-educated and clever young woman, to fathom the thoughts which ran in the young fisherman's mind.

Frank turned suddenly and spoke with a half-smile on his face. "Do you know," he said, "I'll be really sorry to get well again. It means I'll have to go away from here, an' I'll miss you so much."

Miss Denton had been thinking regretfully upon the same question. She too would miss these delightful visits, and for a moment she was at a loss for a reply.

"Yes," he continued with a note of pensiveness in his voice. "I'll miss hearin' you readin' to me. You've been so kind to spend your time upon me—a common fisherman, an' you——"

"A common, ordinary girl," interrupted Miss Denton with a laugh.

"No," said the other; "... an angel!"

The July days passed slowly, and Frank was glad when the doctor said that he could get up and sit outside in the sunshine. The collar-bone had knit nicely, and it was only the arm which really bothered him. But while he was improving in his physical injuries, he was becoming much disturbed mentally over the fact of leaving the young woman who had cheered the long hours of his enforced loneliness. He had given a great deal of thought to her, and a feeling was beginning to take possession of him that it would be a hard thing for him to leave her when the time came. Whether her feelings in that respect were the same as his own he did not know, and he was afraid—much afraid—that he would make another mistake. To reveal to her the unrest which held him in daily suspense might mean a rejection which would be fatal to their friendship. She was, to him, all that was good and beautiful, and with such a woman to work for he felt that he could do great things. The very thoughts of her inspired him, and an analysis of his attitude towards her showed that he was very much in love.

He had been afraid at first that she was in a social position far superior to his own; but when she admitted that her father's affairs would necessitate her taking up school teaching, Frank felt almost glad that such was the case. With no barrier of this nature between them, he pondered as to whether she would look upon him in the light which the other girl had—that of his profession as a fisherman. He wondered, but in a vague way he did not think so. Lillian Denton was a girl of the right sort—free from affectation and social airs. Besides, even if he were a fisherman, he could be a gentleman in spite of his profession. He could earn good money and keep a wife in the best of everything. His mother's estate would fall to him some day—but he dismissed the thought. He knew instinctively that Lillian would marry for love and not for money, and Frank wondered if he possessed the attributes which would be likely to attract a girl of her type. "I'm afraid," he soliloquized, "she'll think I'm a feller that's blown about by every wind what blows. Turned down by one girl a few weeks ago, an' proposin' to another a few weeks after. Oh, but I'll never be able to exist without her. She's everythin' to me now, an' if I don't get her, th' bottom'll be knocked out of my life. I'll be no good afterwards. I'll never be able to stick at anythin' . . . but I'll have to do it an' take a chanst, for I want her badly—aye, badly."

Westhaver was young, and he loved the beautiful in life with his whole heart. It was the way in which he did everything—whole-heartedly. Thrown together so much as they were for many weeks, it is not to be wondered at, his falling in love with Lillian Denton. Frank did not know many girls, and since he was a boy he had lavished all his affection upon one who had proved shallow and false. He was a sailor, and the loneliness of a sailor's life tends to make them respect and honour women more than the ordinary landsman, and when a sailor falls in love he does everything with a rush. Fishermen are said to go the regulation deep-water sailor one better, and there is a saying around the fleets that an extra high-line trip which gives a young fisherman one month's money ahead will send him ashore to marry the first girl he fancies.

The day came when the doctor told him he could leave the hospital on the morrow and go home. Frank received the news with no great enthusiasm, and the medical man— a keen judge of human nature—put two and two together, and made his deductions with a smile. He met Miss Denton on her way up to the institution, and in the course of conversation remarked that "her friend, the Captain, was feeling quite blue about leaving the hospital." The blush which suffused her face when he made the remark sent him off chuckling to himself. "Given a quiet, lonesome hospital; a handsome young sailorman, sick; a pretty girl, sympathetic; daily visits for a few weeks; and the bacteria will take effect. That's the prescription." And smiling to himself at his joke, he went his way.

Frank was sitting by the open window when she entered, and he looked at her with the welcome shining in his eyes. "Got t' clear out t'-morrow," he said when she had seated herself.

"Are you sorry?" she asked with a smile.

"Yes," he replied slowly, "I am."

She apparently ignored his answer. "Dad wants you to come along to the house and stay for a day or two before you go home. Is your suit-case packed?"

"Everythin' is in it, Miss Denton. But it ain't right for me to impose on you——"

"Sh! Hold your tongue," exclaimed the girl. "You're not at sea now, and you'll obey orders."

Frank laughed. "It's a pleasure for me to obey orders from some people——"

She was packing his things in the suitcase. "Do you want your watch out of this vest?" She held up the sea-stained garment. It was part of the suit he wore on the memorable trip out of Portland.

"Yes, if you please. I cal'late it's spoiled, ain't it?"

"No," she replied. "It seems all right. There is something else in the pocket too. Do you want it?"

"What is it? Ain't a roll of bills, is it?"

For answer she stepped across with the watch, chain, and a small velvet box. Frank took them from her slowly, and slipping the watch into his pocket, he took the box in his fingers.

"Th' ring! I clean forgot all about it." He spoke slowly, and then raised his eyes up to the face of the girl standing in front of him. Pulling a chair over, he said quietly, "Will ye sit here a moment?"

Wonderingly she obeyed, and with his eyes gazing into hers he snapped the cover of the box open and displayed the flashing gem.

"What a lovely diamond!" she exclaimed in surprise. "Isn't it a beauty?"

"Yes," he said tensely; "but not half so beautiful as what you are, Lillian. Will—will you put it on your finger?"

With the colour mantling in her cheeks, she picked the ring out of his outstretched hand, and while he watched her with the intensity of apprehension she slowly slipped it on her finger.

"Sweetheart!" he cried joyfully, and reaching over he clasped her to him with his strong right arm, and as he looked into her eyes—bright and shining with the lovelight under their long lashes—he knew that he had won. "Oh, darling! An' 'tis the happy man I am this day now that I have ye for my own. Aye! my very own!"

CHAPTER FIFTEEN

THERE IS NO MAN SO SUPREMELY HAPPY AND CONtented with life as he who has wooed and won the girl of his heart. Frank Westhaver was no exception. He had taken a chance with a young woman whom he regarded as his social and intellectual superior, a girl he had met in an unusual manner a few months before, and upon an acquaintanceship of a few weeks; he had proposed and was accepted. The odds, to his mind, were greatly against him. He was a fisherman and a member of a profession usually regarded by the uninitiated as being of a low type—odoriferous, menial, poor, and degraded. He had no means of knowing what other rivals there were already in the field, but he had "made a set for her," as he expressed it, and he had "hooked his fish."

If Frank could only have read Miss Denton's mind he would not have thought his task such a difficult one after all. Months ago, when she first saw him, he had impressed her greatly, and when she learned more about him and got to know the stuff he was made of she admired him more than any other of her friends. The admiration was mutual, and soon ripened into love.

There is a trite, but oft-times true, proverb which declares that the course of true love runs not smoothly. So Westhaver found when he broached the subject to old Captain Denton. The venerable shipmaster had no objections to Frank as a son-in-law—in fact he would not have wished to see a better man the husband of his daughter—but he had some views upon the subject which he explained to Westhaver at some length.

"I like you, Westhaver," he said, as the two sat on the sun-flooded porch of the Denton house, "but if you were th' smartest fishing skipper on the Atlantic I wouldn't let you have my daughter for a wife. I'm a sailor myself, and I know what the lot of a sailor's wife is, and years ago I vowed if Lily ever got hitched up it would never be to a sailor. No, siree! I know what her mother had to go through when I was away at sea. I've seen her git grey-haired with worrying over me, and every breeze of wind that blows keeps them wakeful and wondering how their husband is faring when he's outside. Then there's th' lonesomeness of it, and—— Well, I reckon I need say no more. You know exactly what I mean, and let me tell ye, a fisherman's life is worse than a deep-water sailor's. Ye may be at home a little oftener, but th' risks you fellows take in them small schooners is more than I'd want any son-in-law of mine to be taking, and there's a sight of poor fishermen's widows around this coast, I can tell you. Then again, I've given Lily th' benefit of a good education, and I've had her brought up well socially. She's not going to throw all that away as a fisherman's wife. When she marries, her husband has got to be living at home, and have a shore job, and a good one. I'm not going to see her living alone and depending upon the earnings of a husband who may strike luck one voyage and make nawthing in another. That's too precarious."

Frank nodded. "Yes, sir, I kin understand th' way you look at it, an' I see your point, but I don't plan fishin' at sea all my life. My uncle an' me are plannin' t' start a little business up in Long Cove. We've bought a vessel— th' *Kinsella*—an' I cal'late runnin' her while uncle looks after th' shore end o' th' plant."

The old man nodded. "Yes, that's all right, but you're going to be doing the sea end of it, and that's what I object to. You're a smart lad, I know, and I think if ye'd look around a little you can do more than fossick around with a little bit of a business. Use your brains, and look for something bigger, my lad—I'll give ye two years—and when you've got into something that'll keep you ashore and earning enough to keep my girl as she should be kept, I'll say nawthing. But 'til then—no marrying.''

Frank accepted Captain Denton's decision as final, and Lillian was too dutiful a daughter to dissent from anything her parent said. "You'll find something, Frank," she remarked when the situation had been explained to her. "Dad is right. I couldn't bear to have you away out at sea. You've got two years before you—two years is a long time, but I'm sure you could do a lot in that period. You're young yet—twenty-three isn't old—and we've both got plenty of time before us. Get your wits to work now, and I'll help all I can."

And as Frank looked down into her lovely face he felt that his task would be inspired by his love for such a woman. "Oh, dearie," he whispered as he pressed her to him, "I feel that I shall do great things for your sake. With such a prize to win, I c'd go through anythin' t' make you happy." Her face was very close to his; her hair brushed his cheek, and, looking into the depths of her brown eyes, he saw her admiration for him glancing from under the long lashes. There was a warm glow in her face and a fascinating disorder in her silky hair, when her father's voice came from the verandah.

"Oh, Westhaver! Come out an' try one of my Antwerp manillas!"

Frank rose. "Jest another, sweetheart!" and with the touch of her warm red lips upon his he went out to join the old man with a little regret at having to defile the lingering sweetness with such a thing as a smoke.

It was a glorious August day when he landed upon the string-piece of the Long Cove wharf. A fresh breeze was blowing in from the sea, and the tang of it, coming in over the weed-strewn rocks, with the sight of the fleecy clouds racing athwart the blue of the sky, filled Frank's young heart with the ecstasy of living, loving, and being loved. All the Long Covers were working upon the new additions when he stepped ashore, and they threw down augers, saws, adzes, and hammers in the rush to greet him. There was

Long Dick, rangier and more bronzed than ever, pumping the hand off him, and shooting questions like a rapid-fire gun. Jud Morrell, Uncle Jerry, Zeke, and Lem Ring were surging round him with the light of welcome in their eyes. Oh, but he felt good to be home amongst them once more!"

"Waal, waal, an' here's our Skipper Shorty Westhaver!" cried Long Dick. "Home at last, after settin' th' whole coast a-talkin'. A reg'lar dog of a rip-roarin' driver from T Dock, with yer rough an' tough gang, an' th' *Mabel Kinsella!* Lord Harry! boy, but ye've sartainly been paintin' th' water, ef all what we've h'ard is true. Blest, but I'd be 'most scared t' be one o' yer gang, ef ye're th' dog of a feller they say ye are!" Such were the greetings —rough, jesting, but sincere—and it was all he could do to break away from the mob and get up to his mother and home.

He found Jules behind the house making horses for supporting fish flakes, and the honest fellow's joy at seeing him again was truly cordial. "Oh, Frankee, but I was thinking you never coming home. I jest say to Cap'en Clark dis morning dat I be for go to Yarmout' to-morrow for see what come over you."

"Come up th' field aways," said the other. "I got somethin' t' say t' ye—you cute ol' dog."

Jules threw the hammer down and followed his friend. Frank walked on for a few yards and sat down under the shade of a giant spruce. "Here, you blame' ol' trawler," exclaimed Frank, with a twinkle in his eyes, "what d'ye mean by goin' aroun' Yarmouth an' tellin' my whole history to every girl ye meet?"

Jules looked up questioningly. "Er—ah," he stammered awkwardly. "Did *she* tell you dat?"

"Yes, she did," replied the other. "An' a nice scrape ye've let me in for—you an' yer gossip."

Sabot's large eyes opened wide. "What have I done, Frankee?" he said in hesitation. "Is—there anyt'ing wrong?"

"Is thar' anythin' wrong?" reiterated Frank. "Waal,

I sh'd jest say thar' was! Do you know what you've gone an' done?"

"N-no." The Frenchman's reply was apprehensive, and his eyes showed his trepidation.

"Waal, I'll tell ye then," said the other with mock severity. "Ye've jest gone an' tied me up t' th' finest little clipper what ever left th' ways—meanin', that I've put th' ring on Lily Denton's finger——"

Jules gave a whoop of joy, and in his delight he embraced his old dory-mate with all the fervour of his inherited Gallic temperament. "I knew dat she was de girl! I knew it—I knew it. Oh, Frankee, but I'm glad—veree glad." And when his outburst was over, he explained the affair to his friend. "I knew dat Dexter girl was not for you, Frankee. She was too *perfide* — *orgueilleuse* — proud — flirt, I t'ink you call dat. She want everyt'ing —never give nawt'ing. W'en she went to *hôpital* at Boston she get worse. I see dat—you no see. Now, w'en dat lofely girl come off de wreck I say dat de girl for Frankee. I see dat she like you by her eyes on de *Kinsella,* an' w'en you go *hôpital* in Yarmout' I go for see an' tell her. She was ver' 'fraid w'en I tell her how you hurt, an' w'en I see dat, I tell her w'at fine feller you was. I tell her dat everee tam I take her to *hôpital,* an' she ask me lots of question 'bout you. Den I lef' you to do rest, an' I feel glad —so glad."

Frank reached out and clasped Jules's hand. "Say, ol' Sabot, I owe you an awful lot, an' I'm a-goin' t' try an' pay it back. You're my best friend, an' I want ye t' stick by me. I've got some big work ahead o' me afore I kin call that little girl my own, an' you're goin' t' help me out, an' I'm goin' t' help you as well. How about it, ol' dory-mate?"

"I'm de man, Frankee," replied the other gleefully. "I'll stick wit' you 'til de *enfer* freeze over for skate on!"

Frank lost no time in getting down to business. He was unable to use his arm—it was still in the sling—

but he could use his head, and having plenty of ideas he planned out schemes for the future. Taking his mother and Uncle Jerry into his confidence, he told them of his engagement to Miss Denton and the conditions attached to the engagement by her father. Mrs. Westhaver thought the desire of the old captain was only right. She was a sailor's wife herself, and understood, but Uncle Jerry thought the stipulations were a little harsh.

"I was plannin' on you takin' th' vessel while I'd dry th' fish down on th' beach below here, an' ship it inter Anchorville or Bayport, but maybe you kin suggest a better scheme."

"I can," replied Frank decisively, "but I'll need money t' carry it out. If I'm goin' into a fish business, I'm goin' th' whole hog, an' not mess aroun' with a small, one-horse affair."

Mrs. Westhaver nodded over her spectacles. "If your ideas are good, Frank, you can use my money for it, if it'll keep you to home. It'll be yours some day, an' you might as well use it now."

Uncle Jerry grunted. "What's your plan, Frank?"

The young fisherman procured paper and pencil before replying. "Now," he said, "we'll sum up our assets. You hev a good vessel in good condition. She's worth, we'll say, five thousand dollars——"

"She's an American vessel," interrupted the uncle, "an' for gittin' her register changed t' Canadian in order t' land fish here 'twill cost quite a sum in duty."

"Aye, I know," answered the other, "but she ain't a new craft, an' they'll value her very low, so I cal'late th' value I've put on her'll about cover her under th' new register. Now, for th' shore plant, we hev no place as yet."

"Waal, I was cal'latin' t' use th' beach alongside th' wharf," said Uncle Jerry. "It'll be handy for unloadin' an' loadin', an' 'twon't cost nawthin' for rent."

Frank tapped the paper with his pencil. "That's all

very well in a way, but that won't do for th' future. That bit o' beach really belongs to Cap'en Asa Crawford, as well as does th' land to th' south side o' th' wharf. Everythin' 'ud be all right s'long's Cap'en Asa's alive, but we don't know who may git that place when he's gone. S'pose someone was t' come along here an' start a business like ours. What's t' hinder them buyin' Asa's place an' shovin' us out? Nawthin' at all."

The other nodded slowly. "What's your plans, Frank?"

"Waal, in th' first place, we'll start a company. You'll put in so much capital, an' mother kin lend me some o' her money at interest. Then we'll buy out Cap'en Asa's land 'longside th' wharf an' th' wharf road. On that land we'll build our fish shed. Now, thar's Cap'en Ring with a business on the other side of us. We'll git him t' come in along with our company, an' then we'll make contracts with Long Dick, Jud Morrell, an' the other fellers shore fishin' 'bout here to sell their fish to us. We'll pay them cash on delivery, an' in order t' do that we need ready money. Now, with Cap'en Ring in partners with us, we won't be competin' with one another, an' we'll have all th' land on both sides of the Government wharf, which'll stop anybody else from comin' into Long Cove an' settin' up. Seein' that th' Government is makin' a harbour for us here with them new additions to th' wharves, we've got th' best place for a fish business anywheres along this coast from Anchorville to Port Stanton—'most forty mile."

"How much money d'ye cal'late this is a-goin' to cost?"

"It ain't so much th' cost, but what are we a-goin' t' put into it? I'll borrow five thousand dollars from mother an' pay her a good rate of interest for the use of it, an' I'll buy that strip from Cap'en Asa. That'll count as my share o' th' business. You'll put in th' schooner, an' ef ye like, some cash as well. Then we'll git Cap'en Ring to value his place around th' wharf, an' we kin take that into th' company. Whatever amount we put in, we'll divide th' profits in proportion to them every year. You an' me an' Cap'en Ring an' Lem an' Zeke kin go on wages for th' work we do. That'll be arranged later. Now we'll start makin' up th' company."

Uncle Jerry lit up his pipe, gazing the while through the smoke at his nephew's face. The scrutiny pleased him mightily.

"Now, Uncle, we'll call ourselves th' Long Cove Fish Company—that's a good-soundin' name, eh?"

"A good name," assented the person addressed.

"That's settled," continued Frank, writing it down to see how it looked. "Now I'll buy Asa's land first. We can't do anythin' without it, an' when I've got that, we'll work out the other details later. I'll go'n see Cap'en Ring after I buy th' land——"

"D'ye think he'll come in?" interrupted the uncle.

"Waal, I'm not sure, but I think he will. It'll be better for him, though ye kin never tell how he looks at it. I'll put it to him, anyway, an' ef he don't want t' go partners with us, we kin go ahead ourselves."

"Who's a-goin' t' run th' schooner, Frank?" queried Captain Clark. "You say you ain't a-goin' to handle that end."

Young Westhaver looked across into his uncle's eyes.

"No, I'm not a-goin' t' handle that end. I'm a-goin' t' run th' office part o' this company, if you'll agree—"

The old skipper laughed. "Waal, Frank, I cal'late you're the only one in th' comp'ny what kin. I can't, nor Cap'en Ring can't, so I reckon you're th' one t' run th' writin' an' figurin' part. But who'll take th' vessel? I don't want t' go vessel-fishin' any more. I've had my share of it, an' I'm hungry for th' shore now."

"Uncle, th' man I propose t' make skipper o' th' *Kinsella*—I'm a-goin' t' change that name with your permission—is a feller what has a good long head on him, and a man what has proved himself as true as steel—Jules Galarneau.''

The other whistled. "Jules?" he said. "But Jules knows nawthin' about navigatin' a vessel."

"No," answered Frank, "he never had a chanst t' learn, but I cal'late it won't take th' same boy long t' pick it up. He's got lots of nerve; he's a bird at steerin' an' handlin' a vessel, an' I'll bet ef you take him out a couple o' trips an' learn him th' chart an' how t' lay a course he'll soon be able t' take th' vessel anywheres. Try him, anyway."

"I will," replied the other. "An' I believe you're right. He's a fine feller, an' he sh'd git a chanst. I'll take her out an' show him th' ropes. Er—by th' by, ye said somethin' 'bout changin' th' vessel's name. What d'ye want her called?"

The young fisherman blushed a little. "Waal, I was thinkin' that *Lillian* 'ud be a mighty good name——"

"Ha, ha!" guffawed the uncle. "*Lillian*, eh? That's *her* name, ain't it? Waal, I reckon we'll hev t' do that for ye, Frank. The original *Mabel Kinsella* don't signify anythin' to us, so when we take out th' new register we'll change th' name. *Lillian*, hah!" And the stout skipper winked over at his smiling sister.

Next day Shorty—though he had really grown to be an average-sized man he was still called by the boyhood nickname—went and called upon old Captain Asa Crawford. The ancient shipmaster was still pretty hale, in spite of his years, and he greeted Westhaver cordially, and bawled for the housekeeper to bring a chair out to the gallery in pretty much the same manner as he would have sung out to a sailor to bring him a ball of spun-yarn.

"An' they tell me ye hed a tough trick out in th' Bay a while ago?"

"Yes, I did hev quite a time, Cap'en."

"Goin' back a-fishin' again soon?"

"No, Cap'en, I'm plannin' t' stay 'round home now. Mother wants me here, an' Uncle Jerry an' me's tryin' t' start a bit of a business in dried fish in th' Cove. That's what I've come t' see ye about, Cap'en. Would ye be for sellin' me that field o' yours what runs up from th' head o' th' wharf to th' road?"

The old man looked at him sharply. "What d'ye want it for?"

"To put my fish sheds up, an' use for a flake-yard. I'd want all th' field ye've got fenced off, ef ye'd see yer way t' sell it to me."

The other nodded, and seemed lost in thought, and suddenly he changed the subject. "You're th' man what pulled ol' Denton off that barque o' his, ain't ye?"

"Yes, Cap'en," answered Frank wonderingly.

"Um!" Captain Crawford grunted. "Jest got a letter from a nevvy o' mine. Morrissey—my sister's child—ye'll remember him. Say's he's marryin' that Dexter girl what used t' live this ways."

Frank reddened. "Yes?"

"Aye!" replied the old man. Then, with one of his sudden motions, he barked out, "Warn't you goin' with that young woman?"

"Er—yes, I was at one time," stammered Frank, "but I'm engaged to Captain Denton's daughter now."

"I know it," replied the old sailor brusquely.

"You know it?" gasped Shorty in astonishment.

"Yes—condemn it—yes!" snapped the other. "Saw ol' Denton day afore yesterday. He was askin' me 'bout you. I was down to Yarmouth on some business. I told him you uster be th' damnedest imp aroun' th' place——"

"Nice character," murmured Frank, at a loss to know how to take the old skipper.

"But," continued the other, "I said you had more sand in ye than anyone I know. What kind o' girl is this Dexter?"

"Very nice girl," answered Westhaver quietly.

"How'd ye come t' break away from her?"

"She threw me down," replied Frank slowly and without emotion. "I didn't break away."

"Huh!" Captain Asa grunted. "An' she threw you down for that nevvy o' mine? A dam' fore-an'-aft turnpike sailor with as much blow in him as 'ud fill a balloon. Good judgment on her part. All he's fit for. Runnin' a fore-an'-after. Gaffer o' Fielding's gang. Comes up here an' tells me how sailorin' is done nowadays. I don't know anythin' about it. I'm out o' date. An' th' swab couldn't tell th' difference between a Spanish fox an' a jewel block. No! but he c'd tell how many yards o' canvas it 'ud take t' strop a dead-eye. C'd you tell me that?"

"Indeed, I couldn't, Cap'en," answered Frank in mystification. "I don't see what ye'd want t' strop a dead-eye with canvas for, anyhow."

"No, nor anyone else. But he's master o' a four-mast abomination all goose-wings an' jibs, an' he comes shinin' it over me what was chewin' my biscuit in a packet ship's fo'c'sle with ol' Bully Peabody aft afore that sojer was ever thought of. Yes, boy! We made sailors in my day— real stuns'lyard, ring-tail shell-backs—none o' yer Paddy Westers or Danny Devine's Liverpool tailor A.B.'s. But you're a smart lad, Westhaver—a smart lad."

"Thank you, Cap'en."

"An' ye want t' start a business ashore? You're sensible, m'lad. Most sensible thing I've h'ard a man say for a long time. Any man what 'ud go t' sea for a livin' nowadays 'ud go to hell for pastime—that's a fact."

He stopped, and seemed lost in reflection, and Westhaver watched him, wondering what all his curious conversation was going to lead to. When the old man spoke again, there seemed to be a strange note in his voice.

"I may be slippin' my shackle 'most any time now," he said. "I'm about due for my long port, I cal'late, but I don't want no sky-pilot dancin' in my wake with his devil-dodgin' yarns. I've got clean discharges, an' I reckon there's plenty o' my ol' shipmates in Fiddler's Green as 'ull testify to ol' Bluenose Crawford when he steps up. But afore I go, I'll leave all my gear coiled down an' canvas snug. Ye want th' lower field, ye say? Waal, ye'll need t' buy th' whole place, this house an' all, an' ye'll let me live here free o' rent until ol' Bosun Gabriel pipes my watch below. What d'ye say?"

"Waal," said Frank hesitatingly, "how much 'ull ye be askin'?"

"Two thousand dollars!—house, grounds, an' all. Ye'll need a place like this when ye splice up with Denton's gal. Th' furniture is t' be sold, an' th' money given to ol' Jane thar'."

Frank nodded. The price was very reasonable, as the house was a good one, and there were fully sixty acres of land, which ran from the shore to the mountain behind.

"What d'ye say?"

"All right, sir, I'll buy it. I'll come an' fix it up with you on Saturday."

The old skipper grunted. "That's settled then. *Captain* Morrissey don't finger my money ef I kin help it. Ye'll give me a check for th' whole amount, an' I'll live in this house here until I slip. Th' money 'ull go to th' Sailors' Orphan Society over in Liverpool. Good day, m'lad, an' good luck t' ye!" And Frank left the old sailor—relic of a hard, daring deep-water type now extinct—with feelings of joy at his good fortune at making a deal with a man characterized by all as being irascible, cranky, and impossible to do business with.

Mrs. Westhaver, Frank, and Uncle Jerry drove into Anchorville next day, and the mother made arrangements for a sum of five thousand dollars to be transferred over to her son's account at the local bank, and on the Saturday Westhaver went up to Captain Crawford and gave him a check for the sum of two thousand dollars. The deeds were in possession of an advocate in Anchorville, and the old shipmaster promised to write him about the sale.

"I'll give ye a bit of a note, ef ye'll write it out for me," said he. "That'll keep ye shipshape ontil ye git th' deeds."

Procuring paper and pen, Shorty made out the bill of sale and handed it over. Cap'en Asa shipped his glasses.

"Ah! 'This is to certify that I have sold my property, with house and buildings thereon, to Francis James Westhaver, of Long Cove, Nova Scotia, for the sum of two thousand dollars. I am to have use and occupancy of house until my death free of rental. After that it will belong entirely to the purchaser. Signed this thirtieth day of August in the year one thousand nine hundred and ——' That seems all right. Gimme th' pen!'' And, painstakingly, he appended his signature and handed the paper over.

With the purchase of the property necessary for the business, Frank felt that he was in a position to approach Captain Ring, and on the Sunday, after church, they strolled over, Uncle Jerry and he, and the young fisherman outlined his proposition.

Captain Ring—a rugged, quiet-spoken man of about forty-five—was rather astonished at the idea, and still more astonished when he heard that they had already purchased a vessel and the land necessary for the business, but during the interview he was very non-committal. "I'll want t' think it over a bit first,'' he said finally, "an' I'll be lettin' ye know in a day or so.'' That was all they could get out of him.

On the Monday, while Captain Clark and Jules were busy transporting lumber down to the land for the purpose of constructing a fish shed, Frank set out to interview the boat fishermen to make his contracts with them. Long Dick Jennings was the first man he approached.

"Ye're for startin' a fish business, Shorty?'' exclaimed that worthy, scratching his head. "Waal now, it's a pity I didn't know sooner, for I've promised Cap'en Ring that I sell all my fish t' him this winter.''

"Ye did?'' ejaculated Frank. "That's too bad. How about Jud Morrell?''

"He's made a contract as well to sell th' Rings.''

"Tarnation!'' Westhaver was nonplussed. "An' th' Muise boys—how about them?''

"All sellin' t' Ring.''

"Tom Archer?''

"Yep," answered the long fisherman, expectorating neatly at a fly crawling over a log. "All th' crowd boat fishin' 'round here is sellin' to Cap Ring. He's plannin' t' do a big business, I understan', an' he got after us all while you was to Anchorville Tuesday."

Frank was crestfallen. With the boat fishermen tied up with a possible rival—and Frank had an intuition that Captain Ring had something up his sleeve which kept him from throwing in his fortunes with Jerry Clark and himself—there would only be the vessel to depend upon for a supply of fish. And before she could be reckoned with, she had to get a gang to fish in her.

"I'll go an' hev another talk with Cap'en Ring. Maybe he'll be for comin' in with us."

But when Westhaver broached the subject, the other man shook his head.

"I cal'late I got enough t' do myself," he replied, "an' I ain't plannin' in joinin' nobody."

"You got hold o' all th' fellers fishin' hereabouts," said Frank. "I'd like ef ye'd let me git Dick Jennings an' Jud to run fish for me."

Captain Ring smiled a slow, inscrutable smile. "I'll need them all, I reckon. What d'ye want with them, anyway? Ain't you got that big vessel?"

"Aye," replied Frank, "but I ain't got a gang for her yet."

"Oh, you'll git a gang." The older man spoke in a bantering tone which jarred a little upon Westhaver, but he pretended not to notice the evident jeer in the words. Frank knew that Ring was a clever man in his own way, and he was well liked by the Long Cove folks, but he had a reputation of being as deep as the hole off the Nor'-west Ledge.

"Waal, it's too bad," he remarked. "You must be cal-'latin' to do a big business, eh?"

The other grunted, "Aye, maybe."

Frank took a long shot. "*D'ye think ye'll git that contract?*"

The older man looked up sharply. "What contract?" he asked.

Westhaver looked surprised. "Didn't ye hear about it?"

"Waal—er—no, I haven't h'ard nawthin'. What is it?"

"D'ye mean t' say ye don't know about that big dried-fish contract?"

Ring looked narrowly at Frank's face. "How did you git to hear about it?" he asked slowly.

Westhaver laughed. "Oh, I heard," he said. "D'ye reckon ye stand a chanst?"

" 'Bout as good as——" He stopped suddenly. "Say!" he began, but Frank was walking away.

"Waal, I wish ye luck, Cap'en," he returned. "It'll be a big thing." And while Ring was cogitating over Westhaver's words, the latter was laughing to himself over his conversational bluff.

"So Cap Ring's plannin' on gittin' some big dried-fish contract, is he? But he ain't got it yet. I wonder now jest what it is?" And while he worried over a possible solution, he had some satisfaction in knowing the reason why the other man had refused to join in. If, by any chance, he did not get it, it was possible that he would be only too glad to get rid of the fishermen he had contracted to buy from, and Frank consoled himself with the idea.

For the balance of the week Frank, Jules, Uncle Jerry, and a carpenter busied themselves in constructing a large two-storied fish shed. The lower floor was to be used for cleaning, washing, dressing, and salting the fish as soon as they were unloaded from the boats and vessels, and the upper floor would be utilized for stacking and storing the dried and salted hake, haddock, cod, and pollock. The building was placed close enough to the head of the south wharf so that there would be a minimum of labor and time in transporting fish between shed and vessel, and far enough back to be clear of damage from the sea during spring tides and inshore gales. Behind the shed was the flake yard, extending up to the main road—a good two acres—and when the fish came in they would be prepared and salted in the building and spread upon the lath-built flakes to dry in the sun.

Frank had informed his uncle of Captain Ring's determination to run his own business, and he also mentioned that the boat fishermen had all been secured by the other. "It's too bad that he prefers to keep out of our concern," said Westhaver, "but we don't need to worry. What fish we git from th' vessel 'ull keep us a-goin' pretty well, ef we kin git a gang for her."

"That's just it," remarked Uncle Jerry. "Where are we goin' to git a gang? Ef you or me was runnin' her ourselves we might git men, but with a green skipper like Jules there's liable to be some difficulty. We'll hev t' pick up a crowd up n' down th' coast. Thar's none o' th' Cove men that'll go vessel-fishin' now that Cap'en Ring has got them all shore fishin' for him. Hev ye any idea what contract he's plannin' to git?"

"I've bin puzzlin' all week t' find out," replied Shorty ruefully. "I've pumped all th' fellers, but they know nawthin' about it, an' Ring ain't givin' out any information. Ef we c'd git a big order in dried an' salted fish we c'd bring him over with us without a doubt. As it is, we'll jest hev to fossick aroun' with what we kin git, an' sell to th' fish company over to Bayport."

The shed was practically finished and ready for use when Frank strolled over to purchase some barn paint from Captain Ring. Lem was in the small store when Shorty entered, and he looked up at his old chum with a glum visage.

"What's th' racket, ol' sock?" asked Frank cheerily. "You're lookin' as ef ye'd not a friend left in th' world. Ain't she good to ye?"

Lem gave a grunt. "I wanted t' take a run over to Anchorville to-day an' see her, but the ol' man's taken th' team an' told me to stay to home."

"Oh?" exclaimed the other. "Why didn't he take you with him?"

Lem shook his head. "No, he wouldn't, an' I don't see why. Said he had some important business down in Yarmouth to-morrow an' I was to remain at home. An' th' Town Hop comes off to-night, an' I told her I'd be down in Anchorville for it sure. Darn shame th' way the ol' man treats me. Thinks I'm nawthin' but a kid."

When Frank took the paint over to his own place he was thinking: "So Cap Ring's off to Yarmouth, is he? Wonder ef it has anythin' t' do with th' fish contract? I—wonder—now?"

That evening at supper Mrs. Westhaver handed him a letter. "The mail-driver jest brought it this afternoon," she said. "Looks like a young lady's handwriting."

Uncle Jerry laughed, and Frank turned away to read the epistle. It was from Lillian Denton—a proper lover's note, encouraging, and full of sweet phrases—but it was the postscript which caused him to jump to his feet with a shout.

"What's th' matter?" exclaimed mother and uncle at once.

Frank answered excitedly. "Now I know why Ring has shot off for Yarmouth, an' th' reason for all his close ways! Here's a line from Lily, enclosing a piece from the Yarmouth paper. Listen! Here's what she says: 'The enclosed may interest you. Why not try for it? You may get something out of it.' An' this is what th' paper's got: 'Senhor Ignatio Rucz of the Brazilian Government Commissariat Department and Captain Giovanni Castromento of the Brazilian Navy were passengers on the Boston steamer today. These distinguished gentlemen will remain in Yarmouth for a few days for the purpose of receiving tenders for a large quantity of dried salted fish to be supplied to the Brazilian Government for the use of the army and navy and the penal settlements. It is expected that a number of local dealers will tender for these important contracts. The eminent representatives of the great South American

Republic will leave for Boston again on Saturday evening.' Now, what d'ye think o' that?"

"It aint a-goin' t' do us any good," said Captain Clark dejectedly. "It's too late now—too late. Ef we'd ha' known yesterday you c'd ha' gone t' Yarmouth this mornin' an' made a bid for that. It 'ud ha' bin a good thing t' git a contract like what they'd want. Too bad!"

Frank had left the table and was pacing up and down the room absorbed in thought. "Oh, if he'd only known a day before! Such an order would have given him a great start. And Captain Ring was even then down in Yarmouth placing his tender in———" He made one or two turns in his pacing and stopped.

"When does the freight train leave Anchorville for Yarmouth to-night?"

"Leaves at eight," answered Captain Clark. "Ye'll never catch that. It's seven now, and Anchorville's fourteen miles away."

"An' th' first train in th' mornin' is . . . ?"

"Half-past two in the afternoon. It'll arrive jest a few minutes afore th' Boston boat pulls out."

Frank grunted, and resumed his pacing. "High water now, I cal'late?"

The uncle nodded.

"Jud Morrell's schooner is lyin' to th' wharf, ain't she?"

"Yes," answered the other.

"That's enough for me," shouted Frank. "Git me a lantern, ma! Come along, Uncle! Quick now! We'll make a shoot for Yarmouth to-night!"

"In that bit of a schooner?" cried the stout skipper in amazement. "It's blowy outside t'-night for sich a small hooker."

"Never mind," snapped Frank. "Git your boots on. Gimme a coat! Come on— let's beat it!" And before Uncle Jerry could protest he was hustled into his coat and boots and dragged down to the wharf by his energetic nephew.

Jud Morrell was not at home when they called, but Frank left word with his wife. "Tell Juddy I'm borryin' his vessel to go to Yarmouth. I'll make it all right with him when I git back!" And they ran down to the deserted wharf and tumbled aboard.

"Throw off th' starn line, Uncle, an' drag her down to th' head o' th' dock! So! That'll do! Let go all, an' jump aboard!"

In fifteen minutes from the time they left the house they had hoisted sail and were leaving the cove behind in the darkness.

Frank ran the jib up and belayed the halliard. "Sheet down yer jib!" he cried as he ran aft. "Now, Uncle, we'll drive her! I'm goin' t' make Yarmouth afore noon t'-morrow or know th' reason why. We'll make a bid for that contract or bust. Give it to her now!"

CHAPTER SIXTEEN

THERE WAS A FRESH OFF-SHORE BREEZE BLOWING across the Bay, and in the smooth water under the lee of the land the little forty-foot schooner slipped along as if she had an engine running in her. The night was clear and starlit, and after he had coiled the gear and trimmed the sheets of the foresail, mainsail, and jib, Frank entered the little forecastle and brought out the compass and binnacle.

Coming aft he squatted down in the well or cockpit where his uncle was steering. "Th' sidelights are out in th' brackets, an' here's th' binnacle, lit an' ready for use. Now, ef this breeze'll hold as it is 'thout droppin' or stiffenin', I cal'late we'll run th' hundred miles to Yarmouth in jig time. Ef I git thar' by noon I won't mind. Let me git in Yarmouth an' I'll bust my way inter them Dagos' room an' make my tender. Kinder cold, ain't it?"

The other grunted. "Ain't thar' no oil-clothes aboard?"

"Can't find any," replied Frank. "We sh'd ha' brung ours along, but, never mind, Uncle. We won't mind th' cold ef we land that contract an' beat that ol' fox Ring out." And Frank commenced to sing a little song to himself—a little love ditty which turned his thoughts to the beautiful girl he hoped to win. "Yes," he murmured when the song ended. "A man kin do a power o' things when it's for a girl he loves——

>Dearie, my dearie!
>Nothing's worth while but dreams of you,
>An' you kin make every dream come true.
>Dearie, my dearie!
>Give me your hand,
>Say you understand—
>My dearie!——

Huh! nice song that. Mus' git a piano when I git married so's Lily an' me kin hev some sing-songs——"

"Start yer jib a grind! She's got too much lee helm. So!"

They passed Anchorville Lower Head light at half-past ten, and Frank made a remark. "Good goin'! Twenty miles in two hours. Hope th' tide'll let us down easy when we make th' Sou'-west Ledge."

At midnight the eastern sky became obscured by clouds, and in a little while after it commenced to rain. The two men aboard the tiny craft were drenched to the skin in the downpour, and Frank cursed his thoughtlessness in coming away without oilskins.

"Goin' t' breeze up, I'm afraid," remarked Captain Clark, puffing away at his pipe. "Hope it don't come too strong, or we'll hev t' run in for shelter."

"It'll blow ol' blazes afore I run in for any shelter," growled the other. "B-r-r! but I'm soaked. Gimme th' wheel, Uncle, an' you go below in th' fo'c'sle. I'm younger'n you."

The older man, afraid for his rheumatism, relinquished the wheel and dropped down for'ard to kindle a fire in the tiny stove. It was becoming chilly and cold on deck, and Uncle Jerry felt it in his bones.

Buttoning his coat up, Shorty twirled the spokes and glanced every now and again at sails and the twinkling flash of Gull Island Passage ahead. "Look's jest like a star," he remarked. "A star of the sea!" And he began to croon to himself an Italian sailor song.

> "Star of the Sea! Oh, bright shinin' star!
> Guide ye my mariner home from afar.
> Light ye his barque o'er th' waters to me,
> Estella marina! Star of th' Sea!
>
> Star of th' night in th' heavens so high,
> Light ye our way from th' dark of th' sky.
> In gale or tempest keep shinin' for me,
> Estella marina! Star of th' Sea!

> Oh, far is our barque from th' dear ones we love,
> So pilot us home with thy light from above.
> Light clear th' path that will lead me to thee,
> Estella marina! Star of th' Sea!

"An' th' man what wrote that little song was a sailor, I'll bet," commented Frank. "He knew what it was t' be homeward bound an' steerin' by th' stars twinklin' jest above his home. Aye, aye—Estella marina! Star of th' Sea! Um! Some heft in that puff!" The little vessel rolled down to her rail in a gust which swept down from a clearing in the spruce-clad hills to windward. "Oho! here's another! Nicely, now nicely! Comes up like a whale, she does!"

Uncle Jerry's head appeared in the square of light from the fo'c'sle hatch. "What're ye tryin' t' do? Roll her over?" he bawled. "Lord Harry! She hove a shovelful o' hot cinders a-top o' me. Let her come up in them puffs—she ain't no Bank schooner remember!"

"All right, Uncle," laughed Frank. "I'll let ye know when she's capsizin'."

The wind came away stronger when the Gull Island light came abeam, and, much as Frank regretted taking any sail off her, both men turned to and reefed jib and mainsail in the light from the gas buoy a few yards to windward.

"Handy things is gas buoys sometimes," remarked Frank facetiously when the shortening down was finished. "Reg'lar Gov'ment lamp-posts for th' small craft t' see when tyin' out a reef ear-rin'."

Uncle Jerry looked hard at his nephew while he was speaking, and as he went below again he murmured, "Can't scare that feller nohow. Got no nerves at all, an' I'm 'most scared t' death in this bit of a boat. Eh, eh— as we git older we lose our grit an' th' young 'uns give us th' dare."

All went well until three in the morning, when they fetched well down St. Mary's Bay and had the Brier Island light astern. The breeze had hauled a little more southerly and was blowing athwart the now returning tide. There was some sea running south of the island, and the little

BLUE WATER

vessel began to plunge and sweep her decks in the rips.

Uncle Jerry fastened the fo'c'sle slide and came aft, and Frank and he nursed the small craft among the breaking crests. It was black dark and blowing squally with rain, and when the puffs hit in they had to shoot the schooner up with sails slatting and booms snatching at the tackles.

"I'm scart o' this punt," bawled the older man. "She's old an' hardly able for a drag like this. Them ol' sails o' hers ain't up to much, either."

Frank was not singing now. Both men knew the vagaries of the tide-whipped Bay of Fundy and the dangers of the whirling rips, and they realized that the breeze now blowing and the set of the tide would call for all their skill and seamanship. The wind would hardly have bothered a large fishing schooner, but an old forty-foot craft like Judson Morrell's was not to be driven through tide rips in squally weather.

"Lookin' dirty," remarked Captain Clark.

"Aye," returned Frank; "but thar's th' red flash o' th' Sou'-west buoy to loo'ard. Once git clear o' that an' well down past Trinity an' I ain't worryin'. Up! wa-a-tch aout!"

A curling crest broke aboard and flooded the schooner in white water. Loggy with the weight of it on her deck, she shipped another, which hid the deck from sight, and Captain Clark yelled, "It's a-goin' t' be too much for her! We'd better shoot back inter Brier Island——"

"No! we'll drive her!" bawled Frank. "This ain't nawthin'——" The whine of the wind and the roar of the breaking rips drowned his utterance, and with the spray and rain lashing them they hung aft by the wheel, while the little craft reared and tumbled among the turmoil.

The mournful hoot of the buoy whistle to leeward barely reached their ears, when the little boat rolled down to a puff and shot up into the wind with a slatting and banging of sails. Frank put the helm up again, but the schooner did not fall off and the slatting continued. "What's th' matter?" he shouted. "Jib sheet parted? Take aholt an' I go'n see." Handing the wheel over to his uncle, he clawed his way for'ard in time to see the jib rip itself into ribbons. "Blazes!" he snapped out. "Jib's gone!" He tumbled aft again and communicated the intelligence to his uncle. "She'll never head up for Yarmouth now. Blest ef that rotten ol' mains'l ain't startin' t' split as well——"

"We can't make it now!" shouted the other. "In with th' mains'l and we'll run for Westport. Quick, or she'll swamp in this howlin' drink. We're 'most a-top o' th' blame' buoy!"

Ripping out healthy Bank anathemas on Judson Morrell's sails, Frank clawed the mainsail down and tied it up. "By the ol' Judas!" he said bitterly. "Ef I ain't the original ring-tailed Jonah, I don't know who is!" He started the foresheet, and the schooner wore round and headed for Grand Passage. "Slam now, you ol' barge! You'll run home a sight quicker'n ye'll head th' way I want t' go!"

It was just breaking daylight when they shot in through the eastern passage and glided in alongside one of the Westport wharves.

"What are ye plannin' t' do now?" enquired Uncle Jerry, after his nephew had slipped the mooring lines over the posts.

Frank wrung the water out of his coat before replying. He was drenched from head to foot, and the good suit of clothes he was wearing was visibly shrinking upon his stocky frame. Heaving the coat over a pile of lobster crates, he asked suddenly, "Who's that friend o' yours what owns that motor dory 'round here?"

"Bill Matheson, ye mean?"

"That's th' feller," said Westhaver. "D'ye know whar' his place is?"

"Yes—but what d'ye want him for?" enquired Captain Clark, crawling painfully upon the wharf.

"I'll git him t' run me down t' Yarmouth. Come on, Uncle. Show me his house an' I'll rout him out. Heave ahead!"

The two men walked along the deserted water-front street, stumbling over lobster crates, buoys, and old broken-down dories. Everything was quiet, and as they strode along the road Frank shivered in his wet clothes. "Fine place t' die in is this Westport," remarked he. "I've h'ard nawthin' but a rooster a-crowin' sence we landed——"

"Here's Bill's place," interrupted the other, and they stepped up on to the porch of a neat shingled cottage.

The lobsterman was roused out, and the two explained their errand.

"Run me down, Mr. Matheson, an' I'll make it worth yer while——"

"Oh, that's all right," said the other sleepily. "When d'ye want t' go?"

"Now—right now," replied Frank. "I don't want t' waste any more time. We've bin all night a-comin' from Long Cove in a little bit of a vessel, but we bust our jib off th' Sou'-west Ledge an' had t' make a shoot for here."

" 'Tain't a very nice mornin' for runnin' down," demurred the man. "Th' south cone is h'isted up to th' Signal Station thar'——"

"I don't care a hoot for storm cones," ejaculated Westhaver. "You run the engine an' I'll steer yer boat."

Matheson laughed. "All right, skipper. Wait till I git my clothes on an' a bite to eat. Draw to th' stove thar' an' dry yerselves. I'll git the ol' woman out t' make ye some hot tea."

Within half an hour he was ready, and Frank turned to his uncle and said, "Thar's no call for you t' go. Stay with th' boat 'til I come back, an' try an' git a new jib. I'll show up this afternoon or to-morrow mornin'."

"Go an' turn in, Cap'en," said Matheson. "Th' wife'll give ye a bed, an' dry yer clothes."

And Uncle Jerry, feeling his rheumatism, gladly availed himself of the offer.

It wasn't just the weather suited for a twenty-foot motor-dory to wrestle with, and when the little craft swung through the eastern passage she was met by a tumbling broil of sea which almost pitch-poled her as she swooped over their crests. Both men sat aft; Frank steering by the tiller, and Matheson, with the engine hatch drawn almost to, nursing the coughing motor as she plunged in the seaway. The rain had ceased, but it was blowing stiff from the south-east, and when they left the bare loom of Brier Island astern all sight of land was shut out by a damp, fog-like mist.

Frank had never been in a motor-boat before, and he spoke to his companion. "How quick'll she make it?"

The other pondered before replying. "It's 'most thutty mile down to th' Cape, but with this south-easter an' tide settin' agin us we ain't a-goin' to make th' run in less'n five hours. I got a good strong engine here what kin shove her along 'bout ten mile in slack water, but with wind an' tide in our teeth we kain't make more'n six."

"Um! 'Tis five o'clock now. Waal, ef we git in by noon, I won't mind; but drive her, Matheson, as I'm in an awful hurry."

They laid a course over towards Cape St. Mary's to run down in the lee of the land, and it was ten miles of water which Matheson is not likely to forget. Twice the little dory was deluged in a sea, and only frantic bailing upon Westhaver's part saved them from sinking. Twice the lobsterman wanted to turn back, but Frank would not let him. "Jest a few minutes more, Bill," he would say, "an' we'll be out o' this. You keep that engine a-goin' an' I'll keep th' dory top o' th' water. She'll be all right!" And even as he spoke the words she almost filled to the coamings. Luckily the engine was enclosed inside a water-tight bulkhead, and whatever water poured into the cockpit of the boat it failed to enter the engine compartment.

When at last they fetched up under the lee of the Cape, Matheson wiped the sweat off his face. "Blazin' Hades!" he ejaculated. "I jest about planned on never gittin' acrost, skipper. Lord Harry! I'll never be hauled out o' my bunk t' make a run like that again—not even ef th' King of England sh'd come an' ask me."

"Ha, ha, ha!" laughed Westhaver. "Never mind, Bill! Ef he sh'd ever ask ye, ye kin send for me an' I'll help ye take him acrost. I'm a great hand at bailin', I am." And the other looked over at him in astonishment.

"I kin understand now," he murmured to himself, "how that young shaver got his reputation. Frightened his gang 'most to death in th' shoal water o' th' Lurcher in a sou'-wester, did he? Huh! I believe it, for he's a dog— a proper, rip-roaring dog, an' scared o' nawthin'."

It was eleven o'clock when they fetched to windward of the North-west Fairway gas and whistling buoy and headed for Cape Forchu, five miles away. The wind had died down to a light breeze, but there was a tremendous swell rolling in from the south'ard—a swell which hove them up sky high and hid them between hills of black-green water. Like a steeple-chaser rushing the hurdles, they swooped over the great undulations with sickening plunges, until Cat Rock bell buoy clanged a warning at them. Then the engine, which up to that time had been running like a clock, gave a few coughs and stopped. Matheson shoved the hatch back and started cranking the fly-wheel, but the engine remained quiescent, and in the haste born of fear the lobsterman yanked the movable bulkhead out and commenced to prime the motor. While he was working away to find out the trouble a sullen roaring came to his ears and he blanched. "What's that?" he ejaculated hastily.

"Nawthin', nawthin'," answered Westhaver calmly. "Only Cat Rock down to loo'ard doin' a bit o' caterwaulin'."

Matheson stood up and glanced at the white water thundering over the great black bulk of the cat-like monolith a scant thousand feet to leeward, and the sight gave him a chill. "God Almighty!" he cried fearfully. "We're gone coons!"

Westhaver nodded. "We are, ef you don't git that engine a-goin'. We ain't ef you do. Water ain't warm for swimmin' these days."

The lobsterman bent to the engine again and overhauled

it in feverish haste, and every time the rock spoke its thunderous warning the beads of perspiration dropped off his face.

"It's no use," he said at last. "Batteries hev give out, an' I ain't got a spare set aboard——"

"Then ye kain't git that engine a-goin'?" interrupted Westhaver.

"No," the other shook his head and glanced at the nearing rock. "It's dead an' so'll we be."

Frank fully realized the desperate position they were in, but he was not one of the kind to sit down and wait for death, no matter how near it was.

"Come on," he yelled. "Paddle her out o' this!" And as he spoke he ripped up two of the bottom boards of the flooring. Tossing one of the planks to his companion, he said, "Lay to it now! We'll weather it yet. Now, bust yer heart out! Sock it to her! Now! Now! And while the surf was thundering in their ears, he shouted encouraging words to the frightened lobsterman, and both paddled with all their strength.

The rock was very near now, and as they rose on the summit of a mighty swell Frank could see the great black bulk glistening in the faint sunlight for a fleeting moment, then a giant upheaval of green water hurled itself upon the adamantine pile, blotting it from view for a few seconds, and with a thunderous roar which caused the very air to vibrate the black fangs of the rock appeared through the welter of froth and white water streaming from it. It was an awe-inspiring sight, even when viewed from the safety of a steamer's deck, but to the frantically toiling men in the motor-boat it appeared as the portals to Eternity.

Frank, with his left arm still weak from his accident, began to feel all in, but to falter in his stroke would be to lose everything. Life seemed very dear just then, and, gasping with his exertions, he snapped huskily, "Keep it up, Matheson! We're slippin' it by! Sock it to her! Now! Now!"

The rock spoke again and the boat seemed to swirl in

the backwash of hissing froth which swept from the ponderous bulk. It seemed to loom almost overhead, but as Frank looked he saw that they were clearing the danger. One minute more and they would be safe from being smashed to atoms between the hammer and the anvil of the sea. One minute more—Frank's heart was pumping like a steam-engine now, and his breath hissed through his shut teeth in rasping gasps. "Keep a-goin'!" he croaked. "Keep a-goin'——" Once more the rock was blotted out. Once more it appeared blacker against the froth of outraged sea, but it was cheated of its victims, and when it roared again there seemed to be a note of ineffectual rage in the boom of the conflicting elements of stone and water.

Matheson collapsed in a panting heap. "Lord! what a shave! What a shave!"

"Come on! Lay to it," snarled the other, still paddling. "We've got t' shoot her up on that strip o' beach afore we're out o' th' muddle. Go to it!"

The lighthouse people had seen them and were running down to the shore, and with the swell driving them in, they neared the breakers rapidly. "Steady now!" panted Westhaver. "Look out we don't git rolled over in th' surf——"

The words were hardly out of his mouth before the plank in his hands broke in halves. The boat swung round; a curling comber caught her and rolled her completely over, and the two men were thrown out into the frothing water. Luckily, the light-keeper and his men had brought a rope with them, and, grasping it as it was thrown to them, Westhaver and Matheson were hauled out sputtering, gasping, and almost half-suffocated. The dory was grasped as she came in on the crest of the next wave, and, none the worse, it was hauled above high-water.

"Waal, ef you two ain't had a session!" remarked the keeper. "I sure thought ye'd git smashed on th' rock out thar', an' we hadn't a boat or a thing 'round here this mornin'——"

Westhaver looked over his sodden clothing. "Lend me

a hat an' a dry coat," he said after he had recovered his breath. "I got to git over to Yarmouth right away. Good, that'll do fine, thank you! I'll bring 'em back to ye later——"

"Won't ye come up to th' house an' git dry?" enquired the keeper.

"No," answered Frank. "Can't stop a minute. Thank ye kindly. I must go now. I'll see ye later, Bill. I'm awful sorry I got ye into sich a mess, but I'll fix it up." And he ran along the rough rock road to the Markland ferry.

Matheson turned to the keeper. "I've been in some tight corners in my day," he remarked as he walked up to the keeper's cottage, "an' I've bin with some all-nation tough skippers a-Bankin', but, by the ol' Judas, that Westhaver has 'em all skun a mile for downright toughness. He ain't got no nerves at all, but, believe me, he's a terrier an' a mighty fine man to sail with. Aye, he's th' man what come in here all stove up after luggin' his vessel through th' Lurcher in a sou'-wester—dories, mains'l, an' mainm'st gone. A holy terror!"

Clad in a lobsterman's oil hat, a coat too large for him, trousers which shrunk on his muscular legs, and tan shoes which squelched water at every step, Frank strode into the rotunda of the Grand Hotel at precisely one o'clock in the afternoon. With a trail of water in his wake soaking into the carpet, he walked up to the hotel clerk.

"I want t' see these Brazilian gentlemen stayin' here," he said shortly.

The clerk looked hard at him. "What name, please?"

"Tell them Captain Westhaver of th' Long Cove Fish Company wants a few minutes."

While a bell boy ran off to deliver the message, Frank was the object for a great deal of astonished scrutiny from the guests lounging around. Captain Ring and some other men were talking and smoking over in a corner, and the former stared at Westhaver with eyes open wide in surprise. "Waal, I be darned!" he ejaculated.

"Who's that? What's th' matter?" enquired one of the others.

"Oh, nawthin'," replied Ring hastily. "I was wonderin' how that feller come here."

The page returned in a minute. "Step this way, Captain," he said, and Frank was piloted along the corridor to a room in which two well-dressed gentlemen were seated at a table smoking cigars and looking over some papers. One of the Brazilians was an undeniably handsome man of forty-five or fifty, with a swarthy skin, black, grey-streaked hair, and a heavy black moustache. The other was fat, clean-shaven, and very yellow as to skin, and his age would about rank with his handsomer companion's. They looked up when Frank entered and surveyed him with an expression of astonishment on their faces.

"Good day, gentlemen," said Frank. "My name is Westhaver—Captain Frank Westhaver, and I am representin' th' Long Cove Fish Company. I understand you gentlemen are here with a view to receivin' tenders for supplies o' dried fish for th' Brazilian Government?"

The yellow man nodded courteously. "We are, sir."

"Waal, ef ye'd be good enough t' tell me what ye want, I will be able t' give ye a price."

The gentleman made a gesture of regret. "I'm sorry, Captain, but all de tenders were to be receive by noon. Eet ees now one of de clock, and we have nearly given de contracts out."

Frank dropped dejectedly into a chair. After all he had gone through it was hard—very hard—to have lost the chances of the venture by the narrow margin of an hour. The swarthy man seemed sympathetic, and he spoke quietly to the disheartened young fisherman twirling the oil hat in his hands.

"Senhor! you are wet? What has happened to keep you from arriving here in time?"

Westhaver looked up at the other's face—it was a strong, yet kindly countenance, and to Frank it seemed to be strangely familiar. "I did not know that you gentlemen would be here until late last night," answered Frank slowly. "I live a hundred miles from here—up above Anchorville—an' I was too late to catch a train, so my uncle an' me took a small schooner an' tried t' make th' passage. It come on t' blow a bit an' we lost one of our sails an' had to run into Brier Island——"

"Yes, Brier Island, I know it," interrupted the gentleman encouragingly.

Frank was a little astonished, but continued. "We got there 'bout five this mornin', then I got a motor dory an' came down here as hard as we could, but the engine stopped when we got off Cat Rock, an' we were nearly hove up on it with th' swell. We got clear, but capsized in th' surf at th' Cape. That's how I got wet."

"And it blew veree hard last night, and you were out in it?" said the other. "And your engine stopped off Cat Rock in this southerly swell?"

The gentleman spoke English with a very slight foreign accent, and Frank's eyes were riveted upon his face. "Where had he seen this man before?" The tone of the voice and the eyes were strangely familiar. Frank replied, "Yes, sir. We had a tough night in gittin' down here." He paused and stared hard at the swarthy Brazilian in front of him. "Excuse me, sir," he said, "but I can't help thinkin' I've seen you somewheres before. I've never bin in your country, but I'll swear that I've met you years ago."

The other laughed, showing a mouth of regular white teeth. "That may be, senhor. I am no stranger to this country. I have been a sailor in ships coming into Yarmouth and into Anchorville——"

"Now I have it!" cried Frank delightedly. "Now I know who you are! Sir! Do you remember two little boys comin' off to an Italian barque one winter's day 'bout ten years ago an' pilotin' her in to Anchorville?"

The other rose to his feet. "Why, to be sure I do," he replied, smiling. "And you were the pilot, were you not? West-haver! West-haver! Yes, yes, I know you now.

You wrote your name down in my book, an' gave me a little souvenir for my lady——"

"Margarheta in Spatechea!" interrupted Shorty.

"Yes, yes! Margarheta of Spezzia! She's my wife now. Well, well, this is curious!" Turning to his wondering companion, he said, "An old friend of mine—Capitan Westhaver—Senhor Ruez. My name is Castromento—Capitan Castromento, of the Republican Navy."

The ice was broken at once, and over the cigars, the onetime Italian sailor and Westhaver went over the incident of the piloting, while Ruez listened with a smile on his gamboge countenance. "Yes, Capitan," continued the naval officer, "I left that old tub in Rio Janeiro the voyage after, and entered the navy. I had done naval service in Italy before I went in merchant ships, and having rendered a little service to Admiral Robeiro during one of the revolutions, I soon got on to commissioned positions through his influence. Ha, ha! I laugh when I think of that pig of a capitan on the barque. How frightened he was! And how he hated to pay the pilotage money until your Anchorville harbour-master came aboard and made him pay. It was very funny."

When a lull came in the reminiscences, Senhor Ruez politely made a suggestion which sounded like music in Frank's ears. "Probably the Capitan weel make hees tender for the feesh supply. One must consider one's friends. Eh, Capitan Castromento?"

"*Caramba!* Yes!" replied Castromento. "But why talk business while dinner awaits? Let us eat first, and you will honour us by joining in dining with us, Capitan."

Frank looked down at his sodden clothing. "I would like to, but my clothes ain't jest right for goin' into a dinin'- room."

"*Por Dios*, then we will have it brought up here," returned the other heartily. "Ruez, my friend, you have no objections?"

"Eet ees a pleasure to eat wit' your friends, Castromento. Let us have eet set here."

Captain Ring lounged around the rotunda with a watchful eye on the corridor, but he did not see Westhaver coming out. "Guess he slipped out th' back way so's I wouldn't see him," he muttered. Then, spying the bell boy, he called to him. "Say, young feller! What became o' that man ye showed up to them furriners a while ago?"

"Westhaver?"

"Yes, that's th' name."

The bell boy put the proffered cigar into his pocket. "Why, Cap, he's still up with them. That rough neck, an' them two Dagos are all eatin' together up in their room——"

"What?" barked Ring.

"Sure enough, Cap! He's dinin' with them, wet an' all as he is."

The fish-dealer looked at the clock. It was within a few minutes of train time, and he was undecided as to whether he would wait to hear who had got the contracts or depart for home.

"Waal, they said they'd mail th' papers from here, so I cal'late ain't much use waitin'. What gits me is how Westhaver sh'd ha' bust in an' got so mighty thick with them. I wonder now?" And with a great respect for his younger rival, and still wondering, Captain Ring regretfully left the hotel.

Frank enjoyed that dinner as he never enjoyed a meal before. The Brazilians were hospitality personified, and it was not long before Castromento and he knew each other's whole history. Frank's plans for the future were heartily commended by the naval officer, and when, in answer to a question, Westhaver admitted that he was engaged to a girl, the gentleman laughed.

"*Per la vita mia!*" he exclaimed, turning to his stout companion. "Friend Ruez, we must do something for our ambitious young man here. He loves—*capite?* And should we not help those who love, senhor? We have been young once. You won your Eugenia from the mob of *revolutionarios* in Para. I stole my Margarheta from under the eyes of her savage papa—a merchant in Spezzia—and ran across the sea with her. Shall we not help our friend, Ruez?"

The other nodded smilingly and stared at the blushing Frank. "Can you supply us weeth a large amount?" he said. "The contract weel be for three years, an' for my department of supplies we weel require at least feefty thousand dollars American worth of bacalao per year——"

"Fifty thousand dollars!" gasped Frank. "Lord, but that's a big contract, but I cal'late I kin supply some of it."

"Why not take eet all?" queried the other. "Three years—one hondred and feefty thousand dollars. I weel make dees contract out for you, and you weel see that we get the shipments regular. By doing thees, eet weel save me the trouble of giving many separate contracts. I weel deal weeth you only, and you can let sub-contracts out to oder men. Our prices weel be fair, and the Brazeelian Consulado een New York weel pay you when the shipments are made to Rio Yhaneiro. You weel communicate weeth heem, and all arrangements weel be made from there. I weel take your references—but one knows a gentleman even though hees cloak be faded—and I weel hand you thees document. Eet specifies everytheeng. Weel you take eet, my friend?"

"Will I take it?" almost shouted Frank, his eyes alight with untold joy. "Waal, I sh'd jest think so! Oh, gentlemen, but you've made a happy man of me this day——"

His ingenuous delight pleased the temperamental Latins, and they smiled paternally upon his ebullition of spirits. When he left them, he had the precious paper in his pocket, duly signed and sealed by the representatives of the mighty Estados Unidos do Brazil, and their good wishes were ringing in his ears. "When you marry, Capitan," said Castromento at parting, "come to Rio for your honeymoon. We will show you our incomparable Bay, our Corcovado, and the botanical gardens. *Adios, Capitan! Vada con Dio!*" And the yellow-skinned Ruez was just as cordial in his farewell wishes.

Frank found himself out in the rotunda in a daze. Was it all a dream? No, there was the paper crackling in his breast pocket. For a minute he stood—a rough-looking, sea-soaked figure—and made a mental retrospection of the afternoon's events. At last, after a summary of the wonderful happenings of the day, he become aware that the loungers in the hotel were staring at him.

"Let's git out o' this. I must be a sight. Now for Lillian. She must hear all about it an' what she has done for me!"

She was tying up some vines at the side of the house when Frank swung in through the gate, and, heedless of time, place, or circumstances, he threw his arms around her and gave her a hug and a resounding kiss.

"Why, Frank, you great bear!" she cried in astonishment, with her brown eyes wide and her beautiful face flushed with the publicity of her lover's caresses. "Whatever sent you down here—and in those wet clothes?"

Westhaver took her by the arm. "Come over to th' summer-house, sweetheart," he said. "I'm jest about bustin' with joy. Another kiss, dearie, an' I'll tell ye all about it!"

She made no resistance. It would have been some task to resist such an enthusiastic young lover as Westhaver, and while she was blushing rosily and arranging the stray wisps of disordered silky brown hair he pulled the paper out of this pocket. "See this, sweetheart? That's th' result o' th' tip you gave me—a hundred-an'-fifty-thousand-dollar contract from th' Brazilian Government!" And he told her the story of his adventures since he left the Cove the night before.

When he finished she looked up into his radiant face, and there was a hint of fear in her eyes. "Oh, Frank dear," she said softly, "I'm so glad you got that, but you frighten me with what you went through. What if you had lost your life out there in the darkness last night, or on the rock this morning? Oh, promise me you'll never do such things again. Promise, Frank, for my sake!"

Frank clasped her in his strong arms and gazed into the pools of her dark eyes. "Sweetheart," he said with the adoration of her in the tones of his voice, "'Twas you that nerved me to do it, an' I knew you'd be near me. I c'd see your face encouragin' me to do my best, an' I did. 'Twas you that put the idea my way, an' 'twas you that made these gentlemen give me th' contract. Darling, ye've made a man o' me, an' I love ye more an' more. Oh, but I'm happy, Lily!"

Old Captain Denton was pleased to see him, and still more pleased when he saw the contract. "I'll want your help, Captain," said Frank. "When I'm ready t' ship a load, I'll ask ye t' look over a likely vessel for me to charter."

It was late in the afternoon when Westhaver left the Denton home for the Cape, and with the touch of a soft cheek lingering on his lips, and the crackling document in his pocket, he seemed to tread on air. The sun was shining, and a light southerly wind was blowing when Matheson and he left for Westport again in the motor-boat. Cat Rock gleamed golden in the light of the westering sun, and the wavelets, lapping around its weed-strewn base, were murmuring a lullaby. Everything seemed to have changed— even the rips over the Sou'-West Ledge had calmed down into great oily slicks of smooth sea—and when, in the starlight of a clear September evening, they puttered into Westport wharves, the little village was transformed into a hamlet of Arcadia—restful and beautifully home-like, with the warm glow of the house lights dancing in the calm waters of the harbour.

Uncle Jerry was nervously pacing the narrow interior of the local post office and general store, and when Frank entered he gave way to a most undignified whoop of joy.

"Lordy, Frank, I've bin 'most scared to death about you!" he cried. "I've jest bin a-tryin' t' git Yarmouth on th' 'phone t' find out ef they'd seen ye. An' what's th' news?"

For answer, Frank drew out the contract. "One hundred an' fifty thousand dollars' worth, an' three years' delivery," he said quietly. "We'll hev t' git right down to work now, Uncle!"

CHAPTER SEVENTEEN

IT WAS LATE ON SUNDAY EVENING WHEN UNCLE AND nephew arrived back in the Cove, and after securely mooring Morrell's little vessel they went up to the house. Mrs. Westhaver had been anxious, and after the greetings were over she said in a hushed voice, "Well, Frank, poor old Captain Crawford must have known his time was come when he sold you his land. He was found dead in bed this morning."

"Dead?" ejaculated Frank in awed tones. "Poor—old —man. Aye, he must have known—he must have known. Poor old Cap'en Asa. We'll miss him sorely." While Frank was genuinely sorry to hear of the old shipmaster's demise, yet the joy of the huge order he had received swamped the feelings that otherwise would have possessed him at the death of an old neighbour, and when he communicated the good news to his mother that worthy lady cried in her pleasure.

"Now, Uncle," said Frank, after the supper things had been cleared away from the table, "we'll hev t' do some plannin'. We want t' carry out th' most o' this contract ef we kin, an' it'll need a lot o' money. All th' money we've got, in fact——"

"How about Ring?" interrupted Uncle Jerry. "He's got all th' boat fishermen tied up to him."

The other laughed. "An' what kin he do with them? He ain't got th' business nor th' money to employ them all. He'll come in with us, never fear. I'll fetch him around tomorrow. Now, th' question is—how much cash kin ye scrape up, Uncle?"

"Six thousand dollars an' th' vessel, I cal'late."

Frank noted the amount down. "Good!" he said. "That means you hev invested a sum of eleven thousand dollars in th' business. I've put in five thousand—two thousand five hundred in land an' th' new shed we've built, an' two thousand five hundred in th' bank. Thus our combined cash amounts to eight thousand five hundred dollars with a plant an' a good vessel. Now, I'll git after Ring to-morrow an' I'll see what he says."

"Hev ye got th' deeds yet for Cap'en Asa's property?" enquired the other.

"No," replied Frank; "but I've got his receipt for my check. He'll have written the advocate down in Anchorville about it, I reckon. I hold his receipt an' he's got my check—so it's a deal."

The uncle nodded. "Yes, I guess so. Poor Morrissey! I cal'late he'll be some mad when he hears that his uncle hez sold his property an' sent th' money to an orphan society instid o' leavin' it to him. An' th' very furniture is t' be sold for old Jane, his housekeeper. Waal, the ol' man never did like Bob. He useter rattle him too much. Poor ol' man."

Breakfast on Monday morning was scarce over before Captain Ring strolled into the Westhaver homestead. When Mrs. Westhaver announced the visitor, Frank winked over at his uncle. "No need t' go to him. He's bothered with all th' fishermen he's got tied up an' he'll be wantin' t' hear about th' contract an' who's got it."

The shrewd fish-dealer greeted Frank reservedly when he entered the living-room.

"Waal, Cap'en," said Shorty with a smile, "got that big contract yet?"

"No," answered the other slowly. "I saw ye down t' Yarmouth an' I thought I'd jest blow over an' see ef ye'd h'ard anythin'. They tell me ye were dinin' with them furriners?"

"Oh, yes," remarked Frank off-handedly. "They were ol' acquaintances o' mine, an' I had a bite o' dinner and a cigar with them."

Captain Ring grunted, and, scanning the other's face through half-closed eyes, he ventured a question. "You'll maybe hear who got all them orders?"

Frank reached for his pipe, filled it and lit it before replying. "Oh, sure," he answered with studied unconcern, which was intended to impress the other, "I got th' whole thing."

Captain Ring's hat rolled on the floor. "You—got—th' whole—contract?" he gasped in open-mouthed astonishment. "Ye're jokin' surely?"

"Oh, no—no joke," replied Frank. "I got it right enough."

"How—much—is—it?" The fish-dealer had picked up his hat and was nervously twirling it around in his fingers.

"One hundred an' fifty thousand dollars."

"One—hundred—an'—fifty—thousand—dollars! Holy Mackerel!"

The brim of the hat was broken off in his excitement as he repeated the amount, and as he stared at the nonchalant expression on Westhaver's face he almost trembled as he asked to see the paper.

"Here it is," said the other, tossing it over as if it were only a circular.

Captain Ring picked up the document reverently and scrutinized it from title to signature. The Brazilian arms and the seal impressed him mightily, and when he handed it back he knew that he had been beaten.

"Aye, you've got it all right," he said slowly; "but are ye plannin' to supply th' whole o' that?"

"Oh, certainly," replied Frank.

The other grunted and a shrewd expression came into his eyes. "An' where d'ye plan gittin' men t' fish for ye?"

Frank knew this was coming. "Th' fellers aroun' here 'ull fish for us, I reckon."

"Oh, will they? It happens they're all workin' for me. I kin use them all myself in spite o' your contract."

Westhaver reached for a match and relighted his pipe.

"Waal," he drawled unconcernedly, "I've got th' vessel——"

"But ye ain't got no gang for her yit," interrupted the other.

Frank laughed. "I won't depend on Bay Shore men for my gang. I'm writin' acrost to Glo'ster for my old crowd, an' they'll all come. I kin scrape up a gang aroun' T Dock any time I sing out an' so kin my uncle. Th' gang don't worry me none."

The older man said nothing, and as Westhaver glanced at his face he could see that he had bluffed him to a standstill. He twirled his hat for a few more long seconds, and spoke at last. "Is yer offer still open, Frank?" he said hesitantly.

"Waal, yes I reckon so," answered Shorty, as if the subject didn't interest him. "But I'll want t' know how ye'll come in an' how much cash ye're willin' to put up."

"I'll throw my whole plant—buildin's an' flake-yard an' three thousand dollars cash in with ye——"

"On a partnership basis?" interrupted Westhaver.

"On a partnership basis," reiterated the other; "an' I'll value my land an' buildin's at a thousand dollars. That'll be four thousand in all."

Frank arose with a laugh and held out his hand. "I knew ye hed t' come, Cap'en," he said. "We'll do better together than runnin' opposition. Ho! Uncle, come in here an' we'll draw this thing up."

Thus the Long Cove Fish Company was formed; but Frank remembered the contract he had secured, and he claimed two thousand dollars for it. "That'll make my share come to seven thousand. This contract's worth that easily, as I figure we sh'd clear nigh eighteen thousand a year on it."

'I'll put in another thousand," said Ring. "Now what'll that be?"

Frank read the paper. " 'The Long Cove Fish Company. Total capital $23,000, of which I own $7000, Cap'en Clark owns $11,000, an' Cap'en Ring owns $5000.' Our profits will be divided in proportion to our shares every year. Now, we'll elect our official positions in th' Company. D'ye agree t' me bein' manager an' runnin' th' books an' the office end o' it?"

"Sure!" assented both unanimously.

"All right! Now I propose that Cap'en Ring superintends th' flake-yards, an' th' saltin' an' dryin' an' storin' up at th' buildin's, an' Uncle Jerry looks after th' vessel, th' boats, an' all th' wharf work. How's that look t' ye?"

"Suits me fine!" exclaimed Captain Ring heartily.

And "Jest what I like, Frank!" from Uncle Jerry.

"Good! Now, with all th' work thar's goin' t' be aroun' here, we must start a store. A store with rope, canvas, trawl gear, oil-clothes, an' all that stuff, as well as gasolene for th' motor-boats, an' batteries—we won't forget batteries ef I know it—an' a lot o' general stuff. A reg'lar store with everythin' in it same's ye kin git in Anchorville, an' th' vessel kin bring th' stuff acrost from Bayport atween seasons. That'll mean another source o' profit an' a good one too."

The others nodded, while Frank continued.

"Of course we'll have to buy some dry fish from some o' th' small dealers up th' Bay, an' I think it will be a good thing for Captain Ring to go on a trip an' make some deals in that connection. Our place ain't quite big enough to store all th' fish we'll git this winter in pickle, but next year, maybe, we'll buy a presser an' a steam-dryer, an' we'll be able t' cure fish all winter 'thout dependin' on th' flake dryin'. Now, Uncle, when will we be able t' git th' *Lillian* a-goin'?"

"Waal, anytime now, Frank. Her register hez bin changed an' she's all fixed up an' ready. Hev ye told Jules?"

"Not yet, but I will to-day. We'll all go down to Anchorville to-morrow an' have our Company drawn up ship-shape by a notary, an' we'll transfer our cash to th' bank. Is that satisfactory, gentlemen?"

The others nodded assent.

"Good!" said Frank. "We'll adjourn th' first meetin' then o' th' Long Cove Fish Company."

That afternoon Westhaver went down to the wharves where most of the Long Cove men were working, and calling them together, he explained to them what he and his partners proposed doing. "It'll be a big thing for th' Cove, boys," he said. "There'll be lots of work for three years at least, an' after that I have no doubt but what we'll be able t' build up a big business. As things progress, it is our intention t' branch out into other lines o' fish products. We'll smoke an' prepare finnan haddies for th' western market. We'll put up boneless cod an' canned fish. We might put in a lobsterin' plant as well, but for th' first year we'll confine ourselves t' supplyin' th' Brazilian Government contract. That'll be a big job for a new concern, an' I am relyin' on all you fellers to help us out. I know all of you, an' you all know me. I'll treat you right, an' I'll look for ye t' do th' same to th' Company. We'll help ye every way we kin. We'll keep a first-class store where ye kin buy yer gear at th' same rates as ye'll git in Anchorville or any other town. We'll hev gasolene an' engine oil to supply yer motor-boats, an' we'll bring herrin' bait over from th' weirs an' keep it always on hand, so you won't lose time huntin' for bait. Now, kin I count on you fellers?"

There was an affirmative roar which left no doubt in Frank's mind as to the loyalty of the crowd, and when Long Dick got up on a barrel and called for three cheers for Shorty Westhaver, he knew that he could depend on them. The rangy fisherman's speech was something in its way and pretty well voiced the sentiments of the Long Covers assembled.

"Fellers," he said, "this young man was eddicated by me"—a roar of laughter from the crowd. "Right ye are, Schoolmaster Dick!" shouted someone who knew Jennings's views—*"in th' business o' fishin'.* He was in my dory for quite a spell, an' I allus knowed then that he hed a long head on him. He's an eddicated man, which most on us ain't, an' I 'low that eddication an' book-l'arnin' is a good thing—*sometimes.* I say *sometimes,* 'cause it ain't allus a good thing, an' it ain't every man what kin git eddication an' be any good as a fisherman. Readin', writin', an' 'rithmetic don't count in haulin' trawls. But, we hev here, a young man what is eddicated, an' what kin haul a trawl or sail a vessel with th' best on 'em. He was a holy terror when he was a kid, an' he was a holy terror when he was skipperin' a vessel, but I say thar's some pleasure in workin' for a man what hez gone through th' mill same as all on us. We know Cap'en Clark an' we know Cap'en Ring, an' we're a-goin' t' act square with them. Any man what tries t' double-cross 'em is a-goin' t' bump up agin Dick Jennin's, an' I'll bump 'em good an' hard. Ye know what sort of a dog I am. I kin be as nice as Devil Dodger Westley, or I kin be a hog, an' when I'm hog, I'm all hog——"

A strident female voice came from the rear of the laughing mob. "Yes, you're all hog, Dick Jennings! Haow about my kindlin' wood, you lazy good-for-nawthin' scaramouch? Come off that bar'l an' git t' home at wunst, or I'll warm yer skinny hide for ye, you blather-skite!"

The aggressive look faded from Long Dick's face, and he reddened under his tan. Dick's wife was a noted virago, and many a time the worthy fisherman had slept in his fish shack in preference to going home. Humbly he crawled off, amid the titters of the crowd, and with his great masculine better half in his wake, the men could hear her laying down "petticoat law" to him. "You lazy, big-mouthed ballast fish! All ye're fit for—makin' a fool o' yerself. An' me waitin' for a bit o' kindlin' t' light my stove with, while you're talkin' about bein' a hog. Yes, you're a hog, all right!"

For the rest of the week Frank busied himself around the buildings of the plant. A bridge was built across the creek in order to connect Ring's place with the new section, and Bill Daley's little packet—still running and looking the same as she did in Shorty's boyhood days—was chartered to bring supplies for the proposed store. Captain

Asa's funeral came off—all the Long Covers following the body to the little cemetery; and the day after the interment an auctioneer came up from Anchorville and sold the furniture and household goods. Frank and his uncle and Captain Ring went to Anchorville, and the papers of the Company were duly drawn up, though there was some little hitch owing to Frank's inability to produce the deeds of the property he had purchased from the deceased shipmaster.

"Of course," said the lawyer finally, "you may receive them within a few days, seeing that the transaction was only made within the last two weeks. At any rate you hold his receipt and you have given him your check for the amount. He was to write his notary about it, wasn't he?"

"Yes," replied Frank;' 'but I don't know who he is, or I'd ha' called an' seen him."

"Oh, well," returned the other, "I suppose it'll be all right. But I'll hold these papers until I hear from you."

While they were in town the three partners managed to scrape up a six-dory gang for the *Lillian,* and when they arrived back in the Cove Frank called Jules to one side.

"Waal, Sabot, ol' sock! An' how's Jessie Leblanc these days?"

Jules grinned. "Veree well, Frankee."

"Now, I cal'late you'll be wantin' t' git hitched up some day, eh?"

"Oh, lots of time—lots of time," answered the other. "I mus' git good job before I marry dat girl."

Frank laughed and slapped his old dory-mate on the back. "Waal, I've got a good job for you."

"What's dat? Down at de fish-house, Frankee?"

"No, sir. I'm not a-goin' t' make a flake bird out o' you, Sabot. I want you to go in th' vessel as skipper."

The big Frenchman gasped. "Skipper?" he ejaculated.

"Why, t' be sure," replied Frank. "You kin handle that vessel all right."

"But—but, Frankee, I'm no good off de shore," stammered the other. "I don't know how for navigate——"

"That's all right, Sabot. Uncle Jerry'll make th' first two or three trips with you, an' he'll show you th' ropes. It'll not take you long with the experience you've had."

"Oh, Frankee!"

"Now, we want her t' git out right away. Thar's a six-dory gang waitin' for her down to Anchorville, so git you down thar' to-morrow. Git yer stores aboard—John Watson's goin' as cook—an' bring her aroun' to th' Cove here. D'ye understand, Captain Galarneau?"

"*Captain* Galarneau?" Sabot rolled the title over on his tongue. "*Captain!* Oh, Shortee, but I'm please. I hope I be good skipper. I'm glad! I'm glad!" And he danced around and snapped his fingers in the exuberance of his delight, while Westhaver watched him with a secret pleasure at his friend's gratification.

"Can I go an' tell Miss Leblanc about dat, Frankee?"

Frank nodded. "Sure thing! Go ahead! You'll sure be able t' git a few kisses over that bit o' news. Run along now, or some other man'll be cuttin' ye out!"

And with a whoop of joy Jules snatched his hat and ran out of the house.

Westhaver watched him go. "Waal," he murmured, "ef any man deserves it, 'tis him. He's true as steel, that feller, an' it's me that knows it."

September passed in all its languor of cool nights and joyous sunlit days, and when October came in, tinging the foliage with the gold and brown of autumnal colours, there was a louder murmur in the crash of the surf on the rocky beach when the winds of the equinox blew inshore. The wharf and breakwater were completed; the buildings of the Long Cove Fish Company were painted and ready for business; a store had been constructed at the head of the wharf, and Frank had fixed up an office for himself at the rear.

With the completion of the harbour work, a general holiday was declared, and Long Cove gave itself up to rejoicing. Flags flew from the Fish Company's buildings; the upper floor of the store-house was scraped and waxed ready for a dance, and a sort of indoor picnic was held on the lower floor. It was a beautiful October day, with a fresh breeze ruffling the waters of the Bay, and when the *Lillian* was sighted coming up the coast there was a general exodus to the wharf-end to view the first large vessel entering the harbour of Long Cove. The schooner looked remarkably spick and span with her newly painted hull, houses, and deck gear. There were new dories upon her deck; her new mainmast was a splendid spar, fitted with a topmast from which flew a red flag with "Lillian" on it in white letters, and new lettering on the counter—LILLIAN of ANCHORVILLE, N.S.

Long Dick Jennings, as harbour-master, was there in all his glory, and his termagant of a wife was strutting proudly by his side when the rangy fisherman greeted Captain Galarneau with a little speech, and presented him with a silver-mounted umbrella for being the first vessel master to open the new harbour. Of course, Frank was responsible for all this, and it was he who directed everything.

The *Lillian* was securely moored, and the Anchorville gang aboard of her followed their new skipper up to the buildings and participated in the fun. Everybody, young and old, men, women, and children, had congregated at the Cove from all up and down the coast, and the Company's grounds almost represented a country fair. There were running races, high jumping, dancing competitions, weight throwing, and even a dory race out in the Bay, which caused a great deal of excitement. In the breathing spells between his organizing duties, Frank gazed over the happy, laughing and shouting throng, and wished he had Lillian Denton by his side and viewing the fun.

In the evening a great "hop," or dance, was held in the storage loft, and in the light of the lanterns and with the fiddlers working full steam ahead the Long Covers tripped the light fantastic until the small hours. It was certainly a day of days in the settlement's calendar, and when a deputation of the guests came to thank him, Frank said that the gathering would be an annual affair—an assurance which was enthusiastically received.

Long Dick—almost three sheets in the wind—clasped Westhaver affectionately by the hand. "Shay, you ol' dog! You've done more t' wake up this place than any man I knows on, so ye hev. Long Cove's a-goin' t' be some place after this, m'lad, an' 'tis you what's done it. You're my boy, Frank, an' I mus' shay I've enjoyed myself more t'day than ever I did sence I was shingle." Then in a confidential whisper. "Shay! This Lillian what th' vessel's named after—she ain't one o' them Bay County Irish women, is she?"

"No, Dick," laughed Westhaver.

"Das all ri' then," replied the other, looking around half-fearfully. " 'Cause my ol' woman is one o' them, an' she's a terror, Frank—a holy old red-headed terror. I'd sooner see ye bunk along o' th' devil himself, horns, hoof, an' tail, than hev a Bay County Irisher for a wife. Steer clear o' them, son, 'cause I know!" And he winked knowingly as he strode off home.

Before he retired that night Frank looked out of his bedroom window. The murmur of the surf on the beach below rose to his ears, and his eyes drank in the glory of the clear starlit sky. Below, everything was dark, and naught pierced the opacity of land and sea but the red light at the head of the wharf, a lantern hanging in the main-rigging of the *Lillian,* and the green starboard light of a sailing vessel standing up the Bay. For a pace he stared out into the night, and when at last he turned away he murmured, "Aye, Lily, we're started now. Everything is shapin' my way, so wish me smooth sailin' until th' day when I go to claim you, sweetheart!"

Next day while the partners were engaged in unloading salt out of the *Lillian's* hold, a team with two occupants seated in it came driving down the wharf road. Everybody knocked off to have a look at the strangers. "Who kin that be?" queried Captain Clark.

"Thar's Jim Henderson from Anchorville a-drivin',"

answered a man; "but I don't know th' feller that's with him."

The visitors hitched their horse up at the office, and while the other remained seated, Henderson, the driver, came along to the group on the wharf.

"Is Cap'en Frank Westhaver here? Oh, you're th' man, sir! Waal, here's a party wants t' see ye, Cap'en. I've jest druv him over from town."

Frank handed his tally board over to Uncle Jerry and went up to the buggy. Its occupant was a clean-shaven, lantern-jawed man, with an exceedingly pale face and faded grey eyes. He looked at Westhaver, and spoke in a perky voice: "Captain Frank Westhaver?"

"Yes, sir!"

The other leaned forward in the seat. "Ah—ahem! You're the party who purchased the property of the late Asa Crawford, master mariner, of this place?"

"Lawyer by his talk," mentally noted Frank, and aloud, "Yes, sir. What about it?"

The other ignored the question. "Ah-ahem! You can prove your title to the property, Captain?"

"Yes!" replied the other, wondering what was in the wind.

"Have you got the deeds?" The stranger gazed hard at him.

"No—not yet," answered Westhaver. "But I expect they've bin put through all right."

The other nodded. "Ah—ahem! What have you to show that you purchased the property?"

Frank resented the interrogations. "What d'ye want t' know for?" he asked. "Who are you, anyway?"

The other gave a dry smile and handed Frank a card. "Pardon me—my card!"

"Wrigley an' Wrigley, Advocates and Public Notaries, Anchorville," Frank read. "Um! An' who are you representin'?"

"Ah—ahem!" The lawyer cleared his throat again. "My client is the legal heir to the Crawford estate, and he wishes to ascertain if the property has really been sold."

"Then you'll be representin'——"

"Captain Robert Morrissey, of Boston, and nephew of the deceased."

Westhaver knew it instinctively. "Waal," he said, "come into the office an' I'll show you my paper."

Frank produced the receipt written out by him and signed by Captain Asa, and he also showed the stub of the check. The lawyer produced a notebook and pencil. "You have no objections to me making a copy of this receipt?" he said.

"No!"

"And the number of your check was 'three,' and dated exactly the same date as this receipt—thirtieth day of August?"

"Yes!"

The other made the copies, and strutted outside. "These buildings are all upon the property you purchased, Captain?"

Frank nodded. The lawyer looked around. "Tell me," he said, after a scrutiny, "what did Captain Crawford say regarding the deeds and the disposition of his chattels and real estate?"

"Waal, as regards th' deeds, he told me that he'd write to his advocate in Anchorville an' hev them transferred to me. I understood him to say that the money he got was goin' to be sent to some Sailors' Orphan Home. His furniture was sold by auction an' th' money was handed over to his housekeeper. He left instructions with th' minister an' some others that this was to be done."

"Humph!" Mr. Wrigley grunted and climbed back in the team again. "All right, Captain. Good day!" And he drove away.

"So Bob Morrissey's a-tryin' t' find out what become of his uncle's property, is he? Waal, I don't blame him in a way. It's kinder hard t' be done out of it like he has. I ain't got no quarrel with him now." Dismissing the incident from his mind, Frank went down to complete his tallying.

It was nearly two weeks later when the mail driver handed Frank a long blue envelope. "Another letter from th' Brazilian Consul?" he murmured as he scanned it. "No, 'tis Anchorville postmark."

It was a long letter, and as Frank read it his cheeks blanched. "Lord Harry!" he muttered, and calling his uncle, he said, "Remember that lawyer feller what drove over here a couple o' weeks ago enquiring about th' property I purchased from Cap'en Asa?"

"Yes?"

"Listen to this what I've jest got from them: 'F. J. Westhaver, Long Cove. Dear Sir,—Acting in the interests of our client Captain Robert Morrissey of Boston and nephew of the deceased Captain Asa Crawford of Long Cove, N.S., we must ask you to relinquish all claim to the property lately owned by the deceased and said to have been purchased by you for the sum of Two Thousand Dollars.

" 'Upon enquiry at Messrs. Smith and Crosby, the advocates who hold the deeds of the property, they inform us that no order or communication from the late Crawford has been received by them, and similar enquiries at your Bank shows that check number three, purported to have been made out in Captain Asa Crawford's favour by you, has never been drawn against your account, and no check for two thousand dollars has been debited to your account in the books of the bank.

" 'The receipt which you hold and supposed to have been signed by the deceased as an interim until the deeds were transferred is valueless, as the supposed signature has never been witnessed by a third party.

" 'Our client, as sole heir, lays claim to the estate, and empowers us to lay proceedings against you if the buildings which you have erected upon the property are not immediately removed, and the estate left as before the presumed purchase.' "

"What d'ye think o' that, Uncle? said Frank. "Ain't that jest one whale of a muddle?"

The other stared vaguely into space. "Whatever will we do ef them lawyers kin prove that? It'll jest about ruin us, Frank."

Frank's teeth snapped and a determined light came into his eyes. "Not if I know it, Uncle," he said. "I'm not a-goin' t' be bluffed out by anythin' like this. I'll go'n see a lawyer to-morrow."

Frank worried over the communication a great deal that night, and having all of a sailor's dread and ignorance of the law and legal procedure he began to fear that he had made a blunder somewhere. His interview with Henry Stevens, one of the smartest advocates in Anchorville County, did not tend to make him feel any happier.

"I'll defend your case, Captain," he said after Frank had told him all the facts; "but I can't say that we have a bright defence. All that you have for proof that you purchased the property is that slip of unwitnessed paper, which is valueless as a piece of legal testimony, and the fact that your check has not been cashed, and your having no proof of delivery, invalidates the sale. If you could prove that you had delivered that check to Captain Crawford, and produced the honoured check after it had been endorsed and cashed by the deceased, there could be no doubt but what you had purchased the property, even though you did not possess the deeds. What we will have to do, is to find the check. Captain Crawford's notaries still hold the deeds, but they have received no advice from him regarding the sale of the property. Everything hinges on your check. D'ye think you could get a chance to overhaul the Captain's house——?"

"Furniture's all bin sold," answered Frank dismally. "It'll be scattered all over th' Cove now."

Mr. Stevens nodded gravely. "Well," he continued after a pause, "I'd advise you to send around a notice to all those who purchased goods at the auction to have a look for any papers or documents. You might have a look around yourself. If you can't produce anything more than what you've got here, I wouldn't advise you to fight the case. You'll lose, sure, and——"

Westhaver's eyes snapped with a steely glint in them. "Mr. Stevens," he said determinedly. "I put th' deal through as ship-shape as I knew how, an' I'll fight to th' last ditch. I won't allow any man to bluff me out of that property, so let it go to court."

The other tapped the desk with a pen. "All right, Captain. I'll do all I can for you."

When Frank arrived back at the Cove, he called a meeting of his partners and outlined the situation. "Ef they win out, we'll hev t' clear out o' this," he said bitterly, "an' all our work'll ha' gone for nawthin'. Th' buildin's will have t' be pulled down, as we couldn't move acrost to Cap'en Ring's land owin' to th' creek. I don't know but what I might make a deal with Morrissey t' buy th' place again ef he gits it, but I cal'late he'll squeeze us good when he knows he's got us in a tight corner. It's my fault entirely. I sh'd ha' seen that Cap'en Crawford cashed that check I gave him an' got th' deeds. Very likely he misplaced it, or lost it, or forgot all about it."

Uncle Jerry was looking very blue, but it was Ring's attitude which was giving Frank the most concern. How would he take it? Frank waited for him to say something.

"Waal," drawled the Captain philosophically, "I cal'late you did yer best. Ef th' property is taken from us we'll work out—never fear. I wouldn't worry, Frank."

Westhaver felt relieved. With his two partners behind him, he was nerved to stand to his guns, and without any delay he started on a search for the missing papers. Notices were sent to all the houses in the Cove, and a reward offered; but, though all kinds of papers from seamen's discharges to newspapers were brought to him, nothing in the shape of the required documents turned up.

It was with a feeling of utter dejection that Westhaver opened a letter from his lawyer.

"Come to Anchorville on Tuesday next. Your case,

Morrissey versus Westhaver, comes before the County Circuit Court at ten in the morning. Trust you have been able to secure more substantial evidence.''

Frank threw the letter down upon the table. "Waál, onless a miracle happens atween now an' then, we're a-goin' t' lose, an' t' lose now means a hard blow to all my hopes. Lord! but I've had my share o' dirty weather in my time. Dirty weather at sea, an' now dirty weather on land. It's hard—mighty hard. I wonder what Lily'll think?"

CHAPTER EIGHTEEN

THE *LILLIAN*, WITH JERRY CLARK AND JULES ABOARD, was fishing down off the Seal Island and Cape Shore. They had made a few good sets, and with sixty thousand of mixed fish below, they were jogging ten miles south of the island while a dense fog prohibited fishing. Captain Clark was lying on a locker, smoking and wondering how Frank was coming along in his case; Jules was studying a chart, and the men were enjoying a "lay off" in reading, playing cards, and gossiping.

One of the Anchorville men had a ditty box which he was fooling with, and Captain Clark, noticing the manner in which the fisherman was scrutinizing the article, enquired, "What's th' matter with yer ditty box?"

The fisherman rose and squatted down on the locker beside the skipper. " 'Tis a trick box," he said, "an' I'm tryin' to open it. It looks jest like a block o' wood, an' I can't find out whar' th' cover is nohow."

"Whar' d'ye git it, Jim?" enquired one of the gang.

"Mrs. Taylor up to Long Cove give it t'me," answered Jim, turning the box around in his hands. "She said she'd tried to open it——"

Captain Clark reached for the article. "Let me hev a try at it," he requested. "I useter be some hand at openin' them trick ditty boxes."

Giving the box a sharp tap with his fist, the side of the box flew back, and a number of papers fell out. Captain Clark laughed. "It takes me to open them puzzle boxes. What letters are them what fell out?"

The man picked them up. "Why, they're all addressed t' Cap'en Asa Crawford, an' here's a closed one with a stamp on it what hez never bin posted——"

Captain Clark jumped to his feet. "What?" he shouted. "Lemme see 'em!" And he grabbed the envelopes out of the man's hand. Rapidly sorting them out, he scrutinized the closed one, stamped and addressed in old Captain Asa's heavy fist.

"What's the address on this here?" he asked.

"Messrs. Smith and Crosby, Advocates and Notaries, Anchorville, N.S.," answered the other.

The stout skipper gave a whoop. "All out, fellers!" he bawled. "Git under way! By th' Lord Harry, ef this ain't luck. That's bin ol' Cap'en Asa's ditty box an' he's put that letter in thar' for safe keepin' ontil th' mail driver came down to th' Cove. I'll bet Frank's check is in that. Rouse out th' gang for'ard!" And he stamped on deck.

It did not take them long to swing the *Lillian* off, and under her four lowers and staysail she headed in for the land.

"Yarmout' or Anchorville, Captain?" asked Jules.

"Anchorville," answered the other. "No use makin' for Yarmouth. Th' train'll be gone by th' time we arrive. Due no'the, th' course, an' drive her!"

Though it was as thick as mud with fog, there was a fresh southerly wind blowing, and the old *Lillian* began to show her heels. Everyone aboard knew about the trouble their young employer was in, and with the loyalty to their friends common to the fraternity the fishermen exerted all their nautical skill in order to get the vessel home as quickly as possible. Sails were jigged up every half-hour, and never was there such a trimming of sheets and careful steering upon a fishing schooner before. Men lounged around the streaming decks with eyes for ever scanning the set and trim of canvas, and when so much as a wrinkle showed, they sweated on jig and halliard until the sails were set without a slack to mar their bellying contours. Captain Clark and Jules had held the envelope up to the cabin lamp, and the silhouette of the check was discernible against the light.

"That's Frank's check in thar' all right," remarked Uncle Jerry.

"Git de cook for steam de ongvelope open," suggested Jules.

The other shook his head. "No, no; we'd better jest leave it as it is. Ef some o' them lawyers thought we did that they'd swear it was a put-up job on our part."

It was four in the afternoon when they swung off, and allowing for the set of the tide against them, they figured in doing the ninety odd miles in twelve hours. None of the *Lillian's* crowd knew when the hearing of the case was due to come off, as they had left the Cove before the date was set, and ignorance of the date gave Jules and Captain Clark a great deal of anxiety. What if it had already been before the court? What if it had been decided against Frank? The buildings might even then be torn down and Morrissey in possession. The suspense was agonizing, and throughout the long night as the gallant vessel stormed to the northward both men kept the deck, consumed with anxiety.

When they made the Lurcher by soundings, the wind hauled to the north-west and freshened. The fog vanished with the advent of the colder wind, and, close-hauled, the *Lillian* was dragging her lee rail through the smother, and the gang rejoiced in the weight of the breeze.

"Go it, you ol' peddler!" they shouted. "Tear th' patch off yerself!" And Jules walked the quarter and prayed for wind and plenty of it.

Their prayers were answered, and when the maintopmast snapped off at the masthead and fell in among the gear with the staysail thunderously flapping in the breeze they actually laughed as they crawled aloft to cut the raffle away.

While the *Lillian* was beating up the Bay in the teeth of a norther, with her decks awash and every plank and beam in her protesting at the press of sail she was carrying, Frank was tossing around on his bed in an Anchorville hotel. He had secured nothing but what he already had, and though he had brought the late Captain's housekeeper down with him to testify that he had been at the Crawford house on the date of the supposed sale, yet he knew that his case was decidedly slim. Another drop in his cup of bitterness was added by the fact that his opponent had declined to make terms. "On no account will I sell my land to Westhaver," Morrissey had written, and in the words Frank felt that the spite and hatred of boyhood days were still rankling in the man's mind. And Wrigley had spoken about an offer being made by a Bayport company for the property. In fact, he had already given the option to them.

Looking very pale and anxious, Westhaver entered Lawyer Stevens's office promptly at nine, and the advocate was none too enthusiastic about the outcome.

"I made your offer to Wrigley, agreeing to pay two thousand dollars for the strip of land you require for buildings and flake-yard, but he says that his client will not sell to you on any account. He also tells me that he has given an option upon that property to the Bayport Fisheries Company."

"So I understand," answered Frank dismally.

"How will that affect you, Captain?" enquired the other kindly.

"It'll ruin me pretty near. I've got a big contract to fulfil, and without that land I'll have to hand th' bulk of it over to someone else. All th' money we've invested in th' buildin's will be a dead loss, though th' Bayport Company might take them over——"

"Yes, they may," nodded the lawyer; "but a great deal will depend upon the leniency of your opponent. He can, if he likes, enter a restraint against you forbidding you to remove a single thing off the land. He can claim everything you have put up on it——"

"Is that th' law?" queried Frank huskily.

"Yes!"

"Then that's jest what that feller'll do ef he knows it. Oh, but I've bin several times a dam' fool in this business! I sh'd ha' stayed at sea until I l'arned t' move about ashore 'thout gittin' foul o' things like this. Yes! I'm some mug when it comes t' business." And feeling utterly dejected and depressed in spirit, he walked along to the Court House with the advocate.

Promptly at ten the case was opened. Mr. Wrigley, of Wrigley and Wrigley, respectfully saluted the Judge and stated the facts for the plaintiff, Captain Robert Morrissey, of Boston. "My client is the sole relative of the deceased shipmaster, and as no will was made regarding the disposal of the late Crawford's property, my client lays claim to it."

"What does the property consist of?" enquired the Court.

"Ah—ahem! The property consists of some sixty acres of land, house, and barn, situated in the village of Long Cove, Bay Shore County."

"Had the deceased any personal property or moneys besides the real property?"

"Ah—ahem! The deceased Captain was living upon an annuity which ceased at his demise. His household goods were sold by his own instructions to responsible parties, and the proceeds of the sale were given to his housekeeper. My client has no interest in this."

After some additional statements regarding Westhaver's supposed purchase of the property in litigation and which Mr. Wrigley declared was never consummated, Mr. Stevens stated the case for the defence.

"You state that your client gave the deceased a check for the amount of the sale?"

"Yes, your honour!"

"Then you will produce the honoured check for the proof of delivery."

This, of course, the defence was unable to do, and all that Stevens could show was the receipt, which being unwitnessed was practically worthless, the check stub with the number and date of the check, and the testimony of the housekeeper, who proved that the defendant had called upon her master that afternoon.

"Did you overhear any of the conversation between them?" enquired the Judge.

"No, sir. They was out on th' porch an' I was in th' kitchen."

"What do you suppose your late master did with the check?" enquired Mr. Stevens.

"I dunno, sir," replied the woman. "I never see no check. Th' Captain was a very particular man, an' he'd never 'low me t' touch or see any o' his papers or letters. He'd swear awful, sir, ef I did."

Even though he was fighting for a lost cause, Mr. Stevens made a great effort in Westhaver's favour. "We have here, your honour, a young and ambitious man who is a victim of circumstances and ignorance of the law. Captain Westhaver is a native of Long Cove and one of that fine breed of Nova Scotians who have made our fisheries famous the world over. He has an unblemished character, and there is not a man who knows him but will testify to the same. My client, wishing to give up the sea and remain near his widowed mother, formed a little business up at his home, and with this object in view, he called upon the deceased with a proposal to purchase a strip of land from him. After some conversation, the deceased master mariner offered to sell all his property for the sum of two thousand dollars, and two or three days later my client handed him a check for the amount, and the deceased gave him the receipt which is now before the Court. That this piece of paper was never witnessed by a third party is due to ignorance of the law on the part of my client and the late Captain. Unfortunately, while my client was away upon a business trip the Captain died, and investigation showed that he had neglected to advise his notaries in Anchorville regarding the transfer of the property, and he had also neglected to cash the check. The papers necessary to substantiate my client's claim cannot be found, with the result that Captain Westhaver is placed in an awkward position. My client, thinking that everything was all right, went ahead and constructed buildings upon the property, and I think this fact alone should convince the Court that Captain Westhaver was acting in good faith.'' With a few more remarks he closed the case for the defence, and while Frank scanned the face of the Judge, he felt instinctively that he had lost.

Mr. Wrigley was rubbing his hands and smiling all over his face, when the Judge commenced summing up the evidence, and as Westhaver caught the exultant look upon the lawyer's pallid face he felt that he would take a great deal of pleasure in having Mr. Wrigley with him for a trip on the *Lillian*.

While he sat waiting for the inevitable decision there was a commotion in the hall-way, and a mob of sea-booted figures clattered unceremoniously into the Court-room. To Frank's intense surprise, Uncle Jerry and Jules were in the van of the mob, and from his seat he could see the whole of the *Lillian's* gang, cook and all, elbowing their way to the front. Captain Clark, with his rubber boots and oil coat on and a Derby hat on his head, waved a letter and shouted:

"Hold th' case, Judge! Is Mr. Smith here?"

The Judge looked up severely at the interruption, and Mr. Smith, who had been one of the witnesses, stepped from his seat.

"Here's a letter addressed to you which we found in one o' Cap'en Crawford's ol' ditty boxes. Open it quick!"

With the odoriferous trawlers crowding around him and peering over his shoulder, Mr. Smith opened the letter and hastily scanned it.

"Mr. Stevens," he said, "here's something which will interest you. Give it back to me when you have finished."

The Court Usher banged his gavel and called for silence, and the Judge, looking over at the chattering fishermen who had so unceremoniously disturbed the sanctity of the Court House, said severely:

"I have a mind to order the arrest of you men for contempt of Court. Captain Clark, what do you mean by this interruption?"

Uncle Jerry reddened. "Excuse me, Judge," he said.

"I'm sorry ef I've done any harm, but I think I've found somethin' that'll prove my nevvy's case."

While Frank gasped in consternation, his lawyer arose and addressed the Judge. "I have here the necessary documents to prove my client's claim. Here is a letter written by the deceased Captain and addressed to his notaries, Messrs. Smith and Crosby. In it he has written: 'I have sold my house and land to Captain Frank Westhaver of this place for two thousand dollars. Make out the deeds and send them to him. I am also sending you his check, which I want you to get cashed and send the money to the Treasurer of the Sailors' Orphan Society of Liverpool, G.B., saying that it is a donation from Asa Crawford, late master of the Liverpool ship *Guinevere*.' Now, your honour, I would ask you to compare the signatures on this letter and on the receipt which my client holds——"

Mr. Wrigley jumped up. "Excuse me, but is that check endorsed by the deceased?"

Frank waited in a cold sweat for his lawyer's reply.

"The check is made payable to bearer," replied Mr. Stevens slowly; "but I see that Asa Crawford has endorsed it as well. That gives us three signatures for comparison, and I think that Mr. Smith, who has handled all the Captain's legal business, will certify as to their authenticity."

The Judge nodded. "How came this letter to turn up?"

Captain Clark stepped forward on a nod from the lawyer. "Your honour," he said, "one of my men had a ditty box given to him by a Mrs. Taylor of Long Cove, who bought it at Cap'en Crawford's place when th' sale was held. It's one o' them puzzle boxes, an' I managed to open it while we were lyin' to off Seal Island in th' schooner *Lillian*. As soon as I opened it a number o' letters fell out an' th' one which Lawyer Stevens has was among them. When I l'arned who 'twas addressed to, I cal'lated it might be th' letter my nevvy was a-lookin' for, so we hung out th' patch an' hooked for port as hard as we c'd slam. Ef th' wind hadn't ha' headed us in th' Bay we might ha' bin in afore."

"All right, Captain!". The Judge looked over the papers laid before him. "I think we have conclusive proof that Captain Westhaver purchased the property in litigation. The endorsed check and the letter to Messrs. Smith and Crosby bear out the testimony of the defendant, and the signature on the receipt is identical with the signatures on the letter and the endorsement on the check. You will swear to the late Crawford's handwriting, Mr. Smith?"

"Yes, your honour!"

Mr. Wrigley, the smile gone from his cadaverous features, arose and spoke. "Your honour," he said, "I beg for a postponement of the case. I wish to prove that the deceased was not in his right mind when he made this disposition of his property——"

"The Judge waved his hand. "Nonsense, Mr. Wrigley. I wouldn't entertain that claim for a moment. I knew Captain Crawford very well indeed, and I know he never evinced any signs of insanity."

And the fishermen assembled sniggered audibly.

Of course Westhaver won his case, and when the Judge gave his decision there was a roar of approval from the spectators, and for a good quarter of an hour Frank was shaking horny fists and being almost choked by the hearty slaps he received on the back from the delighted fishermen. Mr. Stevens was cheered and congratulated until he felt that he had friends for life among the Bay Shore trawlers, and it was a fact, he gained a lot of fishermen's business by his connection with the case.

Mr. Wrigley, knowing that he had lost the day, made the best of a bad job by congratulating Frank upon his success. "I'm sorry I had to oppose you, Captain," he said; "but that's the way of the law——"

"Sorry sulphur!" growled a bulky, red-headed fisherman. "Git away an' leave th' skipper alone, you yaller-mugged sculpin." And Mr. Wrigley wriggled off with the growls and surly looks of a score of angry trawlers hastening his departure.

Mr. Stevens gathered up his papers and placed them in his bag.

"Well, Captain, I'm glad you won out. I'll look after this business for you and see that you don't get mixed up in any more legal complications. It will be some satisfaction to you to know that your friend Morrissey is to pay the costs of this suit. Good day, Captain."

The transition from absolute despair to the ecstasy of joy and renewed hope brought out all the boyishness of Westhaver's nature, and nothing would satisfy him until he had dragged all the *Lillian's* gang into one of the best hotels in Anchorville and ordered a dinner. Clad in their old clothes and rubber boots, they sat down to the meal and ate everything, from soup to nuts, and the commercial travellers and other guests wondered what such a rough-looking crowd could be rejoicing over. At last, when it was all over, Frank drew his uncle to one side.

"Before we go aboard th' *Lillian* an' shoot for th' Cove, I'm goin' down t' buy some books on business, an' one o' them will be a copy o' th' Law. I don't git inter any more scrapes like this again."

When the *Lillian* arrived off the Long Cove wharf next morning, the whole population were down to meet her, and with the ensign fluttering from her main gaff she glided in between the pier heads.

"How d'ye come out?" bawled Harbour-master Jennings.

"All right!" answered Frank, and the crowd on the wharf broke into a cheer which made the hills and rocks echo again.

Chaired on the broad shoulders of two brawny trawlers, Westhaver was escorted to his home by a laughing, shouting mob, who, when they arrived at the house, clattered into the sacred precincts of Mrs. Westhaver's "settin'-room" and demanded to know all about it. If poor Bob Morrissey had been in the vicinity at that time he would have fared roughly, and Mrs. Westhaver had to close her ears to the various lurid and picturesque deep-water anathemas which were levelled against him.

"Now," murmured Frank when they had departed, "I hope I'm through sailin' shipmates with Trouble. Th' clouds hev lifted an' th' barometer's risin' for fair weather. Let's hope I kin steer good courses after this." And he sat down and wrote to Lillian Denton.

The autumn passed and winter came with frost and snow, but Long Cove had passed the hibernating era of coast settlements. The *Lillian* had a full gang of Bay Shore men who came away from the American vessels when they heard that they could fish out of their home port, and as they were in almost every two weeks during the winter the village was by no means lonesome. The boat fishermen, able to procure supplies, bait, and a ready market for their fish, had no call to haul their craft up and go vessel-fishing out of other ports, and the once almost deserted wharf became a daily centre of activity with the men unloading their fares and cleaning and dressing the catch.

The new store, owned and operated by the Company, became a kind of club-room for the inhabitants of the village, and around the big stove on winter nights a coterie of Long Covers smoked, yarned, and argued over every conceivable subject from the build of Noah's Ark to the current war in progress. All the old men of the settlement found the store a great asylum for whiling away the long winter days, and they dropped in after breakfast and read Frank's newspapers and magazines and almost bothered the life out of him until closing time at night.

The chilly months sped away very quickly. Frank came down and opened up the store at eight in the morning, and after sweeping it out and lighting up the big heater he usually retired into the back office and opened up his books. During the day he was kept busy noting the tallies of fish brought in over the wharf and entering the amounts to the credit of the various shore fishermen. The store required a great deal of attention, and as most of the goods purchased were debited against fish supplied, it necessitated quite an amount of book-keeping on Westhaver's part. When the work eased up for an hour or so, he would light up his pipe and proceed to master the art of double-entry book-keeping, and by the summer he was able to strike off an accurate balance and run his ledger, cash-book, and journal in a very creditable manner for a fisherman. There were occasions too when the memory of his legal fight came to mind, that he closed his door against the chatter of the loungers outside and reached down a half-calfed volume labelled with a legal title. It was intensely dry reading, but by patience and exercise of the dogged determination which was part of his nature, Westhaver gained a fairly comprehensive idea of the law regarding property and business transactions.

Almost before he was aware of it, Frank, from his desk at the office, saw that spring had come. The grass was showing brown-green through the patches of snow, and the drip from the roof pattered in glittering drops before the window. In the flake-yard, Captain Ring and Lem were busy erecting the drying racks, and as he gazed out upon the blue of sky and sea, the lure of the season called to him, and he threw down his pen, opened the window to let the fresh breeze sweeten the heated atmosphere redolent of tar and sulphur matches, and went out.

In the flake-yard Captain Ring looked up from his work on Frank's hail. "Aye, it's beginnin' t' look summery again. We'll hev t' git th' flake-yard a goin' soon, as we hev an awful power o' fish t' dry afore th' barquentine comes aroun' t' load."

Down on the wharf, Uncle Jerry, with an oilskin apron around his waist, was standing by the scales tallying the *Lillian's* catch, and Frank stood for a moment and watched the gang swaying on the dory tackles hoisting the baskets of fish out of the hold and dumping them into the scale box. "Waal, you blame' quill driver!" cried Captain Clark. "You're like th' bear, I cal'late. Th' sun hez sure brought ye away from yer desk t' come an' smell gurry again, eh?"

"Yes, I reckon it has," answered the other, smiling. "How much has Captain Jules brought in this time?"

" 'Bout sixty-five thousand, an' all good grade. Brown's Bank fish, y'know, an' all from Jules's favourite spot on th' no'thern edge. He's doin' well for a green skipper."

The spirit of the season was entering Westhaver's blood, and after looking on the scene of activity around the vessel, the gang unloading on her decks, the busy weighers monotonously droning the weights, the wharf hands pitching the fish into wheel-barrows and trundling them away, and old Sailor Dan hitching and bending new rattlins on the *Lillian's* rigging, he strolled with an indefinable feeling of pleasure to the end of the pier.

The waters of the Bay stretched gloriously blue to the far horizon, and the white sails of the boat fishermen could be discerned in the middle distance, while far away to the south a lumber-laden three-masted schooner was sagging lazily on her lawful occasions. In the spring the young man's fancy turns to thoughts of love—so runs an old saying; and Frank felt that way and thought of Lillian teaching school in Yarmouth. He wondered if she had pupils like what he was in his younger days, and he shuddered at the thought.

While he was ruminating over the supposition, he heard footsteps behind him, and Jules's heavy hand on his back almost spitted him on the mooring post upon which he was lolling.

"Hey, you bounder!" coughed Frank as he turned. "What d'ye mean by thumpin' th' life out o' me like that?"

"What you thinkin' 'bout, Frankee?"

"Waal, ontil you come up with that heavy fist o' yours, I was thinkin' of a good many things."

Jules nodded. "So am I."

"Oh, an' what's botherin' you, Captain Galarneau?"

The big Frenchman kicked at a splinter on the cap log. "I want to know when I can get holiday, Frankee?"

"A holiday?" ejaculated Westhaver in mock horror at the suggestion. "A holiday did ye say? An' what do you want a holiday for, you big loafer? Ain't it all holiday with you trawlers aboard th' vessel? Lay-offs an' mug-ups?"

The other laughed sheepishly. "I—I want for get married."

"Married!" shouted Frank. "So that's th' lay, is it? Waal, I cal'late we kin let ye take a day off t' git married——"

"But I want two week for honeymoon," pleaded Jules. "One day no good."

Westhaver slapped his old dory-mate on the back. "Surely ye kin hev yer holiday, ol' trawler! When d'ye plan on goin'?"

"Now. Dis week."

"This week? You ain't in no hurry t' git yer head in a noose, are ye? Will th' gang take a lay-off for that length o' time?"

"Yes," replied Jules. "Two of dem want for get married as well."

The other laughed. "Kind o' catchin' this marryin' business, it seems. Go ahead, ol' man, take yer two weeks. I'd like t' give ye more, but we've got an awful busy summer ahead of us an' we need all hands. We'll give th' *Lillian* her overhaul while you're away."

So Jules Galarneau—the runaway Breton fisher-boy, and now master of a Canadian fishing schooner, a Canadian citizen, and more Canadian than French—got married. It was in proper fisherman fashion, with everybody for miles around invited, and with a big spread in the big barn; much firing of guns and ringing of cow bells, and a dance which lasted until the early morning hours, Jules took the blushing French Canadian lassie for better or worse.

Frank drove the happy couple over to the Anchorville depot, and when they entrained for Boston, he sighed. "Thar's ol' Sabot happy now with th' girl of his heart. Two years yet for me...."

CHAPTER NINETEEN

ON A BEAUTIFUL AUGUST MORNING, FRANK, RIGGED out in collar and tie and a neat blue suit, was driving along the hill road to Anchorville. The buggy, the best double-seated team in Long Cove, was polished and washed until it shone again, while the horse did credit to Frank's pre-breakfast grooming and curry-combing. Before he swung around the Anchorville road, which led up over the mountain, he pulled up the horse and gazed over the vista of village and Bay.

"Waal," he murmured with satisfaction, "I cal'late Lily an' the ol' Cap'en will like th' place. It's lookin' pretty nice now. Giddap, Jess! Twelve miles t' go an' little time t' do it in."

He trotted into Anchorville depot a few minutes before the Yarmouth train pulled in, and his eager scrutiny was rewarded by the sight of the persons whom he sought. The old skipper was the first to hail him.

"Hullo, thar', Westhaver! Lay alongside with that four-wheeled craft of yours 'til I get some of this dunnage stowed!"

And Frank swung the team to the platform and greeted his guests.

"Howdy, Cap'en! Hullo, Lily! Let me see a-hold o' your grips. Cap'en, you won't mind sittin' in th' back seat? Lil and I will drive in front. All aboard! Giddap, Jess!" And with as much skill in driving a horse as he had in driving a schooner, Frank swept down the station road with the dust flying in their wake.

"Oh, Frank, but isn't it just a glorious day?" exclaimed Miss Denton—her sun-browned cheeks glowing with excitement and pleasure. "And what a fine horse you have——"

"Take th' reins an' drive, Lil," suggested Frank, handing them over.

"Naow you jest be careful with that there animal," cautioned the old skipper, "an' see'n don't capsize us into a ditch. She's pluggin' along at quite a clip an' th' least sheer to port or starb'd might have us turnin' turtle——"

"Try one o' my cigars, Cap'en," interrupted Frank, opening his case; and having diplomatically given the father something to occupy his attention, he proceeded to give his fiancée a lesson in driving. The lesson seemed to be greatly enjoyed by both, and considering that it necessitated two pairs of hands on the reins, the horse must have been an unusually frisky quadruped.

The drive over the mountain through the pass opened up some magnificent views of crags and whispering spruce forests, and Miss Denton appreciated the beauties of the scenery to the full. "And just look at that Micmac wigwam in the clearing over there! Look at that old Indian, and the squaws and the little papoose!"

"That's old John the Rain Maker. Him an' his family are makin' baskets an' sweet grass souvenirs t' sell the Anchorville tourists. He's very old—'most ninety, I cal'late. Wait, an' I'll hail him. Hey, John!"

The old Indian came smiling to the halted team. Westhaver pulled out a cigar. "Say, John, show th' lady th' medals th' King an' Queen gave you?"

The Micmac pulled a deerskin pouch from out his pocket and handed the huge medallions over. "Dat one is from King William to my grandfather. The others are from Queen Victoria an' King Edward to me."

Miss Denton looked the relics over with delight. Here was romance! And while her practical parent gave the silver plaques but a cursory glance, she examined them with the reverence of a lover of unusual things.

John was very willing to talk, and after he had crumpled the cigar up and put some of it into his pipe, he told her many things. Yes, he was the last chief of his tribe; he had been across the Big Water to the White Queen's tepee in London, and she had spoken to him; he was ninety-three and still able to carry a guide's pack and paddle a canoe, and he expected to be able to do so for many more years. It was with regret that she bade the royal old Indian good-bye.

As they turned into the Bay Shore road the vista of mountain and sea charmed her eye, and Westhaver felt happy in her delighted remarks. "We'll soon be at th' Cove," he said; "an' I think you'll find it even prettier than any of these places."

"But what could be lovelier than this?" she exclaimed. "Look at those orchards! Look at those pretty houses in among the trees! Who lives in them, Frank?"

"Mostly all fishermen."

"Fishermen?" she ejaculated. "Not the men who go to sea on the schooners?"

Frank laughed. "Sure they do! Some fish off the shore here, but a good many of them go away in th' vessels. Some sail in Anchorville craft and others go to Gloucester. Some nice places, eh?"

"Why, they're simply ideal. I can't understand why they should want to leave such nice homes for the rough, hard life at sea. What are those white things strung on the fences, Frank?"

"Those are hake sounds hung out to dry. They're used for makin' glue, gelatine, and isinglass, an' worth quite a bit. Now, Lily, we're comin' into Long Cove."

"Why, look at the fish, papa!" cried Miss Denton as the flake-yards came into view. "Good gracious! there must be thousands of them drying in the sun!"

Frank pulled the horse up. "That's all ours, Lily. See, thar's our big house near the wharf——"

The old shipmaster in the rear seat was becoming interested now.

"Is that your plant?" he interrupted, pointing to the big red-painted building standing in the midst of acres of drying fish.

"Yes," replied Frank; "an' we own that building an'

flake-yard to the other side of the road as well. Thar's that barquentine you chartered for us, Cap'en. We're loadin' her now, an' ye kin see th' topm'sts o' th' new *Lillian*—th' gasolene auxiliary knockabout we bought after we sold the old vessel. Th' little shed near th' wharf is the icehouse an' bait storage for th' boats an' vessels. Th' low buildin' at th' head of th' wharf road is th' Company's store an' my office—but we'll git home an' have dinner first, then I'll show you 'round.''

Miss Denton looked forward to meeting ''Frank's folks'' with some little trepidation, but her nervousness was speedily dispelled with Mrs. Westhaver's cordial hug and kiss and Captain Jerry's hearty welcome. Within an hour, the young lady's winning ways and sunny smile had so captivated the widow's heart that she could hardly contain her pleasure at her son's good judgment, and the mother felt that she had found a daughter whom she could love.

While Frank, Lily, and his mother were exchanging confidences over the setting of the dinner table, Uncle Jerry had taken Captain Denton in tow, and down at the store with Captain Ring and the young master of the barquentine, they were spinning twisters through the blue haze of cigar smoke—lying, yarning, and laughing with all the hearty gusto peculiar to old seafarers. The Dentons, father and daughter, had indeed fallen into the march of things at the Cove.

Just before the dinner horn blew Frank skilfully piloted his fiancée outside. ''Now, Lil,'' he said softly, ''I've fixed up all this as a little plot to make your father consent to our marriage before the two years are up, an' I jest want you t' watch th' fun. He's no idea what kind of a place we hev up here, an' I'll bet when he sees what we've done, he'll consent right away. In fact, I'm so sure of it that I've got th' carpenters overhaulin' th' house I bought from Cap'en Asa so's t' be ready in a week or so. I've ordered furniture, carpets, pictures, an' books, an' a whole complete fit-out, an' ef your father'll only consent, we'll get married right away——''

"But Frank, I have no clothes ready."

"That's all right, sweetheart—you don't need t' make many preparations, for our wedding'll be a quiet one, with only a few. Ef my scheme works out, we'll be able to take a trip into Anchorville an' git all you want. We kin git th' rest when we come back from our trip."

"Have you planned that too?" laughed Lillian. "Where do we go, Sir Galahad?"

Frank looked mysterious. "Guess!" he said.

"Boston?"

"No, further'n that."

"Montreal?"

"Further south, sweetheart."

"New York?"

"Further still. Give it up?"

"Yes."

"What would you say to Rio Janeiro in South America?"

Lillian Denton gasped. "Rio Janeiro?"

Frank nodded. "Yes, an' I plan goin' down on th' barkyteen thar'. Cap'en Thomas has his wife aboard an' a fine cosy little cabin, an' he said he'd be glad t' take us. We'd call on my friends down in Rio an' I plan on comin' back by Royal Mail steamer to New York. We'll go all up th' coast an' call in at Cartagena, La Guayra, where the people in 'Westward Ho!' went, an' a number o' th' West Indie Islands. Won't that be some honeymoon, Lil?"

"Oh, Frank, it'll be a dream and simply glorious. What a head my fisherman has! He's planned everything! But—what if papa doesn't consent?"

Westhaver waved his hand. "Lil," he said, "I have a hook baited for your dad that he'll be bound to bite on. I'm a-goin' t' show him around th' plant this afternoon, an' you jest say nawthin' but saw wood. He ain't got a chance to dive the twine, for I know jest exactly what an ol' sailor likes."

After dinner Frank took his visitors in hand. "Now, Cap'en, jest let me show you around our plant. All that fish you see dryin' on th' flakes is for th' Brazilian Government. Those with th' long whiskers stickin' out from them are hake; those with th' black lines an' th' devil's finger-marks on them are haddock, and there's a good pile o' cod, pollock, an' some cusk among them. What are they worth? Anywhere from three to five an' a half dollars a quintal or hundredweight. Thar's 'most ten thousand dollars worth o' fish out here now.... The work o' tendin' th' fish layin' on th' flakes is done by a lot o' th' boys an' girls around here, as well as the old men. It's a good job for an old man. He kin potter around turnin' the fish over an' coverin' them up with that burlap ef th' sun's too strong, an' when it looks like rain he jest piles them an' covers them over with tarpaulins. Not hard work by any means."

Captain Denton grunted, and Lillian began to wonder if this was the bait Frank was holding out for her father.

Frank led the way from the yard towards the big building. "Here's th' lower floor whar' we prepare th' fish jest as it comes from th' boats an' th' vessel. They're dressed first, gutted, heads taken off an' then washed. After that we put them into pickle with salt and brine. Those big hogsheads are full o' fish in pickle, and when they've bin in th' salt long enough we take them out, wash them, and after kenchin' to drain off, we lay them out on th' flakes to dry in' th' sun. After they're dried, we store them up in th' loft o' this buildin' ontil we hev enough t' make a shipment."

"An' from here they go down south as bacalao for them yeller Brazilieros to chew," added Captain Denton. "Eh, eh, but it's a great business."

After leaving the fish-house, with its score of busy workers dressing and salting, Frank pointed out how he had brought a supply of fresh water down from the mill dam and installed a carrier system from the wharf to the main building. "Fresh water is necessary in washin' fish properly, while this litter carrier is one of th' best things we've got. It's jest an ordinary farmer's feed an' litter carrier run on pulleys an' a single overhead rail, but I find I kin save an awful lot o' time an' labour by usin' it for transportin' fish from th' wharf to th' buildin' an' dumpin' th' gurry over the end of th' wharf at ebb tide——"

"Do you heave away all th' insides o' th' fish?" enquired the old skipper.

"No. Out of hake we keep th' sounds an' dry them. We save th' livers an' sometimes th' roes of 'most all. Those butts on th' wharf are full o' fish livers tryin' out for oil. Th' sun does that for us an' all we hev t' do is skim the oil off an' sell it for tannin' leather. We sell th' heads an' a lot o' th' gurry to farmers for fertilizer—it's great stuff t' put on th' fields. Th' cod's heads are good for bait in lobster traps. . . . This small buildin' is our ice-house for supplyin' th' vessel. We cut the ice from th' mill dam up above in th' winter time. We also bring herrin' bait acrost an' keep it in storage here. Th' small shed is th' toolhouse, cooper's, carpenter's, an' blacksmith's shop."

They were down on the wharf by this time, and Captain Denton's attention was taken up by the two vessels inside the little harbour.

"Nice little barquentine," he remarked, nodding at the craft.

"Yes, she is a little beauty. We're loadin' 'most three hundred an' fifty tons o' fish in her this trip. She'll pull out in a couple o' weeks, I cal'late. Th' little schooner ahead o' her is th' new *Lillian*. We sold the old one, as she was too unhandy with her long bowsprit, an' havin' no engine it used to be all hands out in th' dories doin' Nova Scotia tow-boatin' every time she got under th' lee o' th' land comin' in here. We got this seventy-ton knockabout pretty reasonable at a sale an' she's payin' for herself mighty quick. With that engine o' hers a-goin' she hauled th' barkyteen up in here as neat's any tug."

Frank made an admirable guide. He pointed out everything and explained its uses, while Lillian and her father listened with rapt interest and attention. "Man an' boy I've sailed th' sea," declared the old shipmaster, "but I never knew so much about fish afore as I've l'arned this day. It's a great business—a fine business, an' next to a little bit of a store, I know of nawthin' I'd like better to be connected with.''

"Why, I 'most forgot t' show you *my* store," cried Frank, as if it had only occurred to him. "Let's git up to it, for I'm sure ye'd like t' see over th' place."

There was the usual coterie of ancient farmers and fishermen lolling upon the empty boxes piled outside under the porch, and when the "young boss" and his visitors stepped up, they nodded respectfully. Frank opened the door and ushered the Dentons into the cool shade of the building, and it was fully evident that the old captain was interested.

"An' what d'ye stock here, Frank?" he enquired after a glance around.

"'Most everything, Cap'en," answered the other. "Provisions, potatoes, butter, eggs, an' all sorts of eatable truck. We supply th' village an' th' vessel, y'know. Then we hev ship's gear, canvas, blocks, fishin' gear, lobster rope, paint, oil, tar, oilskins, cloth, clothing for men, women an' children, an' 'most everything what's needed in a place like this. I hev a post office now an' two deliveries an' collections a week, an' I also brought a telephone line over th' mountain. I'm an insurance agent, gasolene engines, farmin' implements, an' patent fencin' as well—in fact, I'm representative in Long Cove an' vicinity for nigh a hundred different concerns."

The old sailor looked around the piled shelves and the long counters. He scanned the posters upon the wall, and the boxes, barrels, and bales which encumbered the sides of the room. The scent of tar, oil, paint, matches, and oilskins came to his nostrils, and his brain surged with all an old sailor's notions of trade. The fancies of long watches at sea came to his mind, and for a space he pictured himself serving out goods behind that long counter; yarning around the stove on winter days, and lolling with his kind out on the sun-flooded porch in summer. Wouldn't he just like to be holding forth on this particular brand of goods to some customer; advocating insurance and talking fertilizers and horse feed with the farmers. A sailor's ambitions—farming or store-keeping. The old longings came back to him with the sight of the place, and his sea-weary heart hungered for the realization of long-deferred hopes. Timidly, he turned and spoke to the waiting Westhaver.

"You—you must be kep' pretty busy 'round here?"

"I am," answered Frank. "Too busy, in fact. I can't attend to my book-keepin' an' th' fish business 'count o' servin' here. I was thinkin' o' gittin' someone t' help me in lookin' after th' store. To run it, in fact, an' give me a chanst in the office."

The old Captain nodded eagerly. "Hev you planned on who you're goin' t' git?"

"Waal, no, I haven't," replied the other slowly. "I was thinkin', when Lil an' I got married, I'd maybe offer it to you an' keep you near us, but——"

"But?" queried the Captain, with a trace of anxiety in his voice.

"But ye want me t' wait another year yet, an' then, maybe, ye won't take to a job like this——"

"Won't I?" roared the old man. "Jest offer it t' me an' see me snap it up! Lord Harry! this is th' sort of thing I've been hopin' would be my job in Heaven ef stores are run up thar'——"

"How about Lillian?" It was Frank who was anxious this time.

"Take her, son, take her," cried the Captain. "Sink me, but you've got all a man wants t' marry on. I had no idea your Company was so big an affair. An' ye'll let me be storekeeper? Lordy, boy, but I feel as proud as a dog with two tails. Jest what I've dreamed about. Store-keepin'!"

And while Westhaver chuckled to himself and kissed Lillian under the lee of a pile of boxes, Captain Denton was behind the counter and getting on to his job.

It was a hilariously happy family party that sat down to supper at the Westhaver homestead, and while the older folk were smoking and gossiping, Frank and his sweetheart stole away to enjoy a lover's promenade in the moonlight. The smell of the new-mown hay hung drowsily on the summer air, and under the glare of the moon the waters of the Bay shimmered and danced in the silver radiance. Somewhere in the darkness of the spruce forest a night-bird was crooning a nocturnal song; crickets chirruped, and the strains of a violin quavered joyously upon the silence of the night from the home of a fisherman.

"Isn't it glorious, and beautiful, Frank?"

"Aye, sweetheart," whispered the other; "but still more so to me now that I have you here an' soon to be all mine own."

. . . .

The wedding came off on the afternoon of an August day, which must have been ordered exclusively for the occasion. True, there was a proper Fundy fog blotting out the landscape in the early hours, but the sun-dogs soon got to work and ate it up, and when the mist dissipated, it revealed a glorious vista of blue sea and bluer sky.

Down at the wharf lay the barquentine dressed from truck to rail in bright-coloured bunting; her decks scrubbed white, brass shining, painted and varnished like a yacht, and with hatches tarpaulined and battened down, and sails bent ready for sailing with the spring tide that afternoon. The *Lillian* lay astern of her, and she too was tricked out with flags, while ensigns flew from every flag-staff in the village.

It was a general holiday, and all the Long Covers dressed, and shaved, and primped up to do honour to the wedding of the "young boss" to the lovely girl he had chosen for a wife. All the Cove had met her and approved, and Lillian Denton passed the most exacting critic—even Sally Reford, old-maidish and forty, declaring that "she was jest all right an' a mighty nice gal."

The Reverend Mr. Westley officiated at the ceremony. He was whiter of hair and a little shakier now, but he called to mind the boyhood days of the young man he was about to bind in the eternal ties. "Oh, but you were a warrior, Frank. I imagine I see you yet—you and Lem Ring—a proper pair of imps and up to all kinds of mischief whenever you got a chance. Ha, ha, ha!" And the worthy cleric laughed until the tears ran down his face.

And in the presence of four skippers, his mother and Lem Ring, Frank slipped the golden circlet over his bride's slim finger and murmured the most sacred of all vows, "until death us do part."

The tide served at four in the afternoon, and under showers of confetti and blossoms the happy pair stepped down the ornamented gangway and on to the barquentine's poop just as the Blue Peter fluttered from aloft. The *Lillian*, with motor going, chugged alongside; a hawser was passed down, and slowly they hauled out of the little harbour, while the crowds on the wharves cheered and shouted themselves hoarse.

Slowly the land glided away; the crowd dwindled to an indistinguishable mob, and the watchers on the sailing ship feasted their eyes on the panorama of rocky beach, spruce-clad hills, and verdure-hidden village of their home. A string of flags ran up from the wharf staff. "Farewell and good luck!" translated Captain Thomas, and he turned to the rail.

"All right, Captain Galarneau. Let go all! H'ist away spanker an' mains'l! Loose th' sails on th' fore. Up jibs an' stays'ls!"

The *Lillian* sheered off. "Good-bye, Frankee! Good-bye, Mrs. Westhaver!" cried Captain Jules. "Good voyage an' safe home!" And the gang bawled similar good wishes.

"Well yer spanker! Well yer mains'l! Sheet home yer lower foretops'l! Upper tops'l halliards now! Walk her up!"

Frank and his wife leaned over the taffrail staring at the land fading away astern. There was a gurgle and ripple in their wake as the barquentine began to drive ahead under her own canvas, and from the sailors walking the muslin up

BLUE WATER

around the maindeck capstan came a plaintive, yet beautiful chorus:

>Our sails are unfurled and we're over the Bar,
>Away! Rio!
>And we've pointed her bow to the Southern Star,
>And we're bound for the Rio Grande
>Then away! Rio!
>Away! Rio!
>Sing fare ye well, my bonny young girl,
>For we're bound for the Rio Grande!

"Doesn't that chantey sound beautiful on the water, Frank?" She looked up into his happy face, and admiration for each other was reflected in the eyes of both.

"Aye, dearie," he answered, "an' 'tis only on th' water where it really sounds as it should. The sea changes everything, an' 'tis me what owes a lot to it. 'Tis tender an' 'tis cruel; but, oh, it is beautiful! 'Twas from the sea I took you, darling, an' 'twas on it we first met—a ragin' winter sea. 'Twas th' sea what sent me back to you again—'most killed by it. 'Tis from th' sea I earn my bread, an' 'tis th' love of blue water an' you what has kept me to my purposes. Aye! Here's a tribute to th' sea!" And as he spoke he tossed a rose into the frothing wake.

They watched it float astern, saw the great white gulls whirling above it, and as arm in arm they stared at the panorama of spruce-clad hills and rocky beach, their joyful hearts found yet a place for the regret at leaving home and dear ones, which echoed to their ears in the words of the sailors singing:

>We sing as we heave to the maidens we leave,
>Away! Rio!
>You know at this parting how sadly we grieve,
>And we're bound for the Rio Grande!
>Then away! Rio!
>Away! Rio!
>Sing fare ye well, my bonny young girl,
>For we're bound for the Rio Grande!

Sing farewell to mother and old daddy too,
Away! Rio!
And you who are list'ning, it's farewell to you,
For we're bound for the Rio Grande!
Then away, love, away!
Away down Rio!
Sing fare ye well, my bonny young girl,
For we're bound for the Rio Grande!

THE END

FORMAC FICTION TREASURES Also in the Series

Louis Arthur Cunningham
Fog Over Fundy
Fog Over Fundy traces the adventures of a young non-conformist French Canadian woman who returns from Europe to the Tantramar in New Brunswick to fulfill her duties on the family estate and her obligation to the "peasant" workers there.
ISBN 10: 0-88780-710-0 ISBN 13: 978-0-88780-710-7

By Frances Gillmor
Thumbcap Weir
Gid Wyn and his fiancée, Debbie MacQuarrie, are counting on getting her father's fishing weir when they get married in the spring; but there is one villager, Tony Luti, who thinks it's his weir and that it has been stolen from him. Luti sets out to destroy the young couple's dreams and his hatred gets greater with the passing months until one day, under cover of fog, he and his son take revenge.
ISBN 10: 0-88780-645-7 ISBN 13: 978-0-88780-645-2

By Evelyn Eaton
Restless are the Sails
Paul de Morpain, a prisoner-of-war in New England, overhears a plan to send an expedition against the French fortress at Louisbourg. He knows he must do whatever he can to warn the governor. It is 1744 — a dangerous time to attempt a 500-mile journey by sea and overland along dangerous forest trails.
ISBN 10: 0-88780-603-1 ISBN 13: 978-0-88780-603-2

Quietly My Captain Waits
This historical romance, set during the years of French-English struggle in New France, draws two lovers out of the shadows of history — Louise de Freneuse, married and widowed twice, and Pierre de Bonaventure, Fleet Captain in the French navy. Their almost impossible relationship helps them endure the day-to-day struggle in the fated settlement of Port Royal.
ISBN10: 0-88780-544-2 ISBN 13: 978-0-88780-544-8

The Sea is So Wide
In the summer of 1755, Barbe Comeau offers her Annapolis Valley home as overnight shelter to an English officer and his surly companion. The Comeaus are unaware of the plans to confiscate the Acadian farms and send them all into exile. A few weeks later, the treachery unfolds and they are sent to an unknown land as pawns in the Anglo-French conflict.
ISBN 10: 0-88780-573-6 ISBN13: 978-0-88780-573-8

By W. Albert Hickman
The Sacrifice of the Shannon
In the heart of Frederick Ashburn, sea captain and sportsman, there glows a secret fire of love for young Gertrude MacMichael. But her interests lie with Ashburn's fellow adventurer, the dashing and slightly mysterious Dave Wilson. From their hometown of Caribou (real-life Pictou) all three set out on a perilous journey to the ice fields in the Gulf of St. Lawrence to save a ship and its precious cargo — Gertrude's father. In almost constant danger, Wilson is willing to risk everything to bring the ship and crew to safety.
ISBN 10: 0-88780-542-6 ISBN 13: 978-0-88780-542-4

By Alice Jones (Alix John)
The Night Hawk
Set in Halifax during the American Civil War, a wealthy Southerner — beautiful, poised, intelligent and divorced — poses as a refugee in Halifax while using her social success to work undercover. The conviviality of the town's social elite, especially the British garrison officers is more than just a diversion when there is a war to be won.
ISBN 10: 0-88780-538-8 ISBN 13: 978-0-88780-538-7

A Privateer's Fortune
When Gilbert Clinch discovers a very valuable painting and statue in his deceased grandfather's attic, he begins to uncover some of his ancestor's secrets, including a will that allows Clinch to become a wealthy man, while at the same time disinheriting his cousins. His grandfather's business as a privateer and slave trader helped him amass wealth, power and prestige. Clinch has secrets of his own, including a clandestine love affair. From Nova Scotia, to the art salons in Paris and

finally the gentility of English country mansions, Clinch and his lover, Isabel Broderick, become entangled in a haunting legacy.
ISBN 10: 0-88780-572-8 ISBN 13: 978-0-88780-572-1

By Evelyn Richardson
Desired Haven
Mercy Nickerson's father returns from a voyage to the Caribbean with a young Irishman he has saved from a shipwreck. Mercy and Dan are instantly attracted to one another. Rather than go to Boston, Dan decides to stay and turn his ambition to the fishery and ship supply. But his desired haven becomes a more dangerous place than he intended when he turns to smuggling and his wife turns against him.
ISBN 10: 0-88780-675-9 ISBN 13: 978-0-88780-675-9

No Small Tempest
Adria Redmond's life in a sea-faring community is marked by deception and deceit before a tragedy forces her to recognize what's important in her life.
ISBN 10: 0-88780-706-2 ISBN 13: 978-088780-706-0

By Charles G.D. Roberts
The Forge in the Forest: An Acadian Romance
Jean de Mer, an "Acadian Ranger," returns, after three years' absence, to his lands on the shores of Minas Basin to find his son Marc in trouble with the Black Abbé — a French partisan leader. Marc is waiting to be tried as a spy. Together father and son make a daring escape but Marc is wounded and Jean must endure a perilous canoe journey with a young English woman to rescue her child from the Black Abbé.
ISBN 10: 0-88780-604-X ISBN 13: 978-0-88780-604-9

The Heart That Knows
She was abandoned just hours before her wedding. Helpless and shocked, she watched her 'husband' sail away, without so much as a word of explanation. When her fatherless son grows up he sets off to sea, determined not to return to his New Brunswick home until he has sought vengeance on the man who treated his mother so heartlessly.
ISBN10: 0-88780-570-1 ISBN13: 978-0-88780-570-7

By Margaret Marshall Saunders

Beautiful Joe
Cruelly mutilated by his master, Beautiful Joe, a mongrel dog, is at death's door when he finds himself in the loving care of Laura Morris. A tale of tender devotion between dog and owner, this novel is the framework for the author's astute and timeless observations on farming methods, including animal care, and rural living. This Canadian classic, written by a woman once acclaimed as "Canada's most revered writer," has been popular with readers, including young adults, for almost a century.
ISBN 10: 0-88780-540-X ISBN 13: 978-0-88780-540-X

Rose of Acadia
One hundred and fifty years have passed since the Acadians were sent into exile; now, Vesper Nimmo, a Bostonian, sets out for Nova Scotia's French shore with the intention of carrying out his great-grandfather's wish to make amends with the descendants of Agapit LeNoir. Nimmo finds himself immersed in the Acadians' struggles to preserve their culture and language and meets Rose à Charlitte, the innkeeper where he makes his temporary home. Their romance is thwarted by her past; but he cannot leave.
ISBN 10: 0-88780-571-X ISBN 13: 978-0-88780-571-4

By Frederick William Wallace

Captain Salvation
Captain Salvation is a little-known novel of Maritimers at sea, now brought back into print in this new addition to Formac's Fiction Treasures collection. It is an exciting tale of a young reprobate who works his way up from able seaman to mate, skipper and then a ship owner. His strength and intelligence pull him through the violent life aboard ship. Finally, shipwrecked off Cape Horn, he has to face his demons.
ISBN 10: 0-88780-676-7 ISBN 13: 978-0-88780-676-6

Québec, Canada
2006